Ravenous Rhea

ANGRY GREEK GODS SERIES BOOK 3

<u>TRIGGER WARNINGS</u>

Please be advised that this book (and the entire series) will be **<u>gory</u>**.

Other triggers worth mentioning are:

- Alcohol
- Attempted murder
- Blood
- Cannibalism (heavy)
- Emotional abuse
- Gore (heavy)
- Hallucinations
- Incest (Greek mythology)
- Kidnapping
- Murder
- Occult
- Poisoning
- Profanity
- PTSD
- Religion
- Suicide (very mild & brief)
- Torture
- Violence

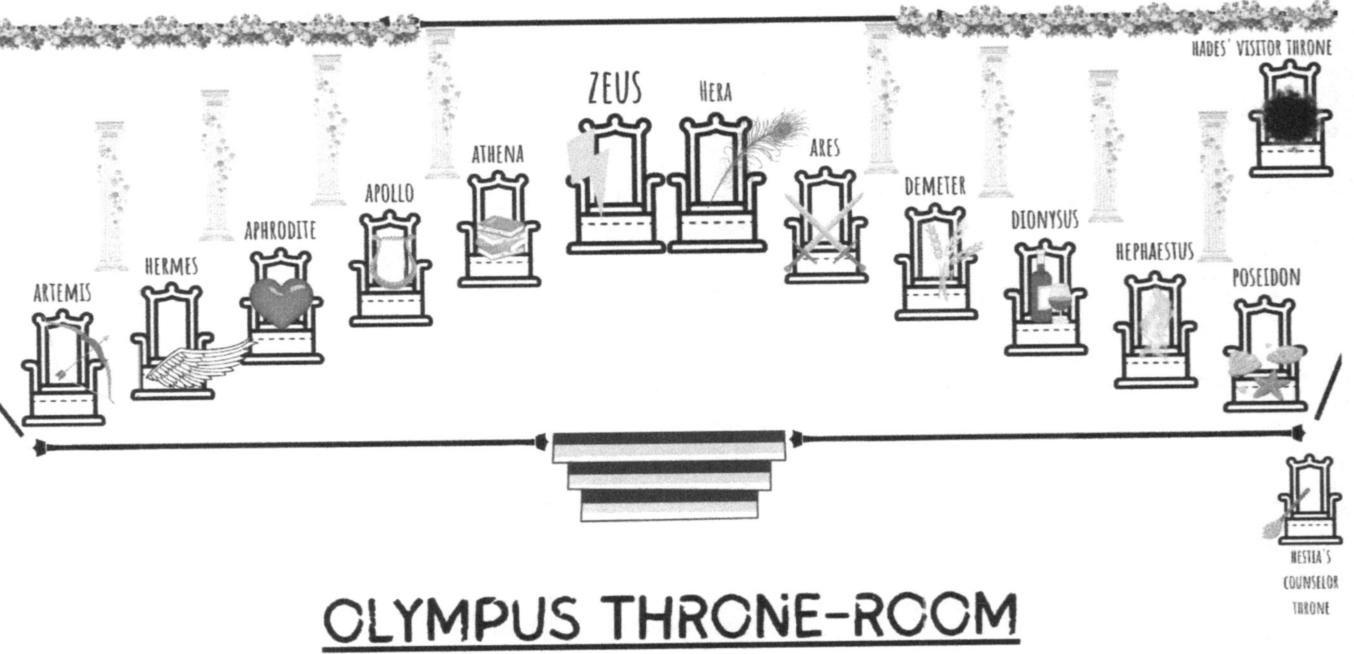
ARTEMIS
HERMES
APHRODITE
APOLLO
ATHENA
ZEUS
HERA
ARES
DEMETER
DIONYSUS
HEPHAESTUS
POSEIDON
HADES' VISITOR THRONE
HESTIA'S COUNSELOR THRONE
OLYMPUS THRONE-ROOM

6 |RAVENOUS RHEA

|| 1. FEED ||

???

The blue-tinted tincture twirled around her tongue as she lapped up its last lingering flavors of blueberry and ambrosia. Its heavenly aroma coated the inside of her mouth with a slippery taste of serenity; a feeling she hadn't been prone to experiencing in recent times.

"If only this were ichor..."

She hiccuped, surprised by the echo in her mind. "No." She twirled the liquid in her cup. "It's tea."

Each slurp swirled down her throat and filled her with an ecstasy she'd forgotten existed, and wished would reappear.

How Olympus had changed. It was a place once loaded with the laughter of nymphs running down corridors to escape lusty gods who couldn't keep their members at rest under their tunics. Once lathered in the unctuous flavor of wine and dripping peaches and spicy finger-foods displayed on silver platters.

And the *sex*. Oh, the sex, how she missed it. Not so much for herself, but for others. How she loved spying on them, overhearing them, basking in their sexy sounds that squeezed down the ivory and gold-laden corridors of Olympus. As a divorcee, she rarely indulged in the act—only in solitude and with the aid of her own fingers—but took pleasure in those around her enjoying themselves. If they were happy, she was happy.

How many times had she stumbled upon Apollo, his beautiful, round butt bared as he thrust against some servant in a corner of the basement kitchen? Thinking to be in absolute darkness in the middle of the night, but forgetting those who—like her—had ambrosia cravings that woke her from her slumber? How many sultry screams had she listened to, coming from Hermes' or Aphrodite's chambers? The harmonies of their satisfaction surging from beneath their doors as she wandered by in her nighttime meanderings?

And of course, the orgies. She'd never partake in them herself, but she'd often snuck a peek at the ones orchestrated by Dionysus. He and his followers got high on hallucinogenic drugs and drowned in grape liquor and went wild. Sometimes he organized such gatherings in plain sight, in a courtyard or orchard or garden. How marvelous to be under the glow of a consenting moon that overlooked his nocturnal frenzies with a watchful but intrigued eye. When he had *invitation-only* parties, she'd eavesdropped near poorly closed doors or peered through key-holes to admire the swaying of bodies in candlelight. She'd licked her lips at the sweat glistening off skin, gliding down backs and thighs and arms in rhythm with the grunts of gratification and the moans of delight.

"Hmm, their blood would have been delicious."

"Hush," she said, sipping on her scalding tea to shut the voice up.

Occasionally, she'd detected someone surprising in the crowd of orgy attendees. Those arrivals always titillated her curiosity more. Apollo had crept in once or twice, focusing on the youthful, virile male guests that Dionysus requested for his nymphs. There were a handful of appearances by higher-level ladies such as Amphitrite—Poseidon's wife, *naughty* girl—or Metis, Athena's mother. And often the ever inquisitive Muses joined the exclusive celebrations. But the one guest that had shocked her most was Hedone—daughter of Eros and Psyche. She'd waltzed in, spreading her powers of pleasure before having her way with a hermaphrodite being with bright bubblegum hair. Oh, how her parents would scream if they knew.

She'd never tell on Hedone, because she'd never want *anyone* aware of her evening discoveries. She'd turn fifty shades of tomato red if they found out about her tendencies, her desires, the acts she spied on, and delighted in watching play out before her. No one in the family would understand it, no matter their disgusting proclivities towards incest and their insatiable natures.

"If they criticize, just dig your fangs into—"

"Quiet, would you?" She shook her head at the annoying noise in her brain. "Let me enjoy this moment of peace."

She loved the rush of emotions. The swelling in her lower half, the tightening of her limbs, the racing of her heartbeat. And her pulse and nerve endings throbbing at the sights and smells and sounds of sex. These self-indulging, unhinged creatures fueled her, fed her, satisfied her. Their actions, their love-making, their explosions of fulfillment covered her flesh with goosebumps and boiled up in her gut with a thrilling tingle.

And then she departed Olympus to venture into the wild, to experiment with her powers. Upon her return, she noticed the palace halls were quiet, empty. The ballrooms didn't overflow with cupbearers coveting half-naked deities. There were no harp-players ogling goddesses with plunging necklines. The lively nymph-driven music had all but disappeared, as the nymphs were confined to their rooms, the toxins they used to ingest considered illicit, and the alcohol confiscated until further notice. No more fancy dinners or backyard concerts or theatrical spectacles.

No parties until the culprit was found.

Those who used to slip into closets and strip and stroke each other's private parts now walked with hesitant steps. Their faces weren't lit up in excitement, but torn in torment as they checked over their shoulders for shadows that weren't theirs. And their worry, their wariness—no matter how warranted—left her hungry, her belly aching, her insides rumbling with rage.

"That is because you haven't fed recently, child."

"Ugh," said Rhea, wishing to dismiss the ominous voice in her head. Why did it always manifest when she was trying to relax?

She'd been so tranquil, lounging in the deserted main courtyard, savoring her berry-and-ambrosia tea, reminiscing the times when Olympus was thriving, alive.

"Why must you always interrupt?" She sneered down at the cooling liquid in her copper cup.

"Because you need to feed. Your belly—it aches."

Rhea set a hand over her abdomen, her fingers pressing into the burnt-orange silk. Sure enough, her insides growled, and despite the beverage she'd been imbibing, her mouth was dry, her throat scratchy.

"That's because it's not tea that you require, it's ichor—"

A noise from the doorway prompted Rhea to sit up straight and drop her feet to the pebbled ground. She'd been sitting cross-legged, with her eyes closed, for a clearer image of her recollections. As her imagination ran wild, she'd been wrapping strands of her chestnut locks around her fingers as she nibbled on her lower lip. She'd been inattentive.

In light of recent events, the Olympians were, for the most part, to stay in their quarters. But there were always a few—like her—who refused to obey King Zeus' commands of staying put, and who crept out once most sconces were extinguished.

Her ears perked up, and she squinted at the glass doors to the palace as they creaked open.

"This is what you get for sitting around thinking of the past and playing at family for hours. You're on edge, and you're famished."

She couldn't reply to the voice now, knowing someone was in the vicinity. Knowing someone was exiting the building and about to come over to her and interact. If they overheard her addressing the being in her mind, they'd know at once something was wrong, something was off about her. They'd suspect her. And she *couldn't* be considered a suspect.

So she cracked her knuckles, re-arranged her hair in a frizzy, lion's mane style, and blinked away the blurriness in her eyes.

"You have a mission, Rhea, and you've been wasting time. You've been here for too long and still haven't—"

"I know," she hissed, too annoyed to recall she wasn't alone, but wishing to get her point across.

The voice didn't command her, usually. It threw out comments, pointed out tidbits of her mission, helped her navigate, and avoid being seen or caught in her acts of thirst. But tonight it had decided to irritate, to push Rhea to her limits. She'd hoped the tea—a concoction suggested by Hecate, when she'd visited a few hours prior—would soothe her brain and put the voice to sleep. But apparently, she'd failed to tame the beast within.

"What's that?" A stern but soulful voice slipped from one of the figures escaping out onto the moonlit terrace. As this individual approached, eyes slitting in curiosity, a few emerald vines made of satin slithered from this voice owner's gown, prodding at Rhea's legs.

Gaia.

Always composed, always a certain scintillation about her appearance, Rhea's mother retracted her gown's tentacles as she passed under an illuminated patch of pavement that turned her muddy eyes to amber, and her scarlet hair to fire. "Rhea, are you all right?"

In her shadow, the eerily quiet Queen of Olympus lingered. The silver pendant dangling from her lovely neck glimmered under the stars. And her gown, its shade the same navy as the sky, swished over the rocky courtyard's ground.

"Mother," she said, her voice a tad too reserved for someone with such power, such energy. "You are perturbed?"

"Yes."

Rhea refrained from snapping at her internal occupant. "I am fine, dear. Taking advantage of the unusual silence for a spell. Crazy how one forgets the noises of nature while living in such a busy place."

With a huff, Hera bypassed Gaia—who'd halted to sniff at a branch of lilies overhead. The queen dropped onto the iron chair across from Rhea and crossed her arms. "Too silent. And cold. I feel so weak, so overwhelmed. Zeus is—" She cringed, likely afraid her husband would come running should she utter his name out loud. "Well, he's being secretive, and I hate it."

"Beware of him. Beware of her, of them all."

Rhea watched her daughter, admiring the sharp curves of her face but frowning at the lackluster hues of her tired brown eyes. She and Rhea were like twins in their appearance, most days. But tonight, Hera was washed out, far from her majestic self, whereas Rhea was packed with vitality and memories and adrenaline.

"Not for long. Not if you don't drink some—"

"You must trust in your spouse, darling," said Rhea, her words worming out before the voice inside could confirm what she already knew. The intuition that she'd been trying to suppress since Zeus had invited her there, along with Gaia. Since he'd begged them to assist with investigating a villain who craved to tear into the gods' peaceful lives and create yet another civil war.

For decades she'd been living out in the wild, acquainting with animals and their behaviors, studying their urges, their feeding patterns, their copulation manners. And despite the progress she'd made, once infused with this voice and whatever its ominous abilities were, she'd been drawn to Olympus. So she'd come, at Zeus' request, and once more took up residence in her old quarters among Olympians.

Zeus had no clue why she'd really showed up, why she'd abandoned her animal analysis. Not to help him, no; but because she was thirsty. And not for berry-flavored tea, nor for the red-tinted blood of measly humans and forest beasts that she'd been sustaining herself with for weeks.

She needed real blood. The flavorful, powerful ichor of the gods. Only one location would provide her with that, in abundance.

"Perhaps a bite to eat?" Gaia had reached the stone table, and tapped two fingers to its surface, summoning a platter of ambrosia cakes, fruit tarts, and the ambrosia-brandy she reserved for special occasions. "To celebrate three generations of goddesses, reunited despite the dire circumstances. How long has it been since we all feasted together, hm?" She took a seat beside Rhea and patted her thigh affectionately.

"Feed. Soon."

"It has been too long," said Rhea, biting back her yelps towards the voice. She gritted her teeth, ignoring the call of Gaia's blood, of

Hera's blood, of their delicate, ivory-colored flesh, of their sugary, soft necks. "This is a lovely idea, because I'm downright ravenous with hunger."

|| 2. GOLDEN GATES OF OLYMPUS ||

LUKUS

With a grunt and an ungraceful bend of the knees, Lukus had arrived. His feet met with the hardened ground, and he waited for his head to stop spinning.

The electricity flickering from Athena's touch still numbed his skin as they landed. She was steady, not a lock of her brown curls out of place; but Lukus wobbled, his knees about to buckle as his shoes planted on the solid stone surface.

He winced, holding in the contents of his stomach as he lifted his chin. Teleporting—*godly traveling,* as Athena had called it—wasn't meant for the faint of heart, and this journey proved to Lukus he wasn't as tough as he'd thought.

"You'll get used to it," said Athena in her cold, matter-of-fact voice; the same she'd used to convince Lukus to let her teleport him in the first place. She released his wrist, leaving a throbbing red handprint on his flesh. "Maybe in time you'll develop your own powers of transportation."

"Right." He sucked in a deep breath of the clean, mountainous air, begging it to erase the queasiness that threatened to take over. "Because I have a 'destiny among the gods', or whatever."

He wrinkled his nose as he peered up at the enormous barrier blocking his view of the palace. The shimmering fence gleamed so brightly it appeared unreal, as if made of pure gold, of sturdy, shiny steel, or of materials not found on earth.

"They *aren't* found on earth," said Athena, fixing her light blue travel tunic, ensuring it flowed near her ankles. "And yes, you have a destiny among the gods. I repeat, you're not mortal, Lukus. You're…" she pursed her lips, "one of us."

For someone so dedicated to her cause of fetching him and dragging him up to Olympus, Athena didn't show much enthusiasm at the revelation of his supposed heritage. Nor did she appear pleased when he'd agreed to come with her. What had she expected? For him to continue arguing, pressing his luck? For him to refuse to accompany her? To ask that she leave him alone and not invade the privacy of his apartment? She was a fucking goddess, dammit. If he were to keep trying to resist her, to obey his urge to tell her to fuck off, she'd strike him dead.

He didn't want to die before understanding why she was under the impression that he had godly blood in him.

"My parents are mortal," he'd said to her, once she'd revealed a tiny glimpse of his heritage. *"I'm not a god, not a demi-god, not even a particle of a god. What the hell are you talking about?"*

Athena's eyes had shifted to yellow slits, by that point. Her veiny, muscular arms had bulged and the aura of trust and confidence she'd inspired had melted beneath a facade of impatience and irritation. *"Well, one of your true parents or ancestors isn't mortal, otherwise I wouldn't be here, picking you up, at my king's request. Though I have no clue which of your progenitors is one of our family members, I would never doubt Father's claims."*

Father. King. God of the skies. *Zeus.* She spoke of him with such reverence, such respect, but with a tinge of a tremble in her tone that made Lukus nowhere near excited to meet with the god himself. Something about how she mentioned her mission, her obligations, her investigation, and how Zeus had ordered her to pursue them, didn't sit well with Lukus. She slurred her speech slightly when mentioning her father, and her cheeks went from rosy to pallid to rosy again whenever she brought up his almighty authority.

She'd spoken for ten minutes, pacing back and forth in Lukus' living room, explaining to him that Olympus was in trouble. The gods were in trouble. And Zeus wanted him there. *Zeus.* The thunder god, the lightning god, the *King* of gods, had asked for him by name. A pinch of pride and heaps of petrification took hold of Lukus' insides, and before he even allowed Athena to snatch his wrist, the nausea had already settled in.

Now, staring at the bold gate before him didn't help. He shaded his eyes, but there was no blocking out that light, and the tiny sparkles that floated on the surface, fluttering like prismatic fireflies. To top it all off, the sour cherry atop this mountain of delusion, was the fact that it was *nighttime.* How could a barrier be so dazzlingly gold under the pale moon? Wouldn't it reflect silver, or white? Wouldn't it—

"The more you question things, the more confused you'll be, Lukus." Athena's voice had softened. No longer as intimidating and stiff, she seemed to relax in proximity to her home. Lukus didn't appreciate how she dug into his thoughts, but he did prefer her in this calmer, less tense state. "Olympus is magical. Everything about this place disobeys the laws of physics that you learned as a human. Corridors expand and constrict, sounds morph, and silence can be overpowering, and what you think you see may be an illusion.

Welcome to Olympus."

Magic. Gods, goddesses, mysteries, memory spells, mortals who weren't mortals, places in the sky that were invisible to the human eye. These were all things he'd laughed at most of his life. Proclaimed skeptic as he was, he'd been in denial of magic and the supernatural for so many years, choosing logic over supposition, proving there was always sense in motives and weapons and criminal behaviors.

That was, until he encountered the bloodthirsty Eros and his impossible-to-resist mother, Aphrodite.

Aphrodite. Her name had sparked a fire in Lukus' heart, starting a war in his mind. She and her erratic son had barged into his somewhat peaceful life and disrupted it, then left him disillusioned and drunk in a hospital bed, his memory wiped, his body bruised and exhausted. And then Athena showed up, reignited his recollections, reinstalled in him all the fear and confusion Aphrodite had so sweetly suppressed for him.

What now? Was he to meet with Aphrodite? How could he confront her, after spilling his heart at her feet and watching her giggle as she declined him because he wasn't a god? After having offered to kill himself so he'd become immortal and share his life with her?

Finding out that he was, in fact, part immortal, could be a game-changer. Would she accept him now, knowing he had the blood of the gods flowing through his veins?

"No." Athena slid in front of him, her bulky beauty barring some of the painful light from destroying his retinas. "I'm sorry I used her name to further encourage you to come with me, but... no, Aphrodite will take no interest in you. She has enough on her plate. Oh, and it's *ichor.*"

"Ichor? What's that?" Lukus swiped a strand of his sleek black hair from his forehead.

"Ichor is god's blood, which is what you have inside of you, according to Father." She turned her back to him, facing the fence without a flinch, its otherworldly luminosity filtering into her being, as if absorbing it.

"According to…Zeus." Lukus huffed, and peered behind him to see if he had room to step backwards.

He'd half expected them to land on a cloud, but was shocked to find that in front of the giant gates of Olympus was a simple slab of boring concrete. Held up by what, he wasn't sure—and he doubted he should lean over the edge to check—but it wasn't the luxurious, heavenly entrance he'd anticipated when agreeing to come here.

"I—" Athena cut herself off and her shoulders hunched forward, her knees bending as if to keep her balance. She was on alert, and so abruptly that Lukus had no clue what to do. His breaths got stuck in his lungs.

Whatever she'd sensed, he hadn't detected it yet, and had no idea how to react. Hide behind her? Crouch? Jump off this stony cliff to his demise?

A voice came from above, as if lowering over them like drops of rain. "Don't you dare." It was deep, but smooth, like an aged whiskey that melted down your throat, then burned and choked you until your next sip. "If you put yourself at risk before I've had a chance to be certain of your identity, I will unleash deadly lightning on the world."

Though he didn't know this thunderous voice, its volume shaking the ground beneath his feet, its intensity rattling his bones, Lukus identified its owner by the words.

Deadly lightning on the world? Is this…him?

"Me." A flowy, foggy figure began to form to Lukus' left,

prompting he and Athena to flip towards it.

Giant arms, bulky legs, and an oval head took shape, with blurry outlines at first, then soon defined into a tall, tenebrous man. His eyebrows were like lines of thick gray fur, and his eyes were blue like a cloudless daytime sky. A heavy mane of curly graying ebony hair unraveled on either side of his light face, and a frizzy beard undulated down to the upper part of his exposed—and *very* chiseled—chest. He adjusted the hem of his sparkling silver tunic, allowing it to settle above his knees.

As he inclined his head, his silhouette became less and less hazy. A radiant warmth emanated from every inch of his bare skin, putting him in a spotlight from the heavens.

"Lukus," he said, his timbre less tremulous, toned down as if to accommodate a half-immortal's hearing. A certain majesty leaked from his posture, straight and formal. "I am Zeus, King of the skies. And as my dear, favorite daughter said: welcome to Olympus."

The dear, favorite daughter in question was cowering in a half-bow, half-curtsy. All Athena's earlier confidence had evaporated as if this glorious being had sucked it all up. Again proving her intimidation from him, she redressed herself, but clearly struggled to keep her legs level and fought an obvious shake of her hands.

Following her lead, Lukus tipped into a bow, unsure of the rules of royalty, never having come close to any kings or queens in his travels as an FBI agent.

When he straightened up, he couldn't prevent the puzzlement from scrunching his face into a grimace. Weren't Athena and Zeus close? In all the Greek myths Lukus had been forced to listen to, he recalled them arguing, yes, but most of the time getting on well and working together. So why was the wisdom goddess so fearful of the father who favored her?

"Oh, that is a story for another time," said Zeus, sending a fleeting glance at his daughter. The blue of his eyes shifted, fluttering between soft sky and deep navy, before returning to its airy light hue. "But for now, we have other matters to worry about. First things first, we must establish if you are indeed half-god, as I was informed."

"Wait." Lukus tripped backwards, stopped from falling by Athena's arm sticking out to steady him. "You're…you're not even sure? What kind of bull—"

"—if you use such foul language in front of me young man I will ignore my curiosity and end you myself." Zeus' tone hadn't risen, but the rapid roar of his words stilled Lukus, pausing his heartbeats. "Ask Athena later what it's like to defy me. Now," his expression morphed to one of a pleasant, grandfatherly figure, "if you would please approach the gate, we will proceed with the testing."

"T-testing?" Lukus couldn't move, but Athena nudged him toward the barrier, and farther into Zeus' shadow, which seemed to stretch on for miles behind them.

"Yes." Zeus' copper-colored sandals slapped on the pavement as he approached. The closer he got to Lukus, the more Lukus' skin covered in goosebumps and his entire body froze over, like dipped into the glacial waters of an ice lake. "You will touch the gate, and if you *are* part immortal, you'll be allowed through."

Lukus gulped. Oh, the things he wished he didn't know. That magic existed, that the Greek gods existed, that there was a palace in the skies that he might be able to visit if he could somehow touch its gates. How he yearned to return to his normal, mortal life of smoking and drinking and bedding women. And investigating gory crimes his FBI colleagues couldn't figure out.

"And what…" He gulped again. The saliva gathered in his throat slid downward, sharp like daggers, scraping his insides, impairing his vocal chords. "What happens if I'm not part immortal?"

Pressing his own large hand onto the gleaming gold gate, Zeus offered a wide but ill-fitting smile. "Oh, you'll die instantly."

Lukus choked, certain his saliva was now a set of swords ripping down the inside of his torso, scratching at his rib-cage, searing through his heart. "W-what?"

Zeus said it so easily, without a hint of hesitation: *you'll die instantly*. Did he not care if Lukus exploded into bloody chunks, staining the concrete in front of this fancy gate? Or if some invisible force slithered under his skin and squeezed his lungs until they were empty, cutting off oxygen from all his organs?

"It would be more like a heart-attack," said Athena with a simple shrug.

A *too* simple shrug; she, too, appeared unaffected by the risk of Lukus dying if their hunch was wrong.

Athena snorted. "Our hunch isn't wrong."

"Because it's no hunch," said Zeus, angling closer, pointing at the gate. "It's destiny, Lukus. But I must assure myself of it this way. If I were to open the doors for you and guide you into my home without verifying my sources first, what kind of king would I be? What if you are dangerous, hm?"

Lukus stopped himself before belting out, *"what the fuck could I do to Olympian gods?"* and took a deep, unsettling breath. The magical purity of the air—like that invigorating outdoors feel of a wild forest before setting up camp, the sensation of one's feet on a never walked-on bank of sand in front of a small stream—reminded him that up here, in this new world, he wasn't in control of anything. He'd been scooped up, transported, and now faced the ever-elusive goddess of wisdom and her all-powerful father, Zeus.

Who was he to defy the gods he once had no inkling were real? Two of them were there, at his side, their presence overpowering, frightening. And they were insisting that he show them he was one of them. Persuaded some prophet somewhere had been right in confessing to them that he, the soulmate-less mortal targeted by Eros and enamored by Aphrodite, was part-god.

Fuck it.

He inhaled another whiff of air, and placed his hand on the gate.

|| 3. SUSPICIONS AND SMELLS ||
HERA

An unfamiliar chilly breeze brushed through the courtyard, coating Hera's olive skin in goosebumps.

"See?" She tipped her bejeweled goblet up towards the wind. "That never used to happen! *Cold?* Unheard of in Olympus. I tell you, whatever is amiss has disrupted everything about this place."

In all her millennia of ruling at Zeus' side, she'd never sensed such a surge of negativity oozing from the depths of her marble palace. Never had she been wary walking down the gilded corridors, nor so scrutinized by the portraits hanging from the ivory walls. Even the bigger, more populated hallways felt abandoned. As if a thick fog loomed and a swamp hid behind one of the copper-framed doors, or a murky lake resided under the tiled floors.

"And Zeus," she snuck a sip of Gaia's glorious ambrosia brandy, "is acting weirder than usual, too." She shivered, recalling her husband's quick retorts, his sneaking around, his summoning of family members without consulting her. "I mean, it pleases me that you are both here." She nodded at her messy-haired mother, and beamed at her beautiful grandmother. "But had he warned me, I would have been able to set up your rooms faster."

Gaia tossed her scarlet mane and arched up in her seat, her vinelike dress hem swaying with her movement. "I don't need such a fuss made about me, my sweet, you know this. If anything, I would have preferred to be out here—"

"—in the cold?" Hera hiccuped. Perhaps she'd had a tad *too* much brandy, if she was raising her voice and interrupting her primordial goddess grandmother without remorse. One usually leveled their tone in Gaia's presence, or allowed her to steer the conversation as she saw fit. But tonight, Hera wanted control, wanted to vent, and wanted to be heard.

"Sweetheart." Rhea's touch wasn't warm as expected, but Hera attributed that to the crisp gust gyrating around their table, as if focused solely on them. "Zeus is always weird. I may have been a bit absent as of late, but I know my son; he's troubled, and with reason, no?"

Hera huffed, her brash breath blowing some of the liquor within her cup out and onto the platter of delicacies. With one of her lengthy royal blue sleeves, she wiped the drizzle, then snagged an ambrosia cake.

"But when he's troubled, he talks to me. He confides in me. I know, everyone else up here hates me—save Ares, my precious—but Zeus usually shares his woes with me. Lately, though, he shares them with—"

She snapped her mouth shut before spitting out the words she craved to use to describe Zeus' favorite daughter.

Wretched, annoying, wisdom-seeking, far from as witty as she pretends to be, trash, opposing my powers—

"Hera." Gaia's bushy but tamed crimson eyebrows lurched upwards. "Watch yourself, would you? I don't need access to your thoughts to know you were about to insult our dearest Athena."

In Gaia's eyes, all Zeus' children were wonders of nature,

marvelous creatures worthy of respect, fueling the earth—*her* earth—with energy and positivity and excitement. No matter their past mistakes or how their offspring often destroyed her beloved planet, Gaia would never stoop so low as to demean a fellow Olympian. And certainly not the revered and perfect Athena.

"Forgive me, grandmother, but I do not see any appeal to her." Hera shoved half the cake in her mouth and chewed, ignoring her mother's narrowing dark gaze in disgust at her masticating.

She'd never normally be so disgraceful, so inelegant in front of anyone else—but Rhea and Gaia knew her too well. They knew that sugary sweets were her preferred way to vent, to ease any tension. The masticating part wasn't in her nature, but she was too frustrated to care, too confused to bother fixing her manners.

She swept the crumbs from the table and tapped her azure nails to the stone surface. "She's like him, you know. Creeping around, prying into our minds to take our every thought and turn them against us. If she weren't so damn pure, I'd assume she was the culprit, feeding us poison and making us act on our most repressed urges. Sure, since she doesn't *have* any urges, little miss perfect—"

"Hera!" In tandem, Rhea's lioness growl and Gaia's turbulent tornado of a tone hit Hera square in the face.

"You've had too much to drink," said Rhea, fetching Hera's chalice before Hera could take hold of it. She sniffed at the contents and gagged. "And this is filled with pieces of your pastry, too. What is the matter with you, daughter? You're the one acting weird."

Gaia nodded. "I've not seen you so disturbed since Zeus' last scandal, and that was centuries ago." She leaned in closer, and her forest and dirt scent soothed past Hera's barrier of anger, its earthy tranquility forcing her muscles to relax. "Is that it? Is he," she cringed, "cheating again? You can tell us, sweetling. We won't hold it against you; it's not your fault."

"Look at you," said Rhea, lifting a few of Hera's dark tresses and rubbing them with the pad of her thumb. "So beautiful. So majestic and poised—" she wrinkled her nose, "—well, in normal times. The most elegant and refined of all goddesses. Mother of marriage, overseer of maidens in their wedding beds. What could stir you so, hm?"

Hera basked in the compliments for a few moments, drinking up her mother and grandmother's admiration. She missed that; missed the goddesses who once prostrated at her feet and begged her for her beauty routine secrets. Missed the gods and cupbearers ogling her as she paraded down the sconce-lit hallways, her lengthy peacock-colored dress trains trailing behind her as she twirled her silver pendant and smiled bashfully. She'd never betray her husband, no matter how many times he'd chosen to wound her by sleeping with other women. But she'd also never deny that she loved the attention and craved the praise of others.

That attention had dissipated in the past few years. Male inhabitants of Olympus shied away from her whenever they heard her clicking heels or detected her vibrant vanilla and magnolia perfume. Maidens scurried off and feigned being busy with other tasks to not curtsy to her. They no longer asked for her counsel, no longer admired her natural magnificence.

And the praise? Non-existent. If anything, Olympians denigrated her now. They demeaned her as *Zeus' wife* or *the wounded one* or some other unpleasant nickname she refused to acknowledge. She was undermined, tossed aside, or feared. There was no awe in the eyes of those who dared to cross gazes with her; there was distrust, loathing, and terror.

But why? All because she had a reputation for easy jealousy? Because she'd trifled with a few heroes and maddened a few gods who'd gotten in her way or taunted her one time too many? She hadn't enacted any curses in hundreds of decades. So what had suddenly inspired her constituents to despise her, after centuries of adoration? Who had spread some foul rumor about her? And why, *why* hadn't Zeus come to her defense?

He allowed the insulting behaviors. He didn't step in to reprimand his people, didn't put his children in their place. Not once did he remind his family that Hera was the queen, dammit, and was to be respected at all times. In a few instances, he'd barked at Athena or slapped Aphrodite on the wrist. But there was no thunder, no lightning, no almighty ability used against his offspring and siblings when they sought to harm Hera's ego.

"It would be easier if I'd caught him cheating," she mumbled. She wished she had her cup to hold, to hide the trembling of her hands. "I'd confront him, we'd have a screaming fit, but at least I'd know what I did wrong. I'd understand that the issue is…me." She sighed, waving at Rhea and Gaia before they both spoke out in her defense. They, along with Ares, were the only ones who ever gave a damn about her, truly. "It's fine, I'm aware he never desired me that much in the first place. His cravings are for younger, more unattainable things, hm? But we'd moved beyond that. He curbed his appetite, he did. Now…he's being sneaky and sly again. And I don't believe it's because of some bare-breasted bitch whispering at him to further undress her. No…there's something else."

"And you think Athena is involved?" Rhea sniffed at something in the air, peeked towards the glass doors, then returned her gaze to

Hera. Her nostrils twitched as she clearly fought to suppress whatever smell she'd detected nearby. As an analyst of animal behavior, she sometimes took on their demeanors. None of the gods were able to figure out what she discerned in the atmosphere that they couldn't.

"I have no clue."

Hera fingered her pendant, peeping down at it as if it would provide her with the answers she sought. But all she saw on its flat, polished surface was her own reflection. Her big brown eyes gleaming with doubt, puckered lips tinted a light blue from the berries inside the baked goods, skin flushed from alcohol.

"All I know is *she* has been defying him a lot lately. She lied to him, did you know?" Gaia and Rhea both gasped. "Yes, shocking. The never naughty Athena fibbing? Unheard of. Only I'm aware of it, though. And I kept it to myself and made an alliance with her, instead. Ugh." She glanced towards her cup, praying it would move from Rhea's proximity and slide back to her.

Rhea, perceptive as ever, grasped the goblet and pulled it farther from Hera's reach. "Alliance?"

"To investigate Hecate." Hera's eyes widened and her shoulders straightened as another chill coursed through the air; but this one wasn't natural. It came from Gaia, whose tentacle-like gown began to wrap around Hera's legs and arms and drew her chair closer.

"Hecate?" A flicker of red flashed through Gaia's once docile eyes. "What about her?"

Hera swallowed. Why did she bring the sorceress goddess up? Gaia adored her, as did most of Zeus' close-knit relatives. To speak up against Hecate put Hera in a delicate position. It would put her up against her mighty, mega-strengthened grandmother.

"She...Athena suspects her," she said, battling to come up with a fib grand enough to convince Gaia. She'd placated Athena for lying, and now she had to lie herself, to protect her hide. "I overheard her speaking to herself about it, debating, and I offered to help. That's the alliance, but I…I don't intend to actually respect it."

Gaia's gown shriveled back into place, and her eyes shifted to their earth-brown shade. "None of that is good, Hera. You're not only betraying Athena, but encouraging her to pursue a lead that isn't correct. Hecate…no, she's not responsible for whatever is going on here."

"But… the poison…" Hera sensed herself shrinking into her seat. How to persuade Gaia something was fishy about her favorite witch friend without offending her to the point of unleashing a tornado in the Olympus gardens? "It was *her* poison, Gaia. From her reserves."

"So?" Gaia crossed her arms over her bosom, pushing her breasts upward, about to spill out from her low collar. "You imply Hecate staged a break-in and is pretending to be a victim? Did she not already disprove this? Or did Zeus lie to Rhea and I when he summoned us here for help?"

"I…" Hera's saliva caught in her throat and her mouth remained agape, her tongue dancing about in search of an appropriate reply.

"No, granddaughter dearest." Gaia stood up, her layers of green silk swishing out, blooming about her like petals of a rose. "I did not come all this way for you—and Athena—to accuse someone who is no more culpable than you or I or Rhea. And I will not sit here while you are inebriated and moaning about your situation. You are a queen, for Zeus' sake! Act like it!" Her voice was ridged with knives, and she raised her arms and glared at the starry sky. "You want respect? Earn it! Cease playing childish games and making idiotic alliances with girls who fancy themselves as detectives. And wait for your spouse to let you in on his plans when he is ready to do so! Be a goddess, dammit!"

Hera clapped a hand over her mouth as she finally found the force to snap her lips together. In the guise of a response—and still unable to formulate sentences in the wake of her grandmother's fury—she nodded once and trained her gaze on her lap, fixing on the remnants of cake clustered over her lush dress.

"Rhea," Gaia snapped, "come, let us leave Hera to reflect on her attitude."

Not daring to disobey, Rhea shot to her feet, again sniffling at the air like a wolf sensing its prey in the vicinity. Her burnt-orange tunic glistened in the moonlight, as if the fabric were fire. The heat radiating from her lips as she pressed a kiss to Hera's temple only accentuated the sweat already gathering over Hera's skin.

"Calm down, daughter," she whispered, combing a few slender fingers through Hera's curls. "A good sleep and some strong coffee in the morning should clear your senses, hm? Your grandmother is right. Things are amiss up here, but you will not solve them by being negative and down on yourself. Eat," she gestured at the remaining delicacies on the tray on the table, "replenish your strength and erase the effects of that liquor. It hinders your abilities, pollutes your blood." She licked her lips, then flashed a quick smile as she hurried after the already departing Gaia.

The lilies swayed overhead and the flowered bushes bristled in the breeze. The temperature dropped considerably, since Rhea took her tropical heat away with her. But Hera didn't budge, continuing to glower at the crumbs in her lap as if they'd offended her. As if they were Athena, Hecate, Zeus.

She swiped them off and stomped on them before retrieving her goblet of brandy, nestling it to her chest as she stumbled over to a swinging chair on the opposite end of the garden. Her favorite place to meditate, to drink—and to plot.

|| 4. THESE SCRUMPTIOUS SWEETLINGS ||

RHEA

After a polite exchange of pleasantries with Gaia—and a few coded comments about Hera's erratic, immature behavior—Rhea chose to meander down the halls of Olympus. To reacquaint herself with the atmosphere of her former home. She kept to a moonlit corridor nearest the side patio-courtyard where she'd once seen Hermes teasing a cupbearer. Peering out the rounded windows, she remembered the exact spot where he'd been tickling under the girl's skirts. Where he'd prompted her to squeal in delight and bite her lip to encourage him.

Such voyeuristic tendencies weren't unheard of in Rhea's family. Many of her children and grandchildren and distant relatives took part in spying on sexual activities, if not attempting to join in. How many times had she stumbled upon Apollo in deep admiration of Aphrodite and Ares while they played in the dark basement corridors? Or when Hebe had waited near Dionysus' orgy-room door, her hand reaching under her tunic as she peeped through the keyhole?

It was all so thrilling to Rhea, but she'd never dare show herself, make it clear that she was there, observing, admiring. To peek in on such private acts was a delicious advantage of living in Olympus, but not all would welcome her attention so openly. Zeus would rage to know his mother took pleasure in watching others in their fantasies. And if word were to reach Hera, or the prudes Artemis and Athena, Rhea's reputation as a mature, matronly figure would be washed away. She'd find herself venturing into the forests and jungles again, forced to feed on animals, instead of the thick, rich-flavored ichor she so craved.

The voice, no matter how brutal and blunt it was, was right, and Rhea was struggling more and more to ignore it. She'd fought hard to not stare at the pulse at the top of Hera's neck, throbbing, begging to be ripped into, to be drained of ichor. And Gaia, her navy veins glowing under her darkened skin, had a rhythm to her heart's pumping that Rhea had to clench her jaw to resist, and had to tighten her fists under the table to not take advantage of.

"Rhea, there you are." The arrival came from Rhea's left, the hallway leading to the main Olympian quarters.

Rhea twisted to it, torn from the images of inky blue liquid dripping from her rosy lips, her tongue coated in the berry-hued substance, the delectable flavor flurrying down her throat in waves of ecstasy.

"Yes?" Heat rushed to her cheeks and her blood boiled. She hoped her thoughts were protected from whoever had discovered her dream-like state, nose pressed into the window.

The figure slithering up to her was none other than Rhea's aloof and alluring sister, Leto. Garbed in her lengthy but quite see-through gown of pale sea-foam, she was like a glowing ghost. Her autumn leaf-colored locks tumbled over her breasts and her feet were, as usual, bare, as she hastened over to grab Rhea's overheated hands.

"I have been looking for you everywhere. Why were you not in your chambers? Zeus said—"

"—you have no regard for what Zeus said, either, since you're here." Rhea clicked her tongue, regretting her harsh tone. Leto was a sweet, nurturing soul, and didn't need to be on the receiving end of Rhea's moodiness. "What is it?"

"This," Leto hugged herself and tipped closer to her sister, "climate, in the palace…it bothers me."

Rhea refrained from rolling her eyes. "It bothers all of us. The breeze is quite chillier than usual, for certain; but what do you expect me to do about it?" She side-glanced at Leto's barely-there outfit and scoffed. "Perhaps a dress with a thicker fabric will help?"

"I'm not referring to the temperature." Leto smacked Rhea's shoulder, and her voice was stern. It was the tone she used for her children, or for her followers when they weren't respecting the proper demure and womanly attitudes she preached. "I mean the environment, the tension, the negativity. You can't deny you've felt it, too? Is that not why Zeus called you and Mother here?"

Rhea bit her tongue before responding. Yes, Zeus had summoned her, but she'd come not to help him uncover his culprit. She'd returned only to get her fill of ambrosia-infused ichor and charge herself with power and energy. Though for what, she wasn't sure. The voice hadn't specified that part to her.

"There's something amiss, and a culprit among us." Rhea's jaw tightened. "Gaia and I are here to assist, yes…but I can tell you now that neither of us has deciphered anything to point us in the right direction."

It was true; upon arrival, Gaia had confessed she'd detected a foreign-smelling yet oddly familiar energy in the air. And she'd smelled an ominous hunch of foul-play after convening with Eros and

Psyche, the principal wounded ones. All her senses were tingling after the brief meeting in the throne-room, where Zeus announced her and Rhea's participation in the ongoing investigation. It made sense, as they both had extensive knowledge of goddesses far and wide, and deep insight on their pasts and goals and motivations.

If Gaia had any suspicions, she'd kept them to herself. As for Rhea, she was so absorbed in her own investigation into whose blood she should drink first, that she hadn't stopped to ponder who might have been responsible for poisoning Persephone, Eros, and Psyche.

And potentially others that we know nothing about.

"Yes, well, I'm coming to you because…you know of safe places, no?" Leto's bushy, untamed eyebrows lurched upward. Her forest fern gaze fixed on the window, on her reflection, but she gripped Rhea's wrist and squeezed. "Areas in deep woods where one's offspring would be protected? Sheltered from all that's going on? Far enough from Olympus that it would take much effort to reach them, to harm them?"

Fighting the fantasy of digging her fangs into Apollo's strong, silky neck, or into Artemis' smooth, unblemished skin, Rhea gulped. "Gaia would know of such places, not me."

"Right." Leto's grip tightened. "But you're her closest and favorite daughter. She dislikes me." Leto shrugged. "Anyway, I was wondering if you'd plead with her, bargain for her to take Apollo and Artemis away from all this. I know they're fierce and wise and can fend for themselves, but I don't trust this dwelling anymore. I…"

"Zeus. She distrusts Zeus. Another goddess confessing this, on the same night? Rhea, you must—"

"You don't trust Zeus?" Rhea spun to her sister, removing herself from her grasp. "Zeus, your king? Your family?"

With a quick peek left and right, Leto gave a timid shake of her head. "I've lost faith in his ability to protect us. Two of our residents were intoxicated during a private dinner. And Hades' wife was also trifled with. There is a being in our midst who has a reach beyond Zeus', a power rivaling if not surpassing his. I doubt he can do a thing to stop them. Her. Whoever it is."

Rhea arched an eyebrow. "You do realize you described every single titaness who dwells here, including yourself?"

"I have an alibi. So does Phoebe, and Themis, and any of the ladies who reside here temporarily or only swing by. You have one; you've been in the wilderness for decades, studying animals, yes?" Rhea nodded, and Leto shoved a streak of auburn and blonde hair from her forehead. "And Gaia has much more important matters to handle. Such as overseeing every single forest and plain and the deities and personifications under her instruction and—"

"—you've made your point." Rhea sighed and rubbed the back of her neck. Not only did her stomach squirm and scream for ichor, but now her other body parts seemed to yearn for it, too. Her muscles were stiff and her organs shrinking, as if thirsty for more sustenance. For the sticky, gelatinous juice flowing through her family members' limbs. "So, you want me to speak with Gaia and get your kids out of Olympus? Is that all?"

"She won't do it. Gaia is preoccupied and will want all inhabitants here to ascertain their culpability."

"Please." Leto clasped her long, thin fingers together. Her foam-green nails sparkled in the heavenly glow from the outdoors.

"We want Apollo—he's delicious. Those arms are bulky and beautiful, rich with healthy ichor."

Leto's breath—a mix of pumpkin spices and pinecones—washed

over Rhea's face. "I never ask you for anything."

That was correct; Leto had sustained herself and her offspring for centuries. She'd birthed them, clothed them, defended them whenever Zeus was unfair. She'd even inspected their conquests—mainly Apollo's, since Artemis took no part in romance or sex—and gave her blessing for their most difficult journeys.

"Artemis' virgin skin would be gorgeous, splattered in blue ichor, tainted with toxins. Imagine the effects of our venom rushing in her arteries, Rhea."

For the first time since the voice had snuck into her bloodstream, disturbed her dreams, entered her conscious thoughts, Rhea hesitated. Since that fateful day a few years ago when she'd sensed its poisonous fumes flowing from head to toe, when its cravings became *her* cravings, when it became *her*. She'd never disobeyed its requests, though it had always been soft albeit persuading about them.

But these folk the voice wanted to drink from were her family. Her grandchildren, her precious nieces, nephews, her sex-seeking siblings or her fun-fulfilling friends. How would they differ from the creatures she'd ingested in the jungle? How would she be able to sink her claws into their flesh and her teeth into their throats without remorse, only heeding her ravenous hunger for their blood?

"I will help you, Rhea. I can tune in, turn your inhibitions off, restrict your vision. Let me take over...and we can devour these scrumptious sweetlings and bring them closer to us."

She still had no true inkling what this voice wanted, why it required immortal blood, and how its feedings never killed the recipient and only converted them into bloodthirsty beings like her. The internal speaker had urged her to test this theory on animals, first, and it hadn't always succeeded. Many beasts died as she drained them, and some died later, unable to survive as zombified beings. But when she'd begun to bite into humans, turning them without fail into hungry monsters who craved blood, she'd shifted her interest towards new victims. A handful of unimportant demi-gods that she'd encountered in the forest, or satyrs and nymphs that she'd come across in her travels.

The memories of Rhea's discoveries, of her rabid drinking spells, aroused her. Her veins engorged at the idea of squeezing the flavorful ichor into her mouth, its lavish lapis shade staining her teeth, its heavenly effects covering her insides in venomous victory.

"Lie. Lie to her, and covet those handsome children for your own desires."

"I make no promises," said Rhea, caressing her sister's chilly cheek. "Gaia is busy with all this madness, and she won't appreciate her offspring requesting favoritism."

Leto paled, and her shoulders slumped forward. It tugged at Rhea's heartstrings to have to pretend, to have to claim Leto's children would receive the safety they deserved. In truth, she'd soon be hunting them down and transforming them into the same ravenous monster she'd become.

"Rest easy, sister." Rhea plastered a peck on Leto's forehead, then marched backwards, toward her guest chambers, on the opposite end of the corridor. "I'll try my best to make a decent argument about this to her. Don't hold your breath, but I'll update you once we've spoken."

Leto bowed, one hand over her heart. Standing there in the moonlight, her comely curves so defined and dazzling, she was so pure, so gullible.

Rhea's lips slid into an easy smirk as she rotated towards the smaller, unlit guest hallway and cruised towards her quarters. Oh, she'd soon savor the substance she'd come all the way from her southern American forests for. She'd soon be loaded with godly ichor, and continuously ravenous for more. And she loved it.

|| 5. NOT CARNIVOROUS CUPID ||

LUKUS

Half-hunched, half-cozied up in the windowed reading nook overlooking the ever-elusive Olympus gates, Lukus fought to keep his chin up, to prevent himself from melting.

To his shock—and not Zeus' or Athena's—he hadn't burst into flames or coughed his heart out after touching the golden surface that blocked him from accessing the palace. Instead, when his fingertips grazed the glitter, a surge of energy shot up his arm, swirled in his shoulder-blades, then raced up his neck and down his back, into his legs. The sensation was like injecting an illicit substance into one's bloodstream. A substance loaded with ecstasy, adrenaline, oxytocin, ADHD medication, vanilla vodka, and countless grams of sugar.

Whatever this power had been, it still coursed through Lukus' insides, charging them, waking them. Whatever this magic was, it roused his limbs to action, gave him insight and intuition he'd never had before.

Like when he'd tripped up the marble stairs leading to the giant palace doors, he'd caught himself, somehow managing to set his foot on the step as if he'd never lost his balance. When the blinding brightness of the doors started to blur his vision, he somehow saw clearly after a few blinks, as if the glow no longer affected him as it had earlier. And as he passed the intimidating, lantern-lit throne-room, sighting its enormous thrones and the navy night sky seeping between the pillars weaved with vines, he'd felt nauseous and nervous. But the energy in him kept him standing straight, stopped his knees from buckling, and his guts from spilling from his mouth.

Now, settled in his guest suite, he fought to control the after-effects of the magic in his veins. His brain worked a million miles a minute, his thoughts were all over the place, and he couldn't sit still.

What the fuck was on that gate, and how did it get in me?

When dropping him off, Athena had informed him he'd adjust to the sensation in time. *"It's your immortality taking root in your core,"* she'd explained, once Zeus had abandoned them to pursue his other tasks. *"The gate recognized you as one of us. It conferred to you the ability to walk our halls and eat our food and see us in our true form without dying."*

Glancing at his luminescent arms, Lukus wondered; was *he* in his true form? Had he become some giant, long-legged, broad-chested creature in the seconds after he'd been accepted by Olympus? Or did he appear as his usual rugged self, with his smoky voice, his messy mane and all?

How will Aphrodite see me?

He shuddered. No, he was far from ready to meet with the woman who'd stolen his heart, but also notified him that she didn't *want* his heart. The gorgeous goddess who'd informed him he had no soulmate, and that his destiny was one only Zeus seemed privy to knowing.

He'd hoped that, once isolated in his quarters, he'd be able to unwind. That he'd be able to take in all the information he'd received, to take a moment to understand what was happening to him. This was when he'd usually crave a cigarette or two, and a glass of whiskey to wash down his emotions. Yet he didn't feel like he needed either of those. Something about that magic that flowed within him seemed to curb his former urges.

Despite being grateful that he'd no longer need to pollute his body to clear his thoughts, once he'd set foot in the elegant entryway of his suite, he knew his mind wouldn't rest in Olympus. Ever. Yes, this chamber had a *private lobby* with a cushioned divan and a coffee table and rows of wooden bookshelves…but such luxuries disturbed him more than comforted him.

He'd never been in a room so ornate, so opulent, with such delicate details along the crown molding, or such polished dressers or copper door-handles. Or lavish sheets that were so soft, so plush, he feared touching them would ruin them. The bed itself could contain five large people, and the pillows looked like clouds, a squishy foam that would envelop his head and mask his thoughts and transport him into realms of lullabies. The fresh linen scent mixed with frosted cupcakes welcomed him inside. And a gentle melody thrummed out of a pearl-shaped speaker in the far left corner of the sleeping area.

After Athena had bid him a good evening and closed his door, he'd crumbled to his knees, unsure what to do. Cry? Laugh? Pinch himself until he woke from this nightmarish dream? Get drunk beyond belief off whatever liquor the gods used to drown their woes?

Why would they roll out such a red carpet for him? What was this destiny reserved for him, and why'd the gods so suddenly realize how important it was? And why did they need to give him such ridiculously overwhelming accommodations? He was used to the grime of greasy motels and peeling wallpaper in rooms above seedy bars with rowdy music and bar-fights. Didn't they, the damned Greek gods, know he didn't require much in terms of comfort?

"It's only a guest room," Athena had mentioned, upon witnessing his jaw nearly tumble to the ground. *"Our other high-notoriety guests receive the same treatment. You're not much more special than them."*

The forced dismissal and fake disregard in her tone told Lukus that he *was* special. But he didn't have the might to prod for details yet, nor to inquire why it apparently disturbed Athena so much.

She'd been tense, her steps robotic as she'd guided him down the sconce-lit hallways of Olympus, mentioning this or that heroic tale, or gesturing towards a door that Lukus would soon be opening for himself. Though she still radiated with otherworldly beauty, and held herself upright with confidence, any time her eyes met Lukus', they were gray, slitted. She'd been so adamant on bringing him there, and now that they'd arrived, she appeared disappointed. She didn't drag her feet, per se, but her paces were nearly hesitant. Her every word to Lukus was short, simple, with little effort to compose her sentences.

Zeus' behavior had been the opposite, especially when Lukus had passed his gate-touching test. He'd clapped, the motion so thunderous it rattled the barrier and quaked the concrete beneath them. Athena had recoiled at the excitement, hurrying them both within the boundaries of Olympus. Zeus looked ready to grab Lukus and squeeze him in a bone-crushing—and likely life-draining—hug.

"Welcome to the family, Lukus." His voice had been ripe with pride and pleasure as they parted ways at a junction in the corridor, after gliding past the throne-room. The King of the skies headed down a darker, dingier appearing hall, while Athena motioned the way towards an opposite, warmth-ridden passage. Its walls were so pristine they appeared unreal, and its paintings seemed to come alive when Lukus glanced at them.

Would he one day be *in* those paintings?

"Nah," he said with a disheartened chuckle, peeling himself from the homey bench that he'd crawled to after entering the room. "Me? A demi-god featured in artwork in the halls of Olympus? Let's be fucking real for a second."

He opted to pinch himself a few times, just in case. But every twist of his skin did nothing but leave a faint red mark in its wake. He felt no pain, no sharp tug. If anything, the pinching woke up more of his profound and repressed memories; those Aphrodite had come to the hospital to erase from his mind.

The gut-wrenching images of him and Aphrodite having sex were the most prominent recollections, the ones that had flashed before him as if they'd actually happened. He recalled how, at the moment, when she'd stuck such pictures into his head, he'd believed them, fallen into them. He'd awoken from his daze nearly convinced he had indeed seen the gorgeous woman naked. That he'd been allowed to touch her fair skin, to lick the sweet spots she concealed beneath her lacy black bra, to sniff in the suntan lotion scent under her chin.

But the visions were only fabrications she'd employed to deter him from his skepticism; they were his deepest desires that she'd used against him. They hadn't worked, since he'd ended up drugged in a warehouse. And moments later, plunging his teeth into her delicate flesh and chomping away on her organs.

"Ew," he said, glaring at the tiled floor, as if expecting a pool of rich, scarlet blood to gather at his feet and invite him to slurp from it.

In the hours since Athena had returned his memories, he'd struggled to forget his carnivorous stint, and fought against the iron taste trickling into his mouth. And then the image of *him*; that blond-haired man in black leather who'd shot an arrow into his heart and turned him into a bloodthirsty, flesh-eating zombie.

Would he have to face him? *Eros?* Would they bump into each other in the corridors? Would Eros cackle at how easily he'd taken advantage of Lukus' mortality and his obvious intense crush on Aphrodite?

Heaving himself onto the bed, he took a lengthy breath and fell backwards onto the sheets. He let their softness caress the back of his neck, and their soothing texture lull him into a state of calm, a place of peace.

Though physically, he appeared to relax—his heartbeat slowed, the sweat coating his skin dried, and his nausea subsided—internally, there was no ceasing the questions, the inability to believe.

How am I part immortal?

Did he have a descendant, somewhere along the line, who'd copulated with a Greek god? Or was one of his parents a nasty, home-wrecking, deity-loving asshole who'd lied to the other about his legitimate parentage? He couldn't envision his mother cheating on Dad; but Dad was a secretive man, who only spoke to scold or poke fun or demean those he claimed to love.

Dad. It was Dad, for sure.

Athena had hinted that the link to his Greek ancestry came from one of his parents. And only now, in the diluted atmosphere of his private room, did he remember how she wasn't much more informed than him.

"Your destiny is valuable, and that is all I was told," she'd stated, before turning the doorknob to his quarters. *"The less you question me, or Father, the better."*

Was Zeus his father? Was Athena his sister? Had he been conceived by accident? Or had a god targeted one of his parents, enchanting them into doing whatever they wanted? That was a signature Zeus trait, if he remembered correctly. Did that make Hera his step-mother, Apollo his brother, and was Aphrodite—gasp—a distant but still somehow bonded by blood family member?

"No, gross." He gagged, holding in the vomit that began to prowl up his esophagus. "She would have said so. Someone would have warned me. No."

He reviewed options in his head, based on the myths and gods he remembered the names of, when a knock resonated from the door in the entryway.

Jumping from the bed—and not stumbling forward, to his surprise—he cleared his throat. "Uh…yes?"

Athena hadn't advised him whether to expect guests, or if he'd be summoned out of the room at some point. Was he supposed to get into pajamas—did part immortal beings wear those?—and snuggle under the covers and wait for a servant to bring him breakfast in bed?

He smirked at that, but his smirk wiped off his face immediately upon hearing the voice coming from the door.

"I'm to bring you to the throne-room," said a harsh yet eerily milky tone that chilled him to the core. A masculine, moody melody he could have sworn had repeated many times in his brain. It had haunted his dreams, bullied him in his waking moments. He'd never quite known who it was and why he couldn't stop hearing him.

It's…him?

He'd listened to that raspy tone over and over in his mind. To the sickeningly sordid laughter that accompanied it, and the roaring rage that took hold of it when Aphrodite had found him, confronted him.

"Sink your teeth into her skin, my friend…"

Lukus took one stable stride towards the lobby, but his brain flickered with scenes of carnage, blood, insides pouring out onto a filthy slab of concrete. He couldn't wobble, because of that damn magic cruising in his veins, but his overheating cheeks and tightening fists weren't from physical ailments. Those, the magic couldn't contain or reverse.

"Feast on her godly body..."

He gulped down the sickness slithering up his throat, getting closer and closer to his mouth. He didn't want to move forward, didn't want to open that door and see the man behind it. To witness the angry Greek god who'd made him into a puppet, a monster to further whatever his sick agenda was.

"Enjoy it."

His feet moved of their own volition; as if the new energy in him didn't give a damn about his former mortal feelings. As if he was a magnet drawn to the visitor on the other side of the door, and would leave no choice for Lukus but to confront his terror, his nightmares. The creature whose actions had haunted him for weeks, without him being able to make any connection, since his true memories were squashed beneath fake ones of how he'd solved his case.

"Eros?" he said, a weak whisper worming from behind his trembling lips. Whatever this godly energy was, it didn't assuage his fear, didn't fix it. It only had an effect on physical weakness, on clumsiness, on pain.

This pain was rooted in his abdomen, but flaring to life in his brain.

The door creaked open, and on instinct, Lukus shielded his face with his arms. He couldn't look. He couldn't visualize the cannibalistic piece of shit who'd been responsible for shaking up his life and fucking with his heart, his soul.

"Lukus," said Eros, his voice suave, smoother than Lukus had ever heard it.

He'd expected the click of big leather boots to echo off the floor as Eros approached. But with his chin dipped down he saw a different kind of shoe coming up to stand before him.

Sandals?

Plain, manicured feet in a pair of sleek, golden sandals, stopped inches from his tennis shoes.

Too curious for his own good, Lukus lowered his arms and looked up—face to face with his nightmare.

Eros, garbed in an off white tunic falling from one shoulder, leaving the other bare, clasped his hands near his navel. The garb drooped to his knees, and his legs were shaven and glossy. His exposed pectoral muscle bulged, and he offered a simple smile as Lukus focused on his glistening skin.

"That's not me, anymore," said the god, batting his long lashes over his rounded, amber eyes. "I don't need access to your thoughts to know you're scared, incredibly so. You always will be. But I'm," he pointed a bulky finger to his chiseled chest, "cured. I'm no longer an arrow-shooting asshole craving soulmate's hearts to fall at his feet. You're safe, Lukus."

Disbelief and distrust wove deep into Lukus' core, but there *was* something different about Eros. The malice in his tone was replaced by purity, by cautious sympathy. The flicker of fury in his gaze had disappeared, leaving room for a twinkle of kindness. And the hardened leathers he once wore were now puffy, pleated layers of white, ironed and emitting a docile cotton candy scent.

He was, all things considered, Cupid; not the carnivorous creature who'd tortured Lukus into eating a goddess's arm.

Thank fuck.

|| 6. MOONLIGHT DRINKING ||

HERA

Rocking herself into an acceptable stupor, thanks to the liquor loading in her blood, Hera tipped backwards in the swinging chair, her gaze fixed on the stars. Of all places to admire the night sky, she'd argue with anyone that the main courtyard was the most ideal location. Its open patio surrounded by tall bushes and its hanging lights from the dangling lily branches gave the area a romantic atmosphere, which she believed was perfect for star-gazing.

But each star she tried to focus on, to identify its constellation— she'd become recently fascinated in human astrology—doubled, tripled. She squinted, then widened her eyes, then rubbed them—but it was no use. Nothing fixed the blurriness.

How strong was Gaia's brandy?

No matter the percentage of alcohol in Gaia's concoction, and how it had filtered with ease into Hera's bloodstream, it hadn't quelled her questions about Athena, her worries about Zeus, her doubts about every other Olympian inhabitant. She'd hoped the brandy would at least shut down her thoughts for a spell. Instead, the images in her mind had grown worse, more vivid, further inducing a migraine she feared would be monstrous by morning.

Especially if she didn't put her goblet down now. Only a few sips of the liquid remained, and she swirled them, admiring the shimmer in the beverage—that hint of magic Gaia tended to tip into her tinctures. *"To soothe the soul,"* she'd say, with a wink of an eye and a smirk.

She hadn't smirked at all that night. Hera deflated in her seat, remembering how she'd embarrassed herself before the marvelous, majestic mother of all things. She lowered her chin, returning her view to the lush divans spread out across the way, near an extinguished marble fire-pit. Feet pressing to the floor, she started to stand, to entertain the idea of lounging on one of those divans and burying her face in the velvet cushions, to hide her tears. Tears of drunkenness or extreme embarrassment or fear, she wasn't sure; but those tears needed to come out.

She wouldn't shed them in the presence of her husband, in their enormous marital bed. Nor would she be caught dead showing such vulnerability in front of her children, adoptive offspring, siblings, or employees. Especially since they'd jump at the occasion to demean her more than they already did. Hera, Queen of the skies, sobbing? Heavens, that would be beyond detrimental for her worsening reputation.

Athena, above all others, would cackle in pleasure at the sight. She'd stop at nothing to ensure everyone knew of Hera's breaking apart and probably take the opportunity to ensure Zeus punished her for it, too.

"Wife?"

The thunderous tone took Hera by surprise, causing her to fall back into the swinging chair. She had stood up, apparently, and hadn't realized it, so deep in her nightmares of Athena's potential accusations and Gaia's disgust at her disgraceful demeanor.

Keeping her profile turned away from the intruder, she

straightened her shoulders. "Zeus?"

She fixed her wrinkled tunic and tugged a few fingers through her curls. They'd been married for eons, but Hera would never appear disheveled in front of her husband, if she could help it. She spun to find him slithering into the courtyard, his hair like waves of silky silver in the moonlight.

Oh, eons of marriage, yes—but how handsome and alluring he still was. Hera's heart skipped a beat at his approach, and her knees buckled under her skirts as his tall, tenebrous figure came closer to her tiny, tormented frame.

"I see my rules still do not apply to you," he said, folding his bulging bare arms over his broad chest. His eyes were their outer-space blue; the shade that could mean anything from arousal to anger.

Deciding not to tempt him into either extreme emotion, Hera hurried to gulp down the rest of her beverage. Liquid courage, was that what humans called it?

"I wasn't alone, but…forgive me, husband. I needed fresh air, a drink, a space to gather my thoughts."

Zeus sniffed the air, the motion rattling his lengthy salt-and-pepper beard. "Ah, yes." He winced. "Gaia was here, I smell her. Where is she now?"

Zeus and Gaia had a tremulous past. Between fighting for the rule of Olympus, and disagreeing on how best to imprison Gaia's unruly children—titans, giants, and monsters—they rarely saw eye to eye. Their tension was the reason Gaia usually steered clear of Olympus, preferring to concentrate on her protégés on earth, and to visit with her daughters and other family members away from the palace.

But such a situation warranted her aid, and Zeus had had no

choice but to summon her. They loved each other dearly, but struggled to tolerate one another for too long.

Hera sensed Zeus' discomfort at the scent of his grandmother, and reached out to caress the coarse but almost see-through hairs on his forearm. Before her fingers could graze his skin, he pulled away, drawing a few steps backward.

"Zeus?" Hera refrained from frowning at his refusal of her touch, and tucked a few locks behind her ears. "Gaia was here, but she returned to her quarters, I believe. To give me time to calm down."

"Calm down?" Zeus' biceps bloated as his veins turned to electric blue under his pale skin; a sure sign of irritation. "What did you do, Hera?" His voice didn't rise in volume, but it was choppy, impatient.

He means "cough up the details, and do not make me beg for them."

"Nothing." She scoffed, dismissing his question with a flick of her thin wrist, moving towards the middle of the patio. Her lengthy dress train slid over the pavement as if to cover her footsteps, as if *they* contained secrets she'd rather he not discover. "I am uneasy, and it's hard to withhold that from her. She disliked my venting, and told me to take some time to myself. But you," she flipped to him, whipping her hair in a sensual motion most men wouldn't dare ignore, "*you* are troubled, too. I can tell. What is it?"

Zeus combed his fingers through his tresses and sighed. "We have more company."

"Ah?" Hera's eyebrows elevated. "More help for the situation? Do I have time to prepare rooms this time?"

"No need." He waved at her to join him at the iron table. Wrinkling his nostrils, he sat on one of the hardened chairs and stretched out his long legs. "Our guest has already arrived, and is settled in the master guest suite."

"The master suite? Who—" Hera inhaled a sharp breath and flurried over to sit beside her husband. "That suite should have gone to Gaia, you know. I didn't understand why you wouldn't give it to her, and now I'm even more confused."

Zeus cracked his neck left and right, then angled backwards to peer up at the sky. "It's Lukus."

"Lukus?" Hera scrunched her nose. She recognized that name; but how and why would he be a visitor in Olympus? "The human? The agent who helped Aphrodite? For what purpose?"

"More help for the situation, like you said." Zeus' nonchalant voice didn't match his twitching toes and the blue veins continuing to shock through his limbs, flickering like lightning.

Hera hesitated to lean forward and cup his knee, hoping to slow his shakiness. Because of his earlier denial of her touch, she refrained.

"How could he help? He's mortal. What could he offer us that we don't already have?"

Zeus' legs jerked to life as he rose from the chair, surprising Hera into releasing a shy gasp. "Because he's *not* mortal, I confirmed it. He...he touched the gate. He passed through, meaning he's part immortal, as my sources claimed."

When Zeus spoke of sources, the identity behind them was often impossible to decipher. The Fates, the Graces, sometimes even the Muses. Poseidon and his gossip from the sea, Hades' whispers from down below, Ares and his overhearing of conversations near battlefields—any of these options were plausible.

"Lukus, the skeptical FBI agent, the one Aphrodite was nearly eaten by, the one Eros tortured? You're saying he's part-god? You..."

Her hands curled into fists, and she slammed them on the armrests of her chair. "Zeus, please don't tell me you went and fathered yet another demi-god. Please don't tell me I have to drown in another cup of brandy to digest this." She got up and pushed past him with a huff, sensing her habitual jealousy jarring through her like a knife splitting her in two. She groaned, then began to shove her sleeves up as she glared at her spouse. "Who am I rendering mad, this time? Which mortal bitch have you seduced, hm?"

Zeus' gaze found hers and immobilized her. Sparks of electricity shot from one pupil to the other, and the inflamed veins in his arms flurried up to his neck, coursing into his cheeks, zooming up to his forehead. His temples pulsed, and Hera recoiled, aware she'd crossed a line.

But how am I to remain calm when he all but confessed his infidelity? Again?

Zeus took three giant-like strides up to her, then snatched her wrists and squeezed them. "You are insolent. That's why Gaia is annoyed with you, I'll bet." He loosened his grip, but his scowl was sharp and concentrated on her, as if seeping under her flesh and burning it, electrifying it. "But no, wife dearest—I've been faithful for centuries, and that is the truth. Lukus is not my son, he's…well, he belongs to someone else, and I'm not at liberty to share that information yet."

Hera swallowed, the insides of her nostrils scorched by his sweet honey and ambrosia scent as it forced its way into her nose. "You know who his ancestor is? Who his real parents are?"

"I do." Zeus released her, and his shoulders slumped a smidgen forward before he rotated and rallied over to the swinging chair. He didn't sit, but instead moved the device front to back, as if the swaying motion lessened his stress. "But that's not why I brought him here. It's his destiny to dwell with us, in time. But he's also a gifted detective, and we could use some outside insight."

"Zeus." Hera tiptoed in his direction, but stopped short of a few feet from him when his voltaic gaze whipped to her. Despite her inebriated state, she wouldn't dare defy Zeus too much, else he'd shock her to sleep for the next few days. "Lukus is skilled at human investigation, not affairs of the gods. I'd overheard he was Greek, and raised in the belief of our existence, but he refuted his heritage. He'll have little knowledge to aid us, surely you…you thought of that?" She tried to not slur her words, yet she felt the liquor gathered in her belly, sloshing about, reminding her she was far from lucid enough for such a conversation.

But we must discuss this. He must understand what a grave error he's making in bringing a mortal here.

"Yes, well," Zeus blew out an exasperated breath, "he's no longer specializing in human investigations. The knowledge is something he'll pick up on; Athena will be investigating with him. The two, teamed together?" He let out a chuckle—a sound of near relief, of partial reassurance. "They'll find our culprit, Hera, I'm certain of it."

Hera had left the goblet on the table, and she now stared at it, wishing it would refill and float over to her hands. "Right, well, you made your decision, hm? You brought him here, you've appointed him to the task—so what do you want from me? You clearly have no interest in my opinion." Her mouth dropped wide open at her last words, but no further sounds escaped. She knew she'd gone too far, this time; but there was no way to repair the damage done.

Zeus would smack her seven ways to Tartarus for such drunken, daring implications. Oh, he'd make her see those stars she'd admired up close, sending her soaring skywards without a second of remorse. His temper, though usually controlled, was never something to test, especially during these trying times.

To her awe, however, Zeus did nothing rash—at least, not comparable to his past fits at her defiance. He unleashed a growl the likes of which Hera hadn't heard in centuries, causing the ground beneath her feet to shake, and her balance to shift, forcing her to her knees. In two quick hops, Zeus towered before her, and grasped her chin to hold her face up, to force her to look at him.

"I want you to come and try to make a good impression on our newcomer, as I'm introducing him to our main inhabitants right now, in the throne-room." His fingers pressed hard into her skin, and she had no doubt they'd leave marks that even her magical make-up would have a terrible time masking. "So you'll figure out some means to erase your intoxication and show up in ten minutes to meet Lukus. Am I clear?"

As swords pierced into her stomach and tingles traipsed from her head to her feet, Hera fought to readjust herself and get up. Zeus meant business, and if he hadn't half-drained her of energy right now, in fury at her back-talking, it meant he needed her. He needed Hera, his wife, the Queen of the skies, to recompose herself and be at his side.

"Fine." She sucked in a deep breath and perked up, swirling her fingers in the air to summon her crown. It swished into the courtyard a few seconds later, and rested atop her head, its razor edges digging into her scalp, waking her. The weight of the jewels seemed to temporarily rid her being of the alcohol, and infused her with her usual strength and poise. "Let us meet this not-so-mortal Lukus, then."

|| 7. INTRODUCING, LUKUS… WHO? ||
LUKUS

He'd seen it on the way to his guest suite, and still the throne-room bedazzled Lukus the longer he sat near its pristine pillars weaved with vivid, verdant vines. The nighttime breeze blowing between the marble brushed through his unruly hair, billowing down his back, stiffening him against the hardened stone of his *guest throne,* set up to face the other seats arrayed in a semi-circle.

Athena had been the one to explain the seating after Eros brought him to the throne-room. *"You're one of us, but we've not established who and how high ranked you are, so…"*

Most invited gods hadn't yet arrived. Eros and a beautiful blonde woman—Lukus assumed it was Psyche, Eros' wife—chatted in hushed tones near a side-door, and Athena showed Lukus around.

She pointed out Zeus' cushioned stone throne, in the middle; Hera's next to it, its surface regal blue, and with peacock feathers at its top. She indicated the puddles beneath Poseidon's luxurious spot, and hinted at the stench of alcohol and illicit substances surrounding Dionysus'.

Thankfully, Lukus' guest chair was far from the foul smells, set up straight across from Zeus and Hera. He'd heaved onto the bland, stony space with difficulty; even as a tall human, it was clear he was small for a god. A *demi-god,* supposedly.

The attendees of the impromptu meeting poured in one by one, sometimes in twos or threes. Two gods with similar, bouncy blond curls and wearing tunics that left little to the imagination sauntered in, deep in discussion. Their muscles bulged as they glared at one another, as a joke or in seriousness, Lukus couldn't tell.

A maiden in a fitted, short tunic paraded in with a dog at her heel. She ordered it to rest by the entrance as she flocked over to her spot— beside one of the barely-clothed blond men.

A long-haired, obscure looking deity swaggered in—more like wobbled—and even from afar, Lukus noticed the violet tint to his lips, and the red lines through his purplish eyes.

That one's Dionysus, for sure. He's the party one, right?

A few more hurried in, not paying Lukus much heed, too busy yawning, complaining about the late summons. Or catching up on gossip, or peering out at the night sky with peaked interest. Some had energies that made it difficult for Lukus to look at them. Or glows about their figures that were hard to penetrate, with features so cloaked in neutrality that he didn't bother to try recognizing them.

Among the final arrivals was *her.* The sea-green-eyed, luscious strawberry blonde beauty who'd captured his heart, stolen his breath, and destroyed his life. She waltzed in, arm-in-arm with a bulky hunk of a man who sported a copper helmet over his dark hair. She was tiny beside him, yet her voluptuous curves drew all the attention to her, and her measured footsteps contrasted his massive, monstrous ones.

Lukus had forgotten all about her and how she'd affect him once they met again. If she'd noticed him, if she cared, she didn't show it. No, she preferred to canoodle in a corner with the barrel-chested deity

Lukus assumed to be Ares, Eros' father, and her lover.

Agnes...Aphrodite. Gorgeous as ever, and unwilling to give me a chance.

When Zeus suddenly stormed in, dragging an olive skinned, crowned but scowling lady at his side, everyone sat and silenced. Including Aphrodite, who gave a brief nod at Lukus in acknowledgement.

Zeus directed the seething woman to the throne by his, and flipped to Lukus, hands on his hips. "Your room is to your taste, I hope?" His expression shifted from the irritation it had harbored when he'd entered, to a calm, genuine smile. He exuded absolute authority, yet allowed a veil of kindness when addressing Lukus.

The woman he'd lugged in with him folded her arms and huffed as she dropped into her throne. A few sleek strands of her chestnut hair slipped in front of her face, shading her eyes as she wriggled to and fro. Like a child throwing a tantrum, she fidgeted, muttering words under her breath that made no sense.

"Oh, Hera is drunk again," whispered one god, likely louder than he'd meant to. He was the second blond deity—the one who'd taken a seat towards the end of Zeus' side. He crossed one leg over the other, and Lukus cringed, positive he'd seen the man's private parts under his too-short tunic. Lukus encouraged body positivity and wasn't against nudity, nor wearing whatever one wanted; but such a sight wasn't the pleasant welcome he'd hoped for in his potential new home.

Athena, in her spot a few spaces down from Zeus' chair, wrinkled her nose, but her lips twitched upward, if only for a few seconds.

Someone else chuckled at the insult, but Lukus didn't have time to see who, as Zeus spun to his constituents and growled. His spine tensed, and his arms tightened at his sides, his skin surging with sparkling blue veins.

"Hera is none of your concern; not tonight, at least," he barked to all in attendance. "So let us not focus on her, please?"

As he marched to the doors, grumbling about *"late arrivals,"* each step shook the mirrored floor, rattled up through the pillars. Most of the deities fixed on him, tense and quiet. They held their tongues, straightened their postures. Some appeared to not even breathe, waiting for their king to return to the center stage and explain why he'd requested their presence.

Hera, shoving her curtain of curls from her face, glanced at Lukus. Her eyes, a cold but chocolaty brown shade, flashed with blue as she adjusted the sapphire encrusted crown atop her head. She didn't glare, yet there was nothing gentle about her gaze as she kept it on Lukus, lingering, as if to dig deep into his brain.

Her hostility furthered Lukus' questions about his parentage. He had a hard time recalling all his Greek myths, but he did remember that Hera, Queen of the skies, was a scorned and often betrayed woman. Zeus had cheated on her with over half the planet—mortals and immortals combined—and she'd spent eons pursuing the culprits and driving them mad. Her demeanor tonight…did it mean Zeus was Lukus' father? That he'd gone astray again, and she'd found out, and was pissed?

Interrupting Lukus' thoughts, she flinched and looked askance once Zeus stomped back to his spot.

"I doubt Poseidon will show; his response to my summons was a bunch of gibberish, but it implied we shouldn't wait for him. So we'll start without him." He kept his back to Lukus, once more addressing his royal family. "I've asked you here tonight because we have a new family member."

He twirled to Lukus, expression awash with an odd pride, a glowing gold growing over his sky-blue gaze.

"Family member?" The voice came from a lady far on Hera's side. Her metal-blue eyes pierced through Lukus before softening and focusing on Zeus. "Brother, are you sure?" Her wheat-colored gown shifted down her shoulder, and she tugged it up, exchanging a quick glance with a flaming mahogany-haired woman off to the side, near a small door. "Sister? Is this accurate?"

The second woman, her attitude off-standish, almost displeased, raised her shoulders. "How would I know? I work in the kitchens now; and I don't chat with the Fates anymore."

"I am sure," said Zeus, snapping at the two goddesses, demanding their attention. "It's unnecessary for me to specify how I know, but I do. Lukus Arvantis is a direct descendant."

"Of whom?" The youthful goddess who'd wandered in with her dog narrowed her light gaze at Zeus. One foot dangled off her mud-covered throne, and she'd drawn the knee of her other leg up to her flattened chest. Leaves in colors of autumn stuck to the armrests, and she set one of her hands atop them, making a *crunching* sound. "Did you have another affair, Father?"

Whoa—that's a pretty bold statement in presence of all these gods, right?

Gasps came from Hera's side of the room, and glowers appeared on several faces.

"You should watch your tongue in such a presence, Artemis," muttered the other blond-haired deity with little covering over his lower half.

She waved him off, an air of familiarity in the gesture. "Everyone was thinking it, Brother; I merely said it out loud to not waste time."

Two women who'd remained out of the way, not far from the kitchen-working goddess, wouldn't remove their eyes from Lukus. Both had reacted to the "affair" claims with a sharp intake of breath, but kept their concentration on the newly introduced family member.

One of them looked like a majestic tree with her layers of emerald satin cloaking a tall, sensuous body. Her hair poked out of her scalp like fiery branches, and her dirt-colored eyes blended into her tanned skin like roots blending into soil. She mumbled something to the woman beside her who, though her dress was a form-fitting burnt-orange and her wild locks were reminiscent of a lion's mane, was an eerie copy of Hera.

Zeus' arms charged with electricity, and though he looked ready to hurl a thunderbolt at the girl on the leaf-battered throne, he refrained, his body wracking with shivers as he contained himself. Lukus feared he'd be electrocuted from the proximity, and he recoiled in his seat, shielding his face, bracing for death.

"No one is dying," said Athena, her tone annoyed as she rolled her eyes at Lukus. She waved at her fellow gods in dismissal. Earlier she'd been so fearful, so deflated in Zeus' presence. But in front of everyone else, she perked up, taking on her role of goddess of wisdom with seriousness. "Father, they're tired. We're all tired. Forgive our reactions, but is there anything you can tell us about Lukus' parentage?"

"No." Zeus replied so fast, with the strength of a lightning bolt, its intensity forcing everyone's mouth shut. "Not that it's anyone's business, but I didn't cheat, as I explained to Hera, earlier. And no, I cannot divulge anything else about Lukus' heritage. Not yet. We have other matters to focus on."

"My King?" A tentative voice grew from somewhere behind

Lukus, soon accompanied by the timid footsteps of Eros. He stepped up to Zeus and bowed. "I made certain claims about Lukus when I…" he winced, "tortured him, and I'd like to verify those."

"What claims?" Zeus crossed his arms, his furious energy dimming next to Eros' surprisingly soothing charisma.

"He said Lukus doesn't have a soulmate," said Aphrodite, with a tremble in her tone. She didn't glance at Lukus, instead admiring her bubblegum pink nails as her fingers twitched near her armrests. "Gods don't have assigned soulmates, so that is further proof of your statement, Majesty."

Zeus kept his arms close to his chest, but twirled his beard with his finger, peering between Eros and Lukus with shifting eyebrows. "Indeed, it is. Well, get on with it, then." He gestured at Eros to work his magic.

Without hesitation, Eros flurried over to Lukus. He offered a flimsy smile, and Lukus flinched, reluctant to let him touch him.

"This will be quick, and won't hurt," whispered Eros, as he used his strength to draw Lukus into a straightened position.

Funny he'd say that, as he once shot an arrow straight into my chest.

Lukus groaned, wishing he could deflect the god's touch; but he had no clue how to use his powers, if he had any.

Eros set his warm palm over Lukus' heart. The lovely lady he'd been talking to earlier shimmied over and placed her hand over Eros'. She was charged with serenity, permitting Lukus to relax for the first time in days.

Together, she and Eros hummed, chanting as they pressed harder into Lukus' torso, and a wave of heat emanated from their touch.

Before Lukus could cry out—the heat rose, charring his insides, and he wanted to curse the deity's name for lying to him—Eros and his wife removed their hands and turned to Zeus.

"It's confirmed. He," Eros scrunched his nose, "he has no soulmate. I never marked him at birth. I never even knew of him."

Though Lukus was already aware of this, the confirmation of it still stung. He'd never wished for a stable lady in his life, nor was he the type to settle down and build a family of his own. But to be stripped of the option, to not have the chance like others did, left him numb, a smidgen disappointed, a tad overwhelmed by emotions he couldn't understand. Sadness? Confusion? Freedom?

"Not having a soulmate doesn't mean not being able to love, Lukus," said Athena, glimpsing him through slitted eyes, clearly the only one reading his thoughts. She held her chin up, her elbow resting on her bronze armrest.

"She's correct. I'm glad she's able to translate what you're feeling." Zeus approached Lukus, his lips sliding into a sympathetic smile. "As a demi-god, you will have your pick at just about anyone—"

"—Father." Athena's voice had changed from reassuring and calm, to overpowered and perturbed. It resembled the one she'd used when rousing Lukus from his stupor, when explaining he had a purpose, a new life that awaited him. Determined, laced with truth.

Zeus twisted to his favorite daughter. "Yes? You have more to add about soulmates? That's not quite your area of expertise, is it?"

Athena rose from her seat, but didn't move forward. "No, I've nothing to add in that domain. We're not here for soulmates and origins; we have bigger matters to investigate, no? So you've introduced Lukus, who is to help me. Now I have news of my own to share, before we proceed."

A silence so heavy filled the room, Lukus could have sworn he heard the wind whooshing outside. He could have sworn he was listening to the gods' breathing, their saliva slipping down their throats, their heartbeats thrumming in their rib-cages.

Zeus, strangely solemn in the wake of his daughter's interruption, cocked his head. "What news? What would you need to reveal here, before submitting it to me for approval, as is the custom?"

Never removing her gaze from her father, Athena whipped an arm out to point to the other side of Zeus' throne. "I have finally narrowed down my list of suspects, and your wife," her slender finger aimed right at Hera, whose jaw dropped, "is my number one suspect."

|| 8. WIFE VS. DAUGHTER ||

HERA

"What?"

Hera's peacock scream seared all ears—including her own. It silenced the room, sobering everyone—including herself—into sitting up straight and staring at her in…disbelief? Awe? Possibly pleasure at seeing someone take her down? She wasn't sober enough to work out *that* part. She glimpsed the blurry figure of Athena, on the other side of Zeus' throne, her stubby finger still pointed in Hera's direction.

"Me? Number one suspect?"

She never employed the English insults her humans often used, but many of them swirled in her brain as she watched her family react to the allegation.

Damn. Shit. Fuck. What else do they say?

Athena remained stiff, upright, her muscular arm not once twitching as she continued to point at Hera. "You heard me."

Zeus, his eyes flashing like a raging tropical storm, peered between his favorite daughter and his wife. "What is the meaning of this? Are you two in another of your spats?"

His voice was too calm for the situation, and Hera gritted her teeth before begging him to speak out in her favor; as his bride, she deserved his protection, no? Yet to prod at him now, before he'd had a chance to digest what was going on, was dangerous.

A throaty chortle came from the doorway, and though she hated to turn her back on her accuser, Hera spun towards the sound.

Her brother, the moody, mean King of the seas, had arrived, in perfect late fashion. His thunderous intrusion roused a few other onlookers from the scene of Athena's morbid accusation, thankfully taking a few glares off of Hera.

Why did he come at all? Zeus hates tardiness.

The brooding brother, Poseidon, stood against the door-frame. "Oh, I showed up in time for the drama, I see."

Zeus barely paid him any heed, fixed on his beloved child instead. "Athena, explain yourself. I'm trying my damndest to stay calm, but your silence is pushing me." The veins glowing up and down his arms, and zipping to his legs, were proof that he was in no mood to be tested.

Even I know that...yet she dares accuse me in front of him?

"We are not on the greatest of terms, but why would you stoop so low?" Hera fought the tremble in her voice. "And without proof? That is unlike you."

Despite her anger, it was sadness that prevailed in Hera's heart, messing with the liquor sloshing in her belly. She wanted to yell, to hurdle up to Athena and strangle her; and yet the accusation wounded her pride, threatening to melt her strong facade.

"You do not know me." Athena wouldn't look at Hera; as if the simplest exchange of glances would dissuade her, weaken her, embarrass her. She concentrated on her father, lowering her arm to her side, at last. "An anonymous witness singled you out, actually. It would be foolish of me to ignore their concerns."

"Singled me out?" Hera gulped, and an acid flavor of ichor

resided in her throat. Her limbs frosted over, and her fingertips became numb. "W-who? I would…Zeus…" She fought to twist her neck to her husband, who remained planted in the middle of the room, solemn and silent as a tree. "Would you please explain to your daughter that I'm not responsible for all this nonsense?"

Zeus smacked a palm to his face and meandered behind Lukus' seat, almost as if fleeing the area, as if refusing to address the issue.

"What in the heavens am I going to do with you people?" The exasperation in his tone was difficult to analyze. Was he annoyed with Athena, for crashing his introductory party for Lukus? Or disgusted at the alternative that his spouse might be involved with the poisoning of the deities under his watch?

The half-mortal, as it turned out, was as frozen as Hera, his jaw about to reach the floor, his striking sapphire eyes wide with wonder. His shoulders drooped as he switched his view from Athena, to Hera, to Athena again. He'd appeared somewhat strong to Hera, earlier, when she'd first laid eyes on him. Sturdy shoulders, a wide but well-built frame; but now he seemed to shrivel, revealing more of his weak, mortal side than she could tolerate.

Not that he matters, but he will back her claims, no doubt.

"This is absurd." Hera gripped the soft edges of her throne and heaved herself up. Though her vision remained foggy from alcohol abuse, she'd regained most of her balance, sobered up from Athena's cruel misgivings. "Surely none of you believe this, right?" She peeped to her left, at her fiercest allies, siblings, children; then dared look to her right, where Athena stood, finally deigning to accord her a glance—loaded with spite and heavy with accusation.

"I'd wager more gods believe it than not," said Athena, her tone sharp like a poison-dipped dagger, shredding into Hera's careful composure.

"You are all absurd," muttered Zeus, resurfacing at last.

He'd been grunting behind Lukus' seat, obviously at odds with himself and unclear on how to handle what was going on between his daughter and his wife. A storm still brewed in his gaze, but it surprisingly hadn't changed to navy—the ultimate proof of his fury.

"This was ill-timed, Athena. Why did you not speak with me privately, first? Why do you continue to defy me? I trusted you; that's why I put you in charge of this investigation. Yet you…you cause trouble, like this? And," he winced as he glimpsed towards the doorway, near where Rhea and Gaia stood still, silently seething, "in presence of important company?"

Athena kept her posture straight, but a smidgen of shame urged her cheeks to twitch and her furious energy to soften. "I—"

"And *you*—" Zeus stomped up to Hera and grabbed her by the shoulders. "Do not look so smug! *You* push her buttons so much, it has brought us to this! To silly, unfounded confrontations in a crowded throne-room, before our newest family member? What will he think of us?"

Hera, though initially shocked by Zeus' electric touch, wriggled out of his grasp and distanced herself from his impulsive irritation. "Who cares? I bet he's aware of the temper of the gods, no?"

With a grunt, Lukus nodded; then shook his head; then nodded again.

The poor sod has no idea what to think. He fears us. As he should.

"You will not even defend me from this preposterous girl's allegation?" Hera snickered, wishing she had the authority to slap her spouse, to demand his loyalty to her—the way he demanded her respect for all his illegitimate children. "Well, I suppose what matters is," she traipsed over to where Demeter sat, and prostrated before her, "that I have other family members who'll stick up for me."

Demeter, steely eyes trained on Zeus, shot to her feet. "Oh, you have me on your team. You always will." Her light raspberry scented tunic swished as she bent over to help Hera stand upright. "I will not sit and watch this idiocy take place. It is, as Zeus stated, absurd." She flipped to Athena, and her skin burned as she held Hera close. "You play with fire, girl."

"Sister." Zeus' timbre was one of warning, baritone and bordering on rage, though low in his throat.

Another hand slid into Hera's, and she gawked at its owner— Hestia, all her neutrality faded, leaving place to a rarely witnessed annoyance, manifesting over her skin in an orange glow. Her eyes never shifted with her moods, but her energy burst forth like a bonfire.

"You are being irrational, Athena," she said, serene despite her flaring temperature. "And you, brother, are putting your offspring before your spouse. By my terms, this is unacceptable."

Hestia never participated in godly wars—whether they be small spats near the kitchens, or downright battles on earthly fields. Her decision to involve herself here meant more to Hera than anything else. Hera squeezed her hand in thanks, and fixed her gaze on Zeus.

"Anyone else care to help deny and dispel such horrific accusations?"

She smelled him before she saw him; Poseidon, swaggering over to the center of the space, leaving murky puddles of water in his wake. His glossy gaze showed he'd been drinking that evening, too, and his seaweed and smoke stench revealed he'd been out and about, not confined to his ocean castle.

That would explain why he took forever to get here.

To Hera's shock, he didn't stop beside her and her sisters—he trailed onward and posed before Athena with a brief bow of his head.

"Sorry, Hera," he snapped, without locking eyes with Hera. "I'm with Athena on this one. You've been sneaky as of late, and I don't trust it."

"How dare you?" Hera's fists bunched as she tried to worm out of Hestia's grip and fought Demeter's clutch—both knew she was prone to engaging in physical combat with her brothers if they demeaned her.

Poseidon shrugged, and sat on the step leading to Athena's throne. He wore leather pants—uncommon for gods, meaning he'd been mingling with humans—and his squishy movements made Hera clench her jaw.

"It's because he still wants Athens to himself. He still thinks he can reverse its preferred god from Athena to him, of course, so he'd flock to her to…how is it the humans say it? Oh yes, to *kiss her ass,*" whispered Demeter, drawing Hera back to her before she did something she'd regret. "We don't need him. He's fickle and, to be fair, he'll change his mind when Athena doesn't give him his heart's desire. Fret not."

Her reassuring words did nothing to soothe Hera. Athena, in her hasty accusation, had started a civil war. Perhaps she'd meant to—perhaps this was a sordid trick to root out the real culprit. But if that were the case, why hadn't she consulted Hera on her plans? Were they not allies? Were they not joined against—

"Hecate." Hera's hiss was inaudible to her sisters, but she'd intended it so. She'd wanted to hear the name reverberate in her throat, for its letters to lather her tongue in toxins, for its sound to surge through her and erase all the brandy that had been clouding her senses.

She made a deal with Hecate, not with me. Now the two are teaming against me?

Several gods hadn't lifted from their seats, and Hera had no intention of letting them sit this discussion out. "Ares!" She clapped at her war god of a son, summoning him to her at once. "Hephaestus; don't even think about it," she said, as she sighted the forge-dwelling deity beginning to rise to his feet, his focus on Athena. "She hates you more than I do, so don't be stupid. Side with your real family; your mother."

Both her sons floundered over to her; Ares with his chin dipped, his imaginary tail between his legs, and Hephaestus leaning on his magic metallic cane but grumbling gruesome insults under his breath. Towards whom, Hera would have rather not known. But grotesque as he was, she needed his support now more than ever.

For the two additions to her army, four others rallied instead to Athena's cause. Hermes, with a blown kiss of spite at Hera, flopped onto Athena's throne in pure defiance. Dionysus—likely not sane enough to make his own decisions—wobbled over to fall beside Poseidon, and they nudged each other while exchanging blubbered, drunken words. Apollo and Artemis—no big surprise there—sent fleeting glances to their unresponsive father before marching to Athena and bowing to her.

"This is ridiculous," said Zeus, lingering near Lukus, as if waiting for the demi-god to express his own opinion, to help the king out. "Return to your seats, all of you." His voice was too tame, too timid; no one listened. "You'd provoke me, again? You'd press this matter and create a divide among us? We've had centuries of peace. This is idiotic." His veins weren't popping out anymore, and his gaze had turned to a rainy winter night; gray and boring. If fury still roamed in his blood, he'd hidden it.

One could say he was used to evenings like these. This wasn't his first viewing of such hostility, of such division among his constituents. The Trojan War had separated his family members and lowered their guard, and Hera knew he was remembering those events with clarity now, as he leered at his children and siblings.

But why not get riled up as usual? Why remain so calm?

Hera craved to run up to him, to grab his upper arms and shake him, much like he had done to her moments prior. Because *he* needed the awakening, not her. He was stuck, lost in transition, overwhelmed by his favorite daughter's accusation and torn between believing it or not.

Would he choose her over me?

Aphrodite sidled up to Hera, her languorous steps about to make Hera gag. She sent a brief glance towards Lukus, then gaped at Ares, and at her husband, and shook her head. "I cannot."

Hera hadn't counted on her alliance; it was no secret the goddess of love and the Queen of the skies were far from friendly towards one another. "Go on, then. But your spouse and your lover stay with me."

Cheeks flushing with a rosy hue, Aphrodite pinched her lips and, with clear reluctance, she swished over to Athena and snuck her hand in hers. She whispered something in the wisdom goddesses' ear, and Athena cringed.

"Do you see how you've divided us, step-mother dearest?" Athena's voice amplified over the chatter, its volume piercing but steady. If she'd trembled earlier, if she'd doubted herself at any point in time, Athena no longer exuded her woes. She stood tall, shoulders pulled back, chest sticking out, with her array of soldiers surrounding her.

When Athena cast a furtive peek towards Zeus, Hera could have sworn she detected a whiff of fear in her expression. Was she worried that Zeus stood unresponsive, still?

Hera sensed two more presences join *her* crew. Two figures charged with disappointment at Athena, and sudden sympathy for the woman they'd abandoned on the terrace earlier, because they thought she'd thrown a fit.

"We're here," said Rhea, her lion's purr pumping into Hera's ears.

"And we apologize," added Gaia, infusing the area with her forest and flower aroma. "We should have listened when you said you smelled something amiss with her."

Athena scowled at them. She had the numbers, but Hera had the power, and there was no mistaking it. And yet, nothing seemed to deter the wisdom goddess and her lack of empathy or regard for the truth.

"Confess, Hera. It'll be easier for all of us. Confess, and we'll rectify this divide and all in Olympus can rest once more. Our activities can resume as normal."

Zeus and Lukus, crammed in the midst of the commotion, breathed in tandem. Insistent as he was that Lukus wasn't his descendant, they were so similar in this moment, it was disconcerting. The same hesitation in their gazes, the same rhythm of scratching at their cheeks, rubbing their chins.

"You have nothing to say, husband?" Hera crossed her arms, glowering at Zeus without remorse.

She'd normally refrain from such measures, but if she didn't press him, he'd never choose. He'd never interfere to cease this nonsense before it went too far. He'd never break free from the strange trance that was keeping him quiet, urging him to keep his feelings to himself. An uncommon reaction; he'd usually storm around and scream and punish, even his favorite daughter. But tonight he was stoic, his lips sealed.

Clapping a hand to his forehead, Zeus again moseyed behind Lukus' chair, his steps quaking the mirrored floors. He groaned, he cursed in ancient Greek, he even let loose a few strings of electricity, aiming them at the walls—but he didn't take sides, didn't speak for his daughter or his wife.

He was too mild compared to his usual self.

What holds him back? Did someone warn him, threaten him if he were to take sides? Does he know something none of us do?

Though grateful for those who'd come to her aid, Hera released her strengthened exterior and shrank away from her protectors.

"It's no use." She sneered at her frail mess of a spouse. "He won't get involved. I told you he was acting odd, and this proves it. He'll leave us all to devour one another, as he has in the past. This," she waved at her group, then at Athena's, "won't resolve overnight."

"Daughter," said Rhea, reaching out to snag Hera's wrist. "Do not let this go. You were right—Zeus is off, but Athena is up to something, and we must act now. Zeus must see reason."

"He won't." Hera didn't fight her mother's fingers, and instead tugged her towards the door with her. "He'll react at the last minute, when he deems it necessary. And when he does, it'll be in *her* favor, you watch. I'm too tired for this." With her free hand, she massaged her temples, headed for the exit.

Rhea let her go.

When Hera arrived at the threshold, she overheard Rhea's mutterings. "I'll keep an eye on her; she appears calm now, but who knows what she'll do once she's alone?"

Snorting, Hera stole into the corridor. She growled at the portrait of Heracles across the way.

Who knows, indeed? At least Heracles knew not to test me—but will Athena learn from his mistakes?

|| 9. A RUSH OF BLOOD ||
RHEA

"Hera, wait."

Rhea was near-breathless by the time she caught up with her daughter, outside the throne-room. Her breaths further choked in her throat when the queen flipped around and glowered at her.

"Unless you seek to help me fight back against that ungrateful child, Mother," Hera's lips pinched, "I'd ask that you let me go." Her eyes were like melted chocolate, on the brink of oozing with tears—from pain or indignation, Rhea couldn't tell.

Their hair aside—Rhea's was more unruly, untamed—they mirrored each other. And more so in how they expressed their emotions. It was easy to see if Hera or Rhea were angered; and there was no doubt here that Hera's rage would soon overflow. From her twitchy, temperamental tone, to the sparks flying off her skin, Rhea knew her daughter was on the verge of an explosion.

"I'm not here to drag you back into that chaos." Rhea pressed a hand to one of the coppery walls for stability, and allowed her heart to resume its regular speed. "Only to assure that you're okay."

"Okay?" Hera's nostrils flared. "*Okay?*" Her skin flecked with sparkles and began to glow gold. "She dares…that spoiled, sniveling little bitch dares accuse me?" She snatched her crown and tossed it over Rhea's shoulder, not once shuddering as it crashed against a statue and bounced to the opposite end of the corridor.

Rhea spun to take a gander at the tiara—the same she'd worn as queen, centuries ago—and winced. "Was that necessary?" It wouldn't shatter, made of the magical, godly material of all royal deities; nevertheless, to see it treated with such impulsive rage was disappointing.

"No, because I would have preferred to hurl it in her face and watch its edges scratch that perfect flesh of hers—"

The word *flesh* woke a growl in Rhea's belly. An animalistic urge to feed, coupled with visions of tearing into necks and slurping up the rich, warm liquid hiding under heaps of fur and feathers.

Still keeping her balance with one hand on the wall, she placed her other over her abdomen, praying her daughter couldn't hear its rumbling. "Enough, Hera. It's an act, it must be. Athena is..." She twitched her lips, unsure what words would soothe her daughter—or at least postpone her fury before she went on a murder spree. "She's seeking attention from Zeus. What I discovered since I arrived is that she's been defiant; and you told us so yourself, remember? Lying, resorting to manners she's never used before."

"But..." Hera sucked in a heavy breath, and deflated as she puffed it out. Her frame rattled and her big brown eyes charged with tears—like they had when she was a child, eons ago.

Rhea remembered the fitful little girl goddess who wanted nothing more than to marry and become the Queen of Olympus. The teenager who threw things when she didn't get her way.

That explains the crown tossing.

"Why would she charge me in front of everyone?" Hera sniffled, and stiffened, as if she hadn't been about to tumble into her mother's arms. As if Rhea had imagined her brief vulnerability. "Why would she stoop so low?"

"For attention. I told you."

Rhea's stomach twisted and roared, and a groan echoed in her mind. The voice—it had been dormant, and it was waking. She had to hurry and end this conversation before it asked her to eat her own daughter.

"She's pressed for time and isn't analyzing her evidence properly. With that...*Lukus*, was that his name? With him around, she'll focus her energy better, I'm sure. I'll talk to Zeus, all right?" She reached out to push a few matted chestnut curls from Hera's face, but her belly brayed in response, forcing her to stay still instead. "You go...sleep, hm?"

"Sleep?" Hera arched a brow. "How could I sleep after all this? The alcohol has drained from my system; that encounter sobered me. I need more of Gaia's brandy—"

"Drink. Now."

Rhea bit her tongue before lashing out at the voice. It had been tormenting her since she'd spoken with Leto, earlier. And somehow, it had remained quiet during the meeting, and uncaring during Athena's outburst. But in this deserted hallway, facing Hera in her anger, it was thirsty.

Rhea had denied it for too long. It had begun to tighten her intestines, to fight with her insides, to remind her *it* was the boss. *It* decided when it was time to feed. And it always had, even in the wilderness...but it had been nicer about it, then. Why was it suddenly so bossy?

On cue, the sound that only Rhea could hear hummed to life in her ears. The one that haunted her until she responded to its gushing, until she ended it by guzzling up the life-juice of the being nearest her. The familiar rush that made her salivate. That *thump, thump* of a heart pumping the delicious liquid, filtering through organs, rushing to extremities. The gurgling of Hera's blood—not an animal's for once; this pull was harder to resist.

I'm not drinking from Hera. I refuse.

The voice crackled through Rhea's brain. *"Naturally. You will take your leave of Hera and find us a drink. At once. Or else I'll—"*

"Mother?" Hera came back into view; Rhea hadn't realized her vision had become blurry, and she'd been wavering to and fro, as if about to faint. She'd spaced out, and needed to get away from Hera, fast. "Are you unwell?"

Rhea shrugged, but Hera took that as a signal to continue speaking—which she'd apparently been doing as Rhea struggled to remain lucid.

"As I was saying, I'm going to summon those on my team—you included—once I've settled my nerves. Probably in one of the smaller ballrooms; I'll send word. Will you be there?"

"I…" Rhea jammed her fingers to her temples, fighting the slurring of her speech, praying to ignore the constant *thump, thump,* and that swishing sound of blood sliding from one vein's end to another. "Yes, sure…I…"

Hera's touch startled Rhea, erasing her fogginess for enough time to barrel backwards, away from her daughter.

"Mother?" Hera squinted, cocking her head. "Perhaps *you* need to sleep, hm? I'll have someone fetch you once I have a game-plan. Go rest."

"I…" Again, Rhea fought to speak. Her instinct was to go to war for her daughter, to be outraged at Athena's overstepping, to ensure her family didn't come to arms over such silly yet serious accusations.

But the longer she lingered in Hera's presence, the more the scent of her became too hard to resist. The pull of her powdery fresh, delicate skin was too much—

"Go, Mother." Hera leaned forward to push Rhea, but Rhea skidded out of reach before they made contact. The simplest touch would send her over the edge, and she wouldn't sink her fangs into her child. She couldn't.

"Right." Rhea whirled around and bolted in the other direction. "Summon me…later…"

She didn't wait for Hera's reply, nor did she turn to view her reaction. She stumbled along the hall, unsure where she was going, unclear on how to control her urges.

"You cannot control this. You're here to satisfy your hunger, grow stronger, remember?"

"But…" Rhea had no means to bar her words from spilling out, and she hoped no one was in the vicinity to hear her talking to herself. How bad would that look? With a culprit on the loose—and her waddling up the corridor, lost and ravenous, they'd accuse her at once. Which would spare Hera…but Rhea wasn't the wrong-doer, was she? And she couldn't be caught.

"You will *be caught if you don't drink. Now. Enough delaying—your body needs this.* I *need this."*

Though its timbre was familiar, and fairly feminine, Rhea still had no clue if it was her voice, or someone else's, oddly morphing inside her mind. What sort of toxins could do such a thing to a goddess of her standing? What magical animal had the power to rouse such screams in her brain without having bit her, poisoned her, demanded that she do its bidding?

"I'm not an animal. Stop fighting me. We need to—"

A shadowy figure appeared in the hallway, a dozen steps from where Rhea had stopped, grasping at a door-frame, in desperate need for somewhere to lie down, to gather her thoughts, to shove her cravings down.

This person's arrival woke her immediately, dissipated her dread, fixed her fogginess. It smelled like heaven on a stick, like sweet buns straight out of an oven. Like ambrosia cakes and honey and roses and those fancy French pastries she couldn't remember the name of—

"Rhea?" The tone, timid at first, came closer. Its owner, a shapely woman draped in an off-white tunic dropping off one shoulder, carried a set of brass scales in one hand, and her other rested on her hip. "What are you doing?"

Only one goddess walked around with scales—in case her judgment, her opinion, was needed.

"Themis, sister dearest." Rhea fumbled to adjust herself, to pretend like she hadn't been about to take a bite from the nearest painting to shut that damned voice up.

Themis, a titaness with a long history with Zeus—and several children by him—was a recurring visitor of Olympus. Often, she resided there, while weighing in on political debates on earth that were too exhausting to witness in person. She kept watch over lawyers and judges and criminals, lifting her scale up, waiting for it to tip in someone's favor. And she yelled if the situation below didn't go the way she'd predicted it.

She was one of Rhea's more serious siblings, who kept to herself and didn't mingle much with the family.

"Oh... then she won't be missed, will she?"

"Shut up," Rhea snapped, before shaking her head. "I mean, *shut up,* you darned migraine!"

"Ah." Themis fiddled with the thick scarlet sash around her upper waist, under her heavy bosom. "I presume you came from the throne-room? I was just headed there, because I surmised something of a commotion happening, and figured my opinions could be of use—"

"—it's over." The pulsing in Rhea's ears amplified, and she flinched once, twice, three times, grinding her teeth. "They…Athena…berserk debauchery…"

"Do it."

Rhea nearly forgot Themis was there, and stood stunned at the voice's urging. "My…my own sister?" Her tongue throbbed with thirst, with hunger, with desire.

"Rhea?" Themis approached, caution in her stance, her darkened eyebrows drawing upwards. "You are paler than usual. Have you eaten?" Leaning in closer, she parted her sheet-white blonde hair with a few fingers, the violet hues in the strands shimmering in the nearby candlelight.

"See? She cares for your wellbeing. So, eat. Eat her, Rhea."

Rhea's speech failed her once more, and though she'd shut her mouth, she felt her teeth shifting. Their edges pointed, elongating like a lion's, digging into her gums and under her lips.

The transformation hurt, and any second now, she'd have no choice but to widen her jaws and—

"Eat! Feast, Rhea! Drink her up, fill your gauge, indulge in her godly ichor. Now!"

"Rhea—"

There was no stopping Rhea once her teeth shifted to fangs. She opened her mouth, unleashing her deadliest weapons, and sank them into Themis' neck. The titaness had no time to squeal, and no room to move, as Rhea crammed her nails into her arms, shredding into her muscles, immobilizing her.

When the scrumptious liquid from Themis' throat finally surged into Rhea's mouth, she sighed in delight. She sucked, slurped, guzzled down every drop as it squeezed from Themis' arteries, spouting from every vein. The taste tingled her senses—the savory spiciness, and the exploding flavors unique to every god. Themis' blood had a hint of berries and a dash of caramel; and Rhea moaned in pleasure with every drizzle that filled her belly.

The blue-tinted ichor dribbled from Rhea's lips as she paused to breathe, then dug her teeth in deeper. The juices streamed down her shoulders, her arms, showering onto the floor, forming a pool at her feet—that she'd lap up later. Not a single drop could go to waste.

"Do it," said the voice, reminding Rhea of her other objective, the one she often forgot about when enjoying her delectable drinks.

Her drinking wasn't meant to kill—it was meant to infect, to share the venom within her while indulging in a delightful treat of sugary blood. The voice had explained it to her—embed her teeth into flesh, slurp up as much blood as possible, and replace it with a large dose of toxins through her own saliva. A few droplets of her spit would fuse into the remaining blood and transform it, and soon the victim would receive the same tendencies as Rhea.

A craving for ichor, and a need to poison.

Rhea's actual favorite part wasn't the aroma of the blood, nor its thick texture, nor how it loaded her with power and fulfilled her. No...it was when she arrived at the tip of ecstasy, the instant when the walls between her victim's consciousness and slumber took hold, and she had access to their memories. Somehow, the recollections she saw, in every creature she drank from, were sexual.

Themis was no prude—surely the insights in her mind would be titillating. Rhea smirked when she came to that peak; when the connection deepened, and Themis' barrier breached, allowing her thoughts to swirl into Rhea's.

Oh, the things she visualized, making her knees weak and her extremities numb with jealous arousal.

"Themis," she said, pulling away to burp and lick her lips, "you naughty titaness!"

The woman's body had gone limp, but Rhea had no trouble holding her up, infused with heaps of wild, wicked energy.

Themis had participated in an orgy, recently. She'd crept into one of Dionysus' parties, experimented with a few attendees, lowered to her knees to pleasure them as they watched her with excited eyes. A titaness, in their frenzy? How insane, how *wonderful!*

She fluttered from cupbearer to harp-player to kitchen-aid, dazzling them with her tongue-work, her hands stroking and squeezing and slipping into crevices as she smiled. She didn't discriminate on gender—her dazed steps took her to men and women alike, and she enjoyed entertaining them with her skill, revealing herself as a sexy, sultry siren.

"Good. You're done."

Rhea wiped the edges of her lips as she retracted her fangs and let Themis slump at her feet with a *thud.*

Did anyone else know? She wondered; had any of the family members been aware of Themis' tendencies? Of her creeping about, taking part in group fantasies with those in the employ of her king?

Rhea's lower lips trembled as she imagined all the terribly tormenting things she'd do if she were ever to brave her fears and participate in one of those festive nights. Oh, the wonders she'd share, the pleasure she'd give, she'd receive—

"*Put your fantasies on hold—we're about to have company.*"

"Hm?" Rhea came to, the world around her becoming clear, her blurriness dissipating. "Oh, crap. I have to go hide. And," she giggled, "wash my face. Take a long, cold shower. Because you, my sweet," she peered down at Themis and her heart skipped a beat, "were beyond satisfying. I should drink from my sisters more often."

|| 10. FAMILY MATTERS ||
HERA

Hera chose a rarely used ballroom as the place for her impromptu, middle-of-the-night meeting. It was a space once meant for small get-togethers and located on the opposite side of the palace from Athena's quarters. From the smell of it—a pungent incense, honeyed oil, and sex—it had been a recent hotspot for one of Dionysus' frenzies.

It will have to do.

None were too pleased about being there; but they weren't happy about the tension Athena created, either. Demeter and Hestia still fumed, their tempers flaring to abnormal levels, though Demeter kept her insults internal, for once. Hestia's skin had returned to its normal pallor, but something about her cracking knuckles and uneasy stance showed Hera that she—the most mature, most demure of all gods in existence—had had enough of this ridiculousness, too.

Gaia was there, physically, but her spirit seemed elsewhere. She'd waded in like a leaf blowing in the wind, and was solemn—much more so than she'd been earlier—and solitary. After acknowledging Hera, she moved on to pace near the windows in the far left corner of the area. She mumbled to herself, but whatever she said, Hera couldn't hear it, and wouldn't dare interrupt.

Rhea hadn't answered the summons, but though her absence disappointed Hera, it didn't surprise her. The mother of the Olympians had been out of sorts, earlier, in the hallway, and likely took Hera's advice to go to sleep. To see her children—and grandchildren—so roused in rage and pitting against one another had to be exhausting, and too reminiscent of her own power struggles with her ex-husband, Cronus. It must have all been too fresh in her memory, and Hera didn't blame the titaness for taking time to herself.

I'll catch her up later.

She'd thought about inviting Hades, but dwelling in his underworld castle, and so far from reach, he likely had no idea of what Athena had done yet. By the time he showed up, if he'd been on Hera's side to begin with, the fickle wisdom goddess would have found a means to change his mind.

The women were clear on why they'd been asked to meet Hera, but it was the boys, Hera's sons, who complained the most. Since they'd stumbled in—side-by-side, despite their hatred of one another—Ares and Hephaestus hadn't stopped rolling their eyes and fidgeting and sighing. Hera had explained to them that they were essential in helping her fight Athena, and that their service would be rewarded. But neither seemed to care, too preoccupied by the fact that the woman they loved—both of them, at the same time—had chosen the other team.

Naturally, they wanted to be with her.

So, while waiting to discover if Zeus would deign to make an appearance, Hera wasted her breath scolding her sons, reminding them they owed *her* their allegiance, not Aphrodite.

"Where do you think your strength of character and logic for battle comes from, hm?" she asked Ares, who sulked, sitting on the edge of a chair with his helm wedged between his legs. His near-black locks of hair had grown longer in recent times, and Hera imagined Aphrodite had requested them that way. She loved tousling long hair, especially her own. But if a war was on the horizon, he'd shorten that hair soon enough, to Hera's pleasure. "Your father didn't impart that on you; *I* did. So you owe me your respect, Ares. You owe me your life. Flurry over to that little bitches' team and see your privileges and powers revoked and limited."

Ares didn't argue, but Hera saw the spite in his snarl as he tapped a foot to the ground and retrieved his gnarly scabbard from his belt. He threw the weapon from hand to hand, grunting, glaring up at Hera as if hesitating to hurl it at her. He wouldn't; yet the image of his violence sent spine-tingling shivers up and down Hera's legs and arms.

Hephaestus would be the easiest to convince, or so Hera believed. "Aphrodite doesn't love you," she said, with a meager flick of her wrist, not bothering to lace her tone with any sympathy.

Her words were cruel, but true, and everyone in the room, in the palace, *in the world,* knew it. Including Hephaestus. He'd vied for the goddess of love for eons, and had even given up on punishing her when she was found with Ares—which occurred every other week—as he wanted her to be happy. Oh, she was happy all right—just not with him.

"Mother," he said, leaning on his cane, wincing as he marched over to take a seat by his brother. "That matters not. What matters is—"

"—would you like me to remind you what happens when you test me, son?" At the front of the room, facing them, Hera barely moved from her chair, unfazed by his talking-back.

She raised one eyebrow, daring Hephaestus to oppose her further.

She glanced at his stubby legs, at his inward-set feet, at the permanent scars on his arms from where his bones had twitched, twisted, broken. From when she'd hurled him from the heights of Olympus, infuriated by his actions.

"Do you need another lesson? Tell me, and I'm happy to push you off the cliff again."

She didn't wish to employ such tactics on him, and refused to look back on why she'd had to in the first place, all those years ago. Thankfully, it appeared she wouldn't have to push. Hephaestus gulped, peering down at his past wounds, most of which would never heal—because Hera had willed it so. She'd wanted him to see his ugliness in any mirror he faced; wanted him to remember what happened when he angered the Queen of the skies.

From that instant, the area became calm, quiet.

Demeter leaned against a wall, twirling a few of her buttery blonde and ashy almond tresses around her fingers.

Hestia peeled at the faded wallpaper near the doorway, mouthing curses at the staff that had chosen to disregard this room and neglect to clean it and maintain it properly.

The boys huddled by one another, so different, yet sharing the same plight. Their features were scrunched and their muscles pulsated as they tightened their fists and clenched their jaws.

Gaia halted her pacing, peeking out at the night sky, watching for dawn's arrival.

Zeus barged into the ballroom during a moment of perfect silence, startling everyone from their positions. "What is the meaning of this?"

Though his steps were booming, his tone was muted, muffled behind his thinned lips. He was the last to arrive, and from the sight of his messy mane of hair and wrinkled tunic, he'd been risen from slumber and forced out of the comfort of his warm sheets.

Had he gone straight to bed after Hera stormed out of the throne-room? And if so, how had he been able to shut his eyes and rest after the tumultuous affair, the accusation of his own wife? Hera hadn't gone to their chambers, but she'd wondered if Zeus really had…or if he'd instead been sharing someone else's sheets.

Hiding something, as usual.

"Hera?" He glowered at her, as she sat pretty on a folding chair at the opposite end of the door.

"Yes, I apologize for the late summons," she said, nodding once at her husband, then waving at her other attendees. "Now that the final guest is here, we can proceed."

Demeter's demeanor had worsened the instant Zeus arrived, her gaze silently implying she currently despised him. Even so, she fluttered over to stand beside Hera, to offer her support. Hestia also padded over and took up Hera's left side. There they were—her fierce but often reserved sisters, hoping to ensure Hera was heard, to prevent Zeus from exploding on her.

Where had they been, of late, when Hera had needed them? When cupbearers had openly mocked her, when serving girls had giggled at her, when they'd believed she was far enough down a corridor and unable to hear them? Or when her own children had ignored her authority, and continued to defy her at every turn?

No time to worry about that; they're here now, and that's what's important.

"Summons, yes." Zeus clicked his tongue, approaching his wife like a snake slithering through the grass, about to attack. "You can *proceed* with an explanation on how, and why, my spouse thinks it appropriate to summon me, the king, from my own bed, in the heart of the night."

Hera shot up from her seat, her breaths choppy through her gritted teeth. "You..."

Her arms tensed, her fingers flickered with energy; and thankfully, her sisters held her back before she pounced on Zeus. Such a dangerous act would be reprimanded, and she was glad Demeter and Hestia were looking out for her.

"Have you forgotten, husband dearest," she allowed her jaw to relax, and her shoulders to soften, "what happened a couple of hours ago? When your favorite offspring," she held in a gag, "pointed her accusatory finger at me? Blaming me, without proof, of the atrocious acts committed within our marble walls?"

Blowing out an annoyed breath, Zeus threw his arms up and spun away from her. "How could I? You all exasperate me, and that's impossible to forget."

Irritated as he acted, he appeared to lack any motivation to become involved with his family's affairs. Especially those concerning his spouse and his daughter in their bickering.

Has he finally had enough of us both?

Twirling one finger in the air—in the international *wrap it up* signal—he paraded over to a vacant seat behind Ares and Hephaestus. He sat with a huff, crossing his arms. Relief flooded Hera's being when she noticed his veins weren't glowing—she had a few minutes to spit out her speech before he became truly frustrated.

"I wish to clear my name," she started, moving away from her chair, spinning on her heels to take in her entire audience; Gaia hadn't stirred in Zeus' arrival. "Because I have nothing to do with this disgusting situation, and you know it. You know me."

Ares coughed, Hephaestus quirked a brow, and Hestia shifted her weight. Zeus grumbled something under his breath that prompted Ares to snort, and Demeter to growl at him.

"What?" Hera squinted at her husband, her sons, then twisted to her siblings. "Do you *not* know me? Or do you disagree that I'm innocent? Come now." She peeped at Gaia, who'd finally removed her gaze from the window, fixing it in Hera's general direction, but with little to no emotion in the depths of her eyes. "I'm strict, and a tad vengeful, true. But I've not endured any betrayals lately, no reason to provoke madness or start a war. And I'd never permit human death by such gruesome means." She swallowed a sour saliva, rehashing the descriptions of Eros' bloodbaths. "Nor the transformation of humans into monsters, or the abuse of gods for some sick game."

"Then why did Aphrodite go against you?" Ares' thighs bulged, his muscles contracting, as if he were about to stand. His helmet, squeezed between his legs, looked ready to burst. "This culprit attacked our son, and she chose Athena's team. Why? Why would she find you guilty?"

Hephaestus, though never one to agree with his brother and rival, sat up as straight as his hunched back would allow. "He's right. She's a good judge of character, and has had front row seats to all this drama, no? So why would she pick Athena? She dislikes her."

Hera wrinkled her nose. "Yes, but she hates me. She chose the lesser of two evils, in her opinion." She blinked at her son's disbelief, displaying over his face as he stared at her. "It's well-known Aphrodite and I never see eye-to-eye on anything, though our quarrels remain more discreet than those I've had with Athena. We never take the same sides in any argument."

"Hm."

A biting breeze brushed through Hera's locks, whipping into the back of her neck. She rotated to find Gaia approaching the other guests, the hem of her dress unfurling around her like a spring flower. Its edges curled inward, and the sleek satin fabric shimmered with her every movement.

"There should be no sides. This shouldn't be an argument."

Unsure what Gaia's purpose was—the mask of serenity over her face was impossible to read through—Hera side-stepped, allowing the primordial goddess the center of the room.

"Agreed, which is why I summoned you here."

"I've held my tongue, preferring to be a silent observer, but the fiasco from earlier has convinced me otherwise." Gaia inclined her head at Hera, one hand pressed above her chest. "Athena was wrong to falsely accuse, but she's right that behaviors at this palace are amiss. And Hera…" She caressed Hera's chin, leaving a subtle scent of grass and rain-soaked mud residing on Hera's skin in the wake of her fingertips. "You're not the culprit. You have vice, you are sinful—no, don't look at me like that, you *all* are—but you'd never poison without making more noise about it. We're all aware how you love the spotlight, and would have craved attention for your actions."

Hera opened her mouth to protest—and yet no sounds escaped. She bunched her lips together, scrunched her nose, and nodded once.

"Now that I've spoken, if you'll excuse me." Gaia bowed towards Zeus. "I'll need to speak with some of the other deities and put some order into this chaos." As she swished out, her brief but pointed glance at Zeus implied that such a task was his job. But if he cared to refute her claims, he said nothing, half-lounging on his seat in utter disregard for the situation.

Before Hera could think to prowl over to him and shake him,

Hestia cleared her throat.

"If it comes to a trial—"

Hera choked, the word *trial* causing her heart to pound harder in her rib-cage. "No. No, it cannot come to a trial. Zeus," she gawked at her unresponsive husband, "please. Say you'll prevent that."

When Zeus kept his lips sealed, shaking his head and chuckling—*chuckling?*—Hestia set a hand on Hera's forearm, her touch filling the queen with a soothing warmth she didn't realize she'd needed.

"*If* it does, I'll speak with the staff. They could testify on your behalf; they've all attended to you and your…" she flinched, "needs. I have no doubt they'll be sturdy witnesses to have on your side."

Without waiting for dismissal, Hestia hastened after Gaia, taking her hearty heat with her.

Left with Demeter, Hera would have felt triumphant, assured that some of her family members were there for her. But with Ares and Hephaestus' sneers, and Zeus' hurtful decision to stay out of things, Hera stamped a foot to the floor.

"Will you not do something?" Her words were vague, but all in the room knew they were addressed to her spouse. She wanted him to react, to divulge what that intricate mind of his was brewing, plotting. "*Zeus.*" She snapped at him, as he'd remained adamant on averting his gaze to his feet. "Answer me." The voice that flew out of her mouth wasn't her own. It was that of a thousand scorned goddesses, of a cluster of disregarded ladies.

Demeter wrapped a warning hand around her wrist, but Hera had had enough.

"Husband!" Hera's screech prompted Hephaestus and Ares to cover their ears, and Demeter to crouch near the floor, whimpering.

Zeus, unafraid of his wife's outbursts, stood up. Not menacing, but not cautious, either, his arms were straight, his shoulders arched back.

"Forgive me, *wife,* but though I won't take sides, I can't dismiss Athena's claims. I dismissed her hunches against Hecate, because we had proof of her innocence. But I have no actual, palpable proof of yours."

Hera's chin sank, and a flimsy squeak slipped from her dry, acidic tasting mouth. "Wh-what?"

"If you are innocent, then you'll have no trouble proving in it a trial." He spoke so easily, unaffected, too neutral for the situation.

Swallowing the urge to claw at his face and demand him to see reason, Hera rooted her feet to the floor and prayed for courage. "I fear tricks. Foul-play and lies and tales spun to put me in a position of guilt. I'm outnumbered and unloved, Zeus."

His earlier spiteful chuckle reanimated for a few painful seconds, before he walked away, headed towards the exit.

"You're unloved because you're the one who likes to dupe others, Hera. Athena will be just."

"Zeus—"

He held out his hand, and a flash of lightning struck through his eyes. So piercing, so real, it sent Hera toppling backwards until she fell onto her chair.

"No. Enough." The veins in his arms began to shock up from his fingers to his upper bicep. "I have too much on my plate already. Before I started the meeting to introduce Lukus, there were rumors of human-zombies disappearing from where Psyche had left them. And after Athena's abrupt takeover, I received confirmation of those rumors. These creatures Psyche created haven't been cured as requested, and I need a few hours of sleep before I interrogate Apollo and Artemis on their slacking." He lowered his arm and turned towards the door. "Forgive me, but I am too tired to mediate your fights tonight. Handle it."

With that he disappeared into the corridor, Ares at his heels, Hephaestus hobbling after them.

Hera grabbed her head and rocked back and forth. Demeter, still on the ground, angled against the chair and rubbed her sister's shins. "We need to find this culprit, Hera. Fast."

|| 11. FRENZIES AND FOLLIES ||

LUKUS

Outside of the throne-room, Lukus sensed air filling his lungs again—as if it had stopped during the commotion.

His mythology knowledge was still rusty, but it didn't take a lot of searching through his brain to know that Athena, pointing fingers at Hera, was a recipe for absolute disaster. More so when Zeus—the big boss, the favored father, the annoyed husband—steered clear of it all. He'd stalked out of the room once Hera had left. He hadn't spoken to Athena, hadn't said goodbye to Lukus, and hadn't bothered to notify anyone of where he was going.

Now, a few hours later, Lukus sat on Athena's plush bed, watching her pace back and forth, her brown curls like an owl's wings flapping in her wake.

Her quarters were simple, with plain but pleasing colors that inspired calm, but the tension in the air did nothing to allow any sort of calm to fill Lukus.

"No." Her sandals clacked on the polished, tiled floor beneath her feet. "Why would he leave?" *Clack, clack, clack*—her rhythm accelerated, slowed, stopped, then accelerated again. "Why would he not take my side? Her side? Any side?"

Uncomfortable, Lukus hugged himself, unsure where to look. He was in Athena's quarters—Athena, a fierce virgin goddess, permitting him to sit on her mattress, to be alone with her in her room. Was she allowed to do that?

"I'm allowed to do as I please," she said, grunting at Lukus' thoughts.

He snapped his neck up to squint at her. Had all the myths about the solemn, stiff goddess of wisdom been wrong? Or was Athena on the verge of a rebellion, exhausted by her family's antics?

He'd never get used to her invasiveness, but she'd clarified to him that he had no choice. For the sake of her investigation, Zeus had made it so only she, of all the gods—including him—could read the minds of her peers. That included Lukus—a half-mortal, half-god, but fully lost man who'd arrived in the heart of a massive family feud.

He wanted no part in it, nor did he want to choose sides. Like Zeus, he was thrust in the middle; and without knowing his parentage, he wasn't sure whose party he'd choose even if he could. None of his mother's lessons or his father's mumblings at the dinner table had prepared him for this.

Lukus Arvantis, an FBI agent, was caught in the beginnings of a civil war amongst the Greek gods.

Fuck, what did I do to deserve this?

Athena whirled to him and grabbed his upper arms, forcing her golden gaze into his. "Deserve? Lukus, it should honor you to be here. Regardless of the state of our family, it's pride you should be feeling, not…ah." She pulled away and squinted at him, seeking the emotions he hid under his flimsy facade of a face. "Fear? Right, that I can acknowledge. Confusion? Yes, yes…this is all new to you." She rubbed her chin and leaned closer to him. "But that skepticism, that disbelief of who we say you are…*that* has to stop. You're here, willing or not, and you're one of us. Accept it—the faster you do, the faster you can assist me."

"Assist you?" Lukus gulped, and wished he'd accepted the cupbearer's offer of a refreshment earlier, when they'd first arrived in the room. Athena had dismissed the young girl with a wave of her hand, and Lukus hadn't had a chance to even think about what gods were supposed to drink when thirsty.

"We drink everything—but often tinted with ambrosia. Oh," she blew out a breath and smacked a hand to her forehead, "that adjustment will take a while, too. I'll have to ensure we have human beverages and food prepared for you until your body adapts to Olympus. To your new status." She dropped onto the mattress, but kept a safe and smart distance between them.

Not that Lukus was prone to doing anything to violate her, beautiful and appealing as she was, but he was happy she didn't squeeze too close to him. After his experience with Aphrodite, he wasn't ready for sentiments to bloom in his cold, soulmate-less heart. And in any case, he worried Athena would punch him seven ways to hell if he showed a slither of attraction towards her.

"Lukus." Athena snapped at him. "Focus, please. You act like I haven't explained this to you; Zeus wanted you here to help me with the case, remember? A fresh set of eyes, a man with detective experience."

"*Human* detective," Lukus added under his breath, covering his mouth to muffle his words. "How can you and your father think I can provide anything to this..." he swallowed down the word *mess,* for fear of offending her, "situation? I was a total skeptic up until a few weeks ago, and to be fair, my recollections of Greek gods and their powers and history...ugh. It won't be up to your standards."

Athena stood and trailed over to one of her closets. She opened the double doors, but held on to the edges, glancing into the armoire but not entering it. "We only have two suspects, for now; you'll have to catch up on your lessons later."

"But..." Lukus cocked his head, watching as she disappeared into the closet's depths. "I thought Hera was your suspect?"

She returned seconds later, her outfit changed to a shorter dress, her chest covered in coppery armor. She carried a worn-out helmet in one hand, and placed it on the bed, beside Lukus, who stared down at it in awe...then into the lap of his wrinkled trousers.

There was nothing Greek about him, and he frowned, feeling suddenly more out of place than when he'd first arrived.

"She's the primary suspect, yes. But there's also the person who planted that idea in my head; the one who thought to exonerate herself by accusing someone else. Hecate."

"Hecate." Lukus ruminated over the name, whispered it a few times, getting used to pronouncing it. It sounded familiar, but he couldn't quite place it; an ancient goddess, perhaps? One lesser known, not as prominent in the stories?

"Goddess of witches, magic, the night, crossroads, and master sorceress of the Underworld." Athena sighed, electing to sit cross-legged on the floor, a few feet away from Lukus. Her eyes had shifted to a slate shade, and with a weave of her fingers through her hair, she braided a few strands around her head, keeping the locks from falling over her face. "It was her poison that somehow escaped out of her guarded dungeon dwelling, and found its way into Persephone's, Eros', and Psyche's food and drink and blood. This poison has different effects based on who it contaminates. We still don't know what it did to Persephone, but it turned Eros into a bloody, heart-seeking monster, and Psyche into a zombie-creating freak."

"Psyche?" Lukus massaged his temples. "That's Eros' wife, right? Fuck. You said I wouldn't need my lessons yet, but that's two names already that I didn't know. Luckily Psyche was with Eros today so I put that together. Are you sure I'm the one for the job?"

Athena's back straightened, and she set her hands on her knees. Her shorter dress revealed her long, muscular legs, and she made no motion to cover them up, to shield them from Lukus' vision.

Of course, she didn't fear him, didn't expect he'd attempt to do anything more than look at her. What was he but an uncultured little mortal who'd discovered he might have a deity as a parent? If he had powers, he had no clue what they were or how to use them; and why would he seek to overpower someone like Athena?

In any case, his heart still belonged to—

"Stop." Athena's gaze darkened as she fixed it on Lukus. "Aphrodite will never love you, and you're not in love with her. You're still under the effects of her spell, and those will fade, in time. For all we know, she's your sibling; and though I know my family tends towards incest, and that's quite normal in our routine, I doubt you'd be inclined to do the same?" Lukus gagged. "Right. So, for now, I need you to stick with me; to keep your thoughts on our goal, okay?"

Her shoulders were tense, but surely she could summon someone to rub them for her, to help her unwind. She was a princess, and a favored daughter; couldn't she get just about anyone to do just about anything for her?

Whatever her preferences, she remained in her spot, uncaring of her physical pain, if she had any. She was focused, determined, and wanted to solve her case.

"Because of Hecate's involvement—willing or not—I instantly

accused her. She proclaimed her innocence, Father protected her, and I pushed." She winced, looking down at her sandaled feet. "That was why you sensed tension between us. Yes, we are usually on the same page, but he disliked my accusation of Hecate. In his eyes, she can do no wrong, no matter her past of frenzies and follies and—"

"—Frenzies and follies? So," Lukus gulped, "she has priors?"

Athena nodded. "She's reformed from most of her insane practices, and only comes out of her potion-making trances to visit earth and spook humans, or so she says."

"But you…you don't believe it." Lukus folded his arms, finally grasping the difficulty of Athena's predicament. "She's a protégée of Zeus, but you see past that—you see her former behaviors and doubt that she's actually gone…*good?* Is that the word? Is anyone good or bad up here?"

With a snort, Athena snapped her fingers, and a cupbearer—a male, this time—entered the room. She ordered some watered-down ambrosia, black coffee, and a bowl of grapes, and urged the servant to hurry.

"Yes, good and bad exist. But it's all convoluted. We have backstories that show us in a specific light. Some of us have been forgiven for our transgressions, some of us bypassed punishment, some are still suffering the consequences. For Zeus, if you've proved your worth, and you don't attack members of his direct family, all is well."

"But…Hera?"

Lukus glanced at the door, begging it to open and reveal the servant with the liquid he'd been needing to fix the dryness in his throat. It was a lot to take in, and he'd need to refresh, relax, review the options before diving into helping Athena. On earth, in his apartment, he'd prepare for something like this by drinking himself stupid, because he saw things clearly when inebriated. But he had a hunch that getting drunk wasn't an option here. He'd have to become a different kind of detective; a legitimate and magical one.

"When defending herself, Hecate implied Hera was involved. And the effort it took to extract the information from her…" Athena huffed. "It leads me to believe Hera does have something to do with it all. Is she the culprit? Doubtful. She has no access to the Underworld, nor does she have the time to go about sprinkling toxins in other deities' food. But she has friends. She has allies, minions—those who helped her uncover Zeus' treacheries, aunts, sisters, and serving girls that respond to her beck and call. Though lately, most have deserted her, they still fear her wrath."

"Aunts, sisters, serving girls." Lukus crossed his legs at the ankles. "Are you only investigating women?"

When the door opened, Athena waved the servant in, took the tray he was holding, and shooed him out. She set the tray on the bed, between her and Lukus, and lowered beside it.

"I suppose giving you all the facts would help. Forgive me, Lukus. It's been quite a night." She plucked a grape from the ceramic bowl and popped it into her mouth. "Psyche confirmed that the voice she was hearing while poisoned—that's an effect of the poison, it makes one hear things—was feminine, and it wasn't her own. So we've concluded that our culprit is a woman."

"And Hecate…what makes her think Hera is behind this?" Lukus pointed at one of the cups, and Athena nodded. He took it, drained a few sips, and let out a breath of relief as the cold liquid trickled down his throat. "Do they have beef?" Athena blinked at him, clearly not up to speed on human slang. "Oh, uh…do they have a negative history?"

Athena shrugged. "Not that I'm aware."

A tingling sensation began in Lukus' extremities, but he didn't fight it or interrogate Athena about it. She had ordered ambrosia in his water, and had warned him it was a substance he'd have to get used to. It tasted like water and quenched his thirst, and that was all that mattered for now.

"I'll need to talk to Hecate, then. You're biased; it's obvious you dislike her." He drained his cup and set it on the tray, wiping his mouth with his sleeve. Dressed in his navy suit pants and his wrinkled baby blue shirt, he didn't fit into this new world he'd been dragged to. Would he have to change into a tunic? A toga? A skirt that barely covered his manhood?

Fuck, I hope she doesn't pay attention to that thought.

To his relief, Athena was too busy chowing down on grapes to address his questions about clothing. "Hm. Smart. A neutral interrogator. Fine." She got to her feet and clapped her hands to dust them off. "Hermes will be much too pleased to have to bring her here again, but it can be arranged."

As she proceeded towards the door, an ear-splitting, wall-shaking, floor-board-rattling screech resonated under the threshold and stopped her dead in her tracks.

She flipped to Lukus, checking if he'd heard it, too—and he had, but it had frozen him, turned him to solid ice.

He hadn't heard anything like this in years; not since a case he'd investigated in Chicago, with a mind-twisting serial killer who liked to jump-scare his victims before beheading them.

Athena pressed a finger to her mouth and motioned at him to follow her out. Once in the corridor, he struggled to keep up with her rapid strides, but to his luck, their destination wasn't far. They passed a few doors, rounded a corner—and there she was.

A woman was sprawled out on the floor, a shiny sheet of white-blonde hair spread about her head like a halo. She lay on her back, legs bent at odd angles, arms outstretched and limp against the marble floors. Her eyes were closed, but her torso moved up and down—she was alive. Which was astonishing, considering her pallor, and the two fairly obvious bite marks on her neck. Gaping, gnarly, the wounds were huge—like a creature with giant fangs had dug into her throat and slurped out as much blood as possible, leaving her neck bruised and pale, drained to the point of sagging.

She gurgled, and more blood—colored blue—discharged from her mouth. Athena hurried to kneel beside her, avoiding any puddles of the inky ichor. She grabbed at the woman's wrist to check her pulse.

Lukus peered around in search of someone else, unsure that this half-dead woman had uttered such a scream. A different person had to have come across the scene and scurried off. But as he scanned the area, all he saw was a silver tray, crashed to the ground, its contents—a plate of grapes—smashed.

"Themis?" Athena's voice was muted as she shoved some hair out of the woman's face; but Lukus was close enough to detect the terror trembling through her tone. "Oh, heavens, you're alive, but barely."

"I…" The woman, apparently awake, lashes fluttering as if trying to open her eyes, coughed. Thick blue liquid—matching the stuff that had fallen from her mouth—pooled out of her gnashes, slithering down her pale neck and gathering on the ground, before Athena.

"No, hush, don't speak." Athena rose so fast, the motion sent Lukus tumbling into a wall. "Someone…something…bit her."

She gawked at Lukus, but he was at a loss for words—what sort of being lurked in the Olympus corridors and chewed out chunks of goddesses' necks?

If this was a goddess at all—Lukus had no idea who Themis was, and didn't recall her from any of his mother's tales.

"She's a titaness. A predecessor of the Olympians." Athena's braided hair had unleashed itself, stringing on either side of her ears, each strand stiff like rope. "She handles divine law and order. I work with her from time to time. A sweet-natured soul, if there ever was one. Oh, dear." She covered her face and grumbled into her hands. "Shit."

Lukus' eyes widened at her curse, but before he could comment on it—or dare say anything else, for that matter—Athena barreled past him and stared out into the abyss of a hallway they'd arrived from.

"Apollo!" Her voice echoed down the passage, morphing. Lukus could have sworn he saw the words as they bounced against the walls and vanished once at the end of the path. Was this a power to summon and send messages?

That could come in handy, if I ever learned it.

"Apollo, come now, hurry!"

Lukus took advantage of her distraction to approach the victim. He was shaky, a bit nauseous, but he needed to control his bowels— he'd seen worse, after all, in the wake of Eros' carnivorous rage.

Themis was still breathing, but she'd stopped trying to speak. The gashes were deep, swollen, and seemed to have become infected; an obscure redness started to swell around them, and the blue-ish blood had congealed, blocking any fresh blood from escaping. If there was any blood left in her—she was so ghastly, Lukus wondered how she was still alive.

Is there a mechanism to prevent her from bleeding out? Do gods have that ability?

Upon closer observation, the liquid that had poured out of her seconds before was a different hue from the blood staining her neck and off-white dress. The latter was near navy, its texture similar to regular blood, but with a scent of something Lukus couldn't decipher. Ambrosia, maybe? He wasn't familiar with the aroma, but the gods drank so much of it, surely it mixed into their blood-stream.

The other color—a dark turquoise tincture, thicker, and eerily smelling of berries—drew his attention. He slanted closer, wishing he had gloves so he could touch it, but Athena grabbed him by the collar and yanked him away.

"Don't get too close. Whatever that is—" she peered at Themis and shuddered, "—I assume it's not safe for humans. More so if it got her in that state."

"Is it…" Lukus couldn't swallow, and wished he hadn't finished his water. Something clogged the top of his throat, and he sampled his own blood—coppery and warm. And disgusting. "Is it poison?"

Athena wouldn't look at him, but she acquiesced with a quick nod. "It has to be. Whatever, whoever did this drank half her blood, and replaced it with toxins. I can smell it in her, similar to the scent Eros and Psyche had. Infected. Meaning our culprit is at it again."

|| 12. WE'RE DOOMED ||
RHEA

The human had been curious; too curious. Noticing the potential of poison, planting the idea in Athena's head…

"Half-human, remember?" The voice prodded inside Rhea's brain, and used its ominous strength to shove her farther behind the wall she'd been using as a hiding spot. She'd placed a spell of invisibility upon herself, but it wouldn't fool anyone looking close enough.

Naturally, when Rhea had picked up on the wail blasting down the halls—a short but deafening sound, reminiscent of wars past and breaking hearts and not tinged with the pleasurable passion Rhea preferred—she'd escaped her chambers, where she'd ran to after ditching Themis' inanimate body. She'd sniffed the air, seeking her victim like a lioness, wondering if she'd remained where she'd dropped her. If any other gods had crawled over for the scraps she'd left, appealed by the berry bouquet of Themis' blood—or if they'd been dumbfounded and petrified at the gruesome nature of the attack.

As they should be; they're not thirsty for ichor, like me, are they?

As Rhea snuck closer, she realized that, sure enough, Themis had been discovered in the same spot where Rhea had sunk her teeth into her neck. Alive, as planned…and poisoned. Also as planned.

Keeping to the shadows of the corridor she'd tiptoed down, and muffling her mind as best as she could—Athena would hear her with ease—Rhea watched the scene. She witnessed Athena's arrival, her eyes like giant sunflowers basked in bright rays of sunshine, illuminating the poorly-lit hall, shining over Themis in her pool of blood. And the human—*half-human,* yes—who'd nearly barreled into Athena, breathless and shocked at what she'd found.

They both inspected the near-lifeless titaness, though Athena didn't give Lukus much time to analyze anything before yanking him away and whispering to him. Then Athena screamed into the void of a hallway she'd come from, beckoning Apollo and his healing arts.

"He won't be able to heal this," said the voice, vibrating with an eerie sense of pride.

A breeze wafted through the halls, and Rhea froze. Someone was coming.

The gentle flutter of wings woke nearby, from an adjacent hall. It came closer and closer to where Athena and Lukus stood, bashfully bewildered by the display before them.

"Athena?" The timbre was Hermes'; tentative and confused, as he deactivated his winged sandals and landed next to his half-sister. "What is—" He gasped and tumbled backwards, one hand over his mouth. "What in Tartarus happened here?" He shook himself and grabbed Athena's wrist, spinning her to him. "The scream reached me, and I, uh…finished my business as quickly as possible to come bear witness to…this?" He released Athena and raised his palms towards the ceiling as he gawked at Themis' near-unconscious body.

Athena scowled at his half-clasped tunic, sliding a tad too far down his waist to be considered appropriate. Rhea knew where he'd been—he'd cornered a new serving girl on the way out of the meeting, and had been wooing her in his chambers. She'd passed his room after her drinking spree with Themis' blood, and there was no mistaking the low moans and the squeaky bed-springs. She'd wanted to linger, to tune in, to watch—but the voice had urged her to her rooms.

"I feared we were the only ones who heard. There's no trace of the person who screamed—I doubt Themis emitted that sound, it wasn't like her. No one else has come but you." Athena glanced at Themis, then back at Hermes. "But your arrival is opportune; I actually needed to speak with you."

Before Rhea could try to tune into their conversation, they hushed their tones and exchanged a few hurried words in ancient Greek—a rarity for them, or so Rhea recalled from her years of living amongst them in Olympus.

Within seconds, their discussion ended, and Hermes reactivated his winged sandals. Without another word, he bulldozed down the corridor he'd hailed from.

A few more seconds passed, and footsteps echoed from the passageway Athena had yelled into. A glowing, godly creature appeared, his steps so airy he seemed to float. Light locks framed his youthful, unblemished face like blankets of golden silk, and his muscular, bare chest shimmered with sweet sweat.

Even from afar, Rhea recognized Apollo, the musical deity and the sway of his hips—a walk she remembered from the times she'd caught him meandering between partners during Dionysus' orgies.

"Athena? I heard your call, and I was—" He stilled at the sight of Themis, sprawled on the floor, drowning in a puddle of ichor and poison. "Oh. Oh, heavens. This…is that…?" He turned to Athena, who'd approached him, motioning at him to lower his volume.

The voice cackled. *That's fine—we can still hear them. And even if they speak in tongues, this time."*

Sure enough, though from her distance she'd not usually be able to listen to mumblings like these, Rhea was able to decipher every word they exchanged.

Thank you, strange voice.

"It's Themis, yes." Athena flinched, the motion so obvious even Rhea could see it from her hiding spot. "She's still alive, by some miracle, though it's evident she's been drained of a lot of ichor. And that other blue substance…well, Lukus thinks it's poison, and I'm inclined to agree."

Apollo's back muscles spasmed as he trod closer to Themis and crouched, the tips of his sandals an inch away from the slowly spreading toxins on the floor. He'd been too young to remember, but Rhea recalled that Themis had nursed him as a child; would seeing her unconscious, wounded self be too difficult for him to handle?

He sniffled, then leaned away and sneezed. "Poison, indeed. But it smells like berries? What in Olympus does that mean?"

Athena folded her arms and walked backwards until she reached the closest wall. She slanted against it, deflating, like a flower wilting.

"I was hoping you'd know. Didn't the stuff in Eros and Psyche smell like this? It's faintly similar."

Apollo straightened up and turned to her. For a moment, his gaze loomed over to where Rhea was, partially cloaked under an invisibility spell, teeth gritted, legs immobilized. She tensed, praying he wouldn't see or denounce her, but his sight returned to Athena, and he sighed. "It had a faint sugary aroma, for both of them. But this one is potent. And the color…it's so like our ichor and yet lighter, and from what I gathered down there, thicker."

Eyebrows rising, he rotated and lowered to the crime-scene

again. From within his loose-fitting tunic, he extracted a vial, and in one swift but cautious movement, he scooped up a few laps of the toxins. Immediately, and without bringing the vial anywhere close to his face or skin, he sealed the tube shut and slid it into his pocket.

"I'll see if I can compare it to the samples I took from Eros and Psyche." He snapped a finger and emitted a melodic whistle—his way of summoning his personal attendants. In the blink of an eye, a crew of three chisel-chested men appeared, and Apollo pointed at Themis. "Transport her to my room; I have a makeshift lab and medical area set up there. Lay her down, but do not cover her up or touch her wound. Even if she wakes and requests you to—wait for me."

The three men obeyed, and with as much delicacy and caution as possible, they took hold of Themis' legs and arms and middle, and heaved her down the darkened passage.

Athena observed them, twitchy and fidgeting as if wanting to follow them; and yet she was glued to her spot, unable to react, to wake from her stupor. Lukus was immobile and silent at her side, and seemed nowhere near as eager to pursue Themis, carried by Apollo's employees.

Rhea squinted at the investigators. Both were in a similar state of shock, though Athena was better versed at concealing her concern. Lukus struggled to keep his jaw from falling. His limbs trembled and goosebumps populated over his exposed flesh—so large Rhea had no trouble visualizing them.

"Go, now. We don't need to witness this any longer."

All too keen to keep away from the commotion, Rhea slithered to the moonlit hall behind her. She stopped in the middle, pressed her hands to one of the cold windows, and took a heavy inhale of the lightly scented air. The candles in the sconces weren't regular wax;

they were coated in ambrosia and spicy herbs, and the aroma tickled Rhea's nostrils.

"What corridor is this?" She didn't recognize the view outside; patches of flowers, rows of high, hanging trees, and a few benches. A new orchard?

"*Does it matter?*" The voice's timbre was strained, stretched thin. "*You were careless, but you won't make that mistake again, right?*"

"I…" Rhea peered out at the bushes blowing in the slight wind, and sighted her reflection, which caused her to gasp. Blue veins pulsed up and down her neck, feeding into her cheeks, falling into the crease between her breasts. "Goodness, I most certainly won't. I can't do this anymore. It's too risky. What we're doing…it's too similar to the culprit they're hunting. I'll get wrapped up in all this; I can't be."

The voice growled, and forced her to press her forehead to the cool glass. "*Nonsense. There's more risk to disobeying me. You will not stop until I tell you to. To avoid being caught, you'll learn to clean up your messes before you run off, hm?*"

Rhea groaned. "But you told me to—"

"*Be smart about this, will you? It's essential to my—to our goals.*"

"If I can't satisfy my hunger more discreetly, if I can't control myself, they'll be on to me in minutes." Her heart hammered in her chest; from fear of being discovered, or anticipating the voice's reaction, she couldn't tell.

To her surprise, the voice remained level, no irritation flaring up as it echoed inside her mind. "*No one will ever accuse you, Rhea. You're the mother of Olympians! A trusted confidante, a wise deity, a respected power among the titans and gods alike. You're safe. And in any case, Themis won't remember who bit her. This strain you injected her with—it'll wipe her recent memories. Nothing to worry about—"*

A muted giggle and a few faint footsteps roused Rhea from against the window. She peeked left and right and, deducing the noise to come from her left, she steered herself into the obscurity on the other side, cloaking herself in shadows—to spy.

Accompanying the giggle and footfalls were Hermes, still in his inappropriate garb that stopped so close to his manhood, one could easily view what he wasn't really trying to hide. And with him was…

Rhea pursed her lips. "Oh, now who could this be?"

The woman wasn't the same Hermes had snuck into his chambers earlier. For one, this lady was clothed, and had a certain dignity about her as she followed him over to the farthest window. Her black hair shone with hints of cranberry and prune in the moonlight. A twinkle sparked in her violet eyes as she twirled an edge of her mahogany-hued gown around her long, slender fingers.

Rhea's limbs stiffened and her heart stopped.

"Her?"

The goddess of witchcraft wasn't easy to recognize for most, as she never left her dungeon dwelling, except to explore forests and moonlit clearings for her frenzies. And less so to visit Olympus— unless Zeus commanded it. But Rhea had encountered her occasionally; enough to be certain of that poised posture and air of mischief that she had difficulty keeping tamed beneath her neutral facade.

This explained Athena and Hermes' hushed Greek words earlier, and Rhea's lungs constricted. "She asked Hermes to summon Hecate, to assist Apollo with Themis, I presume?"

The voice grew restless within Rhea's brain, its fearful vibrations crawling around inside like a caged rat, scratching at the surface to escape. *"This is bad."*

Hermes leaned against the window, toying with Hecate's lengthy locks of hair, and Hecate's cheeks shifted to a rosy hue that clashed with her pallid complexion.

So, there was more to the witches' arrival than Athena's summons? Had Rhea stumbled upon a blossoming relationship?

"Is she not a virgin?" she whispered to herself, stroking her chin, worried but still curious at the scene splayed out before her.

Hermes was caressing Hecate's jawline, his body pressed a bit too close to hers, yet she didn't seem to object.

"She shouldn't be canoodling with him—he'll seduce her into feeling comfortable. Into talking. And she..."

"She knows too much," said Rhea, finishing the voice's sentence in a small whisper.

Rhea had no clue how she knew, but Hecate's presence meant danger. The witchcraft goddess often flashed in her fuzzy memories as of late, and though she never understood why, nor dared to question the voice, a bizarre sensation brewing in her gut told her that Hecate and Hermes becoming too friendly was bad news.

Rhea's blood chilled, sending her teetering backwards, her balance tested by the vision of the two flirting. Clenching her teeth, she hoped Hermes and Hecate wouldn't notice her stalking, and wouldn't report her to Athena. Or worse; to Zeus.

"I messed with her memory of us and what she might have seen us doing, but she's strong enough to figure it out. She'll denounce us, no doubt about it. Her oath on the Styx is solid, but she's never been bound by river oaths before, not for long, at least. Why she hasn't revealed anything yet is beyond me." The voice stuttered, fading in

and out like static, a network losing connection. *"It's a matter of time before she divulges the truth to Hermes. And that foul little fiend will spread the news to everyone. He'll link us to all the other incidents...and frame us."*

Rhea placed a hand to the nearest wall to steady herself. Her breaths were choppy, and the sweet, sensual aroma of Hecate and Hermes' flirtation filtered into her nose, threatening to make her tug her skirts up and settle down on the floor to further watch them. Too many conflicting sensations swirling inside made her nauseous.

"What am I to do about it?"

Her hushed discussion with herself drew no attention; Hermes was too busy plastering kisses up and down Hecate's arm as she blushed and fanned herself.

"Attack them. Poison them before it's too late."

Rhea's eyebrows lurched upward. "Both of them? You expect me to—"

"—Hurry, take advantage of their coziness! They'll not be prepared for this; they think themselves exempt."

Before Rhea had an opportunity to consider the voice's urgent request, the lovebirds detached from one another. They peeped about as if aware someone had been watching them, and scurried off in the direction they'd come.

Just like that, the tasty atmosphere of sex vanished, leaving Rhea heavy and heated, and the voice within yelping in discontent.

"It's too late."

"We don't know that they saw us, so we shouldn't—"

"—panic? Yes, yes, we should. It wouldn't surprise me if they were telling Athena right this instant. Hermes will have convinced Hecate to speak up, I'm positive. No matter how blurry her

recollections may be, she'll share them."

"Weren't you just ordering me not to freak out? That no one would dare accuse me?"

"If Hecate and Hermes go to Zeus with this information, and not Athena...then you may most definitely freak out."

Rhea unleashed a breath and collapsed to her knees, burying her face in her hands. "We're doomed, aren't we? He'll connect us to everything going on..."

"And all my plans will have been for naught."

|| 13. A CONFESSION FROM THE WITCH ||

LUKUS

A faint glow of gold blared into Athena's chambers from the window—dawn had risen, and not a minute too soon.

Lukus sat hunched on her bed, head between his knees. He took deep breaths of the unscented air in her neutrally decorated suite.

The blue ichor, the puddle of poison, the near-dead goddess sprawled on the floor—it was a lot. Flashes of their discovery rambled on through his mind as if he'd been in that corridor mere seconds ago. As if a reel had replaced his brain, repeating the scene over and over and refusing to end.

An hour or so had passed since they found the titaness, Themis, drained of blood and unconscious in an opulent, portrait-riddled passageway not far from Athena's quarters. As if attacking her was a taunt directed at Athena, a warning that she was getting close in her investigation—too close.

Apollo's hot servants had carried away Themis' body. Zeus was informed of the situation—by messenger, because Athena feared rousing him now would create more chaos. Athena took Lukus back to her room to await Hermes and Hecate.

They had stumbled into Athena's chambers minutes prior, fingers flickering with energy, eyes watery with lust, lips slightly swollen. When interrogated by Athena about their flushed appearances and late arrival, they maintained they were distraught. They'd stopped in Apollo's chambers first, to witness Themis' predicament. When Hecate realized what she had to work with, she'd panicked.

Yet the subtle, quick glances between them and their bodies so close but not quite touching showed Lukus that there was more to what they claimed. That there was a clear cluster of feelings saturating the air around them. A lip-biting and eye-averting vibe that Lukus had no trouble understanding, versed in flirtation as he was.

Athena hadn't had to say anything for him to figure out the sorceress goddess and the herald of the gods had a bit of an affair going on. Affairs—a common occurrence in Olympus, or so Lukus recalled.

But he wasn't there to point out the obvious. Athena had already reprimanded him for letting his thoughts wander. Now that he'd witnessed the carnage himself, that he'd seen what was going on in this godly place, he had to get under the facade. He had to piece out the true motives of all these secret-keeping gods.

Why had Hecate accused Hera? Athena suspected her still; so how much did she know, what did she withhold?

Upon sighting Hecate—an intimidating, lithe lady, imbued in mystery and sensuality—Lukus struggled to keep his jaw from hitting the floor for the fiftieth time since he'd arrived in Olympus. Her inky, auburn and purple streaked hair undulated on either side of her ghost-like complexion. He noticed her violet eyes vibrated with emotion—not menace, not spite, but certainly not pleasure at being around. Her bustier barely held her breasts in place—it was evident someone had trifled with the fabric, as if stuffing his hands beneath it—and her obscure skirts cloaked her lower half, concealing its shape.

She contrasted Athena in many ways. Athena was tan, tall, athletic, her features pinched but an air of ease about how she carried herself. Hecate was voluptuous, her skin like creamy velvet, every inch the seductress; more like Aphrodite, causing Lukus to wonder if they were directly related.

At the vision of the witch-goddess, long-repressed memories slowly seeped into his mind. He recalled cautionary tales his mother had recited about Hecate. Mentions of frenzies and malicious spells and sacrifices on altars.

He observed her as she sniffed around Athena's lodgings, her nostrils flaring at the scents—or lack thereof—and her black-coated nails digging into her bodice as she set her hands on her hips. She had the grace of a cat, the senses of a hound, and the secrecy of a slithering snake; and yet, Lukus didn't see her as a foe. Curious as she was, he didn't gather an ominous vibe from her.

No, the ominous vibe came from Athena, who watched Hecate like a hawk, and snarled at Hermes whenever he sent her a loving glance. She huffed, ground her teeth, and glowered at Lukus, as if urging him to do or say something, then settled onto a chair, crossing her arms, eyes slitted in spite.

"I'm sorry, I needed a moment to gather my thoughts," said Lukus, sitting upright and rolling his shoulders. He'd spent five minutes scanning them, and five more crouching over to figure out how the hell he, a half-human, powerless FBI agent, was supposed to interrogate an ancient goddess and expect her to respect him.

"Understandable." Hecate's words were wrapped in chocolate, swift and soft, as if trying to seduce him. She hadn't spoken when they were introduced, and her timbre surprised him. He'd expected it to be croaky, witch-like, despite her pleasing appearance.

Athena grunted, fixed on Lukus—on his thoughts, as usual. "Of course she's trying to seduce you, she'll want you to—"

Despite his lower status and his fear of being trampled by Athena's wrath, Lukus shot her a glare. He set a finger to his mouth, requesting her to be quiet. Her eyebrows lurched up, but she said nothing, clearly too shocked to retaliate.

"Hecate." Lukus cleared his throat. "May I call you that?"

Is she a queen? A princess? What does one call a witch?

Athena snorted. "You call her a witch, that's what you—"

He snapped at the wisdom goddess with one hand, and motioned at a space beside him on the bed with the other, beckoning Hecate closer.

"You may call me Hecate." She peered once at Athena—definitely not kindly—and lowered next to Lukus, leaving a few inches between them. Hermes squinted at them, his mouth twitching, his arms bulging—jealous, much? "And I'm not trying to seduce you. This is how my voice sounds."

"I concur," said Hermes, passing his tongue over his lips, his jealousy evaporating as he ogled his lover. "Sassy and sexy and—"

"Ugh, enough already." Athena got to her feet and padded over to her dresser to lean against it. From there, she could visualize the entire room, and keep an eye on Hermes, Hecate, and Lukus all at once. "Seductress or not, you're a misleading little fiend if you lied about Hera—"

"—Athena!" Lukus jumped off the bed before being able to stop himself. A hunch warned him to address her with caution. He was still a guest here, and she could overpower him in seconds; but he was fed up with her attitude. "What's the point of this if all you do is interrupt me?"

Athena rubbed the back of her head, looking anywhere but at him. "You need to know the facts."

"I do," said Lukus, glimpsing Hecate. She leaned into the bed, splaying her fingers over the bedspread, balancing herself on her palms. She snickered at Athena, then blew Hermes a kiss. The large ruby pendant dangling from her neck shimmered, its surface catching the light from Athena's window. Lukus returned to Athena and gestured at the door. "But not *your* facts. You've told me your side, and I don't need your interference. Go...wait outside, or something."

"Oh!" Athena's squeak came out high-pitched and piercing. Hecate covered her ears, and Hermes tipped backward as if knocked off balance. Athena stormed up to Lukus and jabbed a finger to his chest. "You dare ban me from my own room?"

Gulping down his angst—with one motion, Athena could slice him in half—Lukus nodded once. "I can't concentrate with you constantly interrupting. Forgive me, Athena." He gently took her finger off him, wincing with the contact of her electrifying energy. "I need an unbiased interview. And you are biased."

Hermes chortled somewhere in the background. "That she is. I've been saying that for decades—"

"—right." Lukus peeped around Athena and motioned at Hermes, who'd taken to gazing at his reflection in a mirror near the door. "You're biased, too, so I'd like you to get out, as well."

Flipping to Lukus, Hermes pressed a hand to his heart and batted his lashes. "Me? Biased?"

Lukus glanced at Hecate, then at Hermes, then at Hecate again. "Yeah. You like her, so you'll defend her. Athena hates her, so she'll denigrate her. You're both distracting, either way, and I can't do the job Zeus summoned me here to do if all you do is bicker. So," he took a deep breath, battling his trembling limbs, "please, leave until I summon you in."

Hermes scoffed, but obeyed, and sent a quick wink in Hecate's direction. Athena took longer to depart, spinning on her heels every few steps as if to beg Lukus to reconsider.

Another ten minutes passed before he and Hecate were finally alone. Despite the tension in the room departing, a lingering feeling of confusion and eeriness remained.

"Hecate." Lukus sat back down and shook out his arms and legs, blowing out his cheeks. "Sorry about that—I'm new at this."

"You sounded quite confident to me," said Hecate, turning sideways for a better view of Lukus. A shy smile formed over her darkened lips. "Once an FBI agent, always an FBI agent—regardless of your location and what's in your blood."

He lowered his gaze and tucked a strand of hair behind his ears. She smelled like lavender and spice, and he sensed his cheeks heating—but now wasn't the time for bashful flirting. That wasn't the right method for this kind of investigation. No, he had to be neutral, normal, and listen carefully. Clues would hide in every word when speaking with Greek gods. They employed riddles, poetic sentences, magical melodies to entice and woo. Lukus wouldn't be wooed, not until he obtained details to aid Athena's case.

"Pleasantries aside..." He sighed, stiffened, and grabbed the notebook on his right, that Athena had given him earlier. He'd requested it, since he was unable to conjure magical markings in the air like she'd done to keep track of her suspects. "Tell me everything, Hecate. From the beginning. What is your role in all this?"

The rosiness once spreading over her cheeks disappeared as she leaned forward to grip her knees. "It started with my potion cabinet being invaded. Upon examination, I noticed my special concoction—one that helps forget fears and affects deep desires and wild thoughts, and that provokes irrational behaviors—was gone. I created it, and it was still in testing, too raw to be used by any god or human yet. It was gone."

Lukus scribbled what he could—*fear, desire, wild, irrational*—and acknowledged her, implying she should continue.

"Soon after," she licked her lips and shuddered, "Persephone began acting strange. I recognized the symptoms, the oddity in her movements and speech, and detected the poison in her blood. I healed her, but little did I know, Eros and Psyche had been affected up here, too. She disappeared, he went on a rampage, she created zombies, he murdered soulmates. A nightmare. Caused by *my* experiment." There was actual regret in her tone. A twinge of pain in her shivering posture. A melancholy in her eyes as they lost their luster and brimmed with tears. "This is all my fault."

Lukus was no expert on body language—and less so when facing a goddess—but her demeanor wasn't that of a criminal. It was that of a victim.

"I wouldn't say it's *all* your fault, no." He peeped at his notes—*strange symptoms, blood smells, zombies, soulmates.* "Who has access to your cabinet?"

"Melinoë." Hecate sniffled, and at Lukus' creased eyebrows, she chuckled. "Oh, right, you wouldn't know who that is…my assistant. Persephone's bastard daughter. Not all there in the head and incapable of the crimes our culprit is suspected of." She tapped a slender finger to her temple. "Mentally deranged, but not violent."

Lukus scribbled a few words, then paused, scratching at the scruff on his chin. "And Hera? Where does she fit into all this?"

Hecate crumbled, and she slid onto the ground.

Lukus, alarmed, hopped off the bed to help her up, but she waved him off.

"No, no, I'm fine. I…" she folded over, pressing her forehead to the floor. "I need something cold on my skin. Give me a moment."

Shocked at such behavior—did gods experience anxiety? Fright? Depression?—he fell back onto the mattress and retrieved his notepad, jotting down his thoughts. *Hecate has some trauma, for sure.*

"Hera." Hecate blew a raspberry as she redressed herself, but remained on the floor. Her skirts fanned out around her like a blackened rose's petals, and she clasped her hands in her lap, looking down at them. "Yes, I told Athena that Hera was involved to get Athena off my case. It was hasty and stupid and has caused a lot of drama, I'm aware; Hermes told me."

Lukus lowered his pen and massaged his scalp. "You lied?"

"I lied." Hecate rotated to gape up at him, her eyes drowned in tears, though her voice hadn't shown an ounce of sadness; it was level and unaffected by her revelation. Perhaps, despite all her power, she had no means to control her crying? Lukus didn't have time to ask. "Hera isn't my enemy. We have no bad history to speak of; I did not need to accuse her like that, but I couldn't let Athena berate me. I needed time to conduct my own questioning downstairs, and if I didn't give her another name, she'd continue to hound me until she convinced Zeus of my culpability."

"And you're not guilty?" It wasn't meant as a slight; Lukus really wanted to know what Hecate thought of the situation she'd put herself in. He watched her, waiting for any cues that would prove guilt, that would flicker over her features and show what she was hiding. How could he be sure? He'd interrogated countless murderers and mind-bending criminals, but seeking to analyze a goddess?

Who the fuck believed I could do this?

She shrugged and returned her gaze to her entwined fingers. "No. Only guilty of making the potion. And Hera," she shook her head and moved up to her knees, "she's not involved. It was cruel of me to use her name, but she reminded me of someone I'd seen recently. Someone whose features were blurry but pop up often in my thoughts. Her face was the first to flutter through my mind when Athena questioned me."

"Reminded you of whom?" Lukus' exterior was calm, but inside, his brain exploded with queries and curiosity. He knew little about the gods, the family he was getting himself into; and the more Hecate talked, the more his head hurt. He was unable to formulate the theories grouping within, or uncover any clues that made sense to him.

"Look, I apparently swore an oath on the Styx—she herself took shape to inform me of it."

"An oath? On the Styx?" Lukus' headache became a migraine. A thing one could swear oaths on that then *took shape?*

What the fuck is she talking about?

"Oh, poor mortal. The Styx is a river in the Underworld, one that gods can swear oaths on. She can come to life, take a human form, but rarely does so. Anyway," Hecate waved, returning to the matter at hand, "I don't remember why I swore that oath. My memory was obviously trifled with." She inhaled a heavy breath and stood up, keeping her arched back to Lukus. "There are chunks of the past few weeks that are missing from my recollections. I," she turned her profile to Lukus and blinked twice, "I've not told anyone about this, mind you. My memory is fuzzy, and though I don't believe *I* was poisoned, I believe the culprit did do something to my brain, to my powers. To me."

Lungs constricting—who would fuck with a potent witch-goddess, for crying out loud?—Lukus fidgeted in his spot and scribbled. *Memories messed with, not intoxicated. May have more information if she can get her shit together.*

"So, like I said, Hera reminded me of someone. Someone I saw down there, hovering near Persephone, at one point…my timeline is blurry, I apologize. Before she was poisoned? After? I have no clue." Hecate's spine relaxed, and she twisted to Lukus, hugging herself as she glanced left and right. "That person," she lowered her voice to a mumble, "looked like Hera. Similar silhouette, similar eyes, that same nagging poise and regality about them. But it could have been anyone. Some goddesses can shift their appearances, others can meddle with visions and memories, and I have no doubt there is more than one culprit at work."

"M-more than one?" Lukus' hardened facade vanished. The strength he'd been striving to maintain, to show himself as a dignified, experienced FBI agent, crumbled. "Fuck. Are you sure?"

If she noticed his distress, Hecate didn't make it obvious. She was still, her eyes flashing with scarlet. "It must be. How else would someone poison Persephone down in the Underworld, and sneak something into Eros' and Psyche's food up here, at the same time? There's a collaboration going on; a sordid, sneaky one. The main instigator is in Olympus, for certain. Themis' attack?" She squeezed her eyes shut and shuddered. When her eyelids parted again, the scarlet streaks had disappeared from her irises. "That strain was potent. Violent. Dangerous. What I caught a whiff of when I inspected her body earlier…the base of it was my potion, but deadlier. As if it had been brewing for a while, growing stronger, or infused with *other* toxins unknown to me."

Hecate's confessions weighed on Lukus' soul, mind, and body. Distraught, he ended up fetching Athena and warning her to summon every single female creature living in Olympus, and he'd insisted they were to meet him in the throne-room as fast as possible. He didn't know their appearances, but he needed to put them all next to each other; especially next to Hera.

Anyone who resembled her would be on his suspect list, regardless of their status in Olympus. Serving girl, cupbearer, musician, lower-tier god, or freaking titan—none would be spared from his analysis. He craved to figure out who this poison-injecting, heart-eating, zombie-making, vampiric piece of shit was, and why they were targeting his new family.

|| 14. THE MONSTER'S MESS ||
HERA

Despite his rhythmic voice and his polite manners, Hera would always loathe Apollo. He smelled of pungent petunias and constantly hummed while working. There was an air of vapid virility about him that made her cringe whenever he was near.

Hera didn't want to be in his annoying, aromatic presence, but when she'd heard of the attack on Themis, she'd disregarded all her grudges against the musical god and demanded access to his rooms. He wouldn't deny her; her, the Queen of Olympus, seeking to check up on her wounded aunt? Would he dare?

No, he wouldn't.

So on this dreadful and early morning, with gloom on the horizon and suspicion in the air, she had no choice but to put up with his fake smiles. She had to tolerate the way he hopped from spot to spot, instead of walking, like a normal deity. To overlook his mumbles—while he inspected Themis' semi-conscious body—and that prudent timbre he employed whenever addressing Hera. Prudent, not out of respect or fear; but out of disgust.

He was, after all, on the other team. He was among Athena's illogical, moronic crew of young gods with no experience and no clue what in Tartarus they were dealing with. None had any notion of the level of evil that breezed up and down their halls, unnoticed, like a welcomed gust of wind on a scathing hot day. None were privy to the sort of magic this culprit used, the means by which it crept into Olympus life. How it had put everyone on edge, wary of their own family members, distrustful of the food placed in front of them.

No, they weren't affected—except for Aphrodite and her children—and likely believed it all to be some sick joke. They floundered about, partied, drank, disobeyed, and took sides—*wrong* sides. They believed the goddess of wisdom because of her title, because of her special spot in Zeus' heart. But Zeus himself hadn't even endorsed her outburst or declared himself in her favor.

Yet he still trusts her. He still will not defend me. He—

"This…" Apollo's dramatically deepened voice—the one he used when focused—intruded on Hera's negative thoughts. "This color confuses me."

Hera, who'd been holding Themis' limp hand, infusing warmth into it, hoping it would wake her, sighed. "What about it confuses you? It's blue. A dark turquoise, I'd say. Not that I'm an expert, but I know my blues." She smiled down at her rumpled royal blue gown—her favorite shade.

Apollo shook his head, his light blond and copper curls emitting a scent of cocoa as they whooshed to and fro before his unblemished face. "No, that part I knew. It's this color coming from *inside* Themis that bothers me. It's," he stuck a gloved finger into the substance he'd collected and poured into a small bowl, "thick. Like paint, almost. And has a hint of berry to it. Industrial berry, mind you—fabricated, not natural."

He spoke as if to himself, in terms he'd use when conversing with fellow healers. Luckily, Hera's knowledge was vast. Though she wasn't a healer herself, she'd learned a trick or two about medicinal vocabulary. If he meant to confuse her—which wouldn't be surprising, as he despised her almost as much as she despised him—it wasn't working.

"Is it different from the toxins you extracted from Eros and Psyche?" She perked up, squeezing Themis' hand tighter, praying for her to awaken so she could avoid pointless conversation with Apollo.

"It is." Apollo brought the bowl closer to his eyes and squinted into it. "Eros' was a clear liquid, glowing red. Psyche's was light as air, with specks of purple. This…this is blue."

"Is it the same strain of poison?" Hera set a hand to her hip and bunched her lips as she glared at Apollo, who seemed ready to taste the tincture to be sure. Not that she'd stop him—she wouldn't mind if he were poisoned and off to roam the world in madness—but it would look bad if she didn't at least pretend to care. "Apollo, don't. Hecate will figure it out. Leave the mixture and work on reviving Themis, hm?"

She and Themis were close, though Themis often worked with Athena. She didn't always approve of Themis' extracurricular activities—it wasn't abnormal to find her near Dionysus' frenzies and sneaking into his orgies, though no one else knew but Hera—but she enjoyed their debates. Hera loved when Themis came to her, fuming over a trial taking place on earth that she had no right to interfere on, but that she wished she could storm into and assist with. *"Those idiots! Do they not see the proof under their noses?"* She'd curse, she'd spit, and Hera would sit back and listen to her tirades about political systems and how she detested them.

But the woman lying on the makeshift clinical bed in Apollo's room wasn't the vivacious, opinionated Themis that Hera loved so.

Her platinum blonde hair had turned white, its violet streaks faded, almost vanished. The big, blush circles she usually dabbed onto her cheeks were washed off, replaced with turquoise and navy stains—poison and blood. Her lips were also stained, the liquid near impossible to wipe off, no matter how hard Hera had scrubbed at it. Her gorgeous cream gown clung to her body, instead of flowing in the wind, and her curves seemed deflated, like flattened under a heavy stone.

Why her? Hera didn't understand this culprit's attacks. Persephone, Eros, Psyche—all were lower-level deities. Themis was a titaness, on the upper scale of power, of royalty. She was a passionate and kind soul, and didn't deserve to have her throat ripped into and half her blood drained. How she was still alive shocked Hera, but she thanked the heavens—and her dreadful husband—for their benevolent blessings.

Zeus had stopped by once, glanced over Themis' immobile limbs, nodded, and vanished. Did he not care about his aunt? Did he not care that the villain they hunted was *there*, in their home?

No, he's too busy chasing down zombies on earth.

"It does present the same overall trace of whatever was in Hecate's concoction, so I'd say yes, it's the same poison. But..." Apollo scratched his chin and leaned closer to Themis' bite marks. "No, there's something different about it. Eros' version made him hungry to watch hearts being devoured. Psyche's enabled her to create walking corpses that fed on raw animal flesh. It gave them urges, but kept them distant, conductors of the events but not taking part themselves, not directly. But this? This attacker was direct, and must have been strong to fool Themis. Clearly, whoever had this strain in them and injected it into her was thirsty for ichor. So...I guess there are several strains that all cause varied reactions? It's too much."

Apollo moved away from the table and plodded over to his desk, covered in vials and paperwork and large tomes of ancient Greek remedies. He sat with a huff, and opened one of the books, mouthing words but too quiet for Hera to attempt to understand them.

A timid knock on the door roused him from his seat, and Hecate and Hermes erupted into the room. They'd swung by earlier, to give Hecate a second to view Themis' situation before hastening off to Athena, who'd summoned her for an interrogation with Lukus.

The human is taking his role seriously, it seems. Good for him.

It pleased Hera that Lukus hadn't detained Hecate too long; her expertise was needed here, to help Themis.

"Has anything changed?" Hecate rolled up her lengthy sleeves and tied her chunky curls into a ponytail. She fluttered around the clinical bed, her hand hovering an inch over Themis' body, absorbing its energy waves, analyzing the toxins it still radiated.

"No," said Apollo and Hera in unison.

Apollo frowned at Hera—this was *his* domain, not hers, and he clearly wanted her to remember it, no matter her queenly status.

He planted beside Hecate as she inspected the bites up close, her nose inches from the gnarly, infected gashes.

"She stirred a bit earlier, and nothing else has discharged from the injury…but the stench has worsened."

Hera nodded—inexperienced as she was, even she'd detected the poison's fumes growing harder and harder to ignore. At Apollo's command, she'd enchanted her nostrils to block out the odor, in case the toxin could infiltrate her organs through her breaths.

A shadow loomed behind Hera; Hermes was discreet for once, leaving space for Hecate to operate. He sneered at Hera when she acknowledged him, and rested against a wall with his arms folded and his nose in the air.

He'd chosen Athena's side, too, and was more obvious about his distaste for Hera than the reserved, polite Apollo. But Hera didn't have time to manage his childish behavior; Hecate had lifted her arms, her fingers twitching with power, bracing to start a serious enchantment. Hera had to pay attention.

"I'm going to wake her," said Hecate, as black veins pulsed through her ashen skin. She was shaken, uneasy, Hera could tell. Whatever had happened with Athena and Lukus, it had left her unstable. Her stance was less straight and confident as usual, and her face muscles spasmed with her efforts. "It'll hurt her, but it's the only way to better understand what took place, and hopefully, who did this to her."

After a few tries—she fumbled her incantation several times, her tongue twisting as she wriggled her fingers and became distracted—Hecate set her hands onto Themis' chest and pushed.

Strings of energy shot into Themis' rib-cage, lifting her a few inches off the table before setting her back down. A faint squeak released from her mouth. Her eyes flew open, and her once slackened limbs convulsed, then tightened as she fidgeted side to side.

She started to sit up, but Hecate held her down. "No, don't overexert yourself. You may fall back asleep with too much effort, and we need you awake for a while."

"Hecate?" Themis' voice came out soft, strained. "What happened?"

"You..." Hera flurried closer, standing on the other side of the table, looking down at the reanimated Themis. "You don't remember?"

Themis grimaced, and smacked her hand to her neck, over her

wound. "No, but my neck hurts something fierce. Did I get bit by some rabid animal?"

Hecate swallowed loudly, "Uh…Themis," she swiped the back of her palm over the titaness' forehead, "you were attacked. Bitten. Yes…someone, something, drank your blood and possibly injected poison into your throat. Do you feel anything ominous floating through you?" Themis blinked, thinking on Hecate's question, then shook her head. "Do you have any recollection of someone digging their fangs into your neck?" Again, Themis shook her head.

Hecate spat and spun away, cursing under her breath.

"I'm sorry," said Themis, craning her neck to watch Hecate. She then switched her gaze to Hera, her eyebrows rising. "Dearest Hera, forgive me, but my memory from the past few hours is fizzled."

"Fret not," said Hera, grasping Themis' shoulder and squeezing. "Like Hecate said, don't overexert yourself."

"I was on my way to the throne-room…there was a commotion, involving…" Themis scrunched her nose. "Oh, involving you, no? Is everything all right?"

"Oh…not all right, no, but it will be. Soon. I hope." Hera's speech drifted off as she lost track of Themis for a few instants, tuning in instead on Hecate and Apollo's hushed words near Apollo's desk. They were facing the clinical bed, their heads lowered; but it was clear they spoke to one another, exchanging crucial information.

Luckily, Hera was a skilled lip-reader.

"It's stronger than what got Eros and Psyche," whispered the witch-goddess, her lips moving fast. "There's a vague trace of my original potion, but this is different, steeped in other substances I'm unfamiliar with."

"Substances *you're* unfamiliar with?" Apollo rubbed his face and groaned. "Then we're well and truly fucked, aren't we?"

Hecate shifted her weight. "I need time to analyze it, but I don't think I can cure her, not fully. It's tricky, I can tell. I'm not sure *how* I can tell, but I have a hunch it won't cooperate and spill out of her pores as easily as it did with Eros and Psyche."

"Shit. And that wasn't easy at all. I saw your struggle." Apollo looked up, noticed Hera watching him, and frowned.

Before he could comment, or request Hera to mind her own business, his door blasted open.

Hera fixed her slouched posture in time to view Athena barging in, her gaze at once resting on the queen and narrowing.

"You," she gestured at Hera, then at the door, "are summoned to the throne-room."

Hera snarled and set her fists to her hips, glowering at Athena in defiance. "Oh, to accuse me of yet another crime I didn't commit?"

"No." Athena glanced at Hecate with the same cruelty—because to her, Hera and Hecate were the same; her number one suspects, her enemies. "You're going there, too. In fact, Lukus is asking all goddesses and titanesses and all ranks of female Olympus residents to join us. He has a…well, he needs to inspect all the women."

Hera's fists unclenched as she dropped them to her sides. "Oh. You as well, I hope? I don't see why you'd escape inspection."

Not bothering to reply, Athena began to spin on her heels—but did a double take as she sighted the revived Themis.

"Themis? You're awake?" She glided over to the titaness, who, against Hecate's wishes, had propped herself up and was massaging her temples.

"I am, and—" Themis moaned as she sat up further, "—don't bother asking. I don't remember anything."

"Crap." Athena took her hand and brought it to her lips to kiss it, prompting bile to rise in Hera's throat.

Why were they both such good friends with Themis, yet such eternal rivals with one another? Surely they had something in common, something that linked them to Themis; why did they have to be on such bad terms?

"I'll come, too." Themis moved her legs with difficulty, swinging them over to dangle from the table.

Athena blocked her, and Hecate swooshed over to wag her finger in denial.

"But you said *all* women, right? Yes, I'm the victim, but I should be there. And…" She wobbled off the bed and Hecate grabbed her elbow, Athena seized her wrist. "I'd like to meet this half-human detective who claims to investigate our culprit. Shouldn't he see me? The most recent wounded one in this monster's mess?"

Surprisingly, both Hecate and Athena peered at Hera, questions quarreling in their contrasting eyes. Did they seek *her* approval? Her, the queen everyone detested, the wife everyone ignored, the one accused of such gruesome crimes?

For once, they looked to her for her authority, for her intelligence. For once, they gave a damn about what she thought; and Hera wouldn't disappoint.

"If she's able to walk with us, fine. She may come. But at the first sign of weakness, of fatigue or illness—she's to go straight to bed, and under Apollo and Hecate's careful watch."

Shoulders squared and torso pushed out, Hera smirked on the inside; oh, how she'd sounded like a ruler, like a respected queen. And how she wished it was always so.

It was unfortunate that her family members had to be harmed and bitten for her peers to recognize her dominion over them. Perhaps this horrid situation would eventually work in her favor. Once she proved she wasn't the grotesque monster they believed her to be.

|| 15. A GATHERING OF GODDESSES ||

LUKUS

Aside from Lukus and Zeus—who'd consented to overview the proceedings, in case *"things got violent"*—the presence in the throne-room was feminine and frustrated.

Athena had worked wonders in bartering with every single woman in the palace. She'd somehow convinced them to line up before Lukus, a half-god, half-human commoner of unknown descent.

Surely they were revolted by him, no? He had no powers, no special godly glow about his silhouette, no tremulous voice like Zeus' or an authoritative aura like Hera. No, he was a regular Joe, with a regular—albeit in shape—body. His eyes didn't shift with his mood, and his hair clamped to his sweaty forehead as he stood before his assembly of potential suspects.

He had no issue with public speaking; but this wasn't a normal public. These were goddesses, titanesses. Some were serving staff, others were lesser ladies with fewer abilities—but all had a link to the Olympians. They had a tether to the bloodline, or a vast knowledge of the premises and the ways this community worked.

Lukus knew nothing.

As he cleared his throat, preparing to explain his summons,

Zeus—who sat in Hera's throne, having left Lukus his own, an honor that made Athena gasp and Hera scowl—snapped for attention.

"Ladies," he said, silencing the slight murmur of anticipation among the assembled guests. "Lukus is a detective down on earth, and he's working with Athena to discover who our culprit is. I'm not too sure what his plan is, summoning you all here, but…well, do as he requests." With a huff, he slugged onto Hera's seat, the motion rattling the ground.

Already struggling to stand upright, Lukus did his damndest not to fumble and make a fool of himself. Peeping at Aphrodite for a few seconds too many, he realized he'd already showed himself as an idiot to *her*. He couldn't screw his chances over with the rest of Olympus.

"I've asked you all here to look at you." He winced, and several of the women shifted their positions and raised their eyebrows at him. A rainbow of sparkling gazes glowered at him, and he gulped. "That sounded horrible. Let me rephrase. I received a particular physical description from an anonymous witness that might help narrow down the possible suspects. So, based on your looks, I'll be eliminating those who don't fit the description. All I need from you is to…well, to stand still, I guess?"

The women peered at one another, some in surprise, others grunting their discontent. Of course, they'd hate being pitted against one another because of their appearance—how many times had such situations caused wars? But that wasn't Lukus' intention. This was no competition, and in any case, the ones left in the throne-room wouldn't be winning any prizes. They'd be singled out as main suspects.

He glanced at Zeus for back-up, but the king shrugged, clearly having nothing to add.

"Get on with it," said Hera, rolling her eyes. She was directly across from Lukus, and the most impatient of all, having volunteered to hold up the frail and flustered Themis—the innocent victim of the most recent attack.

Based on that fact—and because she was platinum blonde and looked nothing like Hera—Lukus approached her, first. She could barely stand, and clasped a cloth bandage over her injury. Her pallid flesh made his stomach do back-flips. She resembled a ghost.

"You don't need to be here…ma'am." He flinched. "Miss? My lady? I'm sorry," he fiddled with his shirt collar, "I have no idea how I'm supposed to address you."

With a weak pat of her hand over Lukus', Themis issued a smile, though her eyes creased in pain. "Call me Themis. And thank you." Lukus gestured at the seat he'd vacated, and Zeus acquiesced, granting Themis permission to sit. She was too frail to return to her chambers alone.

To their surprise, Themis refused the chair. "No, I'm…I need…air. I'll be in the hallway, near the windows. Hera," she brushed her fingertips over Hera's wrist, "I'll wait for you."

Hera nodded, and everyone turned to watch Themis limp out of the throne-room, obvious struggle in her steps but a determined rhythm to her stride.

A proud and lovely woman, she is. Shame she had to be poisoned.

Lukus hoped Apollo lurked nearby, in case she manifested any odd symptoms and needed to be attended to. Apollo would have to suffice, for now, because Hecate was among his lined-up guests.

Next, his gaze rested on the bold-chested, curvy figure of the goddess he'd thought to be madly in love with. She lowered her chin as he came near her, and though he craved to reach out and touch her, he refrained. Last time their skin had been so close, she'd provoked fantasy-like visions of them having sex that he still hadn't recovered from. No matter how many times Athena told him they'd never be together, that Aphrodite would never return his affections—and that his affections weren't even real—he couldn't help feeling powerless and infatuated at the sight of her.

"You can go, too." He backed away as she jerked her chin up. "You don't fit the bill, and your son was one of the manipulated victims. No, you have nothing to do with all this."

It was the first time he'd spoken to her since she'd visited him in the hospital, when she'd come to apologize, to notify him he had no soulmate, and she'd wiped his memory. He should have hated her, should have wished to have never met her, and yet he couldn't help but admire her, still. His heart fluttered in his rib-cage as she bowed in thanks and scurried off and out of the room—likely to meet up with the man she *did* love.

Hera groaned and folded her arms, but Lukus didn't have time for her temperament. He moved on to a light, buttery-blonde haired lady with streaks of chestnut in her locks. Though the shape of her eyes was like Hera's, there was little resemblance, so he released her. She hadn't appeared worried in the slightest from the beginning. Whoever she was, she was confident in her lack of involvement in the attacks.

The woman beside her, clothed in drab, gray fabrics and with eyes like fire, watched him as he stopped before her.

"Hestia," she said, as if guessing he was wondering about her identity.

"Hestia," he repeated, squinting at her, trying to recall her place in Olympus. "The one who gave her seat to…Dionysus, yes?"

Hestia inclined her head. "Indeed. And like my sister, Demeter, that you just dismissed, I take no part in the silly civil wars between my siblings. I'd never dare poison a family member. I cook their food." Her gaze narrowed, and she glanced down for a spell, before perking up. "Whoever this monster is, they're making me into a potential villain by poisoning meals and drinks. I dislike it more than most would assume."

Lukus remembered a few tales about Hestia. A virginal but fierce deity who protected her loved ones and demanded respect. She would, as she'd claimed, never harm her own blood. He gave her a curt nod, dismissing her.

She hurried off to the buttery-blonde—Demeter—and together they vanished from the room, through a rear-door.

He let a few more blondes go—including Psyche, Eros' wife, who was a victim, also—and several ladies with dark hair but who had no comparison with the chestnut-haired, majestic, moody Hera. Most of the cupbearers were too timid and trembling to give off the vibe of killers or angry attackers. And a few provided proof that they were nowhere near where Themis had been hurt. Nor did they have anything to do with food preparation or serving.

It felt like several moons had risen and fallen before he had a small group of women remaining, all of which would be difficult to release.

Hecate was there; not the culprit, but still involved, since the poison came from her personal stash of potions. And there was Artemis, who had curls of a texture not unlike Hera's, though the shade was lighter, and her eyes weren't filled with as much malice. And Athena—to her detriment—possessed a similar build to her step-mother, though more muscular.

Another woman, at Hera's side, was nearly Hera's twin, and Lukus' focus drew to her as he wondered what to do about Artemis and Athena.

"I don't even harm animals unless it's part of an official hunt," said Artemis, in her defense, tapping a foot to the floor in impatience. "My twin brother is the healer in this case, and Zeus has entrusted me to help fix the zombie situation on earth. I don't have time for this, to bite titanesses and drink their blood."

She was right, and Lukus knew it; he couldn't hold her here any longer, so he waved her off. With a snickering smile—at who, he wasn't positive—she escaped the throne-room, summoning her bow and arrows halfway to the door.

"And me?" Athena's gaze switched to a blinding yellow as she glowered at Lukus. "I'm the investigator! How could you keep me here among the accused? I enlisted you, and you won't even tell me—"

Zeus coughed in the background, lifting a finger to the air—his first interruption since the start of the meeting. "*I* enlisted Lukus, and he's within his rights to suspect you, too, Athena."

A certain smugness spread over Hera's features, and she seemed to fight a smirk. Lukus glanced at her and his eyebrows shot up. "I wouldn't act so confident if I were you, Majesty."

Her satisfaction melted at once, replaced with a snarl that sent Lukus teetering backwards. "Zeus? You permit this half-mortal to speak to me like this?" Her hands curled into fists at her sides. Lukus could have sworn rage roamed from her fingers, becoming a twitching electricity in the air.

Athena leaned forward, glaring at Hera in warning. "Watch it."

Zeus got up, his thunderous energy weighing heavy in the room. "I permit him whatever he pleases, if it helps us figure out what's going on."

Willing his body to cooperate—his bladder had come close to loosening at Hera's powers activating against him—Lukus marched over to Hecate, who'd been quietly observing, waiting her turn.

"You…I'm not sure I trust you. But you were sincere when I interrogated you. You gave me the description that's narrowed down our list this much. You're not the one, but don't go far. We still need you, and I have a hunch you still have more to tell me."

Hecate's cheeks flushed as she bowed her head and scampered backwards, nearly tripping into another goddess—one Lukus had missed in his dismissals.

Her hair was poofy and red, her eyes were wild but non-threatening, and her green gown gave her the airs of a jungle queen, with vines instead of arms and bark instead of skin. He remembered her from his introduction, earlier. She'd been one of the goddesses off to the side, eyeing him in curiosity. Along with the one who looked like Hera's twin.

Who are they?

He focused on her bushy tresses. "You…you're not it, either." Lukus didn't recognize her, but her aura was strong, destabilizing. She was ancient, for sure; a titaness?

"*The* titaness," said Athena, her voice still tainted with spite and annoyance. Yet, despite her irritation, she and Lukus worked together, and it appeared she wanted to help him not embarrass himself—again. "That's Gaia, the primordial goddess of the earth, the mother of all things."

"Oh." Lukus felt the urge to fall to his knees and worship the woman. Her name was one his father had uttered occasionally, and she was indeed the creator of everything. Zeus oversaw the world, but Gaia had created it. "Oh, shit." His limbs quivered, but before he could prostrate at her feet, Gaia stuck out her arm and stopped him.

"No need. I am grateful for your admiration, but there's no time for this." She scanned the remaining goddesses, standing before Zeus' throne. They were fixed on the scene, fear in their demeanors, questions scattered all over their scrunched features. "Athena, my daughter, and my granddaughter await your judgment, young man."

Hera's twin wasn't her twin; she was—

Gaia's daughter? So is that...

"Rhea." Gaia didn't read his mind—or so he thought; he had no notion of her powers—but she must have caught the confusion in his expression as he peeked between her and Hera and Hera's double. "Zeus' mother, Hera's mother. *Also* a mother of gods and a fearless friend. You'd keep her there? As an accused?"

Lower lip protruding, Lukus was at a loss for words. Gaia's gaze wasn't menacing, but her voice had no tenderness to it, and no hint of her true emotions. Would she strike Lukus for stating that yes, Rhea was evidently a possible suspect? Would she nod and agree and leave him to his investigation? And would anyone interfere and save him if she chose violence?

Zeus hadn't moved. Athena observed with neutrality bordering on frustration. Hera and Rhea looked ready to crumble to the floor and plead their innocence. It was a shocking vision of Hera, who'd so far been so stern, so solemn and impossible to read. Here she was frail, reduced from queen to potential prisoner.

Fuck.

He opened his mouth, praying his words would formulate on their own, when an ear-splitting, earth-shaking scream reverberated into the throne-room, coming from the main corridor. One so like the sound that had drawn him and Athena to the scene of Themis' attack, that for a second, he wondered if it was still repeating in his head.

When Zeus lurched from his spot, hurdling past Hera, and was the first to reach the hallway, Lukus knew he wasn't imagining it. Gaia flew after Zeus, followed by Hera and Rhea, their arms linked. Athena snatched Lukus' wrist on her way out, and yanked him along.

It was like seeing the aftermath of Themis' attack all over again—except it wasn't Themis sprawled on the polished floor. It was a different goddess…with Themis hunched *next* to her, with her teeth out and her mouth stained blue.

Lukus froze, and his guts churned. He'd seen crime scenes, plenty of them. He'd seen blood, intestines spilling out of ripped chests, vomit-inducing scenarios that even the goriest of movies couldn't portray correctly. But this was beyond his usual FBI investigations. Worse than the soulmate heart-eating disasters caused by Eros; and worse than when they'd found Themis.

This was the spillage of godly blood, wounds worthy of a gothic vampire movie, and poison so sweet-smelling it made him sick. It was ultimate chaos, guzzling out in shades of blue, bracing to drown the corridor's walls and floors in blood. It was gruesome, and his abdomen became uncomfortable and tight the longer he looked at it.

"I…" Themis, realizing she had an audience, wiped her mouth, smearing inky liquid all over her lips. She peeked at the unconscious body beside her and pouted. "It…I didn't…"

"Phoebe?" Gaia, calm despite the circumstances, crouched down to check on the victim, shoving strands of the woman's midnight curls from her face.

The woman's skin—it was sparkling silver when Lukus had dismissed her from the throne-room—was sheet-white and stained with ichor. Gaping wounds were on her neck—bite marks, on the same side and with the same depth as those on Themis' neck. Her torso moved up and down, meaning she was alive, but blood continued to pour from the gashes. A puddle of turquoise poison began to gather under her, prompting Gaia to crawl backwards and away from the danger.

Phoebe, Phoebe...who is she again?

Athena, still clutching Lukus' wrist, leaned her mouth to his ear. "Mother of Leto, grandmother of Apollo and Artemis. A prophecy titaness, revered among us all." Her lips pressed into his earlobe, but it wasn't a romantic or sexual gesture, as her tone was thick with fury, despite its low volume. "And there's your proof that I wasn't involved, and you shouldn't have singled me out, comparing me to *them.*" She jutted her chin at Hera and Rhea, huddled in a corner, tears streaming down their cheeks at the view of Phoebe.

"It's..." Themis sniffled, and glimpsed her hands, covered in ichor and poison. "I...it's not my fault!" The lower half of her face was so soiled, it was as if she'd rubbed blood all over herself, wanting it to taint her skin, to shift its color permanently.

Instead of hurling thunderbolts at her or ordering her to be locked up, Zeus kneeled in front of her and grabbed her shaking hands, avoiding touching the areas soaked in blood. "What do you mean? Why did you do this, Themis?" He cringed as he took a gander at Phoebe, immobile, her white dress blotched with navy and splattered with turquoise toxins.

"Someone...something in my mind made me do it." Themis heaved, hunching over, bowing her head to the floor. "I didn't mean to, I couldn't control it. It told me to drink her! To drink *from* her! And then to...to...inject her with...to fill her up with poison!" She sobbed, her words muffled by her mouth glued to the ground. "What have I done?"

Athena detached from Lukus, but remained at a cautious distance. "*It?* Like a voice? Telling you what to do?"

Themis lifted long enough to nod before crumbling again.

"Voices." Athena flipped around, concentrating on Lukus. "Someone instructing her to drink, to intoxicate. Sound familiar?"

Lukus pressed a hand to his dampening forehead. "Fuck." He ignored Zeus' grumble of displeasure at his language. "So…she was poisoned a few hours ago, and is now poisoning others? By the command of someone in her head? Uh…" Lukus closed his eyes and pinched the bridge of his nose. "Okay, so, who can control someone's mind via poison, and remotely?"

The silence that greeted his reply didn't reassure him, and left him with more queries that he doubted he'd get answers to.

|| 16. TRUTHS SPILLED ||
HERA

Lounging in her dining room throne, Hera sipped on her cocktail of ambrosia and sugary wine. Her belly was full—with food or spite, she couldn't tell—and she couldn't settle, couldn't get comfortable.

How did one find comfort in a home where everyone suspected them, and where there were attacks at every corner?

First Eros and Psyche, then Themis, now Phoebe; the pattern of victims made no sense. There was no link between these gods—aside from Eros and Psyche being married—and no means to understand what these attacks meant.

Despite all the chaos, lunch was served, as always, and at its usual time—when the sun was at its peak. Hestia had slaved away in the kitchens, preparing a heavenly feast of gorgeous greens and hearty potages and mouth-watering meats. And though Hera's appetite was hindered by the sickness swelling in her gut, the disgust at her family members, she knew better than to refuse a meal. Hestia was docile and sweet most days, but if anyone declined her offer of food, she'd go mad and burn down the kitchens.

We can't have that.

Not everyone had decided to partake in the meal, however. A few gods hadn't taken up their spots at the massive marble table that spread from one end of the elaborate dining room to the other. The crystal chandeliers illuminated the vacant seats of Athena, Artemis—likely still peeved at being a potential suspect—and Dionysus. The chair beside Hera's was empty, too: Zeus hadn't deigned to join her after the discovery of Phoebe, preferring to pout in private who knew where.

If he wouldn't defend her, Hera would have to find her own means to confirm her innocence. As she drained the rest of her delectable beverage, her gaze zoned in on one deity she might be able to extract information from—a distraught and disturbed-looking Aphrodite.

Sitting straight up in her seat, a few spaces down from Hera, she had a gloominess to her demeanor, more pronounced than her most dramatic episodes of depression—which happened when Hephaestus caught her with Ares, or when Ares was out of the palace on business. Still, during those trying times, she maintained her flirtatious, flighty nature though she snapped at servants and drank a tad too much wine.

Today, she gaped at her plate, having had maybe two bites of her meal, and hadn't taken a single sip from her drink. She spoke to no one, and ignored the cup-bearers that she'd normally fling all her emotions onto, using them as punching bags for her irritation.

She was a perfect target. In such a dreadful mood, she'd have a loose tongue—eager to share her woes with anyone who dared to ask—and not a care for who she confided in.

Hera set down her glass, impatient to pester her into talking. Surely she'd say something to put another god in the suspect spotlight, right? Or reveal a plan of Athena's, or divulge a weakness that Hera could exploit to her advantage, to prove her innocence?

It took one involuntary squeeze of the shoulders and a fake mutter of *"are you okay?"* to convince Aphrodite to spill her emotions out onto the table. An oddity, for certain, though Hera had hoped for her instability to work in her favor. She and Aphrodite loathed each other, albeit in a more quiet manner than she and Athena. So why would she chat with Hera? As if they were friends, constant confidantes? Was she so distressed that she didn't care who she spoke to?

Hera would dwell on the eeriness of the situation later. For now, she had to tune into Aphrodite's rambling and pretend to give a damn about it all. And decipher something in her words that would help her case.

"…and we were, well," Aphrodite blushed, "fooling around, as per usual. Not far; we heard the scream, and it interrupted us at once. Ares was furious." She cringed. "Sorry, he's your son, I'm sure you don't wish to hear about our escapades."

Hera sneered; if only Aphrodite knew how often she'd been privy to Ares' naughty actions. And how many times she'd been spying and caught them in the act.

"It's fine," she waved at Aphrodite, urging her to continue her tale, "I can handle it, for a good cause."

Divulge something that'll clear my name, please. Don't make me befriend you longer than I have to.

"Oh, Hera." Aphrodite sniffled, and her eyes swelled with tears. If she was about to cry, Hera wanted no part in it; but Aphrodite grabbed her hand and squeezed it, barring her from running off. "Why are you being so patient? Heavens, you have every reason to be pissed at me. At all of us. You, the queen accused of participating in all this insanity? How do you bear it?"

Gritting her teeth to refrain from screaming and seizing Aphrodite's perfect curls and ripping them from her perfect head, Hera inhaled, then blew out a deep, trembling breath.

"I don't. It's insufferable. But I have no idea how to get Athena to understand I'm not responsible for this. For any of it." She quirked a brow, seeing the opportunity to sway Aphrodite to her side, to appeal to her past grievances against Athena. "A sly little thing, she is. Feigning innocence but slipping into everyone's business behind their backs. You've dealt with that too, no?"

Aphrodite loosened her grip on Hera's hand. "I have. But…" She bit her lip and lowered her chin. "I've chosen to move beyond that. We have bigger things at stake, and we shouldn't be fighting." She jerked up again, her face illuminated, untainted by the dismay that had been plaguing her seconds ago.

Ah, Aphrodite—the most complicated of us all, snapping in and out of moods in the blink of an eye.

They all dared call Hera the moody, morose deity. The one who threw fits and was never content. But they had it wrong; Aphrodite was the biggest drama queen, and Hera wished they'd all see it. Instead of drooling at her feet and worshiping the ground she walked on.

"Truth be told, I don't think you're part of this, Hera." Aphrodite had tapered her voice, dimmed it to an unusual softness. She was normally loud, squeaky, her timbre like nails on a chalkboard; but she'd grown discreet, and such a shift drew Hera's rapt attention.

"You don't?" Hera squinted at her, leaning away. "Then why did you take her side?"

"The pressure, Hera, *the pressure.* It's evident to all that I'm unloved among the goddesses, and especially the two of you. I thought quickly, and Athena and I had formed a bond in recent times. A tiny one, mind you, but it made more sense for me to pick her instead of you." She picked up her fork and dipped it into her mixed salad, tossing the elements with little enthusiasm. "But I don't believe you did it. You're as innocent as me," she scoffed, "which, in this case, is *very* innocent."

Hera crossed her arms, studying the goddess of love, seeking any sign of malice, any hint of trickery. "Would you ever speak up for me? Is there some bargain we can strike?"

Aphrodite forked a few lettuce leaves and brought them to her mouth, but didn't put them inside. She glided them left and right over her lips, narrowing her gaze as she pondered Hera's question.

"I won't," she said at last, depositing the fork and wiping her mouth with a silk napkin. "But I will tell you something, and you can do with it what you will."

Hera clasped her hands. Keeping her cautious, unreadable composure was difficult, and more so when she sensed that she was about to receive information that might exonerate her. It was tough to tell, with Aphrodite. She played the aloof, alluring goddess card often, but ended up being wittier and wiser than most believed her to be. She was a master trickster, almost as good as Hermes, and if she planned to embarrass Hera now, Hera needed to be ready for her.

Show no emotion. Mask your thoughts. Don't let her get the best of you.

"I saw Themis lurking, talking to herself, acting strange. Earlier, after she left the throne-room." Aphrodite slouched in her seat and peered left and right, as if fearing eavesdroppers. But the dining room was mostly deserted. The only remaining gods were engaged in a serious debate about some human sport Hera hadn't bothered to care about. "I was in too much of a hurry to meet with Ares, so I didn't stop to check on her. Nor did I have time to return to the throne-room and warn someone…so I kept on with my mission." She swallowed, and reached for her goblet, downing half the contents in one nervous gulp. "I should have acted, right? If I'd spoken with Themis, perhaps she…and Phoebe…"

In a true, earnest gesture, Hera placed a hand on Aphrodite's forearm, settling her sudden shivers. "She would have attacked you, instead." Hera scrunched her nose. "I'm not sure the victims are chosen in advance. If Themis wasn't herself, blabbering, her behavior off…I doubt she knew what she was doing. Phoebe was the first person to approach her, I assume, and…well, we know what happened next."

"*You* know, yes. You were there." Aphrodite shuddered, then finished her cup, setting it on the edge of the table. Her tremors threatened to send the thing crashing to the ground, so Hera snatched it and set it on the other side of the plate. "They say it was a horror scene. Blood, *ichor* everywhere. Pools of poison, drool, fangs, gnashes in the neck—" Aphrodite gagged, then swiped a hand over her glistening forehead. "Yes, I witnessed Eros' carnage, and it was gory—gross, truly. But to witness *our* blood spilled, our family members bitten, broken, drained? No, I cannot fathom it."

Hera stood up and took Aphrodite's elbow, gently tugging her up, as well. "Come. Let us get you to your quarters. I doubt a meltdown in the dining room is a good idea, what with all the suspicion and the stress."

Frowning, Aphrodite ripped from Hera's grip and stumbled backwards, as if drunk. "I'm still not sure why you're being so nice, and I don't like it."

Ah, there we go—she's coming to.

"Did you put something in my drink?" Aphrodite glared at her goblet, then at Hera. "You *are* the culprit, aren't you? Cozying up to me, finding out what I know, sweetening me up to better trap me—"

Before Hera could shove a hand over Aphrodite's mouth to quiet her, someone slithered up to them and cleared their throat. Both she and Aphrodite twisted to find Gaia, her eyebrows bunched, her eyes glowing with irritation, and her emerald dress vacillating, as if about to launch spikes into them.

"The atrocity of you," she said, gripping them both and dragging them away from the table. Once far from any potential listeners, close to the door to the corridor, she fixed on Hera. "You, sneakily prying information out in the open. Since when?" She flipped to Aphrodite. "And you, accusing her of poisoning your drink? In front of others who've already put her in the hot spot? The nerve. The audacity. Heavens!" She released them and unleashed a monumental sigh. "These children are giving me migraines, and I don't like migraines."

Aphrodite gasped and inclined her head, muttering excuses under her breath.

Hera, either less intimidated by Gaia, or the alcohol she'd consumed was erasing her inhibitions, didn't cower. She arched her back and returned Gaia's glare. "I'm prying information to defend myself, since no one else will bother helping me!"

Gaia shook her head as she pinched the bridge of her nose. "I'll help—Aphrodite," she motioned at the goddess of love, "Hera didn't put anything in your drink. Or in anyone else's, for that matter. Be smart, and stop taking sides. Stay out of this civil war, will you? You'll soon have other matters to deal with."

"Other matters?" Intrigued, Aphrodite redressed herself, batting her lashes.

"What else is there but the criminal crawling in our home and drinking the blood from our beloved family members?" Hera folded her arms and took a step back, unsure how to interpret Gaia's attitude.

The ever-elusive, but always frank protectress of the earth was disturbed. Her gown only quivered like this—writhing about as if convulsing—when she was on edge, conflicted, annoyed. It had happened the night before, when Hera had upset her. And it had occurred a few centuries ago, after Gaia had caused a giant ruckus at court when in a screaming match with Zeus.

"There's an odd energy in the palace; and no, I'm not referring to the culprit. Something else." Gaia glimpsed the table, the kitchen door, the windows, the balustrade; then she yanked Hera and Aphrodite into the hallway. Once assured no one loitered nearby, she huddled close to them. "Lukus. His presence has destabilized me."

Hera cocked her head. "How so? He's only a half-mortal presuming to be part god. He has no powers, no knowledge…there's nothing threatening about him."

"I didn't say threatening," said Gaia, her voice hissing like a snake. "I said *odd*. And growing. No powers, you say; but they're developing, brewing. I can smell them."

"Hm, I did sense some power in him last time I saw him, in the hospital. But it wasn't that pungent. It was…different." Aphrodite sniffed at the air, as if expecting to detect Lukus' scent. "What does it smell like to you, Gaia?"

Rolling her eyes, Hera focused on Gaia to avoid nudging Aphrodite.

Get to the point, Gaia. What have you discovered?

As if reading her mind—which she might well have, despite Zeus' ban on mind-reading abilities; Gaia was older and stronger than him—Gaia zeroed in on Hera. "He's not just any half-mortal, dear. He's a full-blown demi-god, descended from an Olympian."

Though it didn't surprise her that Gaia had figured it out—as one of the oldest deities in the universe, she had mysterious skills—Hera's jaw dropped. Aphrodite's did, too, but not without a shriek of shock.

This time, Hera *did* nudge her, to silence her. "Hush. Don't attract attention, you fool." She switched to Gaia, who stood so close to them her voluminous hair kept creeping into Hera's mouth. "Not Zeus', right?" She puffed out a breath to move a few strands away, trying not to spit all over her primordial grandmother. "He swore Lukus wasn't his."

"No, not Zeus'." Gaia sucked her lips inward and closed her eyes.

She knew, oh, of course she did. Nothing ever escaped Gaia. Whether she had access to anyone's minds, it didn't matter. She could read faces, sniff out energies, detect lies from thousands of miles away.

"I came from the kitchens, just now, in case you were wondering." Her shoulders rolled back, but she remained close, her earthy aroma intensifying as she shook out her skirts. The hem of her dress separated into two snake-like sashes that expanded and shot in two directions at once, cloaking the ground in shiny green layers. They then spiked upward on both sides, acting as a blockage on either end of the hallway. Floors and walls of silk—a classic Gaia trait to protect an area she didn't want anyone to enter. "I stole a speck of Lukus' DNA during the meeting. Don't look at me like that," she waved at Hera, "I had to. Something about him troubled me."

"Troubled you?" Hera huffed. "Could you please tell us the truth, instead of stringing us along? Your wall of satin won't keep anyone out for long, you know this." It was unlike her to taunt Gaia, but her patience was running thin. She wasn't done proving her innocence, after all, and didn't give two craps about Lukus.

As if responding to Hera's quips, the gown sent a sharp spike at her, pushing her into the wall.

"While everyone was eating or resting, I went to the kitchens. With my ties to the earth and soil—and thanks to the gardens and crops in the basement greenhouse—I resourced myself, I re-energized. Which allowed me to dig into his heritage. I analyzed it. I discovered his parentage."

Hera and the strangely silent Aphrodite gawked at her, both desperate for her to end her story and divulge her findings.

"He has a mortal father," said Gaia, allowing Hera's lungs to untangle and her erratic pulse to relax. She knew it wasn't Zeus, yet a slither of her had been worried. "And his mother…" Gaia entwined her fingers with Aphrodite's, and a soft sweetness weaved into her voice. "It's you, my dear. Aphrodite. You are Lukus' mother."

"Wh-what?" Aphrodite's knees buckled, and she slunk to the floor, her creamy tunic's straps sliding down her milky shoulders. Her lips vibrated as she held in what Hera presumed might have been the most exaggerated sigh of all time. Her eyes bulged and blared like bright, fluorescent marbles. "Me? Lukus'…mother? No. No, you're mistaken. You've got me confused with someone else, I'd know, I'd remember giving birth to him, I'd—"

"—it's the truth. I'm sorry if it disappoints you." Gaia didn't help her up, and tore her fingers from Aphrodite's tightening fists, her kindness gone in a flash. "Forgive the abrupt reveal, but I must go. Please," she glanced at Hera, "inform him. Prepare him. Lukus needs to know and embrace his powers. And fast, because something nefarious lurks on the horizon, I can tell. We'll need all the support we can get in the battles to come."

|| 17. SWEET AND SENSUAL SLUMBER ||

RHEA

Ears still buzzing with Gaia's whispered words—*Lukus is Aphrodite's son*—Rhea tossed and turned in her four-poster bed. Her thick sheets of fake fur wouldn't keep her warm, and her legs were coated in a cold sweat as she fought to find a comfortable position.

Lukus, a son of Olympus. This put him nearly on par with Athena, Artemis, Apollo, Hermes—all full-blooded sons and daughters of Olympians. As a demi-god, he had less power, but he'd develop a few abilities with time.

He *was* intriguing, she had to admit. When he'd stood before her, inspecting her, studying her, she'd gotten a whiff of him. Something potent coursed through his veins, but she hadn't been able to place it until now.

Another son for the goddess of love—what does this mean?

She wasn't sure how this information affected her, and yet Gaia had made it a point to tell her. Was it because Rhea was the mother of Olympians, making her de-facto Lukus' grandmother? Gaia's tone had been ominous, seeped in a sinister tonality that caused Rhea to shudder, still now, swathed in blankets.

"*It means something,*" said the voice, ever so skilled at

interrupting Rhea's rare moments of quiet.

She'd extinguished all her candles and pulled her curtains shut to mute the intense Olympian sun. She'd even sipped on some sweet ambrosia tea laced with chamomile and honey—but she still couldn't sleep.

And how she needed slumber. It felt like she hadn't gotten a proper night of rest in weeks. Strangely enough, her restlessness commenced when she'd first started hearing that damned voice. When it woke in her mind at all hours of the night, whispering at her to go feed, go drink, go explore.

She'd done enough feeding and drinking for a while, she thought. Themis' blood was potent, quenching Rhea's thirst with only a few drops. Yet the voice had urged her to keep going, to leave nothing but a slither of ichor before spurting toxins into Themis' veins.

And exploring? Up here, in this palace where gods would now be more on their guard than ever, tiptoeing down corridors, looking over their shoulders, hiding in corners to ensure the coast was clear? No, Rhea didn't want to venture out with such tension in the air. And more so since she'd been among the last goddesses in Lukus' line-up, when he'd convened everyone earlier. Few had lingered in the throne-room to witness her, standing by Hera, undergoing Lukus' scrutiny, but she wouldn't risk it. Rumors flew fast in Olympus, and it was a matter of time before Zeus sent a horde of muscular cup-bearers to chain her wrists and throw her into the dungeons.

"He will do no such thing." The voice's timbre was sincere, almost sweet; but it wouldn't fool Rhea. It wouldn't stay soft for long. *"No one will accuse you, though they seem to link these attacks to what happened to Eros and Psyche. Hera is a bitch, everyone knows that. That's why they have no issue with Athena's accusations. But you?*

Never."

Rhea sat up straight and smacked one of her pillows. "You call my daughter a bitch? Who are you to speak to me like this?"

The voice chortled; a distorted, demented sound that Rhea knew would haunt her for weeks. *"I am the voice inside you who controls you and knows what's best for you. Your daughter* is *a bitch. Spoiled and demanding and entitled. Let her keep taking the blame while we work in the shadows."*

Rhea opened her mouth to retaliate—Hera was, in truth, a rotten woman most days—but the voice somehow clamped her lips shut and hindered her from speaking.

"Don't waste your breath; I'm in your head, I know your thoughts. Lie back down. You need to rest for a spell."

Though she agreed she needed sleep, it wasn't of her own volition that Rhea curled into her covers and settled her head atop the silky pillows. In the daylight, her room was filled with comforting oranges and peppy yellows and photographs of her beloved felines, her protectors, her friends. But in the dark, she saw nothing but ghosts and smoky figures blurring before her, taking curvy, feminine shapes before evaporating into thin air.

Was that the voice, manifesting to her in the obscurity? *Was* it in her head, or trailing behind her, sticking its shadowy fingers into her brain and whispering into her ears?

She closed her heavy eyelids and yawned. Maybe, if the voice remained quiet, for once, she'd get a few hours of sleep. Maybe she'd be cozy in her guest suite, surrounded by the exotic jungle scents coming from the magical incense on her dresser, with the faint hum of bees and the chirp of wild birds floating overhead, from the enchanted ceiling.

She had Gaia to thank for that. It was her ancient rule that Zeus had adopted and made permanent in Olympus: that all guests were to receive the highest of comforts, no matter their excessive nature, and no matter who the guest was. Potential foe, elegant grandmother, powerless half-mortal; all were treated like royalty.

Rhea knew Gaia liked her quarters filled with soft soil and replicas of pine trees. With flowers sprouting from every corner, spice racks and vines used as plant-holders, and a ceiling of stars.

Rhea liked the humid droplets of a South American jungle to populate over her arms; she wanted sunny floor-boards and vivid wallpaper.

When the delicate sounds of nature failed to help her keep her eyes closed, she moved on to the next tactic she'd normally employ to ease her mind. One most would be shocked at, but how would they know? She was alone in her room, with only the voice as company. The voice wouldn't dare interrupt this, would she?

With a slight smirk, Rhea snuck her hand under her nightgown and crept her fingers up to the crevice between her legs, anticipating a warm wetness to welcome her. To her dismay, she was drier than a lion's fur during a drought.

"Crap." She kept her fingers there, twirling them, rotating, as she once more closed her eyes, this time to picture something that would arouse her. "Come on, Rhea, think. *Think.*"

After a few moments, she conjured an old but still vivid memory, and latched on to it. That time when she'd stumbled upon a harem of jungle nymphs bathing in a sparkling pool, eagerly watched from behind a tree by a lusty satyr. The nymphs were naked, their breasts glimmering with water, nipples erect and plump and delicious to look at, even from where Rhea had been hidden. The women toyed with one another, exchanging kisses, touching each other, moaning in delight. Rhea licked her lips, entranced by the sight. She cared not what gender these creatures were, because she admired *all* Zeus' creations, and reveled in the witnessing of their sexual acts.

Of course, the sly, sexy things knew the satyr ogled them—naturally, they loved the attention—so they splashed and squealed and hopped about, and the satyr's desire only grew stronger. They pretended to be startled when he jumped out of his hiding spot and revealed his enormous, throbbing member, but they invited him to join them. Five nymphs for one lucky, hairy, snub nosed satyr—what a wondrous, legendary vision, no? Rhea had lowered into a nearby bush and tugged her skirts up and—

"Is this necessary?" The pointed, perturbing invasion in Rhea's fantasies prompted Rhea to groan and remove her fingers from the moisture she'd managed to summon.

"Is your *interruption* necessary? You asked me to relax," she smacked her palms on the bedspread, "and this is how I relax. How have you not noticed yet? How have you not reacted to the visions I get when I drink ichor? You cause them, do you not? You arouse me when I sink my teeth in."

"I do nothing. Everyone reacts differently to the poison," the voice said, calmer, but a dash of annoyance still lingering in her tone. *"Drinking blood, and more so potent godly ichor, causes various side-effects. In your case, you become aroused and venture into your victim's past sexual memories. It is enough that I have to suffer through those; please, would you find a different means to unwind?"*

Rhea's jaw dropped, but as she attempted to sit up, an energy came over her, pressing her into her mattress. Like a weighted blanket deposited over her body, keeping her in place, preventing her from fidgeting too much.

"What are you doing?" She glared at the obscurity, waiting to decipher a feminine figure flurrying about before her; wishing to reach out and grab it, shake it, beg it to give her some reprieve for the night.

"I'm helping you sleep. You haven't in weeks, and that's my fault."

The voice was gentle, *too* gentle, and Rhea's intestines knotted. She didn't trust it, didn't trust *her*, whoever or whatever she was. Dictating commands, urging her to drink blood, forbidding her from being aroused, but appeasing her into slumber? It made no sense.

"You should trust me. What I do, I do for the benefit of all. In the long run, you'll see it too."

Rhea scoffed. "I don't even know what you're doing. You don't get candid enough to share your ultimate goals with me. You've never bothered to explain why or how you poisoned me, who you are, why you've made me so damn thirsty—"

"—My, my, aren't we feisty tonight?" The voice's witch-like cackle almost brought Hecate to mind, but Rhea knew *her* laughter wasn't so unpleasant, so ear-piercing. Sorceress she was, but she didn't have a shred of the malice this creature had. *"You've never questioned me so much."*

"Perhaps it's the Olympus air. It refines one's senses and awakens one's conscience. These feedings," she gagged at the reminiscence of Themis in a pool of her own blood, "why do you cause them? If they are so significant, is there no other way to inject our prey with poison?"

"How odd." The tone was swift but cold. *"For someone so sexually inclined, you find no delight in the delicate, sensual extraction of blood from someone's neck?"*

This being's speech was eloquent, proper. She was high-placed, educated, well-informed of how Olympus functioned and which weak points belonged to which gods. She was an insider, for certain; but who?

And she was right. Rhea had never been so inquisitive until now. Until chomping her family members and being overcome with shame and guilt that even the voice's eerie powers couldn't fix. Suckling on animal blood hadn't seemed so horrible to her; after all, humans killed animals for sport and plopped them into their stoves to burn their flesh and eat them. So why would drinking their precious life-juice be a crime?

But drinking from goddesses, revered and beloved women of Olympus...it felt wrong. Rhea had enjoyed the after-math, the arousing flashes that sent her into a frenzy of pleasure, but when she'd come to, when she'd seen the mess she'd made, her insides threatened to hurl out her mouth. She wasn't squeamish—used to watching her wild cats tear the flesh from their innocent prey—but it was something else when *you* were the attacker, and *you* watched your victim bleed out.

And worse—her hunger grew, independent of her disgust. It fought with her logic, with her sanity, triggering her, torturing her. *Drink, infect, become stronger,* said the voice—and her brain told her to refuse, but her gut agreed with the being controlling her thoughts.

She yearned to rebel against it, to ask it to leave her alone; and after all, what could a voice stuck in her head do to her?

Reminded that this very voice had just confined her to her bed and had her stuck under a weighted blanket, Rhea clenched her jaw and stared at the ceiling.

No; this thing wasn't a regular voice. It was a power, a force commanded by someone else, at a distance. It was poison, and Rhea had no means to rid her body of it; not without alerting her family and putting herself in the hot-seat.

She huffed. "Biting necks is sensual, sure; until you awaken and realize you're sucking blood from a family member."

She wished to fold her arms, but the voice kept them crammed to her sides. So she lay stiff as a board, uncomfortable and unhappy. Did this creature expect she'd be able to fall asleep in this position?

"I need you to trust me, Rhea. All these steps are crucial."

"Oh, and including infecting that same family member, causing her to indulge in the same indiscretions as me?" Rhea cringed, craving to sit up, to throw her pillows, to make a point; but she was weak and exhausted, overpowered by a voice cramping inside her mind.

That voice had never exerted such physical power over her before. It had whispered urgently, susurrated, implored; but never took command of Rhea's body and prohibited her from moving as she pleased.

"You should be thanking me for that." She was faded, as if speaking from the farthest confines of Rhea's brain. *"Themis' intervention by chowing down on Phoebe halted that moronic investigation and protected you. Us."*

"You said…" Rhea scrunched her nose. "You said no one would dare suspect us, but now you are grateful Phoebe was bitten and drained to save us?"

"The risk is minimal, but any actions in our favor are not to be dismissed, Rhea." The tone's volume returned, bouncing inside Rhea's skull, prompting her to grimace. *"And now you have minions to keep the blame away from you. If you feed—and you will, you must, soon—they will be automatic suspects before anyone ever thinks of*

you. How lucky are we that I can be in several heads at once, hm?"

The timbre turned almost familiar, nice. Too nice. Like a friend looking out for a friend, but expecting a prize for it. Or a mother protecting her child from her turbulent lifestyle, refusing to quit her addictions. Or an aunt spoiling a niece with gifts and cakes and adoration behind her parent's back, because she herself couldn't have children. The voice had a motive, and it—*she* intended to use Rhea to get to it, whatever means necessary. Sweetness, firmness, terrible truths, a pinch of violence—this monster would get what she wanted no matter who stood in her way.

And she knew none would get in Rhea's way, either. Like she'd known to target Persephone, then Eros, then Psyche—gods who never caused issues and who, if discovered, would be forgiven.

This thing in me…it's the same thing that was in them, isn't it? I had my doubts, but it's confirmed now, with her behavior, her words. But why?

"So it was you…" Rhea gulped, the weight of her realization becoming heavier than the power the voice continued to exert over her body. "You're the culprit. The one on a rampage in Olympus. What I'm doing…what you're making me do…it's all linked to Eros and Psyche and Persephone, isn't it?"

The voice snorted. *"Are you going to pretend like you hadn't made the correlation? Come now, Rhea, you're smarter than that. You poisoned Themis. You act impulsively, commanded by a voice in your head. It is the same thing, yes."*

Rhea gulped again. "Right. I…I knew that."

Her tongue was heavy, her throat dry, constricting. She'd known something was wrong with her, that the voice was abnormal, that her actions would get her in trouble. But to realize that *her* voice and the one that had infused Eros and Psyche were the same came as a bigger shock to her than she'd anticipated.

"And you…*you* spoke to Themis, told her to attack Phoebe? Since I p-poisoned her, you were in her head, too." Rhea squinted at the darkness overhead, at the ceiling she wished was sprinkled with stars, or cloaked with low-hanging clouds covering a navy night's sky. She yearned for the outdoors, for the big cats she'd cuddle up with, for the sounds of exotic birds atop high tree-tops. "That was why you weren't in my mind while Lukus inspected me. You…"

"I was saving our hide, yes." The voice spoke slowly. Not as if Rhea were daft, but elongating each word to make sure it imprinted inside her brain. *"I caused that distraction, and will do it again if I must. Themis, Phoebe—they are one of us now, and though I had to direct Themis' thirst today, she'll figure it out for herself in time."*

"But isn't Apollo working with Hecate to cure them?"

The voice laughed, again in that witch-like resonance that stopped Rhea's heart and choked her. *"That's what they hope; but they won't be able to extract every drop. They may have succeeded with Eros and Psyche, but this strain, the one in you and now in Themis and Phoebe, it's different. It's resilient to Hecate's spells, and it hides until it's summoned. They'll think the titanesses are cured, and even the titanesses will believe so, at first. But when the attacks continue, those two—that fake healer and the semi-decent sorceress—they'll see they're in over their heads."*

"And you want that, right?" Rhea bit her lip. "To cause discord. Their failure will create rage, will worsen the divide, amplify the civil war?"

"Now you're seeing the bigger picture, Rhea. If I didn't know better, I'd say you're learning."

What Rhea tried her hardest not to say or even think was that she saw nothing. She sensed malice, she detected foul play, and she worried what she'd discover if she asked too many questions. Was that why she'd been so neutral, so uncaring back in her jungle? She'd let the voice control her without a complaint; was it because she didn't want to find out who it belonged to? Afraid of the disappointment, the fury, the truth behind its identity?

If she'd been poisoned with the potion stolen from Hecate, it had clearly happened to her before any of the other gods. Her thirst for blood had begun weeks, if not months ago. Whatever, whoever this creature was…it had been planning this for a while.

"You're holding something back, Rhea, and I dislike it." The voice's energy shoved Rhea's head deeper into the pillow. *"Sleep. I can better access your deepest, hidden thoughts when you're inactive."*

Something sprinkled over Rhea's cheeks, as if the voice was covering her in sleeping powder—but it was only an illusion, a taste of the power this being had. Confined in Rhea's brain or not, she had abilities beyond Rhea's imagination; and when Rhea yawned, suddenly sleepier than ever, settling into the mattress, she knew she'd be in trouble when she woke. Because the creature would read Rhea's hesitation, if not downright refusal, to continue this insanity of drinking from gods and lurking about hallways, pretending not to be a part of the dangers in Olympus.

"We need more minions, more allies. We must weaken more…"

Rhea's eyelids slammed shut like two metal doors.

Yet she didn't sleep, not fully. At one point—minutes or hours later, she had no clue—her eyes twitched, and opened halfway to reveal that she was standing. Walking. Moving forward, her nostrils picked up on a delicious scent, a tasty treat nearby. Her sight became clear, and she realized she wasn't in her room. She was in an empty, quiet corridor, looming near large windows. Moonlight pooled over her, like a headlight blaring at her to move, making her shut her eyes again.

Hadn't she been stuck on the bed? Hadn't the voice prevented her from lifting a finger? How had she ended up here?

She tried to move her mouth to speak, but her words caught in her throat and her lips wouldn't budge, glued together.

This wasn't her; sleepwalking while semi-conscious? What sort of sorcery was this? Was she dreaming?

"You're not dreaming. Be quiet. Let me work."

The voice—it was determined, focused. It had released her. Hadn't it read her mind, sensed her terror? Wasn't it angry?

How much time had passed? Where exactly was she? And what in Tartarus was she up to now?

|| 18. FRIGHTFUL FIGHTS ||
LUKUS

The stuffiness in Athena's room grew worse the longer Lukus stayed in there, suffocated by her complaints.

"I told you," he said, trying his hardest not to glower at her, lest she zap his eyes shut forever. "I don't actually suspect you, okay? You fit the profile, and I couldn't discriminate or play favorites."

Athena, who'd spent the past hour or so pacing to and fro in such a frenzy that Lukus had grown dizzy watching her, huffed.

"But I *am* a favorite; Zeus' favorite! Or so I used to be." She snarled—facing away from Lukus—and her fists were so tight she looked ready to punch something.

As the goddess of wisdom but also of war, Athena was easily restless. Lukus would have to learn to hold his tongue and ensure his behavior never irritated her. For someone so revered in history and mythology, she had quite the temper.

Not unlike the step-mother she so hates.

Hearing his thoughts, Athena rounded on him. He'd been sitting on the bed, and she swept over, setting her veiny hands on either side of his thighs, pressing her forehead to his. Her owlish eyes were like two vivid yellow lightning bolts, about to strike through him and murder him on the spot.

"Don't you dare compare me to her."

Lukus flinched, closed his eyes, and lifted his hands, hoping to push her off him. But he trembled so badly that he couldn't raise his arms, and his stomach churned, anticipating his time of death.

Sensing his terror, or revolted by his weakness, Athena backed a few inches away, though she remained in his space, her mouth bunching and unbunching, her biceps bulging with power. The veins protruding in her hands fired up her arms, and for a second, she reminded him of her father. The same moodiness, the same irrational attitude when miffed.

That thought seemed to further calm her as she redressed herself and spun away from him. "I *am* like him. Which is why we keep arguing, lately. He won't trust my hunches. No one will." She stood tall, her spine arched, her legs strong and sturdy. But the slight quiver in her tone showed Lukus she wasn't as unaffected by her father's disappointment as she'd been trying to convey.

"Obviously some do, since they sided with you." He recalled the accusation in the throne-room, and how quickly certain gods had skidded up to pledge their allegiance to her, to assure her they were on her team.

Athena snorted. "Because they fear me. Well, they fear Father. If no one had come forward, he would have questioned it, and would have thrown a fit, no matter his displeasure with me." Her shoulders squared as she twisted sideways, staring towards the half-curtained window. "And they hate Hera more than they hate me. It was easy to pick the lesser of two evils, in their opinion."

Hera.

Lukus perked up at the mention, and gazed at the sparkling list of names Athena had conjured moments ago, at his request. He'd studied his notes so much that his brain hurt, so he'd wondered if seeing the names in massive, floating fonts might help him.

Hecate and *Athena* were shoved off to the side—the former, to Athena's dismay—and in the middle, bright and blaring, were *Hera* and *Rhea*.

"Gaia was so irritated at me, wasn't she?"

Lukus focused on Rhea, conjuring her image to his memory. She was so like Hera, and yet there was a gentler side to her, an air of kindness that was lacking from Hera's stern features. Athena had later explained that Rhea had been in the jungle, living among exotic animals, and actually had a wilder personality than one would think, but she kept it in check.

Rhea had succeeded in this, because Lukus hadn't detected that wild side. Something about her was off, for sure. But he didn't see her as evil, as one to go about poisoning her family members or digging her teeth into their necks, or ordering someone to do so in her stead.

Was Hera capable of such things, though? Vindictive and vicious, as she was described in the legends, she didn't come off as truly malicious to Lukus. Snarky, sure; but not one to intoxicate those in her proximity for no apparent reason. When Hera attacked, it was under a threat, or when offended. So, had anyone offended her lately? Had anyone roused her anger and provoked her?

"No," said Athena, tuning into Lukus' train of thought. Her eyes had returned to a normal, neutral gray as she sat next to him and sighed. "This is what conflicts me, too; it's easy to accuse her of cruelty, but no one has pushed her over the edge, lately. Her and Father have been…dare I say it? Happy. He hasn't cheated, and she hasn't had to drive any of his demi-god sons and daughters mad. But your arrival…I imagine it tore her up." Athena scratched her chin. "I'm sure her thoughts went straight to infidelity; that you were a son of Zeus and that he had, contrary to his claims, strayed again."

Lukus placed a hand to his chest, feeling his heart beating out of control. The simple idea of being Zeus' son woke the eeriest of impulses in him. The name alone seemed to wake parts of his being he didn't know existed, triggered sensations he never knew could be real.

"But I'm not his, he swore it."

"After the first attack…" Athena squinted at the dresser ahead, raising a finger in a *wait a minute* motion. "Who's to say Hera didn't lose her wits before that? Who's to say she didn't already know about you, and acted in a rebellious rage against Zeus? She sought a means to poison Persephone, a treasured member of the family, daughter of her own sister. Then used Eros and Psyche as distractions as she continued to research ways to get back at Zeus. And then got to Themis…"

"But if Hera attacked Themis, that would mean she was poisoned, too. Someone made her do it, right?" Lukus shook his head. "Because she'd have to be nuts to want to drink someone's blood, don't you think? That's some vampiric behavior if I've ever seen it."

He cringed; he *hadn't* seen such demeanors before. In all his years of investigating the most tricky, fucked-up crimes the FBI could throw at him—including Eros' cannibalistic murders—he hadn't come across any vampire-like scenarios. No gashes in necks, no humans drained of blood by drinking. This was new to him.

My knowledge of anything vampire-related comes from books and movies.

"So you're saying, even if Hera is involved, it wouldn't be of her own volition? Someone controls *her,* too?" Athena groaned and got to her feet, resuming her pacing. "That only puts us back at square one.

Who is the mastermind behind all this? Who has the power to break into minds and poison and provoke a civil war? This is senseless."

Lukus narrowed his gaze at her. "*You* provoked the civil war, Athena. By speaking too soon and accusing Hecate, then publicly charging Hera without tangible proof."

He cowered at once, arms over his head, as Athena zoomed up to him, her upper lip curling and her body seeming to double in size. It hadn't, of course; but such was Athena's powerful presence, prompting him to go crazy with fear whenever he dared to speak honestly to her.

How could they be a proper team if she burned with fury at everything he said?

She slid away, scowling at him. "You're right, and my temper is unlike me. But your little congregation in the throne-room, leaving me up there with the main suspects…it embarrassed me. My pride is wounded, don't you see? My credibility is hindered. By implying that you didn't trust me, others will stop trusting me, too." She gulped, revealing the slightest break in her fierce, warrior facade. "Including Father."

Lukus opened his mouth to reply, but a quick, sharp *knocking* sound shook them both out of their argument, and their gazes fixed on the door, instead.

He'd expected Athena to crouch, to tiptoe over, to sniff at the door-frame to detect who'd decided to interrupt their brainstorming. To his surprise, she waved towards the door and it flew open.

At the threshold were two goddesses that Lukus never would have thought to see again that evening. And less so standing before Athena's room, a clear anxiety painted over their pretty faces.

Hera, in a lengthy, royal blue gown worthy of a queen, her crown removed, her stance not as imposing as usual; and Aphrodite, averting her gaze from Lukus, focusing on anything else in the room. She wore a pale, nearly see-through sea-foam tunic that bloomed over her gorgeous legs like silky rose petals, and a slit in the skirt opened up to her thigh, revealing her smooth skin.

"You?" Athena glowered at Hera, then switched to Aphrodite, scrunching her brows. "And you. What do you want?"

"Oh, the nerve," said Hera, beginning to storm into the room, rage racing in her eyes, turning them blue as berries and lit up with flashes of white.

Aphrodite, snapping out of her struggle to avoid looking at Lukus, seized Hera's wrist and prevented her from barging in and battling Athena. "Civility, remember? We're not here for fights."

Athena disregarded Aphrodite's attempt at peace and continued to glare at her step-mother, hands on her hips as she widened her stance. Oh, she wanted a fight; she was riled up and riveted and ready to stab her frustrations out, Lukus knew.

"Ah? What are you here for, then? Make it quick, because Lukus and I are busy."

Wishing to mimic Aphrodite and maintain a sense of calm, Lukus walked up to Athena, to take her wrist and hold her back. Anticipating his act—and prying into his thoughts, as always—Athena whipped a hand out and used her powers to shove him onto the bed. Her cold stare told him to stay put and not interfere.

Never had he craved to figure out if he had any abilities until that moment. How was he to help investigate when his co-detective had a flair for easy frustration and when he had no means to help control her anger spurts? How was he to figure anything out if all he did was clam up and fold into a pretzel whenever he tried to make a point?

Fuck.

He'd never felt so weak, so useless. His fellow investigator only cared about proving herself to her father and demonstrating how her step-mother was a fraudulent, potentially harmful bitch.

Luckily, Athena was too determined to snarl at Hera to pay his current thoughts any heed. He curled into a ball on the bed, waiting for the right moment to interfere; he had no doubt he'd have to, eventually. The tension surging through the air was toxic, and he didn't know if Aphrodite would be enough to separate the two goddesses if they decided to fight.

"Busy doing what?" Hera peered at Lukus, wrinkled her nose, then returned to Athena as she folded her arms. Her silver bracelets jangled, and she shifted to and fro as Aphrodite mumbled words of caution near her ear. "Continuing your case against me, I presume? Since your little Lukus seems to agree with you; I didn't appreciate being lined up in *my* throne-room and scrutinized." She kept her gaze on Athena, but Lukus knew she was speaking to him.

"I—" he started, but Athena waved another blast of energy at him, sealing his mouth shut.

"Don't react to her taunts, Lukus." Athena's fingers pulsated with power. Tiny swirls of gold and orange sparked from her fingertips as she wiggled them, watching Hera, waiting. "She came here to boast, because she somehow got Aphrodite on her side? Hm?" She switched her leer to Aphrodite. "Is that it? Did she convince you she was innocent? Come now, Aphrodite. I thought we were in agreement."

"Athena." Aphrodite's tone grew firm; firmer than Lukus had ever heard it. She'd been slouched beside Hera, but now she slid forward, almost as if she were protecting the Olympian queen from Athena's soon-to-erupt wrath. "Enough of your childishness, please.

I've taken no sides, as it happens. I think neither of you are capable of such chaos. We came here to," she winced, gaped at Lukus, winced again, and flipped to Athena, "talk."

"Talk?" Athena scoffed, and pressed a hand to her heart as she leaned forward. There was mockery in her tone, daring in her attitude; as if tempting Hera to come closer, to walk farther into the room and defy her up close. "Since when do either of you talk to me? Are you acting nice in front of Lukus, worried he'll go tattle on you to Father?"

Hera's eyes closed, and she smiled; but it wasn't a smile of pleasure or happiness. It was loaded with spite, and prefaced a massive explosion of rage, Lukus could tell. He'd seen that sort of smile before. When one had no other means to express themselves, when at the brink of fury. He prepared for the bout of laughter that usually followed; he'd heard it from criminals he'd arrested or prisoners he'd interrogated.

Sure enough, it came. A bone-chilling, raspy, raucous cackle that erupted from Hera's mouth and bounced off the walls and stilled even Athena into silence.

The queen then swarmed up to Lukus, lowering to her knees and snapping at him. His lips parted, and he found that he could speak if he wanted to, though his vocal cords were inactive.

Hera had broken the spell Athena put on him; but why?

"She's a fraud, you know that?" She set her hands near Lukus' legs and twisted to Athena, snickering at her. "Indeed. She lied to Zeus to travel to the Underworld and investigate down there. Clearly, she'd already set her sights on Hecate, to frame her. Why would she have been so insistent, hm?" She jolted back to Lukus, ignoring Athena's arms as they glowed yellow and pulsed with red and flickered with vivid blue veins. "But when she realized Hecate had a solid alibi, and that my dearest Zeus backed her story, well, she had no alternative but to retrace her steps and instead formulate a plan against me. *Me!* She despises me with every fiber of her being, so naturally, she had to place the blame on me, no? She's not the culprit, no, prude and precious as she is. But I don't doubt for a second that she'd rather incriminate me and get me in trouble, than locate the real monster among us!"

"Why, you twisted little—" Athena's hands shot up, and a blinding light began to form in her palms.

Aphrodite skidded between her and her aim—Hera—and unleashed an ear-piercing scream that caused everyone to huddle and cover their ears and moan in agony.

Everyone but Lukus, who fixed on Aphrodite, cocking his head. He'd heard her yelp, but it hadn't made him grit his teeth, hadn't wounded his eardrums.

"Huh?" He squinted at her, unsure why her screech hadn't affected him. He was a powerless half-god; if her shriek hurt the likes of Hera and Athena, why hadn't it killed him?

If Aphrodite noticed his shock and how he'd remained unfazed, she said nothing, and snatched Hera by the upper arm, tugging her away.

"You are impossible, you know that?" She blew out an exasperated breath. "This was not what we came for. Can you not put your grievances aside for three seconds while we do what we were asked to? Seriously." Her cheeks flushed in a rosy hue that woke butterflies in Lukus' belly, and she tucked her voluminous curls behind her ears as she rotated to Athena. "And you! Must you be so irritating? We came in peace, yet you welcome us in such a grotesque way, it makes me wonder if you have manners at all! Come now, Athena. You put Hera in the spotlight, but you require her to be kind and caring when she shows up at your door? Enough of this. How do you expect Lukus to trust you, to trust any of us when you act like this?"

Hera chortled as she brushed off her skirts and headed for the door. "You?" She stared Aphrodite down as she walked past her. "Being mature? Shocking. Surprising he ever trusted *you,* what with your constant mood swings."

The tension charged up again, and, sensing another eruption, Lukus hopped off the bed and squeezed in front of Athena, his back to her as he gawked at Hera and Aphrodite.

"Let me be clear; I trust no one. Not a single god or goddess here has inspired any confidence so far. I may have lined up a few of you and made it appear that you were primary suspects, but in truth, no one is off *my* suspect list."

He puffed his chest out, to show himself as unafraid before these three overpowered deities who could strangle him in a heartbeat. If he didn't make his point, if he didn't stand up for himself, he doubted anyone else would. They'd have to listen; and they needed him, right? Otherwise, Zeus wouldn't have asked Athena to bring him there.

"The more you argue with each other and pick fights and throw each other under the bus, the less likely I am to trust any of you." He moved away from Athena and sank against the dresser, his resolve melting now that he'd said his piece.

To his shock, no bolts of power or sharpened points of weapons pierced at his skin. He glanced at Hera, who'd stopped near the door, eyebrows raised almost in pride. And Aphrodite, whose lips quirked into a shy smile.

Athena didn't change her position at all; her face remained saturated with irritation, and she gestured towards the door. "Out." She narrowed her gaze at them, finishing with Lukus. "Yes, you too, *fellow investigator."* Her nostrils twitched. "I'd rather be alone with my thoughts and *my* suspect list, thank you." She jutted her chin at Aphrodite. "Whatever you wanted to speak to me about will have to wait."

As the three exiled beings exited, Aphrodite turned to Athena and inclined in a polite bow. "In truth, we came to discuss something with Lukus. So thank you for your hospitality, but we'll take our discussion elsewhere."

As they closed the door, Lukus could have sworn he saw a flicker of interest over Athena's features as she softened. But she'd chosen this; to be excluded and to stay in solitude.

Out in the corridor, sconce-light dancing over their faces, Aphrodite and Hera stood side-to-side, both gawking at Lukus as if seeing him for the first time. Any animosity in Athena's room had remained in there; but out here, nothing was quite right, either. There was a brisk breeze, a chilly air of apprehension. As if a big announcement was about to spill from their lips, and it somehow involved Lukus, and it would change his life forever.

Well, his life was already changed, wasn't it?

He frowned; the woman he thought he had feelings for, and the accused, perilous Queen of the gods had him alone, and who knew what they wanted with him.

"Okay…so what did you need to talk to me about?"

|| 19. SLEEPLESS IN OLYMPUS ||

RHEA

Bare feet dancing across the tiled floors, Rhea lurked, sniffling the air, gulping her saliva to hydrate her drying throat.

Semi-conscious, guided by the voice as it indicated which hallways to take, which areas to turn into, Rhea wasn't herself. She had no control over her actions, as if her limbs were animated by someone else, and her soul slumbered, caught in a sex-dream.

But there was no sex nearby to spy on. And certainly no arousing images flashing through her mind as she meandered from corridor to corridor, creeping past sealed bedroom doors, and hiding from passing servants on their way to their various tasks.

Her heart hammered in her chest, and she feared someone would hear it. Someone would detect her uneven steps, accuse her of being drunk, then accuse her of being out on her own. Then, putting two and two together, they'd end up pinning the attacks on her.

"They won't. You're safe, Rhea," the voice cooed, its timbre foreign, too friendly and reassuring compared to normal. It lodged into the deepest cavities of her body and urged her onward, sniffing the air in search of her next victim.

So soon after Themis, and Phoebe? Rhea didn't think it was wise, but was powerless to communicate her thoughts. They drowned in a lake in the depths of her brain, unable to leak out and reach her neurons, to deliver the message to her mouth, to say out loud. This voice had taken complete control over her—but how? What sort of powerful creature had this ability?

She'd wanted to flip around on many occasions, to see if anyone was following her, holding up the strings that would show she was a puppet, an instrument to the true mastermind's plots. Or to visualize the silhouette she'd imagined forming in the darkness of her room, earlier, while she'd tried to relax. Was the voice able to manifest itself, or was it an orb-like energy that traveled from brain to brain, infecting minds and souls and hearts, luring gods into doing horrific things for some unknown motive?

She'd been about to traipse across a narrow hall when whispered words fluttered over to her, coming from nearby. Their urgency stopped her at the edge of the corridor she'd braced to hurry by, her back pressed to the wall. Peeking around the facade, and towards a faintly illuminated part of the area, she noticed three individuals huddled together, two of which kept gaping at each other, then frowning at the third person.

Squinting, Rhea recognized Hera and Aphrodite—standing abnormally close together, for two goddesses who usually despised one another—and in front of them Lukus, the demi-god child. The ladies were sullen, struggling to speak; and Lukus gawked at them, his jaw clenched, his body upright and tense.

"You must understand," said Hera, her tone trembling, unrecognizable. Rhea had never seen her so distraught, and wondered what the half-human had done to put her in such a state.

Her motherly instincts woke in her gut, somehow awakening her senses and bringing the life back to her, and slowly forcing the voice to hand over control.

"Rhea, don't dwell on this—"

"Rhea?" Footsteps came from behind Rhea, and she stilled, her spine stiff as a board. She'd been so distracted by the scene ahead, and unable to use her own limbs and vocal cords to break free from the voice's hold, that she hadn't sensed a presence arriving, intruding on her as she intruded on Hera, Aphrodite, and Lukus.

She winced, her legs sore as if she'd ran for miles—and she might have, with all the gaps in her memory, since she'd apparently slipped out of her room.

Spinning to the person marching up to her, her blood turned to ice, and she fought the scream swelling in her throat.

The voice had been so positive they wouldn't get in trouble, they wouldn't get caught; and yet there strolled Gaia, her elegant steps slowing as she perched before her daughter.

"What are you doing?" Gaia's bushy tresses were tamed, for once, tucked back behind her ears. She wore a silky, earthy green robe that flowed about her like leaves in the wind, and silver sandals adorned her feet. Rhea couldn't see much beneath the tightened robe, but she assumed she wore her nightgown, which meant she'd been awoken from sleep.

To wake Gaia from her comatose slumber was perilous, and Rhea bit her lip.

"I...don't know."

The voice growled. *"Tell her you were sleepwalking. She'll believe that."*

Rhea gulped, and brushed a hand through her hair, trying not to cringe at the moisture pooling at the base of her neck. "I was sleepwalking, because I...have no idea how I got here."

"Sleepwalking?" Gaia crossed her arms and cocked an eyebrow. "I've never known you to sleepwalk, daughter. Are you certain you're not," she pursed her lips, "eavesdropping?"

Sucking her lips inward, Rhea shook her head. It had been centuries since she'd been scolded by Gaia, reminded of her place, told to watch herself. Usually a docile, discreet child, Rhea rarely got into any mischief, and even when she'd conspired against her husband to save her children, Gaia had taken her side. If anything, most days, they were friends, a team that watched over earth and its heavenly creatures in tandem.

Tonight, Gaia had found her in a delicate situation; prompted to wander the halls in pursuit of someone to drink from, and incapable of controlling herself, commanded by a voice residing illegally inside her brain.

Could Rhea tell her? Could she confess to everything and garner Gaia's protection? She'd never let anyone harm her children, fierce mother that she was. She'd stick up for her, come up with decent excuses, then take her away to the jungle to detoxify her.

"Don't say a thing." The voice hissed, quiet, as if afraid of being overheard by Gaia. *"Don't trust her; trust no one at all, Rhea, not even your own mother. You were sleepwalking, you're here, and you'd like to go back to bed, now."*

"It's the truth, Mother," said Rhea, regaining a bit of mobility and fixing her timbre to sound resolved and precise. "And if you'll excuse me, I'd like to return to my room—"

"—which is on the opposite end of the palace, hm?" Gaia's eyes narrowed slightly, a faint gold glow growing in them. She scanned Rhea from head to toe, then tipped sideways, peering down the way at what Rhea had been looking at. "Ah." She sighed and seized Rhea's wrist, tugging her in the direction she'd come from, and away from the mumbling gods in the distance. "No need to loiter here. The news will get out soon enough."

"News?" Rhea's consciousness seeped back into her core, her mind, her heart, and she tried to pull from her mother's grasp. "Oh!" Her memories of earlier, before bed, hit her square in the chest, nearly knocking her backwards. "*That* news. When you were speaking to Hera and Aphrodite, earlier. Outside of the dining room. I saw you, but I couldn't hear. You cloaked the area, blocked me out. Then you told me…"

Gaia side-glared at her, refusing to release her as she continued to drag her down the hallway. "Yes; don't say it out loud. And I blocked *everyone* out, daughter dearest." They passed beneath a bright sconce that illuminated the primordial goddesses flushed features. "Some secrets aren't ready to be discovered by everyone. Hera and Aphrodite have the unfortunate task of delivering that secret, and for now, you need not be concerned by its reception."

"The secret about Lukus? You don't want anyone else to know?" They took a sharp turn down a corridor Rhea didn't remember ever taking—not that night, never in all her eons of existence. A new cut through this wing, for faster travel from one end of the palace to the other?

Gaia's grasp was firm, but not burdening. Her skin was soft as fresh dirt, her scent soothing like blooming blossoms in the spring. Even when angry, she had a calming sense about her, and an aura that bequeathed tranquility and brought one's consciousness into nature, into one's roots, to reflect.

"Something that enormous and that involves Lukus? Yes, I'd rather it remain a secret, for now. It's essential to his investigation, and the more gods know about it, the harder it will be for him to assist us."

"Damn that Lukus." The voice reanimated, but remained small, locked in Rhea's thoughts. Its energy was raw, powerful, but contained; and its rage was directed at Lukus. *"Him and his link to Aphrodite will be the end of us, of this mission. He's too smart, and now the gods are telling him who he really is? I'd counted on him remaining anonymous. This won't do."*

"As I said, nothing for you to worry about. I'm hoping Hera and Aphrodite urge him to keep quiet, to not tell all of Olympus just yet." Gaia slowed her paces and sent a wary gaze at her daughter. "You'll only need to worry if you continue your sleepwalking eavesdropping, in which case you may land yourself in the center of the case." Her grip tightened, and her lengthy, mahogany nails dug into Rhea's wrist. "You were in his final line-up, Rhea. Why?"

"Oh, great." The voice scoffed. *"Now she's suspicious? This is bad. Tomorrow, we'll confront Lukus, understood? We can't let him develop powers, now that he's about to find out what his source is, where his energy comes from."*

Rhea couldn't reply, but willed the voice to be quiet so she could sort through her thoughts. She had to choose the correct thing to say, to persuade Gaia of her innocence. No, she hadn't poisoned Persephone, Eros, or Psyche. But she'd been poisoned herself, and was involved with the current ichor-drinking incidents, and an unwilling participant in the dreadful events. If Gaia were to figure that out, she might forgive her... or Rhea might end up in the dungeons for all eternity.

Or in Tartarus, with my ex-husband.

She shuddered, but covered up the movements by growling, showing her true annoyance at Lukus' suspicions. "Ask *him!* I've never met the boy, and have spent decades with tigers and cougars in the jungle. He must have had me confused with someone else." She focused on her steps, ensuring she didn't trip over her skirts, or over Gaia's robe.

Gaia loosened her grasp. "I've been meaning to, but I was too busy looking into his ancestry." Rhea flipped to her, eyes wide and questioning, but Gaia held out her free hand and shook it. "I can't tell you how I figured it out, not truly. Like I said, it's not the right time, and that news will break out when he's ready. Well…when *we're* ready. The ongoing case should be his priority, not his parentage."

"There will be no time for any of it. No solving of the case, no telling anyone of his identity." The being inside was restless, as if pacing to and fro in Rhea's brain, heels digging into the flesh and ripping into veins with every intense stride. *"We'll corner him alone, set him off the trail. To be safe."*

"I thought you said we were fine?" Rhea clapped a hand over her mouth, realizing too late what she'd done—she'd spoken out, meaning to address the voice.

Gaia halted, and she spun Rhea to face her. "Daughter?" She studied her face, approached her until their foreheads met; Gaia's warm and dry, Rhea's covered in sweat. "We were fine? Sweet girl, are you ill? What are you talking about?" She jabbed the back of her hand over Rhea's hairline. "Are you poisoned? You're speaking nonsense and I worry about you."

"Don't pass your aloofness off for poison. She'll have you analyzed by the healer and the witch, and that'll be your undoing."

"I'm tired. Hallucinating a tad, I admit. No longer used to the air up here, to all the undiluted ambrosia." She blew out a breath and offered a polite smile to her mother. "No doubt the reason I started sleepwalking. Perhaps I need an infusion to knock me out, keep me heavy and in bed?" She batted her lashes at Gaia. "Is that something you can help me with?"

"There you go; smart girl. Lead her astray."

Though she'd narrowed her gaze in confusion and set her hands on her hips, Gaia grunted. "I don't see why not. But there's something off about you, Rhea." Her lips twitched from side to side, and the edges of her robe perked up, swirling upward on either side of her. They twisted, around and around, until forming two straightened pillars that leaned toward Rhea and *sniffed* at her.

"She's wary; of course, with all that's happened. But it's Lukus' fault, it's him we should be worried about." The voice was tentative, nearly impossible to hear, as if keeping her volume down in fear of Gaia's antenna-like robe detecting her existence. *"He evaded Eros, who was too carnivorous and hungry for blood to view his mistakes; too consumed by fury towards his mother to pay attention. Psyche's toxins never reached him, since she decided to stick to Europe. Aphrodite wiped his silly human brain...but we can't be so nice. We have to threaten him, Rhea. He's dangerous, and more so if he's teamed up with Athena. And descended from Aphrodite. Athena's gotten too close already, and if he inherits half of Aphrodite's abilities, those she keeps at bay..."*

Gaia groaned as her antennas lowered, returning into her robe's hem. She walked around Rhea, nose in the air, picking up on the smells in the atmosphere, her fingertips trailing over Rhea's skin.

Rhea trembled—Gaia was stubborn, and she wouldn't give up until she was clear Rhea had no involvement in the poisonous situation; or until she found her guilty for her ravenous craving for flesh.

"Stay still, and show no emotion. I will take over and protect us." A sudden surge of cold energy shot up and down Rhea's arms and legs, and she sensed herself falling asleep again, though she remained standing, enduring Gaia's scrutiny.

Her vision was blurred, her ears clogging as if filled with water; but she managed to hear Gaia's parting words. "I cannot read you. You're not your usual self, and I dislike it. Go to bed; I'll send a tonic your way, and you'd better drink it until the last drop. No leftovers, and make the goblet vanish once you're done. No one can know I gave this to you…it'll raise suspicion."

Through blurry eyes, Rhea watched Gaia's figure grow smaller and smaller as she vanished down the hallway, turning around a corner.

"See?" she said, once convinced her mother was out of earshot. Her eyesight returned to her, and she unleashed a heavy breath of relief. "She's got our back. Mixing up concoctions to help me not sleepwalk." She scoffed. "Sleepwalking, really? You knew she'd never believe that."

"She doesn't want you to be involved, so she'll believe anything you tell her."

"But why was I out here?" Rhea recalled being in bed, weighed down, barely able to move; then flashes of herself wandering, as if struck by madness. "What was the point of taking such a risk?"

A pungent but delectable aroma slithered into her nostrils. It was close, and coming closer; one of pumping blood, of delicious ichor, flowing fast through veins and tinted with—oh, was that wine? Ambrosia flavored?

"That's why."

Rhea rotated towards the source of the scent, and found a

silhouette at the end of the hall. It waddled to and fro, unable to walk straight, tipsy and hiccupping as it clutched a goblet to its bare chest. Its—*his,* Rhea realized it was a man—messy mop of dark hair swished, the ends frizzy and dipped in wine, dripping the liquid in his wake. His breath was so strongly toxified with alcohol that it breezed up to Rhea and joined the smell of his blood, drawing her nearer.

The man continued his trek towards Rhea, and if he'd noticed her, he said nothing nor made any motion to imply he was aware of her presence. He was dazed, maddened, a level of drunk Rhea had rarely seen in anyone—god or human.

The voice chuckled, and Rhea could have sworn a bell rang in her, as if summoning her to attention. *"Dinner is served, my pet. Feast, indulge, and slurp up as much as you can. You know the drill."*

‖ 20. SON OF... ‖

HERA

"It's something…important," said Aphrodite, her voice more muted than usual, her shoulders struggling to remain upright. The usual glimmer about her had faded, and Hera smelled her fear.

She'll need my help with this; that's why Gaia asked us both to find Lukus.

Seeming to suppress shudders of his own, Lukus peered between the two goddesses, his eyes inquisitive but not unkind. Hera saw no resemblance to Aphrodite in him; he must have taken after his mortal father.

"If it's important, and about the case, shouldn't Athena be told, too? Why me?" His cheeks flushed. "She's the lead investigator, not me."

"You must understand," said Hera, her tone trembling, unrecognizable, even to herself. She peeped at Aphrodite, gaining her silent approval to continue the conversation. As Queen of Olympus, she had more experience in announcing dire circumstances, of delivering news that wasn't always to her listener's taste. "You see, this has nothing to do with the case."

Hera pinched her lips, squinting at Lukus, watching as his eyebrows rose.

Or perhaps it has everything to do with the case—who knows?

"Important, but not pertaining to the case?" His gaze shifted to Aphrodite and his cheeks became further inflamed, the color surging up to his temples and covering his jawline. He fiddled with his hands, shifting left to right, front to back. "But about me? What…what about me could be important?"

Aphrodite's chin dipped. She seized Hera's wrist. "You do it," she whispered, barely loud enough for Hera to hear. So faint was her voice that Hera at first believed she'd spoken into her mind, unwilling for Lukus to detect her reluctance, her fear.

Hera turned to her with a brief nod before placing her gaze on Lukus once more. He continued to fidget, but now his focus was on Hera; waiting, wondering. "Right. Well, I'm unsure how much you know of our grand Gaia, but she has powers beyond anyone's understanding. Among those powers is one more ancient than time itself. She can dive into an individual's origins and genealogy based on their blood or a sample of their DNA. Using plants and herbs and spices, and putting herself into a meditative state. She can sort of sniff out ancestors and descendants, and find out who is linked to whom."

Hera gritted her teeth, recalling how she'd employed Gaia's help more than once to decipher the heritage of demi-gods Zeus had sworn he hadn't fathered.

Lukus' battle with finding a position to stand in came to a halt. His limbs ceased their shifting, and only his lips moved. "Oh."

Aphrodite shivered beside Hera, her grasp on Hera's wrist intensifying as if to tell her to hurry, to get this over with.

"Gaia was wary of you, Lukus." Hera winced. "Not that she's easily suspicious, but you're a new arrival at court, dragged in by Zeus. And with unknown parents that Zeus refused to tell anyone about.

She's protective of her family."

With a gulp, Lukus nodded. "I guess that makes sense."

"She scanned you," Hera fingered her pendant with her free hand, sensing her own comfort diminishing by the second.

How to explain to this boy that he was likely harboring more power than he'd ever be able to process? That he descended from one of the most powerful goddesses in existence? Hera would never admit it out loud, but Aphrodite was more ancient and more skilled than any other Olympian…even Zeus.

"S-scanned me?" Lukus blinked at Hera, then at Aphrodite, then ruffled his thick black hair. "What the fuck does that mean?"

Hera cringed at his vocabulary—that would have to change if he were to remain in Olympus—and pressed her fingertips against her pendant.

"It means she read into your mind. She used your DNA—which she stole during the line-up of the goddesses, supposedly—and analyzed you. And with her prowess in deciphering mysteries, she has identified who your real mother is."

"M-mother?" Lukus' jaw looked ready to collapse to the floor. Hera caught his legs wobbling, his knees turning inward, but he fought to keep upright, to not melt before them. "So my…my mother is the goddess? Shit, I…" he let out a quick, wispy chuckle, "I was right; I'd thought my dad was the cheating son of a—"

Hera whipped out a finger and shoved it against his mouth, silencing him. Aphrodite whimpered, and her clutch tightened around Hera's wrist, as if to beg her not to harm him.

"Don't you dare finish that sentence." Hera lowered her finger and glowered at him. "We mind our tongues, in Olympus. Only foul little fiends like Hermes or drunken fools like Dionysus speak like that.

And you're not descended from them, so don't take on their sordid habits, understood?"

Still in shock, his mouth gaping open, Lukus nodded again.

"Swell." Hera ripped from Aphrodite's tightening grip and crossed her arms. "Yes, your mother is the goddess, the one who has given you Olympian blood. And it's..." She side-glanced at Aphrodite, scrunched her nose, then returned to Lukus. "It's her. Aphrodite. She's your mother."

Aphrodite huffed. "You could have done that more delicately," she grumbled, her eyes flashing with violet and cerulean—she was annoyed. Her earlier apprehension dissipated now that the word was out.

"Well, if you wanted it done otherwise, you should have told him yourself! He's your son, dammit!" Hera threw her hands onto her hips. "It was not my responsibility, but you stood here cowering and begged for my help, didn't you? Now you'd dare complain that I—"

"—y-you?" Lukus had lost his battle against his trembling limbs, and had crumbled to his knees. His gaze had widened, the blues of his eyes so vivid, so shiny with tears that Hera struggled to look at him. He clasped his hands and set them behind his neck as he gawked at Aphrodite. "You're my mother?"

Aphrodite fell to her knees, too, though maintaining a distance between them. Her own eyes welled with tears, showing how quickly her moods could change; from fearful, to frustrated, to overcome with emotion, and in a matter of seconds.

How did I get roped into this?

Hera took a few steps backward, to avoid impeding their exchange.

Aphrodite's voice shook, rattling as if she were sitting on a horse bouncing about, ready to hurl her off the saddle. "I am. Lukus, I didn't know, I had no idea, not until—"

"—until after I got here, lured past those damned golden gates while under the impression that I had a chance with you?" Rage tore through him as he violently lowered his arms to his sides and snarled. "Athena dragged me here by telling me I'd see you. She fooled me?"

Hera refrained from laughing; Lukus *had* to be Aphrodite's son, what with how rapidly his moods morphed. Like mother, like son, it appeared.

"She…she did that?" Aphrodite half-turned towards the room they'd exited, a few doors down the bright hallway. "She tricked you?"

Lukus' furious glare remained on Aphrodite. His fists bunched as he swayed his arms, and an irritated energy filtered out of him, so powerful it nearly knocked Hera farther away from them.

"Yeah, she tricked me. Did you know I was in love with you? Because apparently, she did, and she used that against me."

"Oh, my." Hera covered her mouth with her hand—to help hold in another bout of laughter or to prevent herself from vomiting, she wasn't sure. True, her Olympian family tended toward incest, but a son lusting after his mother was another matter altogether. She scoured her recollections, certain there had been occurrences like this; but it had been centuries.

It wasn't his fault, poor thing. Aphrodite was an irresistible creature, and more so for humans. Even with half his blood godly, Lukus didn't stand a chance in resisting her charms. And if she hadn't known he was her son, she wouldn't have known to turn off her powers when in his presence. It was a sticky situation, and despite her amusement and disgust, Hera hoped they'd sort it out. Because a demigod son of Aphrodite might end up developing a tremendous amount of power, in time.

That's why Gaia was so interested in him...his status may be of bigger use to our cause than I initially thought.

"Damn you, Zeus," said Hera under her breath. "You knew this, and that's why you enlisted him. Son of Aphrodite...he'd naturally be useful in our mystery. He'd be a weapon if we came to war; but whose side would he take? His mother's, and Athena's?" Hera flinched. "Or mine?"

"I...I knew, yes." Aphrodite shrank, sitting on the floor. Her skirts swirled around her like petals of a blooming rose, and her creamy skin glistened with soft, sad energy. "I warned her of this, and I assume she decided to use this information to convince you to come here. We needed you, Lukus." She sniffled. "*I* needed you. My son."

Lukus' anger didn't fade, but it didn't worsen. He maintained his glare, and Hera could have sworn she saw a flicker of green in his usually sky-blue eyes. "So I'm not in love with you, like Athena said once she'd managed to get me here." He also sat, but he pushed himself backward until his spine hit the closest wall. "Your image haunted me, did you know that? After you wiped my memory, I still had my notes describing you. You were there, over my shoulder, never leaving my mind, but I had no notion who you were. No clue why this image kept popping up and disturbing me."

"I had no choice," said Aphrodite, looking ready to crawl over to Lukus and prostrate herself at his feet. She had that air about her; Hera had seen it before, when she'd been caught canoodling with Ares and had to beg forgiveness from Zeus and Hephaestus. "Zeus bade me erase your memory. He told me you'd be essential to our plans, in time, and he told me you were part immortal, but he never...he tricked me, like Athena tricked you. We were both betrayed."

"But when Athena gave me back my memories," he hissed through his teeth, as if recalling pain, "it was there again. That strong link to you, that need to be with you, to give myself to you...but I see it, now. It wasn't love, not like that. It was the love of a son for his mother? Is that what I've been feeling this whole time?"

Aphrodite shrugged. "I wish I could tell you, but I have no clue, Lukus. Son."

Lukus growled. "Don't call me that." He shook his head, as if seeking to shed his own skin, to erase the entire conversation. "You made me *want* you! Back on earth, during my investigation of your other son, you touched me and made me see flashes of us...of us..." he gagged, "*having sex!* What the fuck, man?" He switched his gaze to the ceiling, as if addressing someone upstairs, outside. Someone all-seeing.

Does he hope to speak to Zeus?

"How fucked up are you people?" His tone was turbulent, blowing out of him like a tornado; and yet he was shriveled, cut in two, a crumpled mass on the floor of a random corridor in Olympus.

Hera thought to interfere, but what could she say to reassure him? Aphrodite was a tease, and she'd seduce anything that breathed—including her own son, apparently. It wouldn't surprise Hera if she'd caused such sensations in Eros, before.

Holding in a gag, Hera closed her eyes. She'd never wish for her own sons to lust after her. Though she knew, deep down, it was all a misunderstanding, a silly mistake, it still curdled her blood as she imagined Lukus' confusion, his dismay, his distrust of his new family.

"It explains why Athena kept swearing up and down that I wasn't in love with you," he said, taking his head between his hands. He then released it and sat up straight, gazing at Hera. "Did she know? Is that why she was so weird about it?"

Still unsure if she wanted to get involved, Hera cleared her throat. "As far as I'm aware, Athena had no clue."

"I confirm it," said Aphrodite, wiping the tears that had escaped her eyes. She pressed her hands to the floor and heaved herself into a standing position. "Athena had no idea, otherwise she would have said something to me."

Hera scoffed. "Not if Daddy dearest swore her to secrecy. Her bond with Zeus is deeper than the one she has with you."

"And better than the one you have with Zeus, clearly." Aphrodite's gaze narrowed on Hera, a storm brewing in her aura.

Snickering, Hera made a move towards Aphrodite, intent on strangling her, slapping her. Anything to put her in her place for daring to imply she and Zeus were having marital troubles again. They were; but that was none of her business.

"Why, you little—"

Lukus stomped a foot, and the motion shook the entire corridor, sending ripples to race over the floor-boards, and littering dust from portraits onto the ground.

Hera stilled, having lost her balance. "Hm, now that's interesting."

Aphrodite raised her eyebrows, but seemed unable to speak.

Lukus gaped at the floor, at his foot, then slowly lifted his chin to show the fear smearing across his face. "I…uh…did I do that?"

Clutching her hands together against her bosom, Aphrodite flurried forward, approaching Lukus. Yet another mood swing—now she filled the area with joy and positivity, and it made Hera sick to her stomach.

"You're coming into your powers! Oh, your frustration is

bringing them out!" She opened her arms to welcome him into her embrace. "How proud I am, my dear son—"

Lukus hopped backwards and out of her reach "No." He recoiled, slicing a hand through the air, barring her from coming any closer. "Don't touch me. Not…not yet." He massaged his temples as he further slithered out of reach. "I need time to process this. Don't…don't come after me, please." He flipped around and bolted down the hall, disappearing around a corner.

Hera rolled her eyes. "He's going the wrong way, if he seeks his room. Poor thing."

Aphrodite sidled up to her, their spat from seconds ago seemingly already forgotten. "He hates me. Oh, heavens, I have a new son and he *hates me!*"

Sick of her constant shifts and wails, Hera shoved Aphrodite out of her space. "Please, spare me your moodiness for a second, would you?" She pinched the bridge of her nose. "Do you truly think everyone loves you? Come off your high horse for a moment, Aphrodite. He thought he was in love with you, and he found out you're his mother. How would you react, hm? Accept a warm hug, a pat on the back, and be on your merry way? No." Hera snorted. "No, you'd raise hell if you discovered who your true mother was after twenty-something years, no? Give him time. That's all he asked for."

Dabbing at her nose with a silk kerchief she'd summoned out of thin air, Aphrodite sighed. "But seriously, how could I be his mother?" She snickered at Hera's scoff. "Not that I don't engage in physical relations often, but with a mortal? I've not been with any humans since Adonis, and that was eons ago. I gave humans up; Zeus made me, remember?"

As if you always obey his rules…

"Yes, I remember." Hera hated to admit that it puzzled her, too. Since Gaia had revealed Lukus' heritage, Hera had been subconsciously perusing through lists of Aphrodite's conquests—those that Eros had reported to Zeus, as he was asked to, and that Hera had overheard. "You're sure? There have been no slips? I won't tell my husband, but you must come clean to me."

Skilled liar that she was—Hera would definitely tell Zeus, especially if that meant he'd be more lenient towards her and her honesty—she knew Aphrodite would cough up the truth with a bit of prodding.

But there wasn't a hint of guilt or secrecy in Aphrodite's expression. No subtle quaking of limbs, no flinches, no clacking of teeth or pinching of lips. None of the usual signs of her lying—no, Aphrodite was, for once, innocent.

"I'd recall if I strayed from Ares. I swear to you, Hera, I've not been with anyone else in centuries. And Lukus…well he's no more than thirty, do you think? Late twenties? It makes no sense."

Hera tapped a finger to her chin. "Could you have been put under a spell, at some point? Persuaded to lie with a human, give birth, abandon the child, and return to Olympus as if nothing?" She scanned Aphrodite, wishing to access the deepest confines of her insanely intricate inner workings. "Any gaps in your memory in the past few decades?"

Aphrodite giggled. "Come now; with all the drunken debauchery up here, how can one not have a few blackouts? Those pungent strains of pure ambrosia that we imbibe during our festivities…have you not had a few instances of not remembering?"

"Ah." Hera wrinkled her nose. "I can't dismiss that."

"So," Aphrodite crept closer, her sugary scent intoxicating, "what does it mean, then? How is it possible?"

Hera's heart skipped a beat. "It was planned. It was—oh," she snagged the goddess' wrist and wrapped her fingers tight around her skin, "the culprit. Did it…did she do this? Poison you many moons ago, sway you into sleeping with a human, giving birth to a strong demi-god that she'd later deploy to distract us? Or am I…" She sucked in her lips and released Aphrodite. "Am I going too far, looking too much into this? Exaggerating?"

Aphrodite's energy switched to fury once more. Her eyes laced with purple and scarlet, and she leered down the hall that would lead her to the throne-room.

"No, no exaggeration. With all we've seen so far? Persephone giving Cerberus' blood out, Eros shooting his arrows at soulmates, Psyche turning humans into zombies? I wouldn't put it past that conniving culprit to have meddled with my life, too. There's a link between us all, and it might be Lukus. His existence was to mess with us, yes? Is that what you implied?"

"Indeed." She detested getting ahead of herself, and detested formulations with such detail, those that seemed so implausible…but it made more sense the more Hera thought of it. "Lukus is much more involved in this, isn't he?"

Aphrodite didn't reply, and instead zoomed down the corridor, disappearing around the slight corner that concealed the throne-room entrance.

On her route towards her quarters—where she hoped to find Zeus to demand an explanation—Hera came close to stumbling over a huddled form on the ground, near the Artwork Museum on the other side of the Dining Room.

"Hm?" She regained her balance and glanced downward, at the

clumpy form of clothes—that she gasped at when realizing it wasn't just clothes.

It was a person, bathed in a puddle of blue—a puddle of ichor.

"What in the world—" Hera leaned closer, though ensuring she didn't touch or sniff in the scent seeming to fume off the liquid pooling around the body.

The person's tangled locks covered their face, and with a quick *whoosh* of energy from her fingers, Hera moved the hair and gasped again.

Dionysus lay in a pool of his own blood, two distinct bite marks glowing on his tanned neck. Ichor, and what Hera believed to be poison, were oozing from the wound, lathering all around him in a perfect circle. A few turquoise-tinted footsteps led away from his body, heading in the exact direction she'd been going—to find Zeus.

She smacked a hand to her mouth. "Blessed Olympus, the culprit has struck again!"

|| 21. HELLO? ||

LUKUS

It was one thing to run off, to escape a suffocating situation, to blow off some steam, to wish for a reprieve from an intoxicating discussion. But attempting to do so in a place still so foreign as the Olympus Palace, with lustrous halls decked with golden chandeliers, and portraits that glowered at his every move, and with noises Lukus still couldn't quite identify, was another matter altogether.

Lukus got lost within seconds of storming off.

He twisted around corridors. He bumped into cup-bearers delivering various goods on silver platters—all of whom gawked at him in surprise, as if he shouldn't have been wandering around alone. And he nearly knocked over several precious statues of the inhabitants of the palace. Inhabitants that were his family; his aunts and uncles, his cousins, his half-siblings, his grandparents, his mother—

Sensing his legs turning to stone, his breath caught in his throat as he grabbed at the first thing he could to stabilize himself before he collapsed. It was a statue, from the feel of its cool, smooth surface under his fingers; but he didn't look at it, preferring to focus his gaze on the marble flooring. The swirls of gray in the gleaming white were the only thing keeping his eyes open, keeping his guts from shooting out his mouth. Every twirl of charcoal danced across the surface, capturing his attention, drawing him away from his predicament.

But the predicament reappeared in his mind as his eyesight became blurry, and he could no longer see the marble designs that had calmed his conscience.

Aphrodite—the magnificent, glorious, gracious, hilarious, impossible-to-resist goddess of love and beauty was Lukus' mother. The insanely attractive and powerful creature wasn't, as he'd hoped, his soulmate or a woman he'd somehow, by some miracle, convinced to fall in love with him. She was the woman who had, by some unknown means, conceived him.

The more he thought of her face, her plump cheeks, her pouty lips, the curves of her voluptuous figure, the more he struggled to hold in his vomit. Not only because he'd lusted after her—she'd made him—but because apparently, so had his father. His hardworking, stern and solemn as an old willow tree, fiercely loyal father was a cheating asshole.

"That two-faced piece of shit," he spat, recalling his father's long business trips abroad and the lengthy weeks his mother and sister spent missing him. They were fuzzy in his mind; as a child, he hadn't understood what it meant to travel for work. His nostrils flared as he pictured the suitcases, the letters, the brief phone calls to check in. "Who knows how many other women he slept with and fathered kids on, huh?"

He shuddered, realizing that his sister—she was a *half*-sister. His mother, the tender, sweet, though blind and oblivious woman who'd fed him, clothed him, encouraged him; who'd tucked him in and read him bedtime stories of mythology and heroes…she wasn't his mother.

No, a spiteful, powerful, dreadfully beautiful deity of Olympus was his mom, instead.

"Damn her. Damn him. What kind of bullshit is this?"

He hadn't needed a cigarette and a bottle of vodka this much in a while. Anything to numb his senses and feelings, to drown his pain. He didn't think the godly ambrosia Athena had boasted about would do a thing to help him now.

Had she seduced his father? Had his father seduced *her?* Were either of them aware of who the other was? Aphrodite had mentioned something once about never again mingling with mortals; but had she known what his father was? Or had she been swayed, enticed by the young Mr. Arvantis and his flirtatious ways?

Lukus recalled photo albums showing his father as rugged and handsome, a man whose delicate yet chiseled features were impossible to say no to, according to his *human* mother.

Lukus had so many questions, but wasn't ready to confront Aphrodite about them. He thought of seeking Gaia, but feared running into her after having basically accused several of her family members of being the culprit at work in the palace. She had his answers, but she was an ancient deity who surely had little to no time to deal with him; not with a rampant, enraged monster roaming the halls and draining ichor at every corner.

Some myths had mentioned gods or goddesses who disguised themselves, tricked their prey into welcoming them into their home, their bed, their bodies. Was that what Aphrodite had done to his dad? And to what end? What business did she have wooing some random Greek-blooded man who lived in New York City with his wife and daughter?

"Fuck." He nearly broke the statue he'd been holding—one of a youthful man, and his hand had been wrapped around its penis—as he came to another realization.

The pictures of his birth—were those faked? Real? It made no sense. He had photos of his human mom holding him in the hospital. She wore a hospital gown, her cheeks were puffed and sweaty, she appeared exhausted. She'd given birth to him—so how was Aphrodite his mother?

"Too much magic and bullshit," he muttered, floundering around a corner and ending up in front of the ever intimidating throne-room.

He paused, his lungs constricting as he teetered at the threshold, afraid of peering into the grand space. No noise escaped from its depths, and yet he hesitated to get any closer, worried he wasn't allowed to enter it without a full-blooded god to accompany him.

Had he meandered that far from Athena's suite and the corridor where Hera and Aphrodite had told him the truth? How long ago had he rushed off, desperate for space and time to gather his thoughts?

Regardless of how long he'd been gone, his thoughts weren't gathered, and he felt more and more suffocated with every passing minute. With every question that clustered in his brain, squeezing every neuron, conflicting with all his memories—

"Ah, so you've been informed," said a deep, booming voice coming from within the throne-room.

The area was dark, empty—or so Lukus had thought upon aimlessly staring inside as if he'd find the replies to all his queries.

"Huh?" He slowly poked his head in, past the massive doors, and almost smacked into a huge chest covered in a thin, chiffon tunic.

Stumbling backwards and out of the door-frame, he watched in awe as the voice—and the chest—turned out to belong to Zeus.

"Oh, uh, your…uh…Majesty," Lukus began to dip forward into a bow, "sorry, didn't mean to disturb…"

Zeus smirked, his eyes a light, sky-blue, his hair wild on either side of his squared jaw. His tunic swayed over his knees, and covered half his torso in classic toga fashion.

"No need for formalities, Lukus. It's just us No, what you need is a confidante, hm?" He walked backwards into the throne-room and motioned to Lukus to follow him. "A heart to heart, yes?"

Lukus hesitated again at the threshold, watching as Zeus ignited a few sconces with a wave of his hand. The room illuminated in a soft golden glow, and a gentle breeze wafted in from the rear area that was open to the night sky, and where the pillars were spaced out and covered in bristling vines.

The thrones lined up before the pillars, atop a stone and marble dais that elevated them a few feet above ground. They intimidated Lukus despite the seats being quite empty.

"Nah, you have better things to do, right? Like," Lukus gulped and gestured towards the thrones, "be a king, or whatever?"

With a groan, Zeus ruffled through his peppery curls and fell onto his throne. Lukus hadn't budged from the entrance, and Zeus waved at him once more to join him.

"Being a king involves checking on my constituents and my family. You, young man, are both. Sit." He raised his hand and seemed to tug on an invisible string that drew Lukus over to him in a flash, lowering him onto the seat beside him. "Take a load off."

Shocked and uncomfortable on the throne he'd been dropped into—Hera's, with its plush navy and peacock decorations and its unpleasant, overly sweet scent—Lukus scoffed. "Which load?"

He covered his mouth and sat up straight, worried he'd offended Zeus. These gods—they were all temperamental and tormented and threw fits at any occasion. Athena, Aphrodite, and Hera had proven that in the space of a few hours.

Zeus chuckled as he crossed one massive, muscled leg over the other. "You're not wrong. We are fitful beings, it takes one to know one. You're correct to fear everyone here."

Lukus' jaw dropped. "My thoughts? Are you reading them?" He dared a quick peek at the King of the gods. "Athena said…I was under the impression you couldn't…"

Zeus' eyebrows furrowed, and a slight pinch of rosiness surfaced on his cheeks. "I can do whatever I please, and Athena need not know of it. I have turned off the power for everyone, including myself—but we can still read *you*. Your thoughts must be accessible while I assess you, get to know you."

"Assess me?" Lukus huffed, all but forgetting he was in the presence of a monarch, a powerful deity of creation. He'd had enough of being on his best behavior when it was clear no one else was. Demigod, mortal—whatever he was, he was sick of cowering. "Everyone has been doing that. Gaia, Hera, you, my *mother*—"

"—ah, right." Zeus' throat clearing resonated throughout the room, silencing and stiffening Lukus at once. "Yes, so this confirms you are aware of your heritage. Aphrodite is your mother, as you've discovered. And you say Gaia assessed you? So *she* told you?"

Lukus crossed his arms, keeping them close to his torso, hugging himself. A chill had been lingering in the room when Zeus dragged him across it, but it had grown more intense as he sat closer to the openings between the pillars.

"No," he said, gritting his teeth before they started to clack from his sudden coldness. "She told Hera and Aphrodite. And Hera told me. Damn *her,* she couldn't even do it herself, had to enlist your wife to—"

"—I trust she's as confused as you are." Zeus faced Lukus. "I am not defending her, but she did just find out. No one knew but myself and the Fates. And clearly Gaia didn't take long to start digging and figure things out herself. She must have smelled you."

Lukus blinked at the king. "Smelled me? What the f—" he sucked his lips in, inhaled, then shrank into his seat. "What does that mean?"

"Your energy." Zeus uncrossed his legs and leaned forward as if about to stand, but he didn't. He adjusted his gaze on the doors across the way, as if expecting them to slam shut in the continuously spiraling winds whizzing in from behind him. "She detected you were more than a simple demi-god; you were *the* demi-god. A son of Aphrodite. The Fates," Zeus bunched his lips, "my counselors, divine truth-seekers and all-seeing beings, that is. They warned me of a child that would rise to Olympus and be part of a large overhaul, a tremendous surge of power. It was vague, when they first told me, and I'll admit I spoke to Gaia about it many moons ago…so she must have associated your arrival with that vision. I didn't want you to know yet."

"What I'm confused about, among many things, is why?" Lukus gripped the arm-rests, wincing at the softness of the feathers sprinkled over them. "Why didn't *she* know? Aphrodite? If she's my mother, how does she not recall giving birth to me? How did she not recognize me?" He tightened his fists and jammed them atop the rests, trying his hardest not to snarl. "She didn't even remember she'd done it; slept with my father, I mean. Was she put under a spell? Who the fuck would put a goddess under a spell and make them sleep with a married mortal man?"

Zeus cringed at Lukus' language, but didn't reprimand him. He remained calm, though a storm seemed to swell in his gaze, shifting it from baby blue to a coarse, harsh navy.

"I would assume someone who wanted to mess with heritages and powers and blood. Someone obviously more powerful than Aphrodite, and she's much stronger than she appears. She tones her abilities down at my request, but in truth, she's older and more enhanced than she shows."

"She should show it." A flimsy fleck of respect and curiosity snuck into Lukus' mind. Aphrodite—ancient and able, but keeping quiet at Zeus' order? It seemed unlike her, unlike the outspoken, rule-breaking goddess he'd spent time with on earth, while investigating Eros. "Everyone walks all over her—including you. Not that I'm defending her—I'm still pissed—but I'm saying…the way Hera and Athena were bitches to her and to each other, earlier…"

"Ah." Zeus relaxed, squinting down at Hera's throne coverings. "Athena—I fear my daughter has gotten a bit out of hand."

Lukus refrained from jumping up and waving his hands frantically to show his agreement. "A bit?" He slammed his fists to the arm-rests again.

"Her outburst of an accusation against Hera left me quite speechless, I'll admit." Zeus deflated into his stone seat, his breath blowing through his mustache and his curls. "They both expected me to choose a side, but how? Between my vicious, vindictive wife and my hungry for truth and stopping at nothing to find it daughter? I'm proud of her progress, but she goes too far."

Though he almost snorted, Lukus instead wrinkled his nostrils, recalling Athena's temper, and how it had surprised him. Wasn't she supposed to be a level-headed, wise goddess with her wits about her at all times?

"Yeah. She's in over her head and too stubborn to pay attention to facts. She suspected Hecate, then Hecate singled out Hera for no reason, then Hera seems to point the blame back to Hecate…and Athena can't see past them. It's like she can't visualize any other threat but a witch and a queen."

"Ah." Zeus twirled his graying beard around a lengthy finger, turning to Lukus with one eyebrow raising. "And what do *you* suggest, hm? Son of Aphrodite and investigator on this case—what are *your* thoughts?"

***

Armed with a sealed document from Zeus—one he knew would raise hell and cause more chaos at the Olympian court—Lukus halted before Athena's bedroom door, lifting his hand to knock.

He flinched, his knuckles inches from the surface. Zeus' words echoed in his mind, but he couldn't wrap his head around them.

"If she cannot distance herself from her animosity and enemies to analyze the situation, then perhaps I was mistaken in making her the lead investigator. Someone else will need to take over."

Lukus had bartered; he'd begged Zeus to have someone, *anyone* else deliver the news to Athena. But the king had insisted that Lukus, as the co-detective on the case, had to be the one to inform Athena of his decision.

"She will be unhappy and she'll blame you. But you'll show her my note, she'll know the handwriting and the signature, and she'll not harm you."

The mere idea that Athena would get so irritated that she'd literally shoot the messenger didn't sit well with Lukus. Yet he had an inkling that if he didn't do as Zeus requested, he'd be punished by *him,* instead. The King of the skies wouldn't be nice about using his lightning and thunder if disobeyed, Lukus had no doubt.

He fixed his messy mane by tucking its sleek strands behind his ears, and coughed into his hand, checking his breath. He had no idea why it would matter—he wouldn't be kissing Athena, nor would she ever let him get close enough to do so. And in any case, weren't they sort of like siblings, now?

Still, he wanted to look presentable as he delivered the news to her. If he held himself like a half-god—how did one do that?—maybe she'd let him live.

I still don't trust that Zeus' little letter will be enough to save me.

A subtle shuffling from nearby startled him into turning from the door and squinting into the dimly lit corridor.

"Hello?"

The shuffling stopped immediately, and though he waited to see if it would resume, nothing happened.

When he returned to the door, again raising his hand to knock, the doorknob twisted, and the barricade moved, revealing Athena behind it, yawning.

"Lukus?"

She wore her tunic from earlier, and her hair was braided, falling over her shoulder. She'd removed her breastplate and head-gear, and was barefoot. Though her attire was ruffled, as if she'd been laying down, she didn't look like she'd been sleeping. No shininess to her eyes; only an owlish glow in them as she stared at Lukus.

"I…sorry to disturb you, I hope you weren't asleep. I know you threw me out, but," Lukus hid the note behind his back when he caught her looking at it, "can we talk?"

Athena puffed out a short breath. "Goddesses with such work

don't sleep." She leaned against the door, opening it further to let Lukus inside. "Come; I was working on the list."

"Yeah, so," Lukus closed the door behind him and tiptoed into the area, "that's kind of what I'm here to chat about."

A few of the sconces were extinguished, and the glittering letters Athena used for her list were suspended in air, over her bed. **Hecate** and **Hera** were in a bigger font, fluttering around other smaller names.

So she's still on their case; great.

She fell onto her mattress and motioned at a chair she'd gotten out earlier, when they'd had more company. "Of course it is what you're here for. You're the co-investigator on the case."

He didn't bother to sit, well aware he wouldn't be staying long. No, he'd either be expelled from the premises or roasted on a spit, so there was no point getting cozy on her chair.

He pulled Zeus' paper out and unfolded it, sensing bile rush up to the top of his throat. "Uh…actually, that is the exact thing I've come to discuss. Zeus sent me to tell you that…I'm now the lead."

A flicker of fire flashed through Athena's eyes. "Excuse me?"

"Zeus, he…" Lukus extended the letter to her, and she stood up to rip it from his grasp. "He's worried about you, thinks you're overdoing it, that you're in over your head. So he asked me to take over. Completely."

"You? Take over *my* case?" Athena's eyes were now like molten gold, like the hottest of lavas leaking from a volcano, intent on incinerating Lukus until he was nothing but charred bones and ash. She glimpsed the note, brought it up to her face, read it in one breath, then threw it at Lukus' feet. "This is preposterous."

"You're too close to the situation," said Lukus, his voice straining with fear as a phosphorescent halo grew around her silhouette, coating her skin in what appeared to be flames. "Y-you blame the same two people over and over and don't see any other options—"

"—because there *are* no other options." Her timbre was sharp as a serrated knife, its tip dipped in fire as it sliced into Lukus. "You think I've not considered every single inhabitant of this palace? Even those who must be innocent? I have. Hecate has no true alibi, and Hera is a sniveling snake who would want nothing more than to be the sole ruler of Olympus, I'm certain of it. And what if the two worked together? What if—"

"—this." Lukus gulped, sorry he'd interrupted her, and expecting her to shoot arrows into his chest and plunge swords into his belly. "This is why Zeus asked me to take over. You're too deep in your hatred against them. But I don't know them. I don't know anyone. Which makes me less biased."

"No, it makes you a fool." She hissed. "Both of you."

She rushed up to him, but didn't touch or grab him. The tip of her nose rested between his eyes, and her mouth was close enough to eat his cheeks and suck his eyeballs out. Her breath was hot, reeking of rage and blood. She was a tad taller than him, and her energy was overcharged, heated, unbearable. Standing in his space, intimidating and infuriated, she caused Lukus' bladder to loosen and the bile in his throat to transform into something that would soon spew out—

"Ugh," she moved away and gestured at him dismissively, "you're not worth my time or effort." She lowered onto her bed and peeked towards her curtain-covered window. "You're a weak half-mortal who has no clue who he is nor what he wants. I'm not afraid of you and your threats," she sneered, "or of you stealing my case from me. Go ahead, take it; and go tell Zeus you succeeded. But mark my words, boy—I will not give up and will prove my hunches are founded, and you will be made to appear as an idiot."

Lukus unleashed a lengthy sigh, realizing that somehow, Athena had decided to not murder him for his—and Zeus'—defiance. He released some of his tension, but kept his voice low, to not agitate Athena any further.

"You let your warranted but personal feelings get in the way. When I trained for the FBI, they told me—"

Athena whipped her neck in his direction. Her lava-like glare intensified, as if about to shoot sparks and flames into him; but she didn't budge from the bed, her hands clasped in her lap.

"I care naught for your human lessons. Now get out, and don't speak to me again. I wish you luck in your endeavors."

With a flick of her wrist, she sent him whooshing out of her quarters, her door slamming behind him, sealing herself inside, alone.

"Fuck." He blew out a breath and hunched over. "I can't stand these peeps moving me around like a fucking chess piece!"

A faint giggle echoed nearby, rousing him into standing up straight and gawking about him.

"Hello?" Like earlier, the sounds dissipated the second he addressed them, as if he'd imagined them.

He almost regretted having dismissed Athena from her own case. When he'd had her with him to navigate the halls, he never had the impression someone was watching him. Not like now.

|| 22. MYSTERIES AND ATTACKS ||
HERA

Hera's scream caught in her throat. She had no idea if it had released from her mouth, so distraught and disgusted by the sight at her feet. Her legs wobbled, and though she'd seen this gruesome scene before—when they'd discovered Themis slurping from Phoebe—it never got easier. Only worse.

Dionysus was prone to finding himself lying in various puddles—wine, vomit, coins, grapes, ladies, men. But to see him in *this* puddle roused a sickness in Hera that she struggled to contain.

She again tried to scream, but her vocal cords had frozen. They'd twisted into nervous knots as she glanced at her stepson drowning in a pool of blue ichor and turquoise poison.

Lowering to her knees—but keeping a considerable distance from his body—she fingered her pendant as she whispered under her breath.

"What do I do?"

She'd lost all sense of time and space, all notion of logic and normalcy. Because while finding Dionysus unconscious and inanimate in a random corridor of Olympus wasn't out of the ordinary, finding him with blue bite marks in his neck and reeking of the berry-tinted poison that had been rampant in the palace in the past twenty-four hours was worrisome.

His lips were dyed their habitual maroon—from his excess of wine—but with hints of the poison's bright hue, as well. His darkened curls were tangled and matted as always, brushing over his pallid cheeks. Cheeks that were usually tanned or flushed with inebriation and joy.

Dionysus was, most days, a happy and eccentric god who smiled and snorted a lot. He regaled his manic, frenzy-followers with wild tales that captivated everyone's attention. Even Hera, occasionally, had listened to his stories. Though she'd wrinkled her nose at his gallivanting and was grossed out by his madness, she'd found him entertaining.

Here, his chest bared and stained with the turquoise poison that dribbled from his mouth, his violet tunic ruffled, singed, and coated in ichor and toxins, and his legs bent at odd angles, he looked dead. Deader than normal, after one of his nights of drinking and partying. He did so almost every evening, Hera knew. His private quarters were, unfortunately, not far from hers and Zeus'.

"To keep an eye on him," Zeus had said, when explaining why he'd placed Dionysus so close to their luxurious suite.

In reality, Zeus wanted to keep an eye on *all* the gods, which was why he'd expanded the Olympus Palace to ensure everyone had a sumptuous room—and close-by, so he could watch them. The Olympians once had their own homes atop Mount Olympus, but Zeus summoned them all to his palace, instead. None had refused him— who'd dare?—but Hera felt invaded and suffocated at every turn, having to bump into her husband's illegitimate kids and lovers daily.

Hera frowned now, realizing *no one* had kept an eye on Dionysus, this time. For there he lay, likely on the brink of death, or about to awaken and transform into the same ichor-seeking monster that Themis had become after her attack. Because that was how it worked, no? One got bitten, then became the biter.

"Heavens," came a voice from the corridor Hera had been headed for when she'd located Dionysus.

Whipping her neck in that direction, she found two solemn, darkly-dressed women walking towards her. They were slow and cautious, their faces veiled by the hoods concealing their curls.

I only know two ladies brave enough for an evening stroll after so many tragic events.

Hera's sisters—Hestia and Demeter—often cloaked themselves and toured the courtyards of Olympus at night. They'd spread offerings to their fellow deities, to pray for peace and calm. Surely the attacks hadn't changed their routine, yet it shocked Hera to see them here, discovering her crouched in front of Dionysus' bloodstained body.

Hestia removed her hood first, and rested her gaze on Dionysus, then on Hera in her shriveling mess of a panic. "Oh, my," she said, her customary mask of neutrality fading to reveal a pinch of distress. She was, after all, the goddess who'd given her seat in the throne-room to Dionysus. She never particularly liked him, but they were family, and she'd never disrespect or denigrate him. "Is that...?"

Demeter, draped in mustard yellow with a heavy black hooded shawl about her shoulders, clapped a hand to her mouth. Her hood lowered, and her wheat-colored eyebrows shot up.

"Dionysus?" Her neck stretched forward, allowing her a better view of the soon-to-be corpse. "Is he...alive?"

Hera would have hopped to her feet and spewed out all manners of excuses to explain why she was there, inches from Dionysus' immobile limbs, but her sisters needed no explanation.

Hestia, her charcoal gown swirling around her like flames in a hearth, swept over and lowered at Hera's side. "Sister? Are you all right?"

Though she'd been able to whisper to herself, Hera still couldn't get her voice to function out loud. She shook her head and covered her face with her hands.

"Hera." Demeter dropped to her other side and placed a hand on her wrist, her touch warm, soothing like a summer breeze. "It's okay. It's us. You need not fear repercussions."

"By Zeus," Hestia hissed, "can you imagine if *he'd* found her? Or Athena?" She shoved a few of her bushy auburn locks from her forehead and glanced at Dionysus with widening eyes. "Luckily, we were on our promenade."

"Sister." Demeter's touch became too hot to bear, as if she were shocking Hera back to life. "What happened?"

Whether from Demeter's magic, or from fear awakening in her gut at the idea of someone—*anyone*—wandering about the halls and finding them there, Hera found her voice at last. "I…I couldn't scream, couldn't alert anyone."

Demeter smoothed a few locks of hair from where they'd fallen over Hera's eyelashes. "That might be for the best. In your current condition as accused, it would not look good for you to find victims. Not while on your own."

Hestia hummed in agreement, and angled forward, the tips of her sandals millimeters from where the puddle of poison had begun to expand.

"Oh," she smacked a hand to her chest and deflated, "he's alive, thank Olympus. Like Themis and Phoebe—whatever did this to him didn't finish the job. Odd."

What Hestia would know about murders and *finishing jobs* was beyond Hera's knowledge. She gulped at the revelation that the drunken deity was in fact not dead.

"I'm aware how suspicious this looks," said Hera, taking hold of Demeter's arm to help herself up. Demeter stabilized her, and together, they watched as Hestia mumbled a quick prayer of recovery, sprinkling sparks of her positive and heated energy over Dionysus' lifeless limbs. "But I did just find him there. I'd been with..." She gritted her teeth, realizing how impossible her truth would sound to her sisters. "With Aphrodite, speaking to Lukus. They both left, so I was on my way to my chamber to seek my husband, and..."

Neither reacted to her having been with Aphrodite—to her shock. They were more focused on the immediate situation, thankfully. Hera imagined they'd question her later, once the events had passed.

"And Dionysus was here? You did not see who did this?" Hestia turned to them, arms crossed, squinting from sister to sister as if suspecting they'd exchanged secrets behind her back.

"Not seen, nor heard. We were not far, in the hall near Athena's room—"

Demeter and Hestia gasped in unison, and the latter snapped her fingers twice; her means to summon someone in her staff. "No, we must not linger here."

Hera watched as three young maidens dressed like Hestia popped up and bowed to her. They gauged their surroundings, then shrieked at the inanimate Dionysus feet away, slumped against the wall, sprawled all over the marble floor.

The goddess of the hearth waved at them, urging them to calm down, then gestured at Dionysus. "Take him to—"

"—Hestia, no," said Demeter, interfering before the maidens touched him. "We cannot move him. It would pollute the crime scene! What if there are clues, hm?"

Hestia narrowed her muddy gaze on her sister. "So you suggest we leave him here, in plain sight, where anyone can spot him and immediately point fingers at Hera? That we whisk her—and ourselves—away and let someone else find him? We cannot waste time. He must be healed, and if we bring him to his chambers, it'll give us a head start, no? We can discreetly summon actual healers, without alerting anyone else."

"No." Demeter's steely eyes fixed on Dionysus as she rolled her shoulders. "We can't bring him to his room. But if you keep watch, survey the horizon for anyone approaching, perhaps I can initiate the process of analyzing him."

Hera, retrieving her sense of self and regaining control of her shivering arms, scoffed. "You're not a healer. Hestia is correct; we need to fetch that god-awful Apollo, or, curse me for saying it, Hecate."

"I did not say heal, sister." Demeter shoved her lengthy sleeves up past her elbows and extended her arms. Her fingers twitched with an ominous but sparkling energy that Hera hadn't seen her conjure in centuries. Its scent was recognizable, reminiscent of a forest of pines, of a field of dried crops, of wilting sunflowers.

Oh, her mystery powers!

"Analyze. I've not told anyone this yet, but—" she tiptoed closer to Dionysus, her toes inches from the poison's spread, "—I sensed something eerily familiar about this toxin's stench. During Eros and Psyche's healing, and also when standing near Themis, during the throne-room line-up."

Hera approached cautiously—she hadn't witnessed Demeter's mystic powers in so long. Despite her reservations, the surge of sparks emitting from her fingertips captivated Hera.

Hestia seemed to remain on her guard as well, tugging up the hem of her skirts to ensure it didn't coat in poison.

Hera warned them to plug their nostrils.

"Goodness." Hestia chose to pinch her nose shut as she glimpsed Dionysus' rising and falling chest. "Is he snoring?"

"Interesting," said Demeter, her fingers flurrying to and fro, as if absorbing every particle of air, ripping it to shreds with her enchantment. "He's in a much deeper sleep than Phoebe was, don't you think?"

"As if he was given a larger dose?" Hestia cringed, tipping backwards. "Perhaps this was not a good idea, ladies. We've no experience in these matters—"

"—I do." Demeter sent a seething side-glare at Hestia, then resumed her focus on Dionysus. "And yes, a bigger dose, for certain; it's like every fiber, every confine of his being is filthy with toxins. It's much more intense than what I smelled on Eros or Psyche, or even Themis and Phoebe."

Hera snorted. "Naturally." Both sisters scowled at her. "What? Does it not make sense he'd be drugged with a harsher dose? He drinks so much he's probably immune to the stuff." Her earlier apprehension had been replaced with intrigue.

She had a swelling impulse to understand what level of poison would put down the mighty, heavy drinker that was Dionysus.

Hestia continued to back away, and peered left and right down the hall, keeping watch, as Demeter had asked her.

Demeter waved her hands near Dionysus' body, crouching to

better sniff him out, to identify the strain that had been injected into him. The wounds on his neck were pulsating, turning red and pus-like, and Hera worried he may be further infected. Sweat gathered over his forehead, and his eyelids fluttered, but his eyes remained firmly shut.

After a few minutes of sniffling, muttering to herself, studying every inch of Dionysus' exposed skin, and hovering her hand over the pool of poison to gauge its intensity, Demeter huffed. She rubbed the back of her mop of corn-colored hair.

"Crap." She unleashed a heavy sigh and massaged her temples. "It's so reminiscent of my mysteries. But it's dense, too dense for me to analyze on my own."

"I told you," said Hestia, who'd started to pace back and forth. Her usual calmness faded in the face of Demeter's dejection. "It's beyond our comprehension. Apollo and Hecate would be better suited for this. There's a reason Zeus appointed them. Stubborn and stupid as our brother may be, he *is* the king. He had his reasons. So let us take him to—"

"—no." Demeter's eyes swirled with fire, and her timbre turned raspy. It wasn't anger, nor was it directed at Hestia. It was her alter-ego, her *mystery* persona that unleashed itself whenever she drew out her elusive powers. Hera recognized the demeanor at once, and tiptoed out of reach. "We will not move him. I do need Hecate, yes; but I also need Persephone. This…I'm shocked Hecate didn't detect it before. Or if she did, that she didn't tell me. It's all linked to our rituals, our beliefs, our years of secrets. And if we were all together, we may be able to crack this thing, to figure out who's been using our own spells against us."

"Wait." Hera set a hand to her cheek as her eyes enlarged, zooming in on Demeter. "Are you saying this strain is something out of your Eleusinian Mysteries? Sister...have you used this toxin before?"

All Hera knew of the mysteries were that they were about ritual bathing and sacrifices of animals—but she couldn't recall which beasts they involved.

Demeter closed her eyes. "No. Hecate created this, she told us. But the energy she used, the ingredients—they're all tethered to other toxins we've created. And the stuff that's in this, from what I can tell...is *additional* to her original mixture. Someone has added other ingredients, other poisons; someone has accessed our mysteries."

Hestia blinked, stunned into immobility. Her paces halted, and she gawked at Demeter. Such evocative expressions were unlike her. Hestia was a docile woman who kept her emotions to herself and rarely worried about anything except for a badly prepared meal or an unattended hearth.

Hera understood her current shock and mimicked it. Her heartbeat raced in her rib-cage as she dragged her nails down her face until her arm rested limply at her side.

"No...*no one* can access your mysteries. This isn't possible."

Demeter, Hecate, and Persephone had reached levels of power and energy that no other deity—not even ancient ones like Gaia or cunning ones like Poseidon or Hades—had ever attained. Their mysteries were still just that—unsolved and unapproachable incantations. Curses privy only to them, and only contained within their minds. They weren't written in any books, and weren't shared with anyone outside their circle. The three of them didn't even have attendants or servants present during their mystery gatherings.

"It isn't. And yet..." Demeter's sinister aura diminished as she returned to her usual self, her fingers no longer prickling with enigmatic energy. "It does explain how Hecate struggled to cure Eros and Psyche, and how she might not have fully healed Themis. And what obstacles she faces in working with Phoebe. Either this strain mutated and coincidentally took on similarities to the things we use in our gatherings…or someone had access to our secrets."

"Someone had access to your mind." Hestia hurried over to Hera and linked their arms. She was cold, her skin like ice. "This culprit whispers inside its victim's heads, so can it invade *other* heads, too, without poisoning them?"

Demeter drew her hood over her hair. "I must hunt down Hecate, now. To confront her about not confessing to me that this poison has more to it than she claimed. But also to share our theories. Ah," she glowered at Hera, who grimaced, "I know you distrust her, but believe me when I tell you she's innocent. Created the poison, yes; but didn't share it, didn't make it available. She's as much a victim as those who have been attacked. I'll go to her, and we'll chat. But I also need my daughter."

Hera pursed her lips. "Right. Which means you need me to beg Zeus to summon her from Hades. Which he'll be furious about."

Hestia patted her back as she detached from her and proceeded down the hall towards the throne-room. "You're the only one who knows how to quell his fury, Hera. Which makes you the best candidate to pitch our plans to him. We need Persephone, and Hades will have to understand that." She yanked her hood up. "I'll go to the kitchens and start brewing teas and herbal remedies."

"Indeed." Demeter slithered in the direction Hera had come from, earlier, likely headed for Apollo's quarters. Surely Hecate had set herself up there, keeping close to Phoebe, to monitor her. "Once he agrees, come to me. Both of you."

Watching her beloved sisters disappear, scurrying off to their tasks, Hera shrugged. She should have called for someone to protect Dionysus in his slumbering state, but she didn't have time. She needed to locate Zeus and prepare him for the news—that another god had been struck. An Olympian, this time. And that his sister might have solved another puzzling piece of the never-ending mess that had plagued their once somewhat happy home.

She paraded past Dionysus, averting her gaze, and marched towards the hall that would lead her to her room; to Zeus. "I hope they're right, and that I can—"

A large *thump* echoed through the hallway, and a sudden, blasting pain shot up and down her skull, as if it had cracked in two. A second passed before her eyes closed and she fell to the floor, knocked out, and barred from reaching Zeus.

|| 23. UNPLANNED FEEDING ||

RHEA

She didn't have far to drag Hera—there was a secluded, rarely used courtyard nearby, and it would do well to regroup and plan.

Rhea's forehead coated in sweat as she reached the glass doors and pushed them open with her behind. Hera's dress, though light-looking to most, was heavy with brocade beads near her bosom. Rhea could have sworn actual jewels were sewn into the hem and the sleeve edges.

How on earth does she wear such gowns day after day?

Rhea preferred lightweight, absorbent fabrics, and more so after having spent so many years in jungles or studying natural forest habitats. She'd forgotten all the intricacies of the Olympian court. The fight to be the most fashionable, the need to suffer through corsets and layers of material to show off one's status. Granted, not all Olympians were like that—Athena and Artemis wore sturdy but less luxurious tunics, and Aphrodite's were as transparent as possible to entice everyone into drooling over her perfect body—but Rhea didn't miss such frivolities.

Once past the doors, a flowery whiff swirled into Rhea's nostrils and a brisk breeze blew under her hair, over her neck, cooling her down. This was the courtyard she'd always preferred when living in

Olympus—with high, vine-covered fences and flower-beds galore, packed with roses and tulips and gardenias, sprinkling heavenly scents from one end to the other. It was small, with brick pathways and a narrow fountain of a nymph in the middle, spouting silvery streams of water into a half-filled basin.

Rhea huffed and puffed as she yanked the unconscious Hera up to said basin, and sat on its edge with a sigh. Her knuckles ached— that was a rather large blow, and she hadn't had to use such physical violence in ages.

"Okay…what now?" She ruffled her hair, peering at the glass door she'd come through, praying no one would choose that particular moment to wander by. With a wave of her hand, she placed a temporary veil over it, that would dissuade anyone from peeking out and seeing her. She thanked the heavens there were few windows looking into this garden.

"First off—why Hera?" The voice had been eerily quiet once Rhea had banged her fist to Hera's skull and knocked her out. It remained silent during Rhea's exertion of bringing Hera outside. *"You might have picked Demeter or Hestia, who might have been easier to subdue. So why her?"*

"Easier to subdue?" Rhea scoffed. "Hestia has bashed her head so many times on the ovens and burned her hands while cooking; trust me, she's immune to blows. And Demeter? The slightest screech from her would have rattled the skies *and* the Underworld. Persephone would have come running to alert the entire palace that her mother had been attacked. Hera was the easiest target."

Rhea glanced down at her daughter, her features for once soft. While asleep, she had no means to frown, to wrinkle her pretty nose or scrunch her tamed eyebrows. The glow from the full but lowering moon shone over her delicate skin, and for an instant, Rhea regretted harming her.

But she'd had no choice. Someone had to be incapacitated, prevented from digging too deep into the victims and their wounds. With Hera unable to fetch Zeus, to beg him for permission to summon Persephone, Demeter wouldn't get far in her joint analysis with Hecate. Rhea had made the correct decision, she knew.

"Do you question it? Was I wrong?"

The voice chuckled. *"No, you were right. I only wished to hear your logic. And I agree with it."*

"Was there no other way?" Rhea's remorse swelled in her gut. She pressed a hand against her tunic, fingers digging into her belly—and it growled in response. "I thought I was supposed to be hunting down another drink? That damned Dionysus—"

"—Those three sisters are too cunning, and you *were, again, careless with your feeding. We had to interfere, else they traced everything to you, somehow."* The voice was chilly, its negativity vibrating up and down Rhea's spine. *"Your constant carelessness has put us in quite a predicament, dear."*

Rhea refrained from slamming her feet onto the brick ground. Such stamping would rouse attention, she had no doubt. Though the closest rooms were vacant—two of them belonged to Themis and Phoebe, who were both slightly out of commission—she had the power of a couple of earthquakes when her rage awakened.

"You wanted me to feed, did you not? Was my stomach not screaming at me? My throat dry as the Sahara and my tongue growing heavy?" She crossed her arms. "My carelessness is caused by you and your spontaneity. If we hung back, planned my feedings, it would be—"

"*—you cannot 'plan' a feeding.*" The being inside sounded mocking, as if blaming Rhea for not understanding the rules of being poisoned. The rules of drinking blood from gods.

Were there rules? Why hadn't Rhea received that lesson before she'd been requested in Olympus?

"Well, perhaps we should, from now on." Her nostrils expanded as Hera, still unconscious, released a heavy, dreamy breath. The air from her mouth whizzed up to Rhea, swirling around her like an intoxicating cloud of fresh-baked pastries and ambrosia-tinted liquor. There was a sweetness to her scent—a sugary aspect to her blood, Rhea imagined. Especially with all the sweets Hera ate when stressed; and she was, like all of them, quite stressed nowadays.

"*Do not even think about it,*" barked the voice, anticipating Rhea's craving. "*Drinking is not the objective here. Your hunger will have to wait; yes, I know I am contradicting myself, but we have bigger matters to deal with.*"

"Bigger matters?" Rhea snorted. "You weren't so concerned about those before, were you? Nor when you assured that Themis and Phoebe caused a ruckus, or when you pointed out Dionysus. That you now claim was a mistake. Ugh," Rhea gagged, "his blood was toxic, alcoholic, and unsatisfying. If anything, I feel drunk, not satiated."

"*I thought he would taste divine, but it appears tonight he'd been taking shots of human liquor. Ah,*" the voice sounded like it was about to choke, "*vodka, was it called? I apologize. He was disgusting.*"

Hera's scent continued to prod at Rhea's nose and her mouth watered. "Right, so do you understand why I must drink again, and soon? If I don't, I fear—"

"*—if your impulses take over, I'll take control of you again. And we both know how you disliked that.*"

Rhea snickered. Oh, she'd detested that sensation—or lack thereof, in truth. Earlier, when she'd bumped into Gaia and this internal creature had taken command of her body to protect them, Rhea had felt trapped in her own mind. Deprived of proper thought, unable to feel anything and only allowed to watch as her mother sniffed at her, grimaced at her, doubted her.

She should have attacked Gaia, and she'd thought of it several times since then. But the voice had made it quite clear Gaia was off limits.

And apparently, so is Hera?

"Yes." The voice didn't always sneak into Rhea's thoughts but appeared to find it necessary to do so tonight. *"You mustn't drink from Hera. Her blood is precious, pure. Important. I won't have a single drop of it spilled, and certainly not so you can slurp it all up and infect her and start having visions of her sexual past."* If the internal being could shudder, Rhea believed it was doing so at that moment. *"You need not visualize such things. I need not, either; her adventures are strictly with Zeus, and I can guarantee they haven't done much in centuries."*

Shrugging, Rhea noticed her limbs were jittery. She scratched at her wrists frantically, and gritted her teeth. The voice was correct— any images she'd receive of Hera would be far from pleasant.

But the aroma of her, the warmth of her body as it lay at Rhea's feet was harder and harder to resist.

She wished Dionysus' flashes of fantasies would have satisfied her, since his blood hadn't. But all the images had done was confuse her, render her dizzy and sickened. He'd participated in so many orgy-related frenzies and slept with so many gods and goddesses in recent times that it had been hard to focus on any one image.

After guzzling up his sour-tasting ichor, Rhea had smacked into the wall and slid downward, overcome by all the recollections he'd provoked. Oh, she saw a lot of sexual acts that she'd usually revel in—all sorts of positions that would have erected her nipples and created wetness between her legs and sent her heart racing beyond control. But they were too fast, too unfocused, and too blurry.

Surely because Dionysus is always inebriated when he has his parties.

That disappointment, coupled with the foul flavor he'd left in her mouth, had done nothing to quench her thirst. When the voice had told her to sneak up and interrupt the sisters, choose one to knock out, she'd hoped for a quick fix, a slither of something to keep her going until her next full feeding.

Now the voice was telling her no? This malevolent thing seeking to dismantle her family from the inside and poison them into a civil war didn't want her to drink? It made no sense.

She wasn't sure how long she sat there, fingertips dipping into the fountain behind her, eyes closed in concentration. The moon had shifted, shimmying into slumber as the sun slowly rose, its gentle rays of dawn pouring over Rhea's face.

Her neck chords were rigid, her pulse rapid, and her mouth so dry it hurt. And that smell—that delectable, fruit-filled, candied fragrance hadn't ceased. It pried into Rhea's nose and taunted her, dared her.

Feed. Drink. Indulge, would you? What is that voice going to do, hm? You need your strength, that's what it keeps telling you.

She opened her eyes, glanced at her veil of protection over the door—still active, thank goodness—and gaped down at her immobile daughter. Her lips were parted and the rising sun's rays turned her chestnut hair to tawny streaks that looked like shiny caramel. Her skin was white chocolate, her dress a royal blue fondant.

Heavens, this is the worst possible test.

Hera snored lightly, her bosom lifting and falling in peaceful motions. She hadn't slept well in a while, had she? A queen with no love, no respect, she was exhausted, surely. Rhea pitied the poor thing. Stuck with a vagrant husband who disregarded her feelings, with half sons and daughters who despised her, and actual children who didn't understand her. All she had were her sisters, and her mother—

But her mother was ravenous with hunger and too famished to think straight or to care that she was about to sink her teeth into one of her own children.

"Rhea, don't you dare—"

Her hunger too overpowering, Rhea ignored the monster in her mind and fell to her knees. In a swift—and evidently for the voice, unstoppable—motion, Rhea cupped the back of Hera's head and drew her neck nearer. The aroma grew, loading into Rhea's being, infusing her with the power to keep the voice at bay—for now.

"Let go of her! I told you, you're not to drink from Hera, that wasn't the plan—"

Rhea's teeth shaped into deadly fangs, and she plunged them into Hera's sweet, soft neck, moaning in pleasure once her ichor began to drizzle down her throat.

The Queen of the skies tasted like birthday cake, and Rhea would enjoy every second of draining her blood.

|| 24. THE VOICE ||
LUKUS

Though his bed gave him the impression of lounging on a cotton cloud wrapped in silk and smelling of fresh linen, and his head melted into the pillows as if they were made of air, Lukus stirred awake within a few hours of falling asleep.

He couldn't even remember when he'd gotten into bed. No, he'd paced around his enormous guest suite, first, massaging his temples and muttering formulations out loud, doing his damndest to forget the revelations of the night.

He was to investigate a string of godly crimes involving murder, poison, and blood-drinking. And he'd been deprived of his principal ally, who kept accusing the wrong people. And he was a demi-god, the son of none other than Aphrodite, that he'd had a massive hard-on for since the instant he'd met her.

Thankfully, that hard-on had vanished, and instead all he did was cringe when he thought of her. And cringe harder when he realized that she was involved in all this; *he* was involved in all this, and he had no idea how or why.

Why was he conceived? Why had his father cheated, and did he know he had? What sort of illusions and spells were cast to allow Lukus to come to life, and why had they been employed in the first place?

Lukus hated to think of himself as special. Even when working for the FBI, he didn't boast about his skills in the hallways or remind his colleagues how great he was at solving cases. Yes, he was gifted with uncovering bloody mysteries and had been a prodigy among his co-workers, and had impressed his boss more than once. And sure, he'd used that information to seduce several ladies over cocktails that would lead to his bedroom. But he didn't consider himself above ordinary or average. Just a good-looking dude who liked to smoke fancy cigarettes, drink until his brain shut off, and fuck anything with long legs and pretty hair.

Zeus had implied that now, as the recently discovered son of Aphrodite, he was extraordinary. There was something about him that linked him to the criminal offenses in Olympus, and he was more important than he'd been led to believe. He had a role to play, a mystery to solve, and a family to get to know.

All the over-thinking and disgruntled discussions with himself had finally gotten him so tired, he could no longer stand. He'd blown out all the candles, thrown off his rumpled shirt, and snuck under the covers.

He'd expected nightmares—visions of Aphrodite and him from before, when they did not understand what they were to one another. Or visions of her lover, Ares, finding them together and hacking them both to bits. Or of Athena cackling in his ear, reminding him he was part-mortal, not versed in the godly ways, unfamiliar with over half the inhabitants of Olympus, and therefore would never find all the puzzle pieces to this ongoing crime.

To his surprise, his dreams were serene. Blue skies and rainbows, pastel buildings surrounded by halos of golden light, lime green fields of lavender and lilies. When he opened his eyes and remembered the images, he snorted.

"Did I dream I was in *Candy-Land?*" He threw the covers off. "I haven't played that game since I was a kid."

A faint light filtered in through the thick curtains he'd drawn shut that night. Had he slept longer than he'd thought? He could have sworn it was close to midnight when he'd finally stumbled into the sheets; how could it already be morning?

"It's dawn. So high in the heavens, Olympus witnesses it in all its glory. You should go outside to catch it."

"Huh?" Lukus hopped off the bed and glared towards the entryway, unsure where the voice had come from. He squinted at the darkness, but nothing moved, no shapes flurried about. No one was there. "What the fuck?"

"You won't see me. It's okay, Lukus."

Startled by the softness of the voice, he grabbed the candlestick on his nightstand and brandished it as a weapon, gawking at every inch of his room. The pristine walls, the immaculate floor, the ornate dressers, table, and chairs—all were unmoving, untouched. No shapes appeared before him, no one coming out from beneath a veil of invisibility.

He lowered the candle—not that it would have done him any good in such a place. How he wished he'd brought his gun; would a bullet wound a god?

"Who are you?"

The voice seemed to swarm inside his head, its wings flapping against his skull. *"Cute. Bullets wouldn't maim us much, no. You do not need weapons up here. We're all family, Lukus."*

Though he'd stopped aiming the candle at the nothingness before him, he didn't lessen his grip. "You know my name, so it may be that we *are* family. But who are you?" His timbre trembled, and he gulped, noticing his throat was raw, dry. Hadn't he asked for a glass of water before he'd tumbled into bed? He didn't remember receiving it, yet he'd not been thirsty in his dreams.

"I can't tell you, I'm sorry. I am in your head, sweet boy. That's why you won't see me—not unless I will it. And I won't."

In my head...

Lukus' limbs became numb. The candle slipped from his grasp and fell to the ground, cracking in two.

Voices in one's head were a sure sign of disturbance, in regular times. But here, in Olympus, he knew better—all those who'd been poisoned and attacked had been subject to someone talking in their brain. Someone they couldn't identify, and who'd controlled them, forced them into doing unspeakable things.

Had he become the next target? Why?

"Don't fret about all that, darling." The voice was honeyed, sugary like cotton candy, smooth like a raspberry liquor. *"You should get outside and look at that sunrise, hm? I highly encourage it."*

Lukus grabbed at his throat, intending to choke himself, make himself gag. If he'd been poisoned—which seemed more and more likely by the second—he wouldn't let this thing win. He was the lead investigator—if this miscreant got him, all of Olympus would be screwed and stuck with Athena's archaic ways and beliefs.

He began to reach a finger into his mouth, to trigger himself into vomiting; but his lips sealed themselves, and his fingertip went nowhere. It hovered, as if magically stopped.

"Huh?" He stared at his finger and blinked. "What's going on?"

"You need to get out of this room, dearest. I don't think making

yourself sick is a smart idea; what a mess it would be on those pretty floors, hm?" The tone, Lukus realized, was feminine. It had a deeper tinge to it, a sexy rasp he'd have usually found arousing; but something tricky and malicious hid beneath its initial syrupy layers. *"Come, there's a lovely courtyard where you'll have the best view of the sunrise. Trust me, it's worth it."*

"Worth what? I—" Lukus' lips clamped shut again, and he had no means to unglue them.

What in the fuck is this? Does this voice thing manipulate the victim's bodies, too?

He suddenly felt groggy, lacking coordination and concentration. As if someone had dug a needle full of tranquilizer straight into his bloodstream, and the medicine had taken immediate effect. Like he'd been drugged, his brain turned to mush, his body numbing—

Shit. Exactly like when Eros locked me in that warehouse.

He had no occasion to ponder on the link between this situation and the one on earth, because his legs began to move out of his own volition. They were slow, at first, unsteady; then accelerated, taking him to the main door of his chambers.

His arm whipped out, and he wrapped his hand around the doorknob, and he grimaced at the spontaneity of the motion, at how he'd had no idea what he was doing.

"If you promise to quit being so obstinate, I'll let you control your limbs again. But you have to do as I say and go where I tell you to, okay?"

He nodded, almost too fast, much too eager to regain command of himself. It was eerie, sensing himself moving around but not being the one telling his brain to do so. To watch his feet, to feel them pounding against the ground but having no notion how they were doing so and where they were leading him.

"Fuck," he said, when the internal creature allowed him to pry his lips apart. "You're strong, aren't you? Remotely controlling me like that—where are you, huh? Hiding around a corner or something?"

A sound quite like a growl reverberated in Lukus' mind. *"I thought I asked you to stop prodding, hm? All in due time, Lukus. Now go out into the hallway."*

He obeyed, but realized he was bare-chested, and goosebumps prickled all over his skin at the notion of being seen. Not that he wasn't a sight to behold—many women had told him how hot and in shape he was, how his abs were like those plastered on magazine covers—but his physique was nothing compared to the bulky builds and shiny torsos of gods he'd encountered so far in Olympus. Any early rising ladies who'd view him sneaking about would likely be disappointed by him; and he hated being sneered at.

"Worry not about such trivial things, Lukus. Focus on getting to the courtyard. Go towards the corridor that will lead you to the throne-room but stop before turning into it."

Despite the twists and turns of the palace, he somehow remembered the passage to the throne-room. Around one corner, around another, then another, then down a narrow but well-decorated hall with silver sconces. He felt like he'd made this trip several times already since he'd arrived.

The voice hummed inside, waiting for him to arrive at the spot where she'd told him to stop. Her melody was swaying, enticing, and soothing. As if lulling him into a state of trust and comfort, making it easier to dominate him, keep him on track. *What* track was unclear; why did this culprit—if it was indeed the same thing that had harmed Eros, Psyche, and the others—want him to go watch a sunrise?

"Because it's breathtaking, my friend. And as a newcomer to our court, it would be upsetting were you to not see it at least once, before..."

Lukus slowed his paces. He was passing a portrait of Hera, all decked out in her royal robes and surrounded by peacocks.

"Before what?"

A strange silence charged into his mind, as if the being had left or fallen asleep—but it then sighed, reanimating, its sweetness replaced by a slight annoyance. *"Nothing. Fret not about that now, keep going, would you?"*

Had he heard this person before? Rumor had it—and according to some of Athena's retellings—the current culprit could have been an Olympus resident. This voice was faint but familiar; it rang inside as if he'd been acquainted with it once or twice. Was it a minor, lesser-known goddess that he'd overlooked? One he'd dismissed because she didn't look like Hera, like Hecate had claimed?

"You need to stop getting so animated. It's not good for you; you're too new up here, and the Olympian air will choke you if you're not careful."

He scoffed—was that a threat? Sure, this creature could spew poison and transform others into neck-biting zombies, but what could it do to him, really? Stuck inside his head, muttering orders at him, magically barring him from using his arms and legs—how strong was it, in truth?

Arriving at the area that he'd usually turn left at to approach the throne-room, the voice sent him stumbling forward, instead. Passing through a widened corridor of landscapes and lined with statues of the Olympians in all their splendor. He was walking so fast, they passed in a blur, and he had no time to admire them; no time to think.

"Good, because I don't want you thinking."

Though he had some control over his words, he said nothing, unsure how to react to this being's sudden shift in behavior. It had been alluring, kind at first; now it was determined, a tad unhinged, a smidgen angry. By speaking, he knew he'd anger it further—and who knew what monstrosities it would enact to get him to shut up and obey it.

The internal creature lured him farther, towards where he'd remembered chatting with Hera and Aphrodite—where they'd revealed the truth of his heritage to him.

"Ah, so you know, then?" Its timbre was higher-pitched and laced with—dare he believe it?—worry.

"I do." He scowled at the spot where he'd stood, listening to Hera, struggling to avoid Aphrodite's gaze. "I haven't told anyone else, though. Only Zeus is aware."

"Zeus." The tone returned to its irritation. *"Let us not get started on how we feel about him. All the things he knows and doesn't share, and all the cruelties he is responsible for but doesn't own up to."*

He wouldn't say it out loud, and feared even thinking it, but Lukus sensed a surging rage towards Zeus in the way the voice spoke of him. If he hadn't already suspected its main goal was to destabilize and possibly dethrone Zeus, this would have been an epiphany moment for him.

"We're here." The voice stopped him in front of a frosted, glass door, outside of which he couldn't see; as if a heavy fog blocked the view.

"This is where I'm going to watch the sunrise?" He snorted. "How?"

He took hold of the brass doorknob and twisted, and a whiff of flowers and grass hit his face in a *whoosh*. The haze that he'd noticed was gone. He saw a brick-laden, vine-encircled courtyard decked with colorful buds and well-kempt shrubs. A fountain rested in the middle, water spouting from its mouth—from a shapely, naked woman with her head tipped back and her arms distorted at odd angles. As if she were dancing or weaving spells into the air.

The fountain's liquid trickled into a narrow basin at the statue's feet, and around said basin was a bench-like edge. Its bottom facade was stained blue. Or *splashed* in blue, Lukus couldn't tell, as the color's spread was uneven, as if an ocean's wave had washed up over it. He noticed a small puddle glimmering on the bricks, turning an inky color as it mixed with the red tint of the ground.

As he fixed his gaze on the area, trying to identify that bluish hue, the voice inside whipped his neck in the other direction—towards the rising sun.

"See? Isn't it bewildering? Bedazzling?"

Bewildering and bedazzling, sure; but it was also blinding, so Lukus raised a hand to cup over his eyes as he struggled to glance at the sky.

A rustle in the nearby leaves stilled him.

The rustle was accompanied by a voice. "Him?" It wasn't in his head—it was real, and came from somewhere to his left.

He wanted to whirl around to face the new arrival, but the internal voice kept him turned towards the sun. *"Don't worry. Keep looking."*

"That's who you want me to drink from?" said the newcomer. Its footsteps approached him, along with a weak scent of spices and pine trees. "He's mortal."

"*Half*-mortal," said Lukus, speaking before his possessor had a chance to close his mouth.

The figure came into view, placing itself in front of Lukus and blocking the sun from blasting into his eyes. He nearly thanked the person—but upon viewing their features and recognizing them, his vocal cords froze.

"Hera?"

Her chestnut hair was wild, and she didn't wear blue as he'd been accustomed to. Nor did she exude that usual sense of superiority and that nose-in-the-air demeanor that showed she valued herself above all others.

The woman smirked at him. "Ah, so close."

Burnt orange tunic, savage locks like the mane of a lion, a striking resemblance to Hera—*oh.*

Shit. It's the other one—the mother?

The inside voice had no shock to it; had it been expecting this arrival? *"Not Hera, but so, so similar, don't you think?"*

"It's…Rhea." Lukus' stomach did back-flips. The queen's mother—the mother of Olympians in general—stood before him as she had before, in the throne-room. Defiant but calm, gaze instigating but shoulders rolled back and arms stable at her sides. "Rhea? Is everything all right?"

As she grumbled, he detected a hint of blue stains over her lips. "Is everything all right?" She unleashed a low chortle. "No, nothing is all right, young man. I'm hungry, and you're to be my new meal, instead of the delectable, prized blood I'd acquired for myself."

Lukus' jaw dropped, and though he wanted to skid away from her and her slow strides towards him, he couldn't move.

"Damn it, *let me go,*" he said, addressing the voice taking up residence in his brain.

"No. You will give Rhea what she wants and comply, and make

this easier for her. For us."

Lukus coughed, his jaw clenching so hard that pain sliced up from his chin to his temples. "Who is us? Why are—"

Rhea's sharpened fangs digging into his neck cut him off. His eyes rolled to the back of his head as her tongue slicked over his skin, and he sensed a surge of blood—*his* blood—gush into Rhea's mouth.

Even if he had control of his mobility, he wouldn't have been able to budge from where Rhea had clawed into him. Her grip was strong as stone, and her teeth like swords piercing into him with the intention of maiming, killing.

"Oh, she won't kill you—only drain you enough to keep herself sustained. We have a long journey ahead of us."

Lukus crumbled in Rhea's arms as she sucked, summoning his blood into her throat. As he gushed into her mouth, she dropped to the floor, keeping hold of him, absorbing as much of him as she could.

His vision faltered. He had no clue where he was, nor what was happening. His consciousness was slipping, slipping—

A shadow stepped in front of the sunlight—yet another arrival. Its body blocked the blaring sun, allowing him to see once more, if only for a few seconds. He scrunched his eyebrows and fought his heavy eyelids, desperate to see who'd discovered them, who'd come to his rescue, who was about to rip Rhea off him.

The cackle emanating from the shadowy figure made his heart cease beating. "I'm not here to rescue anyone, young man."

It was her—*the voice.* There was no mistaking that milky madness, that tricky silkiness to the timbre, that sly sharpness that had defined her words earlier, when they echoed inside Lukus. Her—the thing that had been locked inside his mind mere seconds ago. Or had it been minutes? How long had Rhea been suckling the juices from his neck?

"He tastes interesting," said Rhea between slurps, releasing Lukus for a moment as she wiped her mouth, "The mix of godly ichor and mortal blood…strangely delicious."

"I know," said the voice, sounding like she was smiling. Her voluptuous silhouette was difficult to attach to a face or a name in such blurriness. All the women in Olympus had lustrous curves—except Athena and Artemis, who were more square-shaped, muscular. This person, this culprit, could have been anyone.

Lukus stared at her, desperate to figure out who she was. If he was dying today, he wanted to go to the grave with that knowledge; so he could come back and haunt her.

But despite the sun's halo surrounding her, she prevented it from fully shining over them, so he couldn't quite detect her features. All he noticed was her poofy hair in shades of a rich, muddy brown, and with light streaks of dirt and a vibrant twinge of red.

Who has red in their hair?

He had a few names starting with H, and a handful of flashes of faces from the throne-room entered his thoughts. But they all died out when Rhea resumed drinking. His vision faded out completely.

"Drink up," said the mystery being, still towering over them, her voice trickling down like the fountain's water, splashing over Lukus' face. "He will have to do, for now, since you can't limit yourself. This goes against our plans, but you've left me no choice, Rhea."

Rhea muttered something in response, but her mouth was filled to the brink with Lukus' blood.

Enjoy it, you bitch.

The voice, still accessing his thoughts, groaned. "Oh, she'll enjoy it. She needs as much of you as she can to maintain her strength. So many plots to set in motion! Come now, Rhea. Let go of him and take my hand so I can teleport us far from this wretched place."

Lukus' hearing buzzed, then it was as if someone had shoved cotton balls into his ears. Everything was black and silent, and he no longer smelled flowers and plants and the fresh outdoors. He smelled nothing.

|| 25. MUDDY MEMORIES ||

RHEA

The familiar floral fragrances of the Olympian outdoors vanished, replaced by a dusty, dirt-riddled scent that infested Rhea's nostrils. As if attacking her insides, infiltrating her cozy warmth, filling her with mud and smoke.

She squinted, but the area she'd been transported to was dark, enclosed. And small, so terribly small. She could sense her breaths bouncing off a wall in front of her, its facade crumpled and earthy-smelling, as if made of wet dirt.

She was still holding on to Lukus, one arm wrapped around him, her fangs plunged into his neck. The instant she understood she was no longer in Olympus, she released him. She slurped up the ichor lingering over her lips and wiped her mouth, twisting her position away from the wall. As she shifted, she felt another presence beside her. It was Hera, still unconscious, her marvelous gown faded and wrinkled, and stained with her own godly blood.

With a hiccup, Rhea raised her chin and attempted to piece out her surroundings. A faint flicker of light suddenly emanated from a chandelier above, but not all the candles were ignited, showering the location in a dim, gloomy glow. The walls were, as she'd thought, made of mud, with green roots poking out, and a few weeds and vines clustered in corners. It was a square space, with a massive copper cauldron in the middle. Beside it was an elevated, rectangular slab of concrete that looked like an altar, a space upon which to lay a sacrifice.

"Oh, heavens." Rhea's belly was full; too full. The contents swirled and swished against her stomach linings, and nausea began to swell up her throat.

She hadn't realized she was holding someone's hand until that hand let go of her. She gasped, turning to her captor, but their outline was so blurred she had to rub her eyes.

"Not heavens, no," it—*she* said. A majestic but morose tone that terrified Rhea. "Quite the opposite."

Rhea suppressed the urge to gasp. It shouldn't have surprised her that the voice inside had finally come out, had manifested itself. She remembered, now; she'd heard it speaking to her as she drank from Lukus, but it hadn't been confined in her mind. It had been beside her, real, in the flesh. But she'd been too busy sucking the juices from the half-mortal that she hadn't bothered to look.

Now that she wanted to look, she couldn't. The voice, though a living, breathing being, was a blur, a ghost. It swayed away from her, its figure impossible to identify, too bright to focus on. All Rhea saw was the outline of a head, and tufts of deep red hair. The silhouette was shapely, luscious—but the color of its skin and outfit weren't visible under the luminous layers it used to conceal itself.

"Y-you? The thing from within? You..." Rhea was unable to refrain from stammering. Despite not being able to recognize this person, they were now out of her mind and there, in front of her. The demon that had taken control of her, whispered eerie instructions, tempted her to drink the blood of innocent animals, to voyage to Olympus to attack her own family members. This was *her.* "You're here?"

"I'm here. And so are you," said the creature, her timbre distant as she headed towards the middle of the room.

Her voice was familiar, *so* familiar, but Rhea couldn't place it. Rhea couldn't place *anything*. She had no idea where they'd been teleported to, didn't recognize any of the scents, any of the energies. She couldn't seem to get her vision to adjust no matter how many times she blinked and rubbed her eyes.

What was in Lukus' blood? Had there been some strain of poison inside that the voice had wanted her to drink, as punishment for daring to stick her teeth into Hera's neck? Or had he been loaded with alcohol, making her drunk?

She glared at the figure as it stopped near the cauldron and waved its cloudy arm over it, causing whatever was in it to bubble and pop.

"Is Lukus a drunkard, like Dionysus? Why another batch of shitty blood?"

The being didn't move, but Rhea caught movement from someone else in her peripheral vision. Another woman, but this one not hazy, and much easier to decipher.

"No one is as much of a drunkard as Dionysus," the lady said, her voice sultry, smooth like a fine wine undiluted with ambrosia. Croaky, but sexy, seductive.

Though not having seen this particular person in centuries, Rhea recognized her as if she'd met with her yesterday. Tall, curvaceous, elegant in her strides, an air of absolute neutrality about her features, a perfection to her olive skin. She was ravishing. An impressive woman with a little-known back-story, who kept out of most affairs and was, to some, a myth. A memory mastermind, a spell-weaving genius, and *not* a witch.

Under other circumstances, it would have pleased Rhea to encounter her after so long. "Mnemosyne?"

She squinted at the woman—her Underworld sister. Mnemosyne was a secretive and often reclusive titaness who rarely interfered in anyone's business unless called upon.

Mnemosyne's fire and ginger hair was streaked with black, as if soot had been sprinkled atop it. Her eyes were a basic, nearly boring brown, but illuminated by the gold eyeshadow on her eyelids. She held herself with grace; like a queen of the shadows, an empress of the underground depths.

Rhea saw her clearly, compared to the other being who remained by the cauldron, her back turned to them.

The hem of Mnemosyne's lengthy, off-white, off-the-shoulder gown trailed over the dust-covered floor as she approached Rhea. "Hello, sister."

Rhea gulped, peering from Mnemosyne, to the blurry woman, to Mnemosyne again.

"Wait—" her eyes bulged, about to tumble from their sockets, "—*you* are the culprit? You are wreaking havoc above ground, enabling a civil war amongst Olympians?"

Mnemosyne's chuckle was almost as sexy as her voice. Part witchy, part subdued and feminine, it sent shivers down Rhea's spine.

"No, my sweet. I'm an assistant to the cause, though. I've welcomed you here, in my hut, as it's one of the safest places for us, right now."

Rhea blinked at her bewildering sister, finally able to understand what the scents surrounding her were. Mnemosyne's hut was described as a structure of dirt and plants packed together, then topped with wood and a sturdy roof. Enchanted with memory spells to dissuade any unwelcome visitors. And located, of all places, in the Underworld.

The Underworld wasn't a realm where one could appear and disappear at their convenience. One needed authorization to pass its gates, to roam the streams that led to it. Even accessing the lake entrance that guided to the Diamond Gates was restricted to only those who had the knowledge and the incantations to open it. So how had they teleported straight into Mnemosyne's hut?

Whoever could weave such power was someone who had access to the Underworld, Olympus, *and* the human planes. Rhea was puzzled about who harbored such magic. Mnemosyne was—though she rarely used the opportunity—a welcome guest at Olympus, and sometimes explored the mortal realm.

She had to be the culprit. Her denial made no sense.

"I...then who is...?" Rhea crumbled, her limbs weakening without the voice inside to guide her. It was an enemy, a cruel entity who'd forced her to do unspeakable things; and yet deprived of it, she felt frail, uncertain, and alone.

"You're not alone," said Mnemosyne, extending a hand to help Rhea up.

It didn't surprise Rhea that Mnemosyne had access to her thoughts. As a titaness of memory, of remembrance, of words, the mind was her domain. If anyone could seep deep into one's brain, Mnemosyne could top that. She delved into repressed images, forgotten recollections, and moments of blackouts otherwise inaccessible by the most powerful deities and healers.

If the culprit had indeed chosen her as an ally, they'd chosen wisely.

"Ah, but you're an ally, too," said Mnemosyne, beaming at her sister as she helped her stand up straight. She dusted off Rhea's dress, caressed her cheeks to erase any remains of ichor, and blew a soothing breath of honey and spice onto her forehead to ease the migraine that had grown there. "You're an essential part of this operation, darling. We're grateful for all your help. Come, let me show you what your assistance has accomplished thus far."

Her timbre was hypnotic, enticing. For one who didn't speak much and preferred to communicate via the mind, Mnemosyne sure had an effect with her phrasing.

Rhea didn't *want* to follow her, didn't want to see what her insane actions had done. And yet her legs moved of their own accord, as if persuaded to by the titaness' voice alone.

The foggy figure had flurried off to a corner of the room, still facing away from them, only her vibrant scarlet locks visible to Rhea. Had she enchanted herself to be so hazy? Was she not ready for Rhea to know who she was? Did she not trust her, after everything?

"Oh, she trusts you, evidently. But it's not quite time yet for such a revelation; a few more moments. Here." Mnemosyne indicated the cauldron and its depths, urging Rhea to gape within. "Take a gander and a sniff, would you?"

Again, Rhea didn't wish to do as Mnemosyne asked, but as she stopped in front of the pot, she leaned forward and dipped her chin to peek inside. A rich, golden mixture brewed inside, sprinkled with swirls of a reddish raspberry, a violent violet, and a berry blue. An aroma of sugary sweetness and flowers collided with her nostrils, and she sneezed.

"Yes, another poison." Mnemosyne crossed her arms over her heavy bosom and smiled. "Even more potent, more intense than the original."

Rhea steered herself backwards and rubbed her nose. "Am I infected with it now, too? Is that why you made me smell it?"

"No, never. The poison in you is something else, dear. Something to keep you compliant when need be; after all, you can be a bit wild and hard to tame, hm?" Mnemosyne giggled, and the unnamed being grunted, muttering under her breath. "Right; so this potion will soon be completed with the blood of three powerful goddesses. Did you notice the three colors inside the mixture?"

Against her will, Rhea nodded. She'd wondered what the hues meant, if they were added syrups for taste or ingredients to further incapacitate whoever the next victim was. But too confused at the situation, too afraid of opening her mouth so close to the brew, she'd kept quiet.

"They represent the three goddesses that we're waiting to drain. The three with blood that'll mix perfectly and work wonders for our cause. One of them is Hera; rendered unconscious, from what I see, but that'll work in our favor. I presume you were stopped before drinking all of her?"

"She was," said the culprit, spinning in their direction at last. The fog about her slowly dissipated as she meandered closer, as if shedding the layers of her concealment, revealing herself to Rhea inch by inch. "I might have been wrong in choosing someone so ravenous, but you're correct, Mnemosyne. Hera's weakness will make it easier for us to take what we need from her. Stubborn as she is, she'd fight the most."

She was no longer a fog of deception, an unknown silhouette of smoke, a mirage. The voice was full-bodied, in color, her image sharp, her identity unraveled at last.

Rhea couldn't breathe. Gripping onto the edges of the cauldron, she fought against her jaw dropping to the ground. She fought the hammering of her heart in her chest, her knees begging to draw inward, to buckle, to make her collapse. She battled the awe and fear and anger meeting in her abdomen, and tightening it into a knot, worsening her earlier nausea.

How had she not known who the voice belonged to? She'd been acquainted with it many times, for many years. It should have triggered something within her, should have been obvious from the start. Yet she'd followed its bloody requests, never questioning its identity until recently. Never noticing its similarities with a very particular member of the family. One no one would suspect though she had the most reasons to be so infuriated with the gods, with the Olympians.

How did she keep us guessing? How did she confuse us all so?

"Y-you?" Rhea swallowed, but her saliva was acidic, burning down the linings of her throat. From disgust or astonishment, she wasn't sure. "It was you, this whole time?"

The evil doer's scent was so strong, it was impossible to mistake it for anyone else's. She set a finger under Rhea's chin, keeping it upright. Her touch sent chills to race all over Rhea's flesh, and intensified all the explosions within her. Her presence was agonizing and grand all at once; empowering but debilitating, enraged but encouraging.

"Yes, my sweet. I poisoned you, I enlisted you to our cause, I initiated you. Yes, I guided you up to this point; I guided *everyone*. It's my plan. I'm the mastermind behind all this." Her voice, though the same as what Rhea had heard inside her mind, was louder, less constrained. Realer. "And now, I ask that you help me finish the deed and prepare this potion. We need only collect the blood, and you can do that with your fangs. Rhea, please; help us finalize this concoction that'll help us target and destroy Zeus."

|| 26. OPEN YOUR EYES ||
LUKUS

"Come forth, minions; enter this hut and prostrate yourselves at the feet of your ultimate master."

The voice was subtle, smooth—and not in Lukus' mind. He'd never mistake it for anyone other than the creature that had inhabited his brain and coerced him into entering a flowery courtyard to witness the sunset.

He had no clue what had happened next, nor where he'd been transported to. He recalled said sunset—glowing and glorious as promised, shattering any image of beachy landscapes and make-out sessions on towels that led to steamy, sandy sex. And he also recalled someone approaching him, and someone speaking to him, and both voices morphing to blend into one—

The one he was hearing now.

"Come inside, minions, embrace us, your masters, and receive your instructions."

Lukus' eyelids were tightly sealed, and as he tried to pry them apart, he felt like a dozen fifty pound weights rested over them. He was a strong, fit human—definitely benched a couple hundred and squatted about the same—but this was a power he couldn't fight. It was godly, for sure; and it reminded him of another time when he hadn't been in control of his eyes, or his arms, or his legs.

When that fucked-up version of Eros drugged me and dragged me to the warehouse, then aimed an arrow into my heart.

A rush of adrenaline—angry, aggravated energy awakening in him at the thought of the evil, carnivorous Eros—helped him finally open his eyes into tiny slits. Wide enough to gauge his surroundings, to steal a glimpse of the situation unfolding before him.

He was slumped against a wall—a wet, thick, pulsating wall. Someone was hunched beside him, but he was too weak to turn his head and see who. Whoever they were, they weighed him down, making it impossible to fidget or even to breathe properly.

Upon sighting what was happening nearby, he figured his immobility might be for the best, for now.

Three rigid beings stood to his left. Stiff as planks of wood, arms tight at their sides, gazes focused on the opposite end of the room. A chandelier swayed overhead, covered in moss, with only a handful of candles lit; the light was dim, soft. One might have considered it intimate and romantic, but the eerie chanting, and the stench of earth and forest and rotting corpses dissuaded Lukus from getting into any sort of sexy mood.

The beings gazed at another group of individuals, their bodies less stiff, but their energies ever so ominous. Three women, from the looks of them. The one in the middle had a blurry but bright outline, and what appeared to be a cluster of red curls surrounding her head like a halo. The other two weren't as glowing, but intimidating all the same. A lady voluptuous as Aphrodite, but with orange hair and hints of gold shimmering all over her olive skin, and the other—

Rhea?

He'd almost whispered her name, but his vocal cords were

frozen, lathered in ice. It was her, no doubt; the same woman he'd suspected for an instant in the throne-room. Who looked so much like Hera that it was puzzling. Her hairstyle was wilder, sure, and she wore orange and yellow-toned outfits and smelled like a jungle, but she was her daughter's twin in all other aspects.

She was here, standing beside the foggy woman who spoke—and whose voice was *that* voice. Haunting, impossible to forget, and anchored forever in Lukus' mind.

"Come, come, my dears. Come bow to me," she said, majestic, malevolent, hypnotizing. Every word rolled off her tongue and swarmed through the air and hit the stiffened creatures square in the face, animating them.

They wobbled up to her, then fell to their knees.

If Lukus wasn't mistaken—and who knew, with his eyes half open and the woman's otherworldly glow so overpowering—two of the three *minions* she'd summoned were none other than those who'd been attacked in the palace. He recognized Themis' red sash around her waist, still stained with her own blood. Phoebe's sparkling silver skin and long, midnight tresses. The third person was a man, with little clothing, and Lukus could have sworn he had burgundy and godly blue ichor stains on his tunic.

Lukus bit his tongue.

Isn't that the drunk one? What's his name...Dionysus?

The three leaned forward, hands pressing to the floor. Lukus wriggled about, realizing said floor was wet and squishy, like mud. Was this some abandoned cabin in a humid woods somewhere? Or were these the dungeons Athena had mentioned? She hadn't described them, but the air had a whiff of death, and Lukus imagined an Olympian prison wouldn't have a delicate flower and vanilla scent. It would be dark, sinister, and depressing—like this place was.

He zeroed in on Rhea, who'd gotten to her knees, as well. She remained beside the iridescent woman, dipping her chin, obedient. But even with his hazy vision, Lukus caught her flinching. She sucked her lips in, her fingers curled and uncurled, her cheeks twitched and shifted from pallid to purple.

Something was wrong. Rhea seemed to fight herself, to not have full authority over her limbs. A few times she peered sideways at the woman by her—her boss, evidently—then clenched her jaw and lowered her gaze to the floor again.

The skin over Lukus' neck stung, and he nearly emitted a squeak in surprise. Something dribbled down to the middle of his chest, and he remembered he wore no shirt. He was lying sideways on a mushy, moisture-filled ground, half-dressed and not his usual self, witnessing an odd ceremony of zombified gods professing their love to a shining silhouette who sprinkled a charcoal-colored powder over their inclined heads.

What the fuck happened after I got to that courtyard?

Again, his neck ached. It burned, as if he'd been on the other end of a cigarette, and someone had shoved it—two of them, it felt like—into his flesh, searing through it until they reached the bone. Two distinct spots, flaring and inflamed and—

Oh. Oh fuck.

He couldn't move his arms, but he didn't need to touch his wounds to comprehend that they weren't cigarette burns. They were bite marks. He'd been bitten by the rampant culprit—and the last person he'd seen in that courtyard was Rhea.

His memories returned in agonizing flashes. Rhea, approaching him, speaking to someone—a foggy figure in the distance, with reddish hair and a poised posture. Then Rhea's fangs plunged into his neck, his consciousness faded, and the flowery and outdoorsy aromas of Olympus dissipated.

Now, he was here, in this muddy space. He was locked in a prison with not only Rhea—who might come back for seconds, to finish injecting him with toxins—but also *the* voice. The culprit. The nefarious goddess who'd contaminated family members, used them as distractions, and floated from mind to mind, multitasking herself into success.

Oh, yes, she'd succeeded. She'd confounded all the gods, drugged them, messed with their sanity. She'd tricked Lukus, teleported him to a woodsy area out of reach of Olympus. She'd fucked with his mind, gotten him infected, halted the investigation. Smart; incapacitating the investigator assigned to discovering her, imprisoning her.

Rhea was subdued, and so were the three minions still bowing before the creature. And that third and mysterious orange-haired lady looked quite enraptured by the scene, too—

Her gaze snapped in his direction, and on instinct, Lukus slammed his eyelids shut. Not knowing who she was, what her powers were, he feared the worst.

Fuck. Fuck. Did she see me?

He held his breath, listening for footsteps, waiting to feel a warm breeze on his cheek, a finger tapping over his eyes to check if he was awake, alive.

To his surprise, no one touched him—but his body heaved upwards in one swift movement. He had a second to understand that he was levitating, then he was being shaken—in the air. Like salt and pepper shakers, suspended and swerving up and down, his insides topsy turvy and his limbs numb and uncontrollable.

"You cannot fool me, half-mortal boy," said a deep, stern, feminine tone. If it hadn't terrified him, seeping into his core and tangling up his intestines, he might have found it sexy.

"What is it, Mnemosyne?" *The* voice spoke. Her little ritual had been interrupted, and Lukus sensed a pinch of irritation in her words.

Mnemosyne? Who the hell is that?

"Titaness of memory, you insignificant speck." The sultry-sounding timbre came closer, its volume cringeworthy.

Lukus stopped shaking, but remained in levitation, turned upright until his feet dangled beneath him. Something grabbed hold of his cheeks and squeezed them hard, and a scent of tangerines and peaches crawled up his nostrils.

"Open your damn eyes, because I know you're awake. I saw you. I hear you." Her deadly voice was so close, her breath washed over his face.

He groaned. Of course she'd heard his thoughts; she was a goddess, which meant she, like most others, had access to inside his head.

"You're damn right I do," she said, her fingers digging into Lukus' skin, crushing his lips, about to crack his jaw and cheek-bones. *"Open your eyes."*

He obeyed, opening one eye, then the other. Her golden-brown gaze was on him, unmoving, unblinking. Unnerving. She held him several inches above ground, with a strength he'd never have guessed her to have. She wasn't muscular like Athena, nor tiny like Artemis. But she had hidden power beneath her gown, simmering under the surface of her lady-like figure.

"Of course I have hidden power—I'm a titaness, you idiot," she spat, snarling.

If he'd found her beautiful before—and he had, in a hauntingly intimidating way—he no longer had any inkling to view her as such. She was snide, snickering, and ready to bite his head off.

"Do not ruin the meat suit," said the voice, its owner still too hazy to identify. The same as earlier, in the courtyard; it appeared she didn't want to be seen by Lukus yet. It was as if she'd made her entire outline a blur of scintillating light, too blinding to gape at, deterring anyone from seeking to figure out who she was. "Be useful and set him on the altar to prepare him, would you?"

Though her bitterness didn't vanish, Mnemosyne lessened her grip on Lukus' cheeks and spun him to levitate sideways. With one flick of her wrist, she sent him onto the elevated stone altar he'd noticed.

His spine smacked into the surface with a *thud.* "Ouch," he whispered, finding that his vocal cords were no longer broken.

Mnemosyne's face then popped up, hovering over him. Long, poofy locks of orange tickled across his bare chest. "Hush. You're to lie here and comply, when the time comes. Why aren't you still asleep?" She pulled away, and Lukus viewed the ceiling, covered in a starchy mud with weeds peeking out and vines weaving to and fro in chaotic patterns. "Rhea? Why isn't he drained?"

"I didn't want him drained, dearest," said the culprit, her timbre tart, impatient. "He won't do anything, poisoned as he is. I needed Rhea to gain strength, since I halted her from finishing Hera off."

Lukus' heart skipped a beat.

Hera?

He remembered there had been another body by him, but he hadn't been able to see it. Was that Hera? Had she been dragged to this foul-smelling place too? Had she been attacked?

Shit—if only Athena were here; this would prove her wrong.

"Now, would you please do something about his thoughts? He's giving me a migraine." The voice's piercing volume screeched into Lukus' head, pinching him, poking him. "Go back to sleep, Lukus. You need not fret about anything yet; it's not your turn."

He heard Mnemosyne shuffle off somewhere—likely to fetch something to knock him out. He cringed as he craned his neck to the side, towards where he'd been slumped moments before. Because he wanted to see it; the proof that Hera wasn't in on all this and was a victim, like everyone else. That she'd been the one lying next to him, inanimate—and innocent.

To his dismay—he didn't *want* Hera harmed, despite her high-and-mighty attitude and bickering and annoying arrogance—she was there, curled in a ball next to where he'd awoken. Her usually pressed and perfect gown was smeared with dark stains—her blood, surely—and her hair was twisted and knotted. Her skin was pale as the moon, with streaks of blue lining up and down her bare arms. And her neck, exposed in her half-lying, half-slouched position, revealed two round bite marks, courtesy of Rhea.

Poisoned or not, Rhea had sunk her teeth into her own daughter. She'd gotten to Themis and Phoebe and Dionysus, too. Now she crouched beside her master, awaiting further command. And in an odd twist, she hadn't seemed pleased about it.

Lukus was about to resign to his fate, to brace himself for another blacked-out, dreamless slumber, when he noticed *other* forms on the other side of Hera. Narrowing his gaze, he detected two of them, two *women*—one in pale lavender pajamas, and the other in a sheer nightgown. Their chins were tucked, and they were propped against the wall like dolls on display. He couldn't visualize their features, yet there was something familiar about them. Something about their contrasting silhouettes, their different skin tones, their outfits.

Before he had a chance to further investigate—drugged or not, it was in his nature to inquire, to research—Mnemosyne reappeared above him, a slight smirk over her gold-tinted lips.

"Cute. Keep on investigating, Lukus." She blew a thick dust over him, and as the particles touched his skin, they forced him to shut his eyes. "In your dreams."

|| 27. CAPTIVES ||

HERA

A sharp and stinging pain drew Hera from her slumber. It was an agony like those nights when she'd mixed too much ambrosia liquor and sweet cakes, and didn't remember stumbling into bed.

This was worse—the pain flared from one temple to the other, then shot down either side of her neck. One side throbbed with such intensity that Hera hissed as she opened her eyes.

Her eyelids were difficult to pry apart, as if glued together, but she saw enough to know that she hadn't stumbled into bed. No, she'd stumbled far, far from her chambers. Far from Olympus.

Where in Tartarus did I end up?

She was met with a semi-darkness that reminded her of the dungeons, and a stench of wet grass and mud that recalled marshes where she'd retrieved Zeus' precious heroes, reluctantly saving them from their mad wanderings.

The back of her head ached something fierce, and she reached up to rub it, but found that her wrists were bound. Whatever material had been used to tie her up was digging into her skin, and she again hissed at another pang of pain in her neck.

Why am I not in bed, and who dared to tie me up?

She squirmed about, but her legs were numb, weak. Her heart

raced as she sought to widen her eyes, but still her eyelids were too heavy, her eyelashes clinging together and blocking her sight.

She squinted through the darkness, trying to replay her last memories, to recall where she'd last been conscious of her surroundings. With a wince, she visualized her last location—in a corridor of Olympus, walking away from Dionysus' limp body, intent on finding Zeus and begging him to summon Persephone, with Hades' permission.

And then—blank. She'd blacked out, and her nostrils wrinkled when she vaguely remembered being hit on the head. Was that what had caused her blackout? Had that been enough to incapacitate the grand Queen of the skies? A mere *thud* on the back of her skull had knocked her out and brought her here, to whatever this dank and foul-smelling place was?

Her eyelids became more mobile, and she blinked a few times. A few unwanted tears slithered down her cheeks—likely from the effort it had taken to keep her eyes open—and she sniffled. She frowned, and instantly regretted letting the odor of soggy dirt into her nose.

Ahead of her, she noticed a large, stone dais, shaped as a sacrificial table. She recognized it; a sort of altar where humans would sacrifice various creatures for her fellow gods. A practice she herself didn't participate in, but respected. But she didn't smell any animals, nor any humans. There was only a slither of part-mortal energy coming from a person lying atop said altar, immobile, its bare arms pale and covered in goosebumps.

As she squinted to analyze the person's essence, she shivered, hearing chants from nearby. A cluster of ominous, dark prayers in a long-lost ancient language she had no inkling still existed.

Peering about the area, she couldn't gauge where the chants came from. They seemed to swirl in the air, whipping up, twirling like a tornado, but had no source, as if seeping inside the room through the walls.

Resigned, she focused on the inanimate half-mortal on the altar, trying to see into its mind, to detect its spirit and understand who it was. It was a man; bare-chested, but his top half was fairly flat, with no breasts from what she could tell. He was on his back, with short waves of black hair undulating around his head. He smelled familiar, almost friendly, innocent.

The sinister chants intensified, and the man began to convulse. His head whipped left, then right—and Hera gasped when she viewed his face.

Lukus?

The half-mortal son of Aphrodite was the poor soul to be sacrificed, unconscious and seizing on the altar; but who had put him there? Why? And why was Hera there to witness it?

The situation reeked of the culprit; the one who'd freely roamed about Olympus attacking Hera's family. Was it now after her and Lukus? It had transported them to a dreadful cabin in a haunted woods somewhere, intending to finish its nefarious acts—acts that involved sacrificing Lukus and incapacitating Hera?

It made no sense. Why would this malevolent creature go to such lengths for *her?* And for a half-god who had no idea what his powers were, and who hadn't quite accepted his heritage?

The mumbled melodies became louder, deafening. Hera cringed as they rang in her ears, and she battled to understand them. The tongue was so old, so powerful, that even she couldn't translate it. But she caught mentions of *sacrifice, blood, purity,* and *revenge.*

Again, she peeked around the space, noticing a chandelier

overhead emitting a faint light—the only way she'd been able to recognize Lukus. It was missing a few candles, and swayed to and fro as three beings emerged from her left, proceeding to march around the altar. They walked in a weird trance, zombie-like, consumed by madness. Hera recognized that stance, that controlled manner of half-stumbling, half-striding, with no purpose, no clear objective. She'd provoked such behaviors before, and wondered who had provoked *these.*

All three creatures had their chins tucked to their chests, at first. As their prayers amplified, they raised their gazes, fixing on the slumbering Lukus as they waded around him, hypnotized.

Hera recognized them, at last. Though their eyes were a vibrant, royal blue, and their moving mouths were stained blue, and their skin emitted an unnatural blue glow, she knew who these mysterious, messed-up souls were.

Themis, with her red ribbon of a belt still tight around her slender waist. Phoebe, her midnight hair gleaming, contrasting with her now silvery-blue skin. Dionysus, his current wobbling quite resembling his usual walking style.

The three victims of neck bites were here, in this room reeking of a rainy, rotten forest, swerving around Lukus as if about to take out chunks of his arms and legs and sink their fangs into *his* neck.

Lukus had no value; he wasn't fully immortal, had no clue what his abilities were, had barely accepted that his mother was the woman he'd had a disgusting crush on. Yet here he was, the object of these infected being's affection, about to be devoured by them—

Hera had to save him. Stupid mortal soul that he was, he was family, and Zeus would have her hanged from the stars if she didn't interfere.

She wriggled about again, praying to break the ropes around her wrists, to somehow regain mobility in her limbs. But no matter how she clenched her jaw, gritted her teeth, and summoned all the energy of the heavens, nothing happened. She'd barely moved a few inches, and had only managed to bump into something squishy beside her.

"Hm?" She jabbed an elbow to her left, into the thing that she'd bumped into, realizing it wasn't a thing; it was another person.

Were there other captives, like her? She inhaled a breath of the stale, mushy air, and glimpsed to her left, bracing to discover who else the culprit had decided to take from Olympus.

That breath remained stuck in her lungs at the vision of Athena, curled into a ball beside her, in her pale lavender pantsuit pajamas. Her lengthy braid was coming undone, curls poking out in messy patterns. The usual sternness about her had all but vanished in her slumber.

Athena was her enemy, the one who'd had no qualms about accusing her in presence of all Olympians and daring to insinuate that *she* would do such things—like placing Lukus on a sacrificial altar and biting into her fellow Olympians for fun—and yet, Hera was relieved to see her. Of all gods to be captured with, Athena had to be at the top of Hera's list. Witty, wise, physically strong, and mentally unchallenged, she'd fix their situation. She'd get them out of there.

"Hey." Hera nudged Athena in the arm. The goddess of wisdom moaned, but didn't wake. "*Hey,* lifelong foe, would you wake up? We're in trouble, here." She nudged her again, harder this time, and repeated the gesture until Athena swatted at her and nudged her back.

"What? What do you want? Why—" she stilled, her arm tensing next to Hera's. "Uh…where am I?"

Hera grunted; their conversation was likely to go unnoticed under the raucous chants still going on in front of them. The zombified gods had accelerated their paces and raised their voices, and Hera couldn't look at them without getting dizzy.

"Where are *we,* you mean." She jutted her chin at the scene ahead, and sensed Athena shudder in response. "It seems we've been kidnapped."

Athena spat out an urgent curse in ancient Greek and shifted about, revealing that she, too, had her wrists bound.

"What is the meaning of this?" She kept her voice at a harsh whisper, surely detecting the danger and not wanting to be caught waking up.

Smart woman—as much as I hate to admit it.

Athena glared at her bindings and scoffed. "This is absurd. Does this thing know who we are? We—" Athena froze, then spun to *her* left. "Ah, there's another of us, it seems."

Grimacing in pain, Hera leaned over and gazed towards where Athena had been staring. Indeed, another goddess rested there, also in her nightwear—an outfit easily recognizable, as only one goddess dared sleep in something so skimpy. A sheer nightgown with straps strolled down her milky shoulders, and a nest of strawberry blonde curls covered her usually delicate features.

"Aphrodite?" Hera cocked an eyebrow. "Really?"

The deity of beauty stirred, her face still concealed, but Hera knew she wasn't asleep. Her breaths weren't shallow and calm like those of someone in a peaceful slumber. No, they were agitated, and a ripple of goosebumps woke across her exposed legs the instant Hera spoke.

"Don't try to fool us, you deranged woman," hissed Hera, wishing she could extend a hand to prod at the fake-sleeping goddess. "We're awake, and you are too."

With a huff, Aphrodite puffed her locks from her forehead and opened her lackluster lapis eyes, batting her lashes as she worked to sit up straight. "Fine, I'm here." She shrugged, then motioned at the chanting zombies across the way. "What are they doing? Where are we?"

Hera slumped into her spot. All three had been set up against a wall, and its surface was gooey, gushy, its texture like a grassy mud. She flinched as said texture rubbed against her back.

"They're preparing their sacrifice, I bet. The language they're using—it's ancient, *very* ancient. I don't know anyone who still uses it."

"Is that—" Aphrodite gasped, and Athena slammed her hands over her mouth to quiet her soon-to-come squeaks of surprise. She puffed out a breath to move Athena's hands, to speak freely, but kept her voice lowered, strained. "Is that who I think it is? Dionysus? And...and Themis? And Phoebe? What...what is happening?"

Unsure whether to inform Aphrodite that she was correct about her assumptions, and that the one they intended to sacrifice was none other than her newly discovered son, Hera shook her head.

"No clue. And no idea where we are, either."

Athena scratched at her chin. "I know." She narrowed her gaze, her pupils darting right to left, then right again, settling on Hera. "I know this scent. Like a marsh, yes? A swamp. It's...ladies, we're in the Underworld."

Aphrodite gasped again, and Hera's heart skipped several beats. "The Underworld? But how?"

Athena, the calmest of the three, hunched against the wall and drew her knees to her chest. If she'd recognized Lukus atop the altar, she also said nothing.

Did he tell her about Aphrodite?

Athena's eyes widened as she watched the altar, then her head flipped to Hera, her eyebrows rising. "Tell me what?"

Hera pinched her lips. She'd forgotten Athena was the only one allowed to immerse herself into their thoughts. Now she hoped, in their predicament, that the goddess would overlook that fact.

"Nothing to concern yourself about at this instant. We have more pressing matters to attend to, no?"

Athena's gaze narrowed on her, unconvinced; but Aphrodite's squirming drew her attention away.

The goddess of love had managed to worm away from the wall, and was crawling closer to Hera. She gave up once she reached Athena's feet, and collapsed in front of Hera, breathless.

"Heavens, that was tiresome," she said, her usual dramatic tone returning to her as she tried to gather her bearings. She heaved up into a sitting position, then launched forward to grab Hera's bound wrists. "Hera, please, I must ask for your forgiveness."

Awed—never had she heard such words escape the pouty lips of Aphrodite—Hera blinked. "Huh?"

"You...you're not the culprit, as some had implied." Aphrodite sent a quick side-glare at Athena. "I wish to beg your forgiveness for having believed them. With you here, bound like we are, it's apparent that you had nothing to do with this. Well," she bunched her lips and glowered, "unless you're tricking us, which you're quite capable of doing."

Hera's jaw dropped, but she had no words appropriate enough for the situation.

Instead, Athena spoke for her. Spoke *to* her; and for the first time in centuries, she didn't sound snide, nor did she snicker. Her eyes were a dull gray, glossing over, and she seemed to fight a quiver of her chin.

"She's right. I'm also sorry, my queen. It was my assumption that put you in such a bad light, and I cannot apologize enough. I should have listened to Father, should have heeded Lukus' hunches—"

"—Lukus?" Aphrodite perked up at this, a sort of pride illuminating across her face. "He had a hunch? Did he solve it? Figure out who the culprit was?"

Athena bit her lower lip and looked ready to gesture at the altar, but an abrupt, violent rustling sound stopped her, and she recoiled farther against the wall.

Aphrodite followed her gaze and immobilized. Hera swung towards the noise, seeing a crumpled creature creeping up to them.

"Ugh." She tried not to squeal as she crammed herself close to Athena, repulsed by whatever was approaching them.

Aphrodite nuzzled nearer, too, as if seeking refuge between them. "That thing has come to eat us? Is this it?"

"No," muttered the creature, its voice raspy but recognizable. It lifted its head—*her* head. She shook out her wild chestnut curls, revealing beautiful, benevolent features. Her olive skin glistened with sweat, and though her eyes were rimmed with red and blue and purple, their regular warm brown shade instilled a brief sense of tranquility in Hera.

"Mother?" Hera's eyebrows scrunched at the sight—at a disheveled Rhea, her tunic stained with so many colors one wouldn't know which to try to identify first. "What are you doing here?"

Rhea redressed herself, tucking her knees beneath her as she bowed to the three goddesses. "I...I'm the one who did this." She opened and closed her mouth, like a fish out of water.

Hera's lungs tightened when she noticed the hints of cerulean around Rhea's mouth.

Is that ichor?

"It's me," said Rhea, keeping her distance, but leaning forward as if to take her daughter's hands in hers. She didn't, instead curling her fingers into her palm. She remained close, her scent reaching Hera's nostrils and infesting them.

Yes—it was ichor. Rhea reeked of it; it poured from her pores and radiated around her as if she'd consumed so much of it that it had *become* her.

"You…what?" Hera wanted to check Athena and Aphrodite's reactions, but she feared turning away from her mother. "What did you do?"

"I was the culprit." Rhea gulped. "Well, part of the culprit. Its puppet. I acted on its whims, I fed on its orders. *Her* orders." She lowered her gaze to the ground. "The real mastermind was, *is*, her."

Athena shivered as she snuck an arm behind Hera, drawing her closer, oddly protective of the step-mother she hated. Hera silently thanked her, though she had no doubt she could defend herself.

"W-who?" said Athena, also drawing Aphrodite nearer to her.

A new figure approached, arriving out of nowhere. "Me," she said, her voice filling the space like water splashing into a cup. Like mud dumped into a pot to engulf a plant's roots.

This woman, this creature, glowed—her outline was womanly and curvaceous, but everything else about her was blurred. As she meandered up to them, she became harder and harder to look at, as the halo about her silhouette was so bright, so shimmering, Hera had to focus on the floor to avoid being blinded.

"Mastermind, what an adequate term, Rhea dearest," continued the creature, halting a few feet away. Which was for the best, Hera thought—her energy was so overpowering and intoxicating, she might swallow up the three goddesses whole without even touching them. "That is indeed what I am, since no one ever dared imagine me capable of such atrocious acts of violence."

Whoever or whatever she was, her presence didn't distract the three poisoned deities still roaming around Lukus, like sharks circling their prey. They were hungry, and they wanted the half-mortal; their master's appearance didn't seem to change a thing in their plan.

"Don't mind them," said the woman, addressing Hera's thoughts.

Right, this thing can enter minds at will.

"That's true." The woman's timbre was snappy, likely frustrated with Hera's constant interruptions. "Now you're going to let me talk, and you're going to listen until the end, understood? You three are essential, but I'd like you to know what I need from you before I take it."

|| 28. MOTHER ||

RHEA

The mix of Dionysus' alcohol-infused ichor, Hera's pure ambrosia and sweetened flavors, and Lukus' potent half-human blood swirled in Rhea's belly. All three tastes lingered on her tongue, but a fourth one persisted there as well, sour and sneaky—the poison the culprit had injected into her minutes before all the captives began to awaken.

"To keep you compliant," the creature had said. Rhea still didn't dare to think her name, for fear that her brain would catch fire and her heart would explode.

It was the harshest, deepest of betrayals. A long-lost rivalry, a heavy hatred that drove this monster to what she was doing. Though Rhea had been a participant of it—reluctantly—she now wished to become one of the victims, instead. She wished to have her mind melted, her limbs controlled, her every thought turned off so she wouldn't have to remember what she'd done. What she was about to do.

Themis, Phoebe, Dionysus—how she envied them, patrolling around the inanimate Lukus, chanting about his blood and his powers in an ancient Greek that pre-dated Rhea's time as Queen of the skies. She even envied Lukus, passed out on an altar and about to be used for who-knew-what purposes.

All of them were unconscious, unaware of their actions, forced to do the culprit's bidding.

Rhea was, unfortunately, conscious and in control of herself, and she loathed every second. Every second of thoughts that strolled through her, prodding at her to react, to do something to bar this creature from reaching her goals. Yet she knew acting out would be perilous to the captives—one of which was none other than her beautiful daughter.

The one that I drank from only a few hours ago. Who am I to be protective of her now?

Such conflict raged inside Rhea's mind, such torment. But instead of doing something to fix it, she huddled in a ball near her daughter and granddaughters, unsure how to protect them from this evil woman's wrath.

"I'm not evil, Rhea," said the culprit, her voice slick with disappointment. Out loud, she sounded more malevolent and majestic than she had when locked inside Rhea's brain, and every word she uttered worsened Rhea's nausea. "You need not protect anyone from anything, and certainly not from me. Relax, would you?"

Rhea almost snorted—*relax?* How?—but chose not to be too defiant in this creature's domain, surrounded by her minions and associates.

And me—I'm her associate, too.

Rhea couldn't bear to look at the prisoners bound before her. Aphrodite had burrowed into Athena's arms—a sight to behold, as they'd never usually come close enough to even breathe on one another. Athena sat upright against the wall, but her arms were littered in goosebumps and her legs shivered against the muddy ground.

And Hera—oh, she was the worst of them. Rhea winced every time their gazes met, for Hera's was pinched, charged with confusion and pain and dismay. Her silence tortured Rhea; she was always so outspoken when expressing her thoughts. To not hear them now, to not be able to read them was traumatizing.

Rhea had earned those gazes, that quiet. She'd bit into her own daughter, began to drain her of her precious ichor, and had dared to savor her. The culprit—the one wanting her to drink ichor in the first place—had had to rip her off Hera before she infected her, and drew Lukus to them instead. She'd been furious at having to do so, as it was too soon.

"He has no clue of his powers yet," the voice, while still locked in Rhea's mind, had said. She'd then slipped out of Rhea's body as if she'd been possessing her, and manifested before her as a cloud of lime-green smoke. Her presence was toxic, and Rhea had coughed, spewing out puddles of Hera's warm blood. *"He's not yet accepted his true identity, still struggles to cope with his half-god status. I wanted to wait, that was why I drew things out, kept throwing distractions to keep everyone occupied. I needed time."*

Rhea had expected a slap on the face—though how, from a puff of smoke, she hadn't been sure—but the creature hadn't budged. Instead, she'd swished out of the courtyard, promising to bring Rhea someone else to snack on. That snack was Lukus, who'd need to be weakened before he could be transported.

The transportation had gone well. Rhea had brought Hera with them, as the culprit had requested, but she had no idea how Aphrodite and Athena had arrived. They'd been snatched from their beds—both wore their pajamas—but not by her.

The minions? Did they do it?

She sighted Mnemosyne busying herself at the cauldron, concealed behind the hazy clouds spouting out of its depths. Rhea's daughter and granddaughters hadn't yet seen the titaness, else they'd have said something. Hera would have; she knew Mnemosyne. She'd employed her services a few times to assist with rendering Zeus' illegitimate offspring mad.

As if hearing her name—or creeping into Rhea's mind—Mnemosyne stepped away from the fumes. "Ah, you wanted them to see me, hm? To understand my collaboration in all this?"

As expected, all three captive goddesses gasped, but it was Hera's face that showed recognition and became pallid as snow.

"Mnemosyne?" She squinted across the area, zoning in on the titaness' familiar frenzied curls of orange and red around her sneering expression.

Mnemosyne had been, at one point, a lover of Zeus—at the sight of her, the rage in Hera was so intense, it caused the blood vessels on her arms to turn gold, shooting up to her shoulders like fireworks.

"Whoa," whispered Aphrodite, nuzzling her nose into Athena's bosom. Athena didn't flinch or shove her off. Both were too afraid to despise each other. "The titaness of memory? Working with…working with *her?*"

"Working with me, yes," said the glowing figure of the culprit.

Rhea bowed, her forehead grazing the ground, as the sniveling woman approached them. She was too hard to look at; only Mnemosyne seemed able to view past her iridescent surface and beamed at her.

Mnemosyne, beaming? That's something I've never seen before.

Rhea remained seated on the ground, where she felt she belonged. Standing would show herself as an ally of the culprit, and she couldn't tolerate that. She couldn't tolerate herself.

"Ah, Aphrodite, I've not yet thanked you for your own involvement in all this." The creature inclined forward in a semi-bow.

Though she kept her face hidden, Aphrodite's spine tensed, and she sniffled. "M-my involvement?"

Athena held her tighter, and Hera leaned in closer, pressing into Athena as if wanting to become a part of her. Rhea would have laughed were the situation not so dire. Three deities who abhorred each other were crammed together as if their lives depended on their connection.

For all I know, that may be the case.

"Why, yes," the glowing being continued, stepping over to the cauldron. She seemed to turn towards it, but Rhea couldn't tell for sure, with her figure so indistinct. Her hair bounced about the outline of her face, the lengths dipping all around her, curling at the ends like snakes. "You gave us Lukus. Unwillingly, of course; but I appreciate your participation, nonetheless."

Aphrodite squinted at the woman. Her eyebrows rose, scrunched, then rose again. "You…you know about that?"

"I made it happen." The woman swooped a hand down into the pot's brewing contents. "I created the illusion around the whole thing, making certain that all would believe Lukus was born to a family of mortals. I trifled with memories, including your own, to be positive none would remember who he really was."

"Why?" Athena had been quiet until then, and her voice croaked as it reanimated. "What does this mean?"

Aphrodite muttered something to her, and Athena's jaw dropped. She flipped to Hera for confirmation—she nodded—and returned her astonished gaze to the culprit.

"No one was supposed to know yet, but our dear Rhea

accelerated the plans. Nevertheless, things are in motion, and I'm in no position to stop them." The shining lady stirred the cauldron's content's with her hand, unaffected by its heat or its poisonous nature. "Lukus is to lead a human army against Zeus. As part-human, he can speak to other mortals, sway them, arm them, inform them. And as part-god, he can confront Zeus. Once he comes into his powers, which I hope my friends are still working on now." She paused, twisted towards the altar and her minions. "Yes, they are, wonderful."

Athena and Aphrodite—the latter hadn't realized Lukus was the one on the altar, apparently—gripped each other tighter. They gawked at the poor, inanimate man encircled by zombie gods.

"They," said Aphrodite, swallowing, "what are they doing?"

"Trying to awaken his powers." The culprit moved away from the cauldron and slithered up to where Rhea remained on her knees. "It can take years, decades, for a half-god to discover any hint of power within, but I don't have that kind of time. I need him empowered as soon as possible. This fight has waited long enough." Her voice shifted, growing deeper, darker, tinted with malice.

"And us?" Hera perked up, squaring her shoulders, evidently doing her damndest to appear brave. Rhea sensed her angst, tasted her worry, and noticed her tremors. She was out of her comfort zone, and in over her head.

Aren't we all? My poor family.

"Ah, you, my dear prisoners." The culprit lowered to Rhea's level, and Rhea shriveled, crawling backwards until her back met with the cauldron. Its surface was scalding, and yet it soothed the frigid sensations that had been spiraling up and down her limbs, petrified by this ancient goddess' malevolent energy.

She could say all she wanted that she wasn't evil, but she sure smelled like it, felt like it, to Rhea.

If offended by Rhea's running off, the creature didn't show it, keeping low to the ground and facing her captives. "Zeus values you much, all three of you. Your immortal blood is precious, more so than others. Rhea can attest to that, since she tried your ichor, Hera."

Hera's eyes widened, and she clapped a hand over her mouth. "Mother?" She scowled at Rhea, but seemed unable to maintain the link for long. She gagged, keeping her hand pressed harder over her lips.

How Rhea craved to rush over to her daughter and swear to her that she'd never meant to hurt her. Never meant to abandon her when she was accused of all the horrid things the culprit had done. How she yearned to embrace her, vow to her she'd make up for it. That she'd do all she could to earn her forgiveness and that of all the Olympians and humans affected.

Hera would never accept her apologies. It was obvious from her recoiling and her struggle to refrain from vomiting that her own mother biting her neck and drinking her blood was unforgivable. Rhea couldn't blame her.

"You are an important component of my ultimate poison, ladies. Because Zeus trusts in you, and has used all three of you to thwart my plans in the past. Using your power, your energy, against him would make his demise much more delicious. He'd never expect it; like he doesn't expect or suspect any of this."

The woman straightened up, and a witchy cackle escaped her mouth; a mouth that was taking form, no longer glowing and blurry. It was pouty, aubergine-colored, streaked with emerald green.

"He's still wandering about Olympus, consulting his Fates, his ancestors. He's even consulted Mnemosyne's Muses. Though they know the truth he's not been able to extract anything from them. His power weakens with every passing second, and I tell you, it feels divine to watch him fail."

The Muses' implication was a surprise to all—even Rhea hadn't been privy to that information. She peeked at Mnemosyne who, she could have sworn, poked her chest out and offered a slight smirk. She was proud of her daughters. That they'd wandered the halls of Olympus with the knowledge their mother had aided the culprit. And knowledge of the culprit, too. Such innocent and lovely women hadn't been among the accused, not once.

Oh, that was sly. Brilliant, but sly.

Hera opened her mouth, then closed it as she shook her head.

The culprit, able to pry into everyone's mind, set her hands on her hips and fixed on Hera. "You wonder about Rhea's implication." The creature's eyes were forming—mud and bark, laced with vines and tufts of crimson. A gaze Rhea usually found reassuring, soothing; but was now loaded with rage and hatred.

Hera said nothing, but her features seemed to answer the culprit's comment.

"Right. Well, she was a mere pawn, dear. A slave in the grand scheme of things. A slave to my desires."

Rhea acquiesced to this, but wasn't certain if she'd wanted to confirm it. To sound so demeaned, so frail, vulnerable enough to let someone command her every move like so; it wasn't like her, and Hera knew that.

"She was lucid, but had little authority over her actions. Ah, yes, she was the one biting everyone in Olympus, in case you hadn't yet guessed."

Though Athena and Aphrodite gaped at Rhea as if they'd never known her, as if they feared her violence now, Hera crumbled. Her head fell into Athena's lap and she sobbed. Rhea gritted her teeth as she sensed her daughter's agony, and was crushed under her disappointment.

"I didn't want to," Rhea spat, desperate for her daughter to understand. "Like she said, I had little control, so I couldn't—"

"—don't waste your breath, darling," said the culprit. "Hera will not and cannot comprehend the depth of all this. Hush, now." She focused on the Queen of the skies, as if reveling in her pain. "What she says is true, Hera. She doesn't even remember everything I had her do for me. For example, she has no clue *she* poisoned Eros and Psyche, with the help of the Muses. They gave her the poison to sprinkle into their food and drink. *She* commenced the distraction, at my behest."

Rhea's heart skipped too many beats to count. Chills cascaded down her arms and legs, freezing her entire body. "What?"

She'd been in the jungle when the two lovebirds were drugged; or so she'd thought.

"That's right." The woman spun to Rhea, all her blurry brightness dissipating. Though this monster *had* revealed herself to Rhea moments before, the stench of the malice in her aura was still terrifying. And to again confirm her identity, to understand it wasn't a nightmare or a figment of Rhea's imagination, was a strike of lightning and a shock of thunder that paralyzed her. "You were much more essential than I let you believe, Rhea. I should be thanking you most of all; but your role is far from over."

Despite the fear tangling in her gut, and the voices—her conscience, her intuition—screaming at her to stay put, to swallow her fury, Rhea couldn't sit still any longer. She couldn't wait and watch as this deity took over minds, polluting them, and ruined souls.

"No." Streaks of fire flew down her limbs, scorching the hairs on her arms and legs, shooting up her neck and igniting her hair. Her fangs drew out. Claws grew from her nails. A lioness' growl brewed in her throat, bracing to erupt, to deafen anyone near.

In a surge of adrenaline and stupidity, Rhea launched herself on the culprit, seeking to pounce atop her and destabilize her long enough for the three captives to escape. She hoped to dig her teeth into the creature's neck and drain *her,* instead, and hopefully break the spell over the minions, over Lukus, and possibly over Mnemosyne.

But she'd over-estimated her strength. With a swift wave of her hand, the culprit threw Rhea across the room, smashing into a wet, muddy wall. Her body squished into the surface, and it broke her fall, but still she collided hard and knocked her head, nearly losing consciousness. As she tried to shake herself back to life, thick, poky vines wrapped around her wrists, binding them; then another set appeared around her ankles.

"Hey!" The vines twisted and looped into deadly knots that she knew she'd never get out of. They tightened, cutting off her circulation. "What are you doing?"

It had been a reckless move; now, instead of an ally, Rhea had become an enemy. Had she listened to her brain, she could have remained on the inside. She could have found another means to dismantle this monster's master plan.

"I'm sending a message," said the woman, pointing at Rhea and making a circle in the air with her fingers.

A glob of mud and leaves wedged itself into Rhea's mouth, shutting her up. She moaned and wriggled about, but it was no use. She'd used too much energy trying to attack the woman, and now she was stuck.

"A message to Zeus. It's time to rile him up." She zoomed over to Rhea with the swiftness of a cheetah, and kneeled down to whisper in her ear. "You tell him you're mine, they're mine, and his precious Lukus will soon be mine, too. You tell him he's already lost, and there's no point. And then, you'll return to me, and we'll finish this job, once and for all."

Rhea's vision faded, and her body elevated off the ground, leaving Mnemosyne's hut behind.

‖ 29. OUR ARMY ‖
LUKUS

Lukus cringed as his senses awakened. First came touch—shocks up his back as the hard, cold surface under him made itself known. Then the flavor of his own coppery blood mixed with the tartness of ambrosia. A scent of mud and grass and sweat—his own perspiration, he assumed, because he'd never seen any of the gods sweat like he did—with a hint of something sweet, something he couldn't identify. Sounds of chants, robotic voices repeating the same garbled mix of words that he didn't understand. Several voices, two feminine, one slurred and masculine.

He opened his eyes, his gaze fixed on the muddy ceiling overhead, with leaves and vines dangling down, like streamers left behind after a crazy party. The chandelier swayed slowly in a gentle wind, and faint light poured over him.

He was groggy, only half-conscious, but his memory hadn't dissipated, this time. He knew where he was—in a muddy cabin somewhere far from Olympus—who was with him, and the danger he was in. Themis, Phoebe, Dionysus—they still ambled around him as he lay on the altar. Still rambling in their made-up language, and still smelling like poisonous drunkards.

There were more voices in the mix, now. One of them had been

Hera's—he knew its sternness, but here it was painful, pleading, asking about her mother.

One was sobbing loudly, muttering incomprehensible sentences between sniffles. Another, strong but trembling, further froze Lukus' limbs.

"What is the matter with you?" It was Athena; she was irritated, but struggling to keep the fear out of her timbre, Lukus could tell. He'd spent enough time with her to realize when she was fighting her facade of bravery, holding in her angst. She'd taken that tone several times while talking about the case with him. "Why would you go up against Zeus? Why provoke him like that?"

"And my son?" The sniffling, sobbing voice revealed itself to be Aphrodite. She was weaker than usual, less imposing and seductive. Not that Lukus retained any more attraction to her, knowing what and who she was, but it wasn't the tone he'd been accustomed to. The melodious but dramatic tune she sang, enticing, enrapturing. No, she was like a dog's squeaky toy; annoying.

"What about him?" This voice was *hers*—the culprit. Daunting, daring, devilish. Lukus had no trouble recognizing her. She might have been in his mind for only a few minutes, but she'd left an imprint on his brain that he'd never get rid of.

Drawing me to the courtyard for a sunrise—bah! Lying bitch.

The voice scoffed, and Lukus winced, recalling she could hear his thoughts. "Trust me when I tell you that you need not worry about him." He sensed her hovering near him, her stench of rain-drenched dirt and mulch invading his nostrils. "He fends for himself, and he'll come to accept his new fate soon enough."

"New fate?" Hera had fixed her plaintive timbre but the irritation still lingered in it, heavy and oppressive. If she feared this culprit, she wasn't planning to show it yet. "Is that what you do, then? Give new fates? You forced one on Mother, then on Lukus, and now you're scheming to change Zeus', too? No. It won't work. He'll retaliate."

"I'm sure he'll try," said the creature, slithering away and taking her odor with her. Lukus had kept his eyes open, concentrating on the ceiling, but he remembered how Mnemosyne had poked her head over him and stared. He was ready to close his eyes at any moment, unwilling to cross gazes with her again; or with the evil being.

"He has always won against you, and he will again." Hera's voice was stiff, unbreakable, but Lukus knew she was terrified. They all were—he detected their terror, as if it crawled along his skin, inching to his mouth where he'd eat it.

Ew—why would I want to eat their fear?

"Sorry, ladies." The voice had swerved to Lukus' other side, and he shivered at the sensation of her arm brushing his. "But this half-human's thoughts are perturbing me. I must address them."

He had no time to seal his eyes. His body was straightened into a sitting position, his back rigid as if placed against a wall of steel. *She* stood before him in her layers of light, her outline blinding, her red hair cascading down like rivulets of blood. Though he wanted to look away from her, to never visualize her again, he couldn't. She'd forced him up, and it felt like she'd put invisible pins in his eyelids to keep them apart.

"My boy, you're not supposed to be awake, are you?" He saw her flip towards someone else—from the corner of his eye he detected the orange-haired Mnemosyne—then returned to him. He had no doubt, from her proud posture, that she was smirking. Her features were blurred, but there was a subtle snideness about her that he didn't need a face to analyze. "Stronger than you look, I see. Perhaps you've come upon your powers already?"

Lukus hiccuped. "Powers?" The blue-lipped zombies had stopped circling him, and he recalled their lifeless chanting. Had they been strengthening him, instead of weakening him or killing him, as he'd thought?

"Yes, Lukus. They were summoning the energy within you, gifted to you by your mother."

"Mother?" His arms tightened at his sides. "You...you know?"

The woman huffed, deflating as she shook her head. "Why is it that everyone doubts me tonight?" She twirled a finger in the air, magically spinning him to face his other audience—three crumpled goddesses on the floor. "Of course I know. I know everything. I'm privy to all knowledge, to all ancestries, to all roots. In truth, I'm quite responsible for yours, for your existence. I created your entire history, dear. I concealed your identity from your own mother and true family. Yes, I created you."

Her words jumbled about in Lukus' brain as he witnessed three of his new family members, all staring up at him with frowns. As if confirming what the culprit had said was correct; that he was indeed a figment of her magic. That he'd been born for her, to satisfy whatever her sick plans were.

Hera was huddled against the wall, with Athena, who lay with her legs sprawled out, and with Aphrodite snuggled in her arms. The former wore her stained royal tunic, and the bite marks on her neck seemed to glare at his wounds, as if recognizing them. He smacked a hand to his neck, to hide his own gnashes, but all three goddesses had seen them—their gazes widened.

"You bit him?" Aphrodite's squeak grew in pitch and rattled Lukus' eardrums.

"*Rhea* bit him," said Hera, nostrils wrinkling. "This monster wouldn't get her hands dirty if her life depended on it."

The creature whooshed to the other side of the altar and threw a jolt at Hera's face. Hera screamed and fell forward, wriggling against something. When she sat up, tears glistening in her big brown eyes, a glob of what looked like seaweed and mush had fastened to her mouth.

"Insolent little bitch. Seriously, you've been worse than usual, child. Learn your lesson and your place." The iridescent figure whirled around to Lukus. "For your information, Rhea did bite you, as I'm sure you figured out by now. She did so on my command, because we needed to take some of your blood to make room for the poison. A different poison; a potent potion that'll strengthen you, amplify your human reflexes, and multiply any powers you harbor deep within. It'll make you a powerful warrior, more resilient than a regular war-god such as Ares. Infused with Olympian goddess blood, titaness ichor, and a few earthly brews I thought wise to throw in there for good measure."

He heard the mumbling behind the creature's bright outline. The goddesses were either trying to help free Hera from her new mouthpiece, or discussing what the culprit had revealed, or plotting how to get out of there.

"No one is leaving, Lukus." The monster's voice was eerily soft, enchanting, motherly. "Only Mnemosyne is allowed to come and go freely. Everyone else is a prisoner, even you. For now."

"For now?" Lukus' throat ached as he spoke, as if knives had grown along its linings and were rubbing together with his every breath.

She kept a distance between them, yet he felt the warmth radiating off her as it coated his limbs in a sticky sweat. "Ah, you'll be a high commander, dear boy. You'll have a serious rank in my army—one of the highest. It's your blood and mixed heritage that will make you my biggest ally. Once we've ensured you don't reject the potion and react to its effects accordingly, that is. It is, after all, not tested yet. An experiment."

Lukus wished he was dreaming, wished he'd fallen asleep in front of some sci-fi movie. Frankenstein? Or some post-apocalyptic TV show that depicted zombies and humans fighting for survival?

It couldn't be real. He'd barely come to terms with the fact that Greek gods were a thing—and they were angry—but now he had to accept he was the son of Aphrodite, and created to lead an army of...

"Of what?" He gulped. "What kind of army?"

"Oh?" The glowing woman leaned backwards and folded her arms; he imagined her eyebrows rising in curiosity. "You're less reticent than I'd expected. This bodes well."

Lukus gritted his teeth. He wouldn't confess to her how disgusted and horrified he was, nor how his fear threatened to engulf him and knock him into a semi-permanent coma that he actually prayed for. A never-ending slumber, or even death, would be better than sitting before her, unable to recognize her, unable to consent to be used as her army general to pursue her wretched goals.

Whatever the fuck they are.

If she'd read his mind, she didn't show it—she didn't become enraged at his defiance or insults, and was relaxed, letting her arms drop to her sides.

"You'll command a human army. Most of which will be composed of the mortals Psyche infected during her travels. And others that you'll recruit yourself, once the toxins are inside you. It'll be your instinct; to gather followers, to hoard them along with you to the final battle site. That location remains a mystery even to me, I'm afraid. But you'll know; you'll smell it, you'll taste it. And you'll come to me, bringing our army with you. You'll be on the front-lines of the war against Olympus."

Lukus' jaw dropped, and any slither of voice he'd mustered up earlier had disappeared.

The culprit flipped to her other audience. "A war that I *will* win, this time, contrary to what my dear Hera believes."

This time? Has she tried to fight Olympus before?

Lukus wished he'd been more attentive to his fake mother's tales when he was a child. Why hadn't he listened, become more interested in all the myths she recited, in all the gods she spoke of with such reverence? Why hadn't he paid closer attention to the curses his father had uttered when frustrated, which deities he preferred, which ones he prayed to most?

He knew the answer was right there, on the tip of his tongue. Whoever this creature was, she was ancient and dark. She was powerful, smart, witty enough to wade through the throngs of gods unnoticed, employing plenty of ruses and minions to enact her desires without stirring anyone's attention.

Which gods had the mightiest abilities, the oldest magic? Titans, right? So she had to be a titaness, of some sort. One above Rhea, above this snotty Mnemosyne lady, above even the most ancient deities in existence. One who'd been around at the beginning of time, and who'd been brewing in her rage for that long. But who, among such creatures, was so mad at the gods that she wanted to dethrone the king and maim him? Who held such an intense grudge, and why? Which titaness could duplicate herself by being in several minds at once, and had access to Hecate's cabinet in the Underworld, *and* access to Olympus, and stealth beyond anyone's awareness?

The woman rotated to him, the fogginess about her starting to fade. "Yes…yes, Lukus, it's time you see me. The real me. Not this mask, this haze that I kept over myself to protect you, to protect everyone. If you're to fight for me and my cause, you should know who I am."

His temples throbbed, searing pain across his forehead. His heart pounded so harshly that it nearly ripped out of his chest. Anxious waves of anticipation caused him to shudder, to convulse. But he sat as upright as he could, his gaze glued to the woman before him as she became visible at last.

The glow was gone in a matter of seconds, as if she'd flipped a light-switch. The candles from the dimmed chandelier above still basked her in a sort of halo, but one not blinding enough to prevent Lukus from seeing her clearly.

And clear, she was. With her shimmering red and mahogany curls like swaying autumn branches. In her vibrant, verdant dress with actual vines seeming to sprout from the hem. Her skin the shade of desert in the dark, with a texture like that of a reptile's hide, as if coated in scales. Eyes like puddles of mud flecked with green and with an ominous scarlet hue surrounding the pupils.

Oh, she was ancient, all right. She was all-seeing and all-knowing and smelled like fresh soil, blooming flowers, wet leaves in the rain. She was majestic like a towering tree, ready to reach her branches out and impale anyone in her passage.

"G-Gaia?" Lukus slurped up the saliva that had begun to drizzle from his open mouth. "You? You're the culprit?"

Gaia swerved to the goddesses below who, it appeared, hadn't quite recognized her themselves. Their eyes bulged from their sockets and their bodies slumped forward as if robbed of life.

"Culprit—such a poor word to describe the work I've done. So ill-chosen; I'd prefer to be called the creator. The savior. The one who will save the innocent from Zeus' clutches and restore order and balance as it always should have been."

Savior. Save the innocent.

Lukus racked his brain, searching for stories, sentences, words— anything that would help him understand what the heck Gaia was talking about.

"Here," she said, waving a hand over him, dusting him with a white powder that melted under his flesh at once.

Electricity rushed up and down his limbs and pried into his stomach, his lungs, his heart, his brain. Millions of flashes flew through his mind. Images of gods, goddesses, mythological monsters, half-human creatures, palaces and forests and lakes, castles in the ocean, oversized cabins in the mountains.

It was all there—every single Greek myth, every piece of documentation he'd needed days ago for this investigation. The tales his human mother told him, the gods venerated by his father, the adventures of heroes burdened by insane tasks they weren't expected to succeed in.

If he hadn't been so stunned, so agonized at the revelation of Gaia's schemes, he would have thanked her for imparting such incredible information.

Fingertips fizzling with new power—*knowledge*—he glowered at her in all her potential glory, hating every speck of her scaled skin and every flicker of her furious eyes. He'd respected her when they were first introduced; he'd feared her for her status as maker and mother of everything.

That respect had vanished, and he didn't think it would ever return.

"Of course," he said, his tongue swelling, his lungs constricting. "You're still mad at Zeus for locking up your children. That's why you started all this? An eons-old injustice that was proven to be correct?"

Gaia snorted and chuckled before blowing out the chandelier and instilling a sinister silence in the room.

|| 30. GLORY ||

???

The instant the candles blew out, tiny fireflies ignited within Mnemosyne's hut, illuminating the mud-covered walls and floors in a soft, flickering glow. The vines and leaves sprouting from the ceiling turned a golden shade, like stars sprinkling across a non-moonlit sky.

In the obscurity, Mnemosyne's dwelling would be fearsome for some, depriving them of their sight, rendering them immobile and uncertain and forcing them to use their other senses. Others loved that darkness. That sense of being lost in a wet forest in the middle of the night, with nothing but nature to soothe one's soul and the outlines of trees to guide oneself home.

It wasn't *that* dark, not now. Not with the lightning bugs flurrying to and fro, silent and solemn, reminiscent of late summer nights camping out in the forests.

The bugs permitted a glimpse of the other occupants of the hut, all bewildered and transfixed at the revelation. The long-awaited disclosure of the identity of the person who'd been tormenting them for weeks. For years, if they counted Lukus' conception.

Gaia hadn't wished to watch their disgusted and distorted features any longer. To view Lukus blinking furtively, new to the godly realm and infused with all its knowledge, thanks to her powers.

Or to witness Athena's scowl, Aphrodite's pouty lips and teary eyes, and Hera's snarl. Even Mnemosyne had winced when Gaia had made her appearance known to all. Only Dionysus, Themis, and Phoebe had remained unaffected, dazed and intoxicated as they were.

So she'd extinguished the candles and conjured fireflies for a softer, more soothing atmosphere. One where she could calmly explain to her family what her intentions were, and justify her reasons.

Not that I should need to—they all know how Zeus has done me wrong over the years.

She had no doubt Hera would barter, deny it all, and stand by her spouse. But Athena had been wounded by Zeus recently. And Aphrodite was always treated like a lesser being in his presence, having to repress her true self, her true powers. They'd see sense in Gaia's rage, and it was possible they'd change sides and back her without having to be poisoned, first.

Regardless of their positions, Gaia needed their ichor to complete the potion. She'd do all she could to ensure she didn't have to *take* it from them. Giving their blood willingly would render the concoction stronger, and would give Lukus a better chance of defeating Zeus.

Thinking of Lukus, she spun to him, cocking her head. "Now you're aware who I am, and you can close your investigation, yes?"

He narrowed his gaze, as if seeking to peer through the semi-darkness. His mouth popped open and slammed shut several times before he resigned to silence.

"Wonderful. I appreciate the lack of argument or push-back, as I'm quite exhausted from all this nonsense." She allowed her shoulders to relax, her heart to settle in her chest, and her ancient arms to sway at her sides in a gentle rhythm.

"Nonsense you created," thought Hera, ever the relentless,

stubborn, spoiled Queen. Her mouth was still covered by a leafy slush, to prevent her from bursting out. But she knew Gaia could read her thoughts and didn't filter them.

Oh, how Gaia had wanted to smack her pretty cheeks eons ago for her insolence. And how that urge had grown in the past few days, being so close to her, listening to all the petty complaints and cruelties roaming through her mind. Seeing Hera at the palace, entitled and mean and insulting her husband, Gaia had, at first, expected she'd be easy to fool, easy to drag over to her team. Yet the spurned spouse of Zeus would never betray him, no matter how many times he'd betrayed her. She retained all her fierce loyalty, and would die for Zeus' position.

She stared at Gaia now, her reluctance drawing over her half-obscured features. Riled up and unafraid of consequences—this was an older version of Hera that hadn't made its appearance in a long, long time.

"You have some nerve, child," said Gaia, not bothering to mask her voice any longer. She'd played with its tonality during her possessions, shifting it from person to person, ensuring no one could recognize her. It had worked. She'd read all their thoughts, and not a single one had had any clue it was her they'd been hearing. Her they'd be tracking, baiting, hoping to catch. "You and all the others. Filthy-minded, crude, reckless children, that's what you are. My, how exasperated I am from all your bickering and blaming."

Hera's eyes burned, turning a shiny copper that lit up the space before her. She was still on the ground, but was no longer huddled to Athena and Aphrodite. *They* were the smarter ones, staying discreet, deciding to leave Gaia to her devices.

But one of them broke from her trance. "Is that not what you wanted? To *make* us bicker and blame one another?" To Gaia's surprise, it was Athena who had spoken up.

Gaia watched her, unmoved, neutral as ever; but she caught the twitch of Athena's cheeks and a spark of yellow in her gaze.

Ah, she's angry, but too afraid to burst out like her step-mother.

"Yeah," said a voice from behind Gaia—Lukus had retrieved his wits. "You were purposely creating a civil war as a distraction, weren't you? Getting everyone good and pissed, diverting their focus on one another, so you could—"

"—that's enough from you, young man."

Gaia snapped, and he levitated in the air before being thrust back onto his altar; the *crack* from his spine hitting the surface nearly made Gaia cringe, but he'd be fine. He was half-immortal, after all.

"Mnemosyne, please, put him back to sleep. He doesn't need to be conscious anymore, and needs to conserve his strength. He's giving me a migraine, again. Ugh," she pinched the bridge of her nose, "how am I to ally with him when his mere presence makes me sick?"

Mnemosyne sidled over and weaved her magic to send Lukus into a state of slumber. He tried to protest, but Mnemosyne muttered a curse-filled incantation that sealed his lips shut and knocked him out.

As soon as she no longer heard his tone traipsing about in her mind, Gaia could concentrate at last on her granddaughter and great granddaughter and Aphrodite.

"Yes, I wanted a civil war," she said, leaning against the cauldron, crossing her legs at the ankles. The heat from the pot seared up her spine and erased all its tension. "But it all back-fired. Nothing has gone according to plan, for many reasons. Mostly because Rhea ended up being a bit stronger than I'd anticipated. All her years in the jungle honed her instincts and aided in her ability at sniffing out the truth. She was on to me too fast, became too hungry, uncontrollable. You were never meant to speak to me. You were, all three of you, to be captured, drained, then deposited in your beds as if nothing had happened. Clearly," she sneered at the three bound goddesses, "that failed."

Aphrodite had grown restless and was trying to get up, her gaze fixed on Mnemosyne, who still worked her magic on Lukus' unconscious body. She was adding spells to be certain he stayed asleep, and didn't awaken in the middle of a conversation and ruin Gaia's plans. Mnemosyne knew; she always anticipated her mother's needs and took care of them, most days before Gaia even had to express them out loud. She was a blessing, and Gaia was thankful she had at least one obedient daughter who'd assist her in her exploits.

Sadly, not everyone in the room agreed with Gaia's beliefs. Aphrodite continued to struggle, and had managed to stand, wobbling to and fro, glowering towards the altar. "You get your gross hands off my son, you piece of—"

"—no, I don't think so," said Gaia, zapping a few vines in Aphrodite's direction, binding her wrists to her ankles. She shouted in protest, so Gaia threw a glob of leaves and mud over her mouth, like she'd done to Hera. "And you'll be quiet now, thank you. I've had enough of all this interference. Why did they awaken, Mnemosyne?"

The goddess of memory—unfazed by Aphrodite's failed threats—shimmied up to stand beside her mother. Her mixed scents of cinnamon and spices, of peaches and tangerines, always gave Gaia a sense of pleasure and tingled her appetite.

"That is a question better directed at Hecate, I'm afraid. It's her original potion we've been using. All our experimenting might have altered the parts that were supposed to keep them inanimate."

"Why?" Athena, the only goddess without a gag, raised her hands in surrender. "No, please do not silence me. I won't yell, I won't give you a migraine."

Gaia nodded, allowing her to continue her train of thought. She respected Athena, to a degree, but she'd quiet her if she got too nosy.

Athena cleared her throat, but her gaze was directed towards someone else. "Why are you aiding her, Mnemosyne? I'm sorry, I know you little, but I didn't know you to hold grudges against Olympus. What sort of spell did Gaia put you under?"

Though Gaia groaned, readying her fingers to send a leafy gag over Athena's mouth, too, Mnemosyne slid forward, her arms stiffening at her sides. "You think I don't hold grudges against Olympus? Against Zeus? My dear, you aren't wisdom personified, as I'd hoped. If anything, you're quite daft. He holds my daughters captive up there, though he says they're free to go anywhere. Yes…anywhere but here, in the Underworld, to visit me. I loathe him for that."

Athena's eyebrows inched up, and as she parted her lips, Gaia decided she didn't want to hear what she'd reply. She hurled a wad of muddy leaves into her mouth, shutting her up.

"No, you'll listen. *All* of you will listen. I don't care how many gags I have to create and how many of you I have to knock out—you'll stop speaking and pay attention." Gaia set an encouraging hand on Mnemosyne's arm. "Go on, tell her your side of things, darling."

"Mother doesn't have me under a spell; unlike my sisters, I saw reason on my own." Mnemosyne had always had a sultriness to her voice that men couldn't resist. Like Aphrodite's sexy timbre, but with a raspy undertone and a maturity the goddess of love and beauty lacked. "I cannot stand that my siblings are still locked up in Tartarus.

Eons have passed, and they've not been forgiven? Not been given a chance at redemption? It's absurd. How many of Zeus' snarky little kids, all illegitimate, have been accorded second chances? It's unfair. Mother's children have endured enough, yet the king refuses to believe they've changed."

Gaia sucked her lips in, absorbed in her daughter's speech of truth. It was as if their minds were linked. She and Mnemosyne were often on the same wave-length, in agreement without needing to say it out loud. It was such a relief to know she'd always have her, no matter who opposed them.

"I've always believed that all men in our lineage should be punished for their toxicity. Uranus, my father, was punished. Apologies, Mother, I know how you still love him." Mnemosyne sent her hand into her mother's and squeezed. "He deserved it. Cronus, my brother, received an appropriate punishment, as well. But Zeus? Zeus has been left alone to tend to his idiocies for centuries, and it won't do. My nephew shouldn't be spared. I'll do anything in my power to assure myself that he's treated the same as the men before him."

As none of the prisoners could reply, they dipped their chins and peered at the ground, mumbling into their gags.

"On that note," Mnemosyne bowed, one hand pressed to her bosom, "I must excuse myself." She switched to Gaia, lowering her voice. "We're running low on ingredients, and with Hecate up in Olympus, I cannot mind-warp her into giving me what I need. I must employ…" her eyes narrowed to slits, "other methods I'm not too fond of."

Gaia knew those methods, but didn't want to risk any of her captives hearing them. She ushered Mnemosyne out with a nod of appreciation and a quick caress of her cheek.

Thank you, daughter. For your contribution and your sacrifices.

Once Mnemosyne had scurried out into the deadly Underworld air, Gaia reignited the candles on the chandelier. She'd grown used to her family's looks of disgust by now. Once more Olympians found out about her ruses—if they hadn't already, thanks to Rhea and her big mouth—more of those scowls would occur. She couldn't let them wound her, couldn't take them to heart.

What she had planned was, after all, for the greater good, and they'd see it in the long run.

If they don't, then they'll be punished with Zeus.

"Right, then," she said, beaming at her prisoners as she rubbed her hands. "Are we ready to play?" They gawked at her, and recoiled farther against the wall, as if hoping to mold into it and disappear. "Will you give me your blood willingly, to further my cause? Or are we going to fight? Because I've told you; I'll win. I don't wish to kill you, but I will, if it's my last resort. No one will step in my way, and I'm done operating from the shadows. Be prepared for Gaia's glory!"

THE OLYMPIANS
HADES
(NO OFFSPRING)
DEMETER
ZEUS
HERA
POSEIDON
HESTIA
(NO OFFSPRING)
PERSEPHONE
HEPHAESTUS
ARES
APHRODITE
MANY OFFSPRING
MELINOE
METIS
ATHENA
EROS
PSYCHE
RHODOS
LETO
APOLLO
ARTEMIS
HEDONE
MAIA
HERMES
SEMELE
DIONYSUS

To be continued in book FOUR

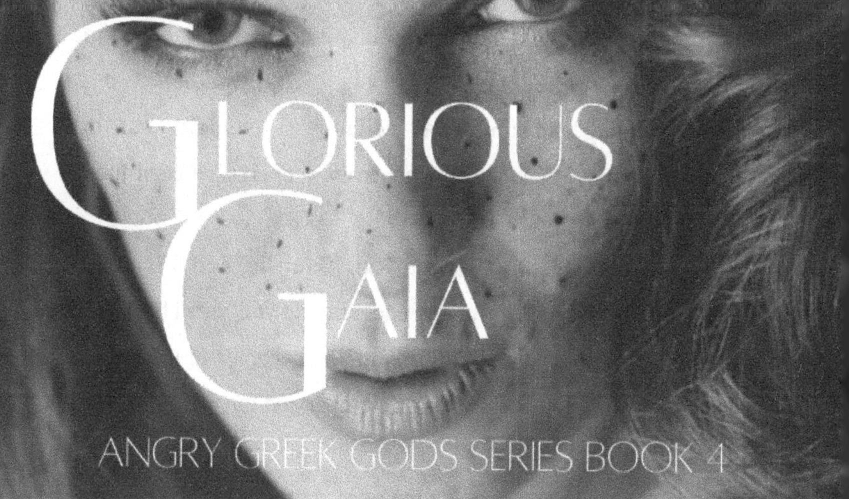

AUTHOR'S NOTE
&
ACKNOWLEDGMENTS

"RAVENOUS RHEA" was a distant dream, a cluster of notes gathered in vague chapters waiting to be written. I had an outline, I had an ending, I had a villain—but how on *earth* would I find the time & motivation to write about it?

Well, finding the time was certainly a struggle; but the motivation was easy, thanks to the generous support I've been lucky to have in my life.

To my betas: **Reanna, Selena, Kat, Danielle, and Viviana**—you have no idea how insightful and encouraging you've all been, and I'm so excited to soon share with you the last chapter in this series. Thank you all for volunteering your time over and over again to read my crazy adventures.

To my love, Matt—for being the most supportive boyfriend I've ever had, and never letting me give up on pursuing my dreams.

To my family, for *always* buying my novels no matter what they're about, and spreading the word to their friends.

And finally, to the women around the country fighting for what's right—I see you, and I dedicate this novel in the voices of strong female characters to you. Keep fighting.

ABOUT THE AUTHOR

Stephanie Rose is an author based in Nevada, but her heart lives in Paris, France, where she resided for almost twelve years. When she's not writing, she spends her time going on adventures with her boyfriend, catching up on TV-shows, or snuggling her black cat, Onyx.

"RAVENOUS RHEA" is the third in a four-book series, inspired by her obsession with Greek mythology. For updates on upcoming works and exclusive content about the Angry Greek Gods world, visit her website: www.stephanierose.online

www.ingramcontent.com/pod-product-compliance
Lightning Source LLC
Chambersburg PA
CBHW010737310726
48971CB00010B/2867